BEAUTIFUL WASPs HAVING SEX

BEAUTIFUL WASPs HAVING SEX

DORI CARTER

WILLIAM MORROW

AN IMPRINT OF HARPERCOLLINS*PUBLISHERS*

This is a work of fiction. The characters, incidents, and dialogues are products of the author's imagination and are not to be construed as real. Any resemblance to actual events or persons, living or dead, is entirely coincidental.

FIRST EDITION

Designed by Jo Anne Metsch

Printed on acid-free paper

Library of Congress Cataloging-in-Publication Data has been applied for.

ISBN 0-688-17464-7

00 01 02 03 04 RRD 10 9 8 7 6 5 4 3 2 1

In memory of Zelda Zuckerman,
whose humor and kindness
are legendary
among her grandchildren

BEAUTIFUL WASPs HAVING SEX

WHO IS GOOD?
1997

I WAS REORGANIZING my life as I do now and then, when I realized with familiar surprise that I no longer speak to most of the people on my Rolodex. Only in Hollywood can you redo your phone list, throw out your friends, and never miss them. My ex-husband calls it my "Scorched Mirth Policy" but I'm sure somewhere across town someone's secretary is taking MY name out of their Rolodex and dropping it into a wastepaper basket. Some executive, producer, agent, or director is deleting MY name from their personal-pocket-computer-data-management notepad. They may even be wondering what ever happened to me. Or maybe not. No hard feelings. It's the nature of the business.

Fortunately, I still keep in touch with a few old friends who are able to dole out a small script rewrite here or a final polish there. I'm on the Hollywood Workfare Program. I don't make a lot of money and the effort isn't particularly rewarding, but I'm also not tempted to take it personally when the scripts get shelved. I'm not looking for fame or fulfillment anymore. Now I write to pay the bills. But I've made peace with that. It's the nature of the business.

I was standing by the kitchen phone, pulling the neatly typed cards off the wheel, dropping all the home phones, work phones, car phones, weekend phones, fax phones, and cellular phones into a Gelson's supermarket bag, when I stopped on Jonathan Prince. I didn't even have his current number. Someone told me he'd moved from his rental apartment in West Hollywood and bought a glass-walled Neutra house with a view of the city off Sunset Plaza Drive. The last time I'd heard from him was six years ago, when he'd sent me one of his trademark Christmas cards, on brown recycled paper, with the latest holiday homily printed on the front:

Herein lies the tragedy of the age: not that men are poor,—all men know something of poverty; not that men are wicked,—who is good? not that men are ignorant,—what is truth? Nay, but that men know so little of men. —W.E.B. Du Bois, *The Souls of Black Folk* (1903)

The word *PEACE* was at the bottom, and typeset in very small, sedate letters, his soft, oddly appropriate name—Jonathan Andrew Prince. Since he sends out hundreds of these brown cards every season and I hadn't received a Nietzsche or Kierkegaard greeting in recent years, I had to conclude I'd been removed from his Christmas list. Hallelujah, amen.

Of all the people I know in Hollywood, Jonathan is the one who finally made me understand I was in the wrong profession, finally pushed me over the edge into sanity. So I guess, in a way, I should thank him. Although he probably wouldn't take my call. Seeing his name again, I was seized by an urge to go into my writing room and turn on my computer, and hardly anything these days makes me want to do that.

But I feel I have to get this down. Not to get back at Jonathan, though a number of people would love to join me in that venture, providing it wouldn't jeopardize their careers. In truth, trying to expose Jonathan would be a waste of time. Everyone's already wise to him, and it doesn't seem to matter. Least of all to Jonathan.

There's only one reason to do this. When I've put in order all the scenes that keep replaying in my head, the sad moments I wish I could rewrite, and the comic tragedy I might have prevented—when

I'm finally finished with this story, maybe I won't have to think about it anymore.

But please don't expect a big Hollywood exposé. As Freyda Wong, my former agent, would be only too happy to tell you, I'm known as a writer of small stories. I'm not the one you'd hire to do your sweeping epics. Or your action-adventure, thriller, mystery, noir, horror, science fiction, western, or buddy movies. My specialty, according to Freyda, is the "well-observed-slice-of-life." In other words, uncommercial, character-driven stories which are overly dependent on casting. Fortunately, this isn't a movie, but it's probably as close to a buddy story as I'll ever get, and it has enough mystery, adventure, and horror to terrify anyone who might think of venturing where I've been.

Even with all that, I apologetically confess this is a mere cautionary tale recounting the years I spent with Jonathan Prince. And the rest of the movers and shakers of Hollywood who were lying on the bottom of that supermarket bag.

IT COULD HAVE BEEN
A CLASSIC
1989

I WAS THIRTY-NINE when this tale began, just separated from my husband of ten years. What shall I say about the prospect of turning forty in L.A. without a loving marriage, nice children, or a wildly successful career to compensate for the lack of the above? It was not a good year.

My ex-husband is also a screenwriter. Only he's annoyingly pro-lific and well known in the industry. As my friend Miriam once said, "Screenplays fall from his fingers." In a way she was right. He could sit down and start typing and I'd hear the clicking of the keys hour after hour, and if he'd take a phone call, the typing would resume the moment he'd hang up. Me, I sat down, got up, made tea, ate pretzels, took naps, took walks, took notes, took out the garbage, thumbed through catalogs, read other writers for inspiration, and in general operated under the paralyzing possibility that I was a fraud, a total sham and failure. When the words wouldn't come I didn't want to go to the supermarket or cook or bank or do laundry or return phone calls or pay bills or write thank-you notes, or have children or buy birthday presents. Because I was afraid I might lose my focus.

And when the words finally DID come, I behaved exactly the same way. Let's face it, I wasn't the perfect wife.

I was the perfect ex-wife, however, because when we divorced I left Hart the house. My first lawyer told me I was crazy to walk away from such a nice piece of real estate and said I'd live to regret it, but I felt it was the only fair thing to do. After all, Hart had paid for it. It's a beautiful Spanish house, which is the only style that really looks like it belongs in Southern California. Sometimes when I'm on Sunset Boulevard heading west toward the ocean, I'll take a slight detour and drive by, but now it seems like another lifetime that I lived there. Recently Hart's new wife moved in and I hear she decorated the hell out of it. Third time out he finally got smart. Not only did he marry a woman who wasn't a writer, but he found someone who was only too delighted to run his life, give gracious dinner parties, deal with the termite men, and attend the always-impending-never-ending award ceremonies: the Academy Awards, the Emmy Awards, the Golden Globes, Directors Guild, Writers Guild, Screen Actors Guild, Producer Caucus, Humanitas, the Vision Award, People's Choice Awards, *TV Guide* Awards, and Environmental Media Awards, all with their beautiful, hand-lettered table-placement cards that read *Mr. and Mrs. Hart Jordan.*

I tried everything not to be Mrs. Hart Jordan. I was resolutely Frankie Jordan, and still am because it beats being Francine Fingerman, for which I'm still trying to forgive my parents. Francine Fingerman sounds like a woman you'd be introduced to at a *bris*, only she can't say hello because (as she tries to explain, pointing to her mouth) she's chewing a large forkful of *kugel*. Francine Fingerman's the chatty woman with the flaccid arms who asks you to zip her up in the Loehmann's dressing room as she squeezes herself into the chiffon dress she's buying for her son's bar mitzvah. *I can give up sweets but it's the BREAD that's my downfall.* Francine Fingerman was born to be the president of Hadassah. Francine Fingerman wasn't a Hollywood writer.

A few days after we decided to divorce, Hart, never one to procrastinate, moved out of our house with the answering machine, his computer, printer, and a duffel bag that had taken him about one minute to pack. He'd borrowed a friend's place at the beach where he could write without distraction (meaning me). I, too, spent my days writing, attempting to get something, anything down. In between marathon naps, I wandered from room to room, stopping in front of mirrors to note how terrible I looked.

I'm the kind of person who, even if I just lose a lipstick, starts to feel disorganized and crazy and begins to question my whole existence. Losing a marriage was more than I could handle. After Hart moved out I was so filled with anxiety and dread that a few times I realized I wasn't even breathing and would have to take a fast walk around the neighborhood just to kick-start my lungs. I tried meditation but was too nervous to concentrate. I had no idea where I was going to live, if anyone would ever find me attractive again, if I'd be able to get steady work, or if I was cut out to be a mother. Not knowing how to deal with any of this, I did what most Hollywood writers do. I called my agent.

I was expecting my agent's old secretary, Adam, but the voice at the other end explained in a friendly manner that he'd replaced Adam as Freyda's new agent trainee. This didn't exactly surprise me. As soon as I develop voice recognition and any kind of rapport with Freyda's secretaries, they leave. But Jonathan Prince wasn't about to let custom or station come between us.

"Is this THE Frankie Jordan?"

"It's the only one I know of."

"I just want to tell you that I'm a big fan of yours."

"Why?" I was immediately on guard, suspecting he'd confused me with someone else. Until he mentioned a movie I'd written when I'd first come out to Hollywood. Not having a lot of experience back then, I thought I'd created a perfect script that couldn't be improved upon. A script constructed as delicately as a ship in a bottle. Until it was sold and the producing team hired a new writer who agreed with every arbitrary change the studio asked for. A director eventually added his own comic touch to the script, and the two stars said they needed to personalize their roles and brought in writers of their own. By the time my movie was launched, I was in that all-too-common Hollywood position of getting credit for a movie I never would've gone to see if my name hadn't been on the screen. Even more embarrassing, it was the only feature script of mine that ever got made and I'd been living off the reputation of that movie ever since. When Jonathan innocently poked at an old wound, I felt compelled to explain in my defensive, apologetic way just what had happened.

"Actually, the movie had very little to do with the script I wrote. I was fired from it."

"I know, but I LOVED your original first draft. You know how boring it is to read most of these scripts? It's like Chinese water torture. But yours . . . I didn't want to put it down."

"You read it?" I was very surprised. No one reads the writer's first draft of a movie unless they're forced to. If they must read something, they read the shooting script. The painful truth in Hollywood is no one really LIKES reading scripts. Scripts are as common as old phone directories and just about as valued. Their brads scratch the finish on good furniture and on bookshelves they're slouchy and disobedient. Even Ana, our cleaning woman, had a certain disdain for the messy mounds of scripts plopped around sofas and beds like so many cow pies. Hart used to say he was afraid of only two things: prostate cancer and getting up to go to the bathroom in the middle of the night and ending his life like the Collier brothers, smothered to death under unproduced movies.

"I laughed out loud and I hardly ever do that," Jonathan gushed. "I couldn't believe they just didn't make your script as is. I can't believe what idiots they were. They went for all the easy jokes. Your version was so much smarter. And funnier. It could have been a classic, I mean it. I've read a lot of scripts lately and yours was by far the best."

So what if he was just a secretary who'd probably be leaving Freyda within the year? I'd accept praise anywhere I could find it. Then Jonathan got down to business.

"Freyda's been in France for two weeks and this is her first day back. She's at a breakfast meeting right now but she'll be calling in for messages. Anything in particular I can convey to her?"

"Yes. Tell her she lives a much better life than any of her clients."

"She certainly eats at better restaurants. See, that's the problem with you writers, you don't have expense accounts. If you did then you'd have more discretionary income for vacations and you, too, could go Relais et Châteauxing through the Loire Valley. That's why I'm becoming an agent. I mean, why not? It's not as hard as writing and the perks are much better."

"I'm glad someone has their life figured out." He was charming, this kid. Smart, too. I heard his other phone ringing. "Do you have to get that?"

"That's one of the drawbacks of this job. You never get to complete a conversation."

It doesn't seem to bother Freyda, I thought. "Just tell her I need to speak with her."

"I'll make sure she calls you this morning. I'm putting your name at the head of her return list. CALL FRANKIE JORDAN," he said as if he was writing it down nice and big. Wow, I thought. Why is he being so nice to me?

Despite Jonathan, by three o'clock Freyda still hadn't returned my call. I finally left the house and went outside with a bag of corn chips, the only food I could get down. I found myself at the end of the garden walking in a circle, around and around the roses like some somnambulant snacker, trying to sort out what had happened with my life.

I'd been feeling for a long time as if it didn't matter to Hart whether I was with him or not. He's a complicated man and he has the passions and demons any smart, creative person has, only he had channeled them into work. He'd found his way to get love and adulation and it wasn't through me anymore. But the ending came as a surprise to both of us.

I'd been wanting to get away for a weekend with him but he'd been too busy working. We finally settled on his birthday. We flew up to Carmel, and in the plane we chatted about the movie he was set to direct. We talked about casting and locations and his unit production manager who played studio politics and whom Hart suspected could be treacherous if not handled carefully. Hart and I had fallen into a pattern. He'd talk about his work and I'd listen. I'd ask questions about his work and he'd answer. Hart wasn't interested in what was going on with me, but I didn't blame him. He was swimming forward in life, churning up big waves, and I was treading water in his wake. It was always the same. I was forever trying to finish my script, forever stuck. It doesn't make for good conversation.

Everything seemed pleasant enough until lunch. We were walking around town looking for a place to eat, when Hart's mood turned black and he fell into one of his angry silences. With almost tacit agreement, we found a small restaurant, sat outside in an enclosed patio, and ordered a bottle of Chianti. Hart was looking off, stewing about something, and I was certain I knew what it was. He was thinking about his movie and that everything might get out of control unless Hart was there to monitor the situation. He'd only been appeasing me by agreeing to get away. Maybe ten minutes we sat like strangers. I studied his profile until it became unbearable, then turned my attention to the bark on a large star pine tree. I felt like one of those old married couples who've long ago run out of conversation. It wasn't the first time we'd experienced this. Maybe that's why so many couples travel with other couples. Why take the chance of sitting in an unfamiliar restaurant in an unfamiliar city with nothing to say? I broke the silence. I said the patio reminded me of a place we'd been to in Santa Fe, a place we both liked, but he said nothing.

"You're going to have to answer me, Hart," I said in what I thought was a light tone of voice. "I don't want to sit here and just talk to myself."

He turned back to me and I thought he'd snapped out of his mood. "Then maybe I should just leave the restaurant." It was said with such hatred I felt the breath go out of me. My first impulse was to flee.

But we stayed, with food untouched, and performed a messy, very public autopsy on our marriage. Too many things were said that couldn't be retracted. Neither one of us knew how to stop it. Hart said I stole from his good times and that he was never allowed to indulge himself in a bad mood because he constantly had to be shoring up my mood. He said I only saw things in black and white, either our marriage was all good or all bad, and that I was ready to abandon the relationship the moment I felt criticized. And he said he was getting tired of it. I countered by admitting I'd lost feeling for him because he gave back so little. I felt there was no room in his life for me anymore, and if I ever got cancer in the middle of production, he would look upon it as an inconvenience. This is why I shouldn't drink wine at lunch. I suppose I wanted Hart to reassure me, to acknowledge that he was distracted with work, under tremendous pressure and afraid of failure, but that we were still okay. What he said instead was, "If you really feel like that then I don't know what you're doing with me. Let's just get a divorce and put us both out of our misery." I can still remember the sick fear: I was going to be alone. But I knew he was right. He was just braver to have said it first.

I was standing in the garden with the empty bag of corn chips when I heard the phone. I was praying it was Hart telling me we'd both been too hasty and he was on his way home. I ran into the kitchen and answered it.

"Hello?"

"You know your fucking ANSWERING machine isn't working."

"Hi, Freyda." She was in her car. Freyda always tried to fit me in between the two movie studios she covered. Or on her way to breakfast or on her way back from lunch. "How's traffic?"

"It's terrible."

"How was France?"

"The food was incredible. You can't believe how we ate. You just don't get a bad meal there. Even in the smallest café we got good food. We stopped at this little place in Vouvray, it's not even in the books, and I had the best french fries I've ever had. They were so good Marty and I were fighting over who'd get the last one. And a poached salmon with a butter-chive sauce that was unbelievable. I don't understand why those women don't all weigh two hundred pounds. They must have a different metabolism than we do. Although their portions aren't that big. Even at the three-star restaurants they don't serve that much for each course. In America the portions are always so HUGE. One day we just decided to stop at a *charcuterie* and get cheese and bread and sausages for lunch and we skipped dinner altogether. Uch. Next time I'm packing bran flakes or Metamucil or something. I couldn't wait to come home and just take a dump. I won't even tell you how many days I went. I think I must have set some kind of a medical record or something. I don't know why I get so constipated over there. It wasn't like we weren't walking. It was probably all the goat cheese. I'm never eating again. You should see me. I'm sitting here on Barham Boulevard with my pants unzipped." We got interrupted by a series of high-pitched squeals of static. I held the receiver away from my ear.

"Freyda?"

"WHAT'S WRONG WITH MY PHONE? I CAN HARDLY HEAR YOU."

"I DON'T KNOW. YOU WANT ME TO CALL YOU BACK?"

"WHAT? I'LL CALL YOU."

She hung up and the next moment the phone rang.

"That's better," she said. "I was on my speakerphone. I don't think it works."

"Why can't you ever call me standing still?"

"Who stands still? And I DID call you before. You were out. Go to Adray's and get a new answering machine. How expensive are they? How ARE you? I miss seeing you. Tell me what's happening?"

"Hart and I are getting . . ." But when I had to say it aloud, the words came out in a teary croak.

"What? I can't hear you."

I grabbed what was left of a paper-towel roll off the kitchen counter and smacked myself across the head, just for distraction. Then I sank to the floor in front of the refrigerator and wept. I had a few moments of bad connection to pull myself together.

"Hart and I have decided to get a divorce." It came out sounding very thoughtful and sober.

"You're kidding? I can't believe it. When did this come about? I leave town for two weeks and your whole marriage falls apart? This is terrible. Are you OKAY? Let's get together and talk. I just can't believe this."

"I need a job." I was still crying but at least my voice was steady.

"What happened to your spec script? When's it going to be done? I was talking to someone a few weeks ago about you."

"Who was it?" I heard nothing but static.

"We're breaking up."

"Freyda? Can you hear me?" Nothing. "Are you there? Are you in a tunnel? Are you alive?"

"Hello? Frankie?"

"I'm still here."

"Talk louder."

"I'M STILL HERE."

"Wait a second. Hold on." I heard her give her name to the guard at the studio gate. Then she came back.

"Hello?"

"Hello?"

"Who's this?"

"It's Frankie. Who do you think it is?"

"You sounded like someone else. I thought someone had cut into the line. Anyway, we should—" The phone went dead.

Jonathan called me a few minutes later. "Freyda would like to have lunch with you this Friday. Are you free?"

"Let me get my calendar." What a joke. "Yes. I'm free."

"Good. She'd like you to come to the office first. And then I get to meet you, too. How's eleven-thirty sound?"

Finally something to write in my calendar. I picked up my pen, and as I began to fill in the hour, I experienced that small rush of affection for life I can get when I feel I'm taking control.

SINGIN' IN THE RAIN LEVEL

WHEN I AWOKE the morning of our meeting, I could tell by the light in the bedroom that the Westside was covered with a blanket of coastal fog. It was September, always the hottest month of the year in L.A., and gloom was a welcome relief. The night before, the dry desert winds had blown into town, hot as a hairdryer, snapping tree limbs and knocking out the electricity. I'd taken to my bed early with a candle and a book, relieved life had suddenly turned so simple. But as I lay on top of the tired sheets that morning like a soggy gingerbread man, I felt a familiar fear creeping in heavy as the fog. It was very tempting to call in sick, claim nausea, delay Freyda for another week until I could fake a happier, bouncier, stronger, funnier me. But I also knew it didn't really matter how confident I appeared. Putting myself out there meant setting myself up for rejection once again.

By the time I eased out of bed, the fog had started to burn off. It was eight-thirty when I got through showering, looked out the window, and saw the sun had returned without a wisp of a cloud in sight. The gardeners were hosing down the patio and watering the impatiens, which were already starting to wilt. The radio informed me it was going to be in the high nineties downtown.

I dreaded driving into Century City because the air-conditioning in my car didn't work. Trying to do my small part for the ozone layer, I'd long ago given up on Freon and returned to windows. Over the years I'd actually tried to schedule all my appointments for the cooler months. I felt like I'd been forced out of reverse hibernation.

I won't go into the nubby, plaid sofa decorating the fast lane of the Santa Monica Freeway or the bumper-to-bumper traffic on Santa Monica Boulevard; that's almost a given. I was already late when I entered the parking structure, sweat dripping down my cleavage, the back of my thighs stuck to my seat. I hate parking in underground garages. Besides the extortion, I didn't want to end my life in the next earthquake crushed to death underneath my agents, however much I liked the symbolism. But I had no choice. Century City was built on what was once the backlot of Twentieth Century-Fox. Instead of the dusty, Wild West streets with their quaint wooden hitching posts, there were now glass office towers with massive, concrete, subterranean parking facilities. I wound my way down and down, getting closer to the center of the earth, searching for a place to park. Every floor of this particular garage is named after a movie and has a theme song playing so you can remember where you've left your car. I finally found a spot on the *Singin' in the Rain* level.

I took the elevator up to the forty-first floor and walked down the hall with my hands held high in the air, like there was a gun to my back, hoping the air-conditioning would dry my T-shirt. I entered my agents' offices through tall double doors and stepped into a cool, quiet, windowless room with an old Oriental carpet cushioning the floor. The walls were paneled in rich mahogany and lined to the high ceiling with leatherbound books. There were hunting prints of hounds and horses and a large antler chandelier that shared the ceiling with the regulation fire sprinklers. Except for the *Hollywood Reporter* and *Variety* fanned across the cribbage table, it was a British gentlemen's club, devoid of gentlemen.

A young receptionist sat behind an Edwardian desk where once a lady arrayed in duchess satin would have written her weekly menus for the cook. It was the kind of desk that might have "braised grouse" or "creamed smoked haddock" etched by the sharp nib of a pen into the faded green leather top. The receptionist looked out of place behind such a desk, with her straight blond hair and the eager, pleasing, cheerful look I'd seen on so many other newly arrived worker bees. She was keeping her antennae out for the important, the famous, the rich, the powerful, but it was useless. The agency handled only writers. I gave her my name and told her I had an appointment with Freyda Wong.

Despite the Pacific Rim flavor of her name, Freyda's just a Jewish girl from Encino, the jewel in the crown of the Valley. She was named Freyda after a dead grandfather, Fred. The Wong came from Freyda's first husband, a name she kept because it sounded more distinctive than Freyda Kellner, which is her maiden name, or Freyda Sobell, which is what she got when she married Marty Sobell. Although when I met Freyda's bemused mother-in-law, I discovered Sobell isn't exactly Marty's real name. She introduced herself to me as "Sylvia SObel, mother of Marty SoBELL." By adding a mere letter, Marty had escaped his Polish-Jewish ancestry and become French. No wonder his mother couldn't keep up.

Hart once said that if Hollywood is a flashy, expensive car, then studio heads are the drivers who sit behind the wheel flipping people off, writers are the humble tires they kick, directors the big engines they admire, producers the shiny hubcaps, actors the smooth bodies, and agents the loud, obnoxious horns. Freyda Kellner Wong Sobel Sobell is more like a friendly little bicycle bell that demands attention with a charming tinkle. Freyda considers herself an indispensable part of your life, not just an agent but a reassuring friend, confidante, psychologist, and morale booster. Her specialty is angst-ridden writers and she has a stable of them who depend on her, of which I was one.

The young, blond receptionist told me Freyda was busy at the moment. I took a seat in a burgundy leather wingback chair because two other people were already on the chesterfield sofa and one of them was talking into the phone in a loud voice meant to be overheard. I looked over and recognized Ian Mandel, a writer Freyda also represented. I'd actually been at a dinner party with Ian only a few months before, sat right next to him in fact, but that morning we both pretended we didn't know each other. If I had anything definite happening deal-wise, I'm sure I would've at least nodded. But when you're not feeling great about yourself, you don't want to find out that someone you don't respect is doing a lot better than you are.

Ian was probably in his late thirties, although he appeared to be headed right toward middle-aged domestication, even then. It was the generous gut and balding pate you first noticed. His thick salt-and-pepper beard balanced his head nicely though, and the AFI baseball cap he was sporting made his hairline anybody's guess. If he'd kept his mouth shut, he could have looked like a big ol' teddy bear, a lovable lug that some women, particularly me, find reassuring to have around when workmen are in the house. But the way he talked on the phone to his secretary, his impatient, self-conscious delivery, took away any illusion. *"Did Lurvey call? Call him back and tell him I've been stuck in a meeting with my agents all morning and I'll call him as soon as I get back to the office. Did you Xerox the script? How many copies? Get one over to Kendel's office. What's happening with my car? HOW much? Jesus. Call them back and tell them to go ahead with it, find out when I can pick it up and tell them they better fuckin' well wash it for that price."* He looked at his watch too many times. It was all tough-guy bravado and synthetic urgency, most likely for the pretty receptionist's benefit, certainly not mine. Maybe she would think he was important.

It was the T-shirt that gave him away. He was wearing one of his credits on his chest, a thank-you memento ritualistically passed out to everyone by the producer at the end of a shoot. I myself have a small collection of these T-shirts and use them to sleep in. The people who wear them out in public are the grips, gaffers, gofers, and wives. Nobody TOO important, like the director, ever wears them because they don't want to advertise what they do. They don't want strangers coming up to them and pitching script ideas. This one Ian was wearing immortalized an MOW with an actor who once had his own series. The producer's eponymous production company was in bigger letters than the name of the movie or the silkscreen photo of the star, and I had to sneak a few peeks to see exactly what it was Ian had written. He was wearing the shirt to remind his agents who he was, a fashion choice which spoke of desperation. It was all too obvious Ian needed another credit. Both the T-shirt and the star had begun to fade.

I didn't know what else to do, so I picked up *Town & Country* from the nineteenth-century pine cribbage table between us. Perusing the pages of smiling wedding photos, smiling party photos, I casually turned to a feature article on a Boston family with a summer compound in Martha's Vineyard. I could almost smell the salt air as I gazed at the old brown-shingled house with its wide porches, wicker furniture, and sparkling white shutters. There was the father, fit, tan, confident as he sailed his boat in the regatta. If I hadn't known better, I'd have thought he'd just stepped out of hair and makeup. His tan, even skin tone looked like it must have been applied with a sponge. And how could he have gotten that stunning contrast of dark hair and silvered temples except by the artful spraying of Streaks 'N Tips? He seemed perfectly cast as the successful patriarch busy conquering the sea on weekends. While mother, very attractive in an Eva Marie Saint kind of way, attended to her garden, picking yellow daisies and tiger lilies for the white ironstone pitcher, which, according to the article, always sat on the outside luncheon table. The lawn that swept to the sea was just the place for their springer-spaniel puppy to romp, and perfectly suited for the charity croquet match they hosted, where everyone present received their own blue-and-white gingham tablecloth and a wicker hamper of "down-to-earth and of-the-moment picnic food." To my surprise, the more I got into that afternoon of croquet, the more I wanted to learn about everyone present. Why was I so fascinated by some polite-looking WASPs with nice hair holding champagne flutes or drinking Pimm's Cup? Because their world was so safe and acceptable, their life so easy, part of me wanted to climb right into it. They looked like they were spending a summer afternoon doing just what they wanted, and even though it wasn't what I wanted, I felt a pang of envy mixed with a dose of contempt. Those people were so different from the people I knew, from the way I felt. They were almost another species.

I was particularly struck by a photo of the hosts' daughter, a young woman in a long white cotton dress and a large straw hat with fresh flowers tucked into the brim. There was nothing particularly unusual about her. She wasn't one of those L.A. creations who can walk into a room and make every head turn. She was pretty in a bland, generic way, but so exquisitely at ease there wasn't any question she knew she belonged. Her untroubled face could only come from someone who traveled light, who had no excess baggage to weigh her down. She was getting ready to drive away her opponent's croquet ball by striking her own ball against it, although she wasn't wearing efficient shoes for such an offensive maneuver. Her children were with her, two little smiling girls in pastel dresses who would probably dance through life. All I kept wondering was, What do these people talk about at dinner?

Their dinners couldn't possibly be as stimulating as ours used to be when I was growing up. At least once a week, every week, my father yelled at my mother for not serving fish more often. Then there was the legendary slotted-spoon fight: *"How many years have we been married, Perle? When the hell are you going to learn to serve things with a slotted spoon, goddamn it."* There was the *"Get your hair out of your eyes you look like a shrunken head!"* tirade, which was aimed at yours truly. My brother got, *"You'll never amount to anything. I'm going to send you to trade school if you don't watch out!"* The birds were blamed on my sister. *"The bird in Queens had a good personality! It would sit on your finger and talk! These birds do nothing! You want to know WHY? Because you don't spend enough TIME with them, that's why!"* According to my father, Grampa Zucky was lazy and a faker because his heart condition wasn't as bad as he made it out to be, and *"If he'd only get out of bed in the morning and do some Royal Canadian Air Force Exercises, he wouldn't be farting around the house all day."* We were all giving my father ulcers and none of us children spent enough time reading the Book of Knowledge.

By the time I finished flipping through the ads for Piaget watches and Mikimoto pearls, thirty minutes and my entire childhood had passed before me and still no Freyda. Ian had slipped out without me even noticing.

There's a certain hierarchy in an agent's waiting room. If you're really important, your agent comes right out to get you in person. If not, you're left languishing with the magazines and Hollywood trades until their assistant calls you in. I knew a very successful writer/director who gave agents four minutes' waiting time before he got up and left. Even though I wasn't successful, if I had any self-respect

I would have done the same. But I wanted my parking ticket validated and Freyda's secretary had the stamps.

I rose and walked across the room intending to reintroduce myself to the receptionist, keeping in mind it wasn't her fault.

"Could you please call Freyda again and remind her—" Just as I was about to say my name, the door to the inner sanctum opened and a young man dressed in a pink Ralph Lauren oxford button-down shirt and neatly pressed khakis glided into the room on butter-soft loafers.

"Frankie!" he said like we were old friends. "Jonathan Prince." He offered his right hand and I tried to shake it but he pulled back slightly and I was left holding only his fingers. They were small hands, smoother than my own. When I let Jonathan's fingers go he turned to the receptionist. "Hey, thanks, Dewey," he said breezily, relieving her of responsibility. Now that Jonathan Prince had arrived, everything was under control.

He didn't look anything like I imagined. From our phone calls I'd pictured him younger, more boyish, but there was a serious, mature aspect enhanced by little round Oliver Peoples eyeglasses. In his shoes he was maybe five-nine at most, with surprisingly broad shoulders. His face was tan with pink cheeks like a healthy child's. He had plenty of hair, which was dark and softly curly and cut short above his ears. His teeth, thirty-two of his best features, were very straight (kept that way, I found out much later, by a retainer he wore at night). I noticed, under his tailored trousers and above his low-profile loafers, his socks were a beige paisley pattern and I was sure he had a drawer full of them. He struck me at that moment as the kind of person who spent a great deal of time at the dry cleaners and who didn't resent paying the prices. I'd wanted to like him, for obvious reasons, but he seemed too polished, way too good at emulating the slick, eager Hollywood agent. It took me by surprise when Freyda told me Jonathan was only twenty-four.

He led me back to the Holy of Holies, past all the secretaries busy in their hall cubicles, just steps away from their bosses, who sat fully visible behind glass walls. It gave the impression of dioramas at the Museum of Natural History. Behind the glass wall each office had been re-created into a perfect little environment for its dweller. There was the Santa Fe habitat, the French Country habitat, the Sherlock Holmes study of dark English walnut with Oriental accents habitat, the Americana painted furniture/Adirondack bent twig/old gas station signs habitat, the Green and Green/Stickley habitat, the Ralph Lauren/Shabby Chic habitat, and the Eames chair, black leather sofa, Billy Al Bengston, Laddy John Dill, Charles Christopher Hill habitat. It was a very expensive Levitz showroom.

"So have you decided on what your office decor will be when they make you a full-blown agent?" I was making idle conversation, passing the time until we hiked to Freyda's office.

"I think I want to sit on a throne. I mean, if your office is supposed to make a statement about you, why not go all the way?" It was said in a manner to make me think he knew how ridiculous the whole business was.

"Where are you from?" I asked, because I suspected I'd pegged him.

"New York. Long Island actually."

"Whereabouts?

"Woodmere?" he answered with a question.

I experienced the satisfaction Henry Higgins must have felt, although it wasn't Jonathan's accent which gave him away, it was an attitude. He was a member of the Five Towns Tribe. Jonathan would have had the air-conditioning in his car fixed the day it broke, because if you're from the Five Towns discomfort is not acceptable. I knew Jonathan all right, or at least his type. It was this familiarity, our not having to break the ice, our sharing those familiar points of reference that made me think him predictable. But right from the beginning, he surprised me. He asked me where I was from and I told him. A town not far from his own but more solidly middle class.

"Tell me, dahlink," he asked, "which beach club did you belong to? The Malibu? The Sands? The Monico?"

"None. We went upstate for the summer. I did experience the Coral Reef a few times with Bobbee Shapiro before she upped and moved to Cedarhurst."

"And? Did you 'experience' being kissed by some tan *shaygets* lifeguard in the sand dunes?"

"Maybe Bobbee got kissed in the sand dunes. I hope so. Her parents bought her every other experience, including an all-girls sweet sixteen party at the Copacabana, where Wayne Newton, at his height, sang 'Danke Schon' right to her face."

"Are you insinuating that the Five Towns is JEWveau riche?" he said.

"Don't take it personally." But I could see he didn't and was only too happy to make his own addendum.

"A friend of mine used to say that if you lived on Long Island and your daughter had crooked teeth, you'd get her braces. If you lived in the Five Towns her parents would say, 'Find out who the best orthodontist is! Get her braces! Get her rubber bands! Buy her a whole new head!' " He smiled at me with his nice straight teeth.

"So did you get a whole new head?"

"If you think I was one of those spoiled rich kids, I wasn't. Hey. Not that I didn't want to be. But I worked every summer vacation. I paid for all my own entertainment expenses at Harvard."

"That must have been really rough," I said, impressed in spite of myself, that he had managed to drop he'd gone to Harvard within the first five minutes of our meeting. I envied him the excessive self-confidence that comes from knowing you can influence people in your favor without doing anything more than naming your college.

"Can't you tell I'm trying to wow you with my Luck and Pluck Horatio Alger routine, Frankie?" I have to say, Jonathan Prince had one of the most charming, one of the most disarming smiles. "Can I bring you any hot or cold refreshments? It's one of my very important duties," he said, reminding me, without having to say it, that he was only paying his silly dues before being promoted to something more befitting a Jewish Prince from Long Island. I asked for a glass of water. "You're too easy," he said, and as Freyda's office came in sight, he turned away and strode down the hall toward the kitchen. He was right, I was too easy. I just didn't know it then.

Freyda Wong was seated behind a fifties breakfast table with a yellow Formica top and chrome legs, talking into her hands-free headset. Behind her, through the large tinted glass windows, was a sweeping vista of the city that went all the way to the ocean. With the headset on and her tower view, she looked like the oft-sighted,

stressed-out Hollywood air-traffic controller who day after day handles life-and-death situations, avoids ego collisions, and guides her
deals through the stormy, dark lies. When she saw me she rolled her
eyes and made a jabbering motion with her hand, indicating a situation on the other end of the line which begged my forbearance.

Freyda is physically a compact woman who tends toward dumpy.
This wasn't always so. When I first met her, she was thin, divorced,
girlish, and voraciously flirtatious. More than once, Freyda had left
me sitting alone in a restaurant while she entertained some man at
another table. As I lined up the bread crumbs with my knife or pretended to be profoundly interested in my checkbook, I would watch
Freyda across the room, presenting herself like an irresistible, naughty
dessert. She kept a list of the men she'd conquered and proudly shared
it with me, along with amusing, sometimes amazing, under-the-
sheets anecdotes. But when the list stopped growing at its prurient
pace and she saw middle age looming, she married Marty. Overnight,
a dramatic change occurred. She decided the best way for her to get
ahead in Hollywood was to appear nonthreatening. Which is not to
say she still wasn't assertive. But like a lot of women in their forties,
she'd gotten tired of projecting any kind of sexuality for men because
of the low return on investment. The attention she'd once been able
to attract by mere femininity was now provoked through elaborate
theme dressing. Displayed with the subtlety of a Sunset Boulevard
billboard, Freyda's wardrobe could have come right out of Western
Costume. Today's motif, apparently, was gangsters. She looked like
she'd just stepped off the set of Key Largo. Or Guys and Dolls. Only
Freyda'd managed to combine both the guy and the doll into one
outfit. She was wearing black baggy pants, wingtip shoes, red suspenders, a black silk shirt, and a white tie held by a tie clip that said
Fred spelled out in marcasites. Pinned to her red suspenders was a
variety of jewelry from the thirties: a Bakelite handgun, a high-
heeled shoe, and a car that looked like the one Faye Dunaway drove
in Chinatown. If you peered inside you might just find a teeny-tiny
Evelyn Mulwray, her head on the horn, a bullet in her brain. A
bejeweled martini glass dangled from each of Freyda's ears. These
outfits declared that she'd closed up the shop, which simultaneously
relieved men and endeared her to women.

In the corner of her office, standing just my height, was a moose on roller skates, dressed as a butler holding a silver tray on which a copy of *The Canterbury Tales* had been laid. Marty had gotten it for Freyda as a surprise birthday present, and although it didn't go with the Eisenhower decor, she kept it there. A gesture of pure love, I'm sure. Originally it came with jaunty helium balloons that now dangled from the moose's white-gloved wrist. I stared at the puckered bags of air and thought of O'Henry's "The Last Leaf." Marty's virility would correspondingly diminish as did those sad, shriveling sacks. As it stood, his manhood had already been deflated, with a little help from Freyda. I squeezed the balloons to confirm Marty's condition and then, out of habit, glanced at the photos on the bookcase, which I knew by heart: Freyda in the Hamptons, Freyda in Paris, Freyda and Marty in tuxedos (his black, hers white) on their way to the Academy Awards, Freyda at her birthday party kissing the moose on roller skates. Some people who never have children seem to become the children they've never had.

Freyda was still on the phone rolling her eyes at me, so I moved on to the various pieces of Hawaiiana that littered each and every surface: the swordfish vase, the palm-tree clock that says *Waikiki,* the ashtray with a surfer on a wave. Just as I flicked the switch on the hula-girl lamp and her grass skirt began to dance, Jonathan came back into the room with my water.

"Did you ever see so many useless, overpriced *chotchkes* in your life?" he said, not bothering to lower his voice. It was a refreshing question, which didn't expect an answer. Everyone else pretended to be so impressed and amused by Freyda's relentless pursuit of kitsch, as if acting otherwise would have been bad sportsmanship. Jonathan was brave enough to say out loud what I'd been privately thinking. Agreeing with people, even before they'd expressed an opinion, is a skill at which Jonathan was remarkably adept.

"I'm supposed to dust them. That's another one of my little duties."

He picked up a feather duster hidden behind the photos and made a couple dainty mock swipes at some ukulele salt-and-pepper shakers. "I told Freyda I need a little white ruffled apron if she's going to make me do housework. I want to join the Betty Furness memorial wall." We were looking up at the framed appliance advertisements Freyda had hung above her sofa, featuring housewives in aprons and high heels, using vacuum cleaners or smiling at their washing machines or refrigerators. It was an odd collection considering Freyda never had anything to do with the cleaning of her own house. Once again, Jonathan had read my mind. "Can you imagine Freyda with a vacuum cleaner? She'd be calling me in a panic every time she had to change an attachment." It was said in a fond way. Freyda always managed to pick secretaries who indulged her without appearing resentful. "You might as well sit down," he said, gesturing at the bamboo swivel chair with vintage cushions of red anthuriums and palm trees. We both knew who we were up against and Jonathan had declared himself sympathetic to my plight. I remember thinking at that particular moment that Jonathan was probably a little too smart to stay a secretary for long. How was I to know I was reading HIS mind?

As the other line rang and Jonathan excused himself to answer it, I took his advice, settled in, and listened to Freyda's phone conversation.

"Marty wants the ocean villas, not the golf villas. There are no ocean villas left? You told them who it's for? Are you SURE? You're sure. Shit. Kona Village doesn't have golf. He wants golf. That's the whole point. Well, what about the Mauna Kea? You can try Kapalua but I don't know if he'll go for Maui. Have you tried the Kahala Hilton?"

Ostensibly, people in Hollywood take Christmas vacations to Hawaii to escape the pressures of the business, but then they all wind up at the same hotels. As much as they say they don't, they like being with each other. Show-business people love nothing better than to talk about the business of show business, and if you're stuck at some lonely civilian outpost, who would you converse with? Who'd even be there to know who you are? No one could understand your hopes, your dreams, your profit participation, your *tsuris* but a fellow *landsman*.

Just as I caught Freyda's eye and pointed to my watch in an obvious gesture of annoyance, Freyda hung up with a frazzled look she's perfected.

"Sorry, but His Royal Highness decided TODAY that he doesn't want to go to Hong Kong for Christmas, he wants to go to Hawaii. It's September, all the good places are gone, I don't even know if I can get a PLANE reservation. He's driving me crazy." She tossed her headset onto some scripts that were sitting on the yellow Formica breakfast table and got up. "Hi," she said. "It seems like I haven't seen you for ages. I've left you alone because you're working on your script but I've MISSED you. I have to go to the bathroom and then we can go. Call the restaurant," she said to Jonathan, "and tell them I'm on my way."

Freyda hurried out, leaving me behind at Jonathan's desk for the perfunctory good-byes. I was still trying to decide about Jonathan. Part of me disapproved of the cocky way he presented himself. I resented his sense of entitlement, as if Hollywood owed him a living. The other part of me admired his confidence because this town abounds in insecure people who suck the life out of you. Both his handshake and his loafers were way too soft and my father had always warned me about limp handshakes. But if a firm, dry handshake is the main indicator of a man's character, my father should have been doing a hell of a lot better than he was. And at least Jonathan wasn't Ian Mandel, whose macho bluster was a substitute for too much paunch and not enough hair. Jonathan seemed like an honest person. He spoke his mind and his observations had some truth. Although I had a feeling he'd pass everything through that Jewish distillery that extracts the usual essence.

"Going so soon?" he said. "You've only just gotten here an hour ago. Tell you what. Just to make up for it, I'm going to give you parking stamps for the entire day." He took my parking ticket and covered the back with stickers. "You can sit in the garage and listen to those lovely movie melodies until midnight or until you go crazy, whichever comes first." He handed me back the parking stub. "Don't ever say this agency doesn't know how to treat their writers. So, when am I going to get to read your spec script? Freyda told me a little bit about it. I can't wait to see it."

It's the thing to say in Hollywood. I can't tell you how many people have claimed to want to read my scripts and, after I've supplied them a copy, never mentioned it again. I knew Jonathan had read my old script but it didn't mean he was going to read this one. "Sure," I said, just to brush him off.

But Jonathan can't be dismissed that easily. Instead of offering me his fingers, he got up from behind his desk and sealed our new friend-ship with a warm good-bye hug.

"Just remember, I want to be the first one to read your script because I'm your biggest fan."

4

STEFANO KNOWS WHAT I'M TALKING ABOUT

FREYDA WOVE HER Range Rover in and out of traffic on Santa Monica Boulevard and I began the saga of my impending divorce, but I couldn't get past the preface before Freyda began her critique.

"So that's it? Hart just moves out? Uch. Men. They disgust me. Not Hart. I happen to like Hart. But men in general. It's like an epidemic." Her thumb hit the horn and she held it there until an old man driving in front of us slowly rolled out of her way into the turn lane. "I know more women whose husbands have decided they just don't want to be married anymore. Some of them had absolutely no warning." Her thumb went to the horn again. "There must be a special place in hell for people who pull into the intersection and THEN signal."

I decided it was best to let Freyda do the talking until we were safely ensconced at our restaurant. I sat back and enjoyed the climate-control air-conditioning blowing in my face.

"Just toss those books in back," she said, referring to the mess of hardcover books my feet were resting on. Her car, backseat and front, was filled with the requisite scripts, but among the reading material were also books. Unlike most people in the industry, Freyda actually reads books for pleasure. Although I wondered if the content was less important than the opinions others had of it. "That biography of Dickens, by the way, is wonderful. You can borrow it if you promise-to-return-it-to-me. It got great reviews. John Updike loved it. Jonathan gave it to me and I read it in France. I think he's going to work out. He's very bright, you know. He went to Harvard."

"So I gather."

"Marty loves him. We took him out to dinner the other night and he recited 'Casey at the Bat.' The entire thing from memory. Marty couldn't get over it. The two of them talked about New York. I think Marty wants to adopt him. I'm sure he won't stay with me long. Jonathan, not Marty. Marty's like an inoperable tumor. As soon as I get them to where they know what I want, they leave. The thing I like about Jonathan is he anticipates. Adam was hopeless."

"He was nice, though."

"He was nice but he didn't anticipate. This is ridiculous. I'm just going to do valet at Neiman's and we'll walk."

When we entered the restaurant, a thin Italian woman who held some menus kissed Freyda on both cheeks and made a big fuss over her outfit.

"Every time you come een you loook so DEEFerent. It take so much thinking. How you haf the time to figure out what you puut on today? You make me feel like I haf no style."

"But I LOVE the way you look. You're so THIN. I just came back from France and none of my clothes fit. I can't stand it."

"No!" she said, sounding almost offended. "You loook the same."

"Please. I wish. YOU'RE the one who always looks so great."

"But you haf such imagination. Doesn't she haf imagination?" She turned to me for confirmation.

"She certainly does." I used to marvel at these effusive greetings Freyda received when she walked into restaurants, presuming it was because she put thousands on her platinum card every month. But then I discovered that in addition to her lunchtime redistribution of wealth, she dispenses Christmas gifts of Godiva chocolates to the hostesses and expensive Scotch and port to the maître d's.

"You secretary, Jonathan, call and I safe you a nice table. You follow me."

We almost made it across the restaurant, but just as our mooring was in sight Freyda spotted someone important sitting in a booth. The hostess wisely placed the menus on our table and went back to work. I had no choice but to stand next to Freyda as she chatted with two men whose accents confirmed they'd both migrated to L.A. from one of the less desirable New York boroughs. One was wearing a very expensive-looking suit with a gold tie bar holding in place a stiff yellow tie. The other was in tennis shorts, his hair pulled back into a little ponytail, always so attractive in balding middle-aged men. She didn't talk long enough to introduce us, just long enough to make me wonder what to do with my hands.

"Where's that *momzer* husband of yours?" the suit said. He was leaning back with his arms hugging the top of the red banquette. A Bulgari watch hung loose on his wrist like a bracelet.

"He's in New York."

No one was supposed to know, but when Marty was between movies, which he almost always was, he sometimes took jobs directing industrials for major corporations. Freyda dismissed them as grandiose commercials. From her perspective, they were on par with army training films. The problem was that Marty's last movie, many years before, had been a hit. Directing industrials was an easy way to make money, and it kept him from having to commit to a new movie, which might ruin his career. As long as he never did anything again, he still retained the cachet. But directing industrials is the Hollywood equivalent of a brain surgeon who does high colonics on the side. The only reason Freyda approved was she liked Marty busy and out of her hair. Unfortunately, industrials don't take much time and then he was "back to being an unemployed, nervous Jew."

"I didn't see him on the golf course last weekend, I thought maybe he'd died," the suit said as he took one of his manicured fingers and began clearing away some food lodged near his back molars. "So when's he comin' home?"

"Friday and he's driving me CRAZY. Will you get him a JOB already? I'm going to diVORCE him if he doesn't get to work soon. You know the way he gets when he's not WORKING."

"He's too fuckin' picky. I send him twenty scripts a week. He's driving YOU fuckin' crazy? He's driving ME crazy."

The one in tennis shorts had snuck his hand down the front of his shirt and was slowly, lovingly caressing his chest hair. "I got a script for him that's fuckin' brilliant. You know Shawn Hively? New writer. Young kid. Very fresh. A lotta humor. I'm gonna have my secretary FedEx it to him in New York. Where's he staying?"

"The Sherry."

"They should name a WING after him there already," the suit said.

As we moved to our table, Freyda slid into the banquette against the wall looking out. I was left with the chair facing a mirror and the hanging salamis. She leaned into me.

"Marty's agent."

"No kidding."

"And the other one is Jerry Slotnick. He might be a good person for you to meet. He's gotten some things off the ground."

"By the grace of God they're not both importing ladies' eel-skin purses from Korea." I could see immediately from Freyda's face that it was the wrong thing to have said.

"Jerry happens to have a deal at Columbia AND Fox. He's in negotiation with ScorCESSI about a project and he's married to a lovely woman who's a terrific artist and a gourmet cook and he has an adorable, smart little girl whom he's crazy about." Freyda almost had tears in her eyes. I'd forgotten what a tireless defender and champion she was of the rich and successful.

"Sorry. I didn't mean to imply that he was a bad father or a bad producer. Only that at this moment he's actually rearranging his balls." I could see him in the mirror above Freyda's head. He had stood up and was trying to get them unglued from his leg without actually reaching into his pants. Freyda glanced at him quickly.

"Men," she said, and the subject was gracefully dropped, which is one of the charming things about Freyda. She can quickly forget any unpleasantness, dodge any contretemps. Grudges and moral outrage never slow her down.

"So tell me what happened between you and Hart? Did anything in particular precipitate this event or was it just a cumulative thing?" I began to relate the birthday lunch in Carmel, when her eyes surveyed the room quickly to see who else she knew. Then she examined the silverware and held a fork up, moving it away from her eyes so she could focus on the tines. I wanted to snap a napkin in front of her face to make her listen to me. Fortunately, a young Italian waiter appeared beside the table. I opened my menu for the first time as Freyda began her query. I knew from experience, Freyda couldn't relax until the food issue was resolved.

"What's the fish today?"

"We have a special swordfish, dipped in bread crumbs and sautéed in olive oil, lemon, and capers with a little white wine. Very good." She was looking up at him in rapt attention, ingesting every morsel of description. "And a filet of sole. Broiled with a very light fresh tomato sauce with just a touch of cream."

"Is the sole REALLY fresh?"

"Very fresh."

Like a lot of women I know who don't actually cook, Freyda whips up her culinary masterpieces in restaurants. "I want the filet of sole but just broiled PLAIN with a little lemon juice and leave the cream out of the sauce and I don't want the potato. I want a double order of vegetables GRILLED. No butter and I want the chopped salad but without the salami or the garbanzo beans and I want the dressing on the SIDE. And iced tea with plenty of ice. And this fork is dirty." She handed the waiter the offending fork. I couldn't help but wish that Freyda was as exacting in my contract negotiations as she was with her lunch.

"And you, signora?" He turned his handsome face my way.

I'd barely gotten through the appetizers on my menu. "I'll just have the swordfish." He disappeared. They brought the bread and water, Freyda took a breadstick, and finally settled in to hear my tragic tale. She was very sympathetic and took my side immediately, as I knew she would.

"I love Hart, I really do, but he's difficult. I couldn't be married to him. Marty has his own *mishegoss* but at least I know how to handle him. Hart's got that cool WASP exterior and you never know what's going on inside. That would drive me crazy." Her voice got lower, more intimate. "Have you two talked about a settlement yet?"

"We don't even have lawyers."

"Well, you shouldn't have to worry. He still loves you, you know."

I could feel my stomach do a rollover. "How do you know?"

"I bumped into him at a screening a couple nights ago."

"What did he say?"

"I'm COUNTING on you," she said to someone over my shoulder. Marty's agent and Jerry Slotnick had gotten up from their booth to leave and had come over to our table to say good-bye. Marty's agent was working a business card between his bicuspids now.

"Tell that *alter kocker* to call me. I'm flying up to Vancouver tonight but I'll be back on Thursday."

"What's happening in Vancouver?" Freyda asked.

"One of my directors is shooting a small independent and I gotta go make an appearance. It's a good thing it's only September. Last time I had to go up there it was winter and they were on location in the middle of the fuckin' woods. I stood around and froze my ass off. I couldn't even feel my feet. I finally had the driver take me back to town and bought boots and a leather jacket on Robson Street."

"It's that damp cold," Freyda said, making a pained face. "It goes right through to your bones. I may have to go up there next month for a miniseries."

"If you want to buy a nice leather jacket I can tell you where to go."

"Everybody's shooting in Vancouver," Jerry said. "Where do you stay when you go up there?"

"The Meridian. It's not a great hotel but it's convenient. I'm bringing my kid up with me this time. Let him see I work for a living."

"Oh, he'll have a fun time," Freyda commanded. "You should bring him to that Italian restaurant that's in the little house. They have very good homemade ravioli with porcini mushrooms and the BEST white asparagus I've ever had."

"What's the name of it?"

She thought for a moment. "It begins with a G. Giardi's, Giovanni's." She gave up trying to remember. "I'll have Jonathan call you with the name and number."

Jerry was still trying to get his balls unstuck. He looked like a Kabuki dancer as he lifted up his right knee and leaned to the left. "Tell Marty I'm sending him the script today."

"Marty got tickets to see Yo-Yo Ma tonight at Lincoln Center. I'm so jealous," Freyda said. Without even signaling, she'd abruptly veered down a new cultural avenue. Tinkle tinkle went her little bell. Everyone pay attention. Freyda Wong's coming through.

But Marty's agent followed her lead and then passed her effortlessly. "Yo-Yo's great. We just saw him in London last month." I could see the tension in Freyda as she tried to regain her advantage.

"Has anyone, by any chance, read that new bio of Dickens that just came out? Talk about London. Sometimes Dickens would LITERALLY walk, I forget how many miles he walked, but it was some AMAZING amount all through London. It's such a fascinating book, it makes me want to go back and read Dickens all over again. John Updike says that of ALL the biographies of Dickens, this one's the best. You're welcome to borrow it. It's six hundred pages but it's a quick read."

Jerry Slotnick, who'd been following this diversion without much interest and whom I suspected wasn't exactly about to immerse himself in Dickens, steered the conversation back on track. "You know, you might want to take a look at that script, too," he said to Freyda. "It needs some work but basically it's all there. We gotta find Marty a movie to direct."

Freyda wilted. "Tell me about it. And give my love to Yoshi."

"You gotta come over for dinner when Marty gets back. She makes this lamb with this sauce. It's unbelievable. The only thing is, I can't stop eating it."

"That's why you're starting to look like a fat Jew," Marty's agent said.

Jerry Slotnick addressed his response to a little wrought-iron chandelier festooned with plastic grapes that hung just above his head. "It's not enough I have to have lunch with him, now I have to take his insults? Fuck you," he said to Marty's agent.

"Do you believe the mouth on him?" Marty's agent looked at me for the first time.

Was I supposed to answer that question? Had I been invited to join in their *kibitz*-fest? I, too, was tempted to say "fuck you" but instead smiled nicely as they said good-bye to Freyda all over again.

Looking around the restaurant at all the men, I suddenly felt scared and lonely. And repulsed. What did all these people want out of life? What made them behave like that? I could feel their desperation and it only added to my own. Not only was I not making a living, I realized it was possible I'd never again be with another man. I'd given up Hart and this is what was out there. The talent brokers who were working the restaurant like a trading floor. These were the new sweatshop bosses with their precision haircuts, smooth shaves, Italian suits, stiff ties, Bulgari Rolex Breitling Cartier watches, who ate lunch on expense accounts and got rich off the workers who actually created the product that made the money that fueled the business that allowed the people in that restaurant to exist. Freyda turned her attention back to me, the reference to Hart's affections completely forgotten.

"I'm putting you up for a couple of rewrites but I'm going to be honest with you: I'm a little worried because you haven't worked in a while and your sample script is old. I wish you could come up with a very, very commercial idea we could try to get a development deal on."

"So do I."

"How's your spec script coming?"

"It's coming,"

"Well, when am I going to SEE it?"

"It's not ready. There are parts of it I still don't like."

"Show it to me and we'll talk about it. But FINISH it already."

"It's almost ready. I need one more pass-through."

"So why do you want to get into the whole pitching game if you're almost done with your script? You must be tired of it by now."

"I'm sick of it."

"Stop being such a perfectionist and just get it DONE. So I can sell it for a fortune and retire to the south of France. We have some new agents I want to have meet you. They're terrific. But finish your damn script."

"Just out of curiosity, what do you think about me doing television?"

"Do you really want the pressure of TV? I think you're better off sticking with features."

"I know, but television at least gets made. They need product," I said, realizing I sounded like an agent myself. "Why don't you call Shepard Blum? Tell him I've decided to do TV again. He likes my writing." Shepard Blum was the wealthiest TV producer I knew. He basically did schlock and he went for the numbers but I'd worked for him once and we'd gotten along.

"Finish *Ivy and Men*. Then we'll talk about TV."

She was right. I didn't want to write Movies of the Week anymore. Who even watches them? But at that moment I just wanted to be wanted by someone.

"I can't wait to see your script. But keep it big. You have a tendency to write small."

"It's big," I lied. "It's the biggest thing I've written lately." Jonathan Prince will like it, I thought.

When her food came, Freyda took one look at the fish, poked it with her new fork, and then turned to the waiter with a displeased expression.

"This is swimming in oil."

"Just a little olive oil so it doesn't stick to the grill, signora." Obviously he'd never served Freyda before. There are certain women who always return their food. It's a control issue. They have no control over their husbands, their age, or the tactics employed by the studios. But at least they have control over their fish.

"And where's the tomato sauce?"

"It has cream in it. You said no cream, signora."

"I wanted the tomatoes sautéed without oil. Just in the pan. They do it for me like that all the time here. Is Stefano here? Stefano knows what I'm talking about. The sauce is what gives it the FLAVOR," she explained to him, then turned to me. "Otherwise it's dry."

The waiter left with her plate. Freyda had become director, producer, editor, and critic of her own lunch. She had sent it back for the needed revisions and all she could do now was wait in frustration.

"So when do you think I'll have your script?"

"Soon, I hope. I just have to do one really unpleasant thing before I can get back to work."

"What's that?"

"I have to go tell the Fingermans I'm getting a divorce."

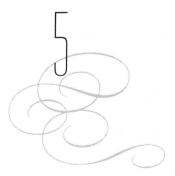

WHO GETS THE MERCEDES?

I LEFT EARLY the next morning. All the way to New York, I kept asking myself why I didn't just make a phone call and be done with it. My parents hadn't even liked Hart when they first met him. Louie and Perle didn't approve of our relationship because he wasn't Jewish. He'd quit teaching to become an unemployed screenwriter. And he was divorced. Louie referred to him as "used merchandise." But after Hart won an Academy Award, he suddenly became the standard by which my SISTER'S husbands were judged. "If only your sister would marry someone like Hart instead of the men she picks. Honestly, I don't know what's WRONG with her. She ALWAYS chooses men she has to take care of." Louie and Perle were much prouder of Hart than they were of me. And for good reason. He'd allowed them access to his success, which bestowed on them a certain situational celebrity they'd never had before. Perle was especially proprietary toward Hart's career and brandished her prestige by proximity as she replayed the rivalry with her sister, Lucille. Aunt Lucille might have had the money, an ocean-view apartment in Boca, and a face-lift, but HER children had never given her an Academy Award. Lucille had been to Europe, taken cruises, and done some spas in Mexico, but HER children didn't write movies that people discussed in line at the checkout stand. It's true, Lucille had a third husband who once directed floor-wax commercials, but HE was never written up in "Arts and Leisure." It's a little like the old joke Grampa Zucky used to tell about when Gittel finds out that Sammy is having an affair.

"*Who is she?*" Gittel screams at Sammy. And he confesses the woman in question is a showgirl.

"*But I'm not the only one,*" he tells her in his defense. "*Your brother Harry, he ALSO has a girl.*"

"*I don't care about Harry, I want to see the* nafka *YOU'RE* shtupping." So Sammy brings her uptown to the burlesque house and they sit down and the girls dance onto the stage, all feathers and legs. "*Which one is she?*" Gittel whispers to him.

He points. "*She's the third one from the right.*"

"*And which one is Harry's?*" she asks him.

"*The fifth one from the left,*" he answers.

She looks both girls up and down and then she turns to her husband and says, "*I like ours better.*"

Now with the impending divorce their Academy Award had been stolen and I was coming back, like the repentant thief, to ease my guilt. I realized this as soon as we were in their rust-pitted Honda on the way home from the Amsterdam train station.

"Who gets the Mercedes?" was the first thing Louie said after he heard the news.

"What has that got to do with anything?"

"How old is that car?"

I had to think. "It's twelve years old."

"It still looks good."

Perle turned around in her seat and said, "Three children. Three divorces. What did we do wrong?"

"I wonder," I said.

"What are you going to do for a job?" she asked me. "How are you going to make any money?"

"I'll write. I'm a writer. What do you think I do?"

"Are you even in the WRITERS Guild?" she said with the annoying way she has of referencing Hollywood.

"Of COURSE I'm in the Writers Guild. What are you talking about?"

"Well, I don't KNOW. When was the last time I saw anything with your NAME on it?"

I'd traveled two days to get there and it had taken only three minutes in their company to really regret it.

My divorce wasn't mentioned the rest of the way from Amsterdam. After the initial shock it was as if I'd never told them, as if I wasn't even there. I sat in the backseat carrying on a furious private monologue, going through my repertoire of grievances, cursing myself for coming. You think Jonathan Prince has parents like these? I asked myself. I'd only just met Jonathan, seen him once, gotten a glimpse of his life, but it was enough to make me know we came from very different stock. It was crazy, but I was imagining Jonathan's parents welcoming him home. I saw them standing in front of a large house, a mother who knew how to take good care of herself, a father who also knew how to take good care of her. There were open arms, big smiles, hugs, kisses, pats on the back. They were delighted by their own creation. My son from Harvard. Jonathan could do no wrong. Of COURSE he saunters down the hall radiating confidence. Of COURSE he feels deserving. Look where he comes from. He wasn't supposed to make his parents feel better about themselves. He wasn't supposed to be compensation for his father's failure.

When I tuned back to what was going on in that car, Louie and Perle were in the middle of a familiar argument. It was now my grandmother's turn to be the focus of Louie's unhappiness.

"I don't want her around anymore," Louie said in the disgusted tone he used when referring to his mother-in-law. "I'm tired of it already." As if he was talking about a dog who was having too many accidents in the house.

"So what am I supposed to do with her?" Perle asked plaintively.

"Send her to your sister's. Let Lucille take care of her for a change. Your sister's selfish. She always has been. She only thinks of herself."

"Well, she's the only sister I have," Perle said, her oddly protective response to any criticism of Aunt Lucille.

Poor Gramma Dora. When Grampa Zucky died many years before and she'd come to live with my parents, Louie's feelings toward her turned, vacillating unpredictably between anger and contrition. I couldn't figure out what she'd done to make him dislike her so. It was a mystery to everyone who knew her. It was particularly nervy of my father because Dora owned the summer cottage where she'd always welcomed us and now was no longer welcome herself. I wanted to point this out to Louie but he'd never appreciate the irony.

It had been years since I'd visited the little house and I was sure once we got there I'd find everything had changed for the worse. Another confirmation I should've stayed home. But when we pulled down our road and I spotted the cottage, I could've yelled out loud, if my joy hadn't been killed by the company. The quaint Victorian houses with their white gingerbread trim and front porches were exactly as I'd remembered them. The only indication time had passed was that the saplings Grampa Zucky planted to shield our pale yellow house from the dusty dirt road had grown into trees as high as the second-story roof. I was stunned by a sense of continuity I didn't know I'd been missing. For almost twenty years I'd lived in Los Angeles, where house remodels are done as routinely as Pap smears. Now I was back where the air smelled of autumn sun and warm pine needles, and I saw Dora waiting in a rocking chair on the front porch where she'd always waited. She was crocheting a pair of pink booties, what every woman in my family wears on cold nights.

Louie parked the car in deep shade. As a cloud of dust settled behind us, I climbed out of the backseat, feeling as if I'd just returned to Grover's Corners. At any moment I might see myself as a ten-year-old, running out the screen door on my way to the lake.

I dragged my suitcase toward the front porch and Dora, her face lighting up with delight, got up from her rocking chair and carefully placed the booties on the cushioned seat. She'd dressed up for the occasion in a royal purple double-knit pant suit with brass buttons and a purple print blouse. She had on white deerskin slippers, which Perle bought every summer by the dozen from the leather factory in Gloversville, to give as birthday gifts throughout the year. Dora's broad square face was tan from the Florida winter sun and so famil-iarly etched in wrinkles that she never seemed to get any older. Per-fect strangers regularly came up to Dora to admire her hair, which was silvery white with jet-black strands that refused to turn. And so thick I don't think she owned a comb with teeth that weren't broken. She wore it short, setting two pin curls on her forehead, carefully sculpted with Dippity-Do, or sometimes beer. Her glasses, the only pair I ever remember her wearing, were smeared with fingerprints. I don't think she noticed. She was getting cataracts and probably thought it was just her eyes. She was only about five feet tall, barely reaching my shoulders, and even though I could look down on the top of her head, I never thought of her as particularly short because she carried herself so unapologetically. We hugged each other and she smelled of face powder, the way women don't anymore.

"Your hands are like two chunks of ice, *mamelah*," she said, putting my hands between her warm palms. "It's chilly in the shade. In town it's ten degrees warmer. Are you hungry? You want I should heat you up a piece of meat loaf?"

For the first time that day I smiled. If only she knew how exotic meat loaf was to me. Whenever it appears on a menu in L.A. it's greeted with cries of ecstatic delight: "*Oh, look. They have MEAT loaf.*" Then everyone at the table relates their childhood memories of meat loaf, and those whose mothers put hard-boiled eggs in the center share an especially close moment. But curiously, as much as they claim to love it, I've never seen anyone I know try to replicate it at home. If they're hungry for nostalgia, they go to a couple of well-known restaurants that serve comfort food for a hefty price. I was so happy to be offered meat loaf by someone who wasn't charging.

As I was about to give myself over to her, Louie stepped up to the porch and threw Dora a dirty look on his way into the house. I could see she caught it, but before either one of us could acknowledge the sentiment, we heard him at the stove banging some pots. She didn't want to go into that kitchen and I didn't either.

"I'm not hungry just yet, Gramma."

She understood. "Maybe later."

I brought my suitcase up to my old bedroom, the one with the upstairs porch; a room barely big enough to accommodate my bed, a dresser, and a night table, all of which I'd painted the same pale yellow as our house. After opening up the three dresser drawers and inhaling the tiny balls of camphor that rattled around in the empty corners, I stepped into the bedroom across the hall. There were the three single beds with white chenille spreads that had been occupied by my brother and any other male visitors. His pennants were still thumbtacked to the wall: Tufts, Princeton, and the University of Pennsylvania. I don't think my brother knew anyone who actually WENT to these schools, nor could we have afforded to send him. It was just inexpensive decoration. The rooms had been thoughtlessly thrown together and forgotten about, but the effect was a house that looked like a movie set. Dora had no idea that her painted, chipped furniture, cherry-cluster tablecloth, Nancy Drew books, and Aunt Jemima cookie jar were selling on Melrose Avenue as high-priced Americana.

The set had remained the same for thirty years but all the familiar characters were long gone. The old Jews who used to stop by our cottage. Mr. Weinseider, the tailor, his skinny arms sticking out of a short-sleeved shirt, stooped over like he was still pinning hems. Mr. Finkle, who made his living selling day-old bread, so happy just to *plotz* on our front porch with the newspaper, a glass of tea, and his Flit gun. The widow, Ida Mink, who insulted babies so the Evil Eye, *kayn aynhoreh,* wouldn't get them. "*Oy, what a* pisherkeh. *Whoever saw such an ugly face on a baby?*"

The old Jews LIKED that the cottages were so close together. You didn't have to shout. If you wanted to visit, you didn't kill yourself walking a mile. They called each other by their last names, even when they sat around our dining room table playing kaluki. "*You call those cards, Mr. Pincus? Bist meshugeh?*" The place hadn't changed, it was the Jews who'd changed. They wanted different vacationlands now. They summered in the Hamptons, Fire Island, Martha's Vineyard, Maine. The only old Jew who was still around, who'd managed to endure, was Dora.

I came downstairs just in time to witness Louie's eruption, which had been building since the train station. It was an anger I knew so well, but never failed to be shaken by. "I'm tired of you," he spewed at Dora. "Why don't you go live with your other daughter? Go live with Lucille for a change." Dora said nothing but I knew what she was thinking because I'd heard her say it in Yiddish enough times.

"Vos vainiker me ret, iz als gezunter." The less you talk the better off you are.

I followed her wise advice and detoured into the kitchen just as Perle opened up the refrigerator and saw that Louie had laid a large bottle of Soave Bolla right on top of the flimsy plastic container holding a premade pie shell. It was filled with lemon chiffon she'd concocted, for my arrival, out of instant pudding and Cool Whip. It was now as squashed as if it had met with a clown's face. When she protested, Louie yelled at her, too. "Have you looked at yourself lately? You need lemon chiffon pie like a hole in the head." Personally, I hate lemon chiffon pie and avoid it at every opportunity, but my mother had gone to the trouble and my father had carelessly ruined it. Dora was the only one who would have scraped the gelatinous mess together and eaten it without complaint. Maybe it was too hard to live with someone so good.

Perle wiped yellow goo off the refrigerator shelf, and we could all hear Louie in the living room now, dialing Aunt Lucille in Florida. Perle stepped out of the kitchen, the lemon chiffon sponge dripping into her hand, and told him to please calm down. It was amazing to me how quickly I could get back into feeling exactly the way I did as a kid: trapped and suffocated. I wanted to call someone and tell them how depressing my parents were but the only person I could think of calling was Hart, and he was the reason I was there. I know from experience that unhappiness is highly contagious and I had enough of my own at that moment without coming down with theirs. I escaped to the small back porch.

The limp socks and brassieres and paint-stained khakis strung across the shaded yard looked like the same laundry that had hung there forever. Shayna, their dog, was lying at the top of the steps. Her tail slapped the gray wood a few times and she looked up at me with her worried brown eyes but she never lifted her head as I sat down. I could still hear Louie on the phone with Aunt Lucille: "You're a cheapskate! You don't even offer to contribute to your own mother's upkeep!" I suspected that Shayna, like me, was out there to avoid a house full of tension. I wanted to be reassuring, but she was an old dog and she smelled, so I just patted her head lightly. "Poor Shayna,"

I said. "Poor Shayna dog," and she licked my wrist where I'd sprayed cologne that morning.

"What kind of a daughter ARE you? You're selfish! You only think of yourself!" Louie was right about Aunt Lucille, although it wasn't the way to deal with his sister-in-law. Poor Louie never understood how to play to her narcissism, how to get what he wanted. Even rudimentary manipulation was beyond him; a promise, a wheedle, a coax, a white lie. He just didn't have the device in his head to slow down the impulse while he considered the consequence. He tossed remarks over his shoulder like Molotov cocktails; he was the mad bomber of the thoughtless insult, a terrorist in his own home. Except his intended target, Aunt Lucille, must have lobbed a canister of mustard gas right back at him. Louie uttered an uncharacteristic expletive—"go fuck yourself"—and slammed down the receiver. "Why is Hart never around when I need him?" I said to Shayna, and her ears cocked when she heard his name.

I hadn't had anything to eat or drink since the train. I'd lost my appetite but now I was getting woozy and needed a glass of juice. There was no choice but to venture back into the house. Perle was busying herself at the stove, putting aluminum foil around the broiler pan as if nothing was amiss. She wore old brown polyester pants stretched tightly across her bottom and brown-and-white saddle shoes polished a dull, chalky white. The yellow cardigan Dora had knit for her about twenty years before gave off a whiff of mothballs. Unable to confront the current situation, Perle began complaining that the man from town they'd hired years before to make the kitchen cabinets had made them too shallow. "You can't even put the DISHES in there," she said as if she'd just discovered it. "It's so riDICulous that anyone would think to make kitchen cabinets like this." She opened the cabinet to prove her point. The only small glasses I could find were used *yahrzeit* candleholders, row after row of them. On every anniversary of every death in the family, they had lit a candle in memory and come away with a juice glass.

"Jake Stern worked for the post office for all those years," Perle said, more to herself than to me, "and we used to think he was such a dope because only the *goyim* had jobs like that. Now he has a nice government pension coming in and what have I got to show for anything?" The croquet players in *Town & Country,* drinking from champagne flutes, flashed through my mind. As I raised the *yahrzeit* candle glass to my lips I thought, This really is a house of the dead.

A moment later, under pressure from Louie, Perle was on the living room phone, making arrangements with a relative in Yonkers to take Dora for a few weeks. Dora was sitting on the sofa with her hands resting calmly in her lap, listening as her fate was decided. Louie, who'd exhausted himself and everyone around him, had gone upstairs to lie down before the next bout. I took Dora's hand. "Come on, Gramma, let's take a ride into town." I wanted to get her out of that madhouse. I wanted to tell her about my divorce. I needed her consolation, her gentle words. She squeezed my hand and I saw the look on her face. She thought I had come there to rescue her. But I was expecting YOU to save ME, my eyes said back.

She went into the downstairs bedroom to put on her sneakers. Perle waited until Dora was out of the room and then, seizing the moment, put the receiver to her yellow cardigan, and whispered, "Don't tell Gramma about you and Hart. She hasn't been well lately. It will only make her SICK."

6

GOOD-BYE AND GOOD LUCK TO YOU

DORA WAS VERY quiet as we headed toward town and I didn't really feel like talking either. I was thinking about Gregory Peck in *To Kill a Mockingbird*. (About a year later, as I watched the movie with Jonathan Prince, he would voice more pointedly what I was feeling in that car. "Can you imagine if all of us Jews had Atticus Finch as our father? Half the shrinks in New York and L.A. would go out of business.") As the car did a slow bump and grind down the root-rutted road, I imagined a middle-aged Scout coming back home to tell Atticus she's getting a divorce. I pictured Atticus in his cardigan, sitting on the front-porch swing with a glass of lemonade and Scout across from him in the rocker. *"You always were a fighter, Scout,"* he says to her in his strong, quiet voice. *"Even when you were small and lived in your tree house, I always knew that if you fell out, somehow you'd land on your own two feet."*

"But, Atticus—"

"Marriage is a complicated business, Scout. It's like a flower that has to be watered and weeded and tended to. But sometimes the flower dies in spite of all you've done. Maybe it means it just wasn't a strong enough plant to begin with, maybe the roots didn't go deep enough. I trust that you've tended

your garden as best as you knew how and that's all that really matters." He takes a small sip of lemonade. *"And when you have a chance, you might want to stop by and say hello to Mr. Arthur Radley. He's been asking for you."*

We came to the bridge that spans the lake and I recognized the spot where I used to stop on my lonely walks back from town to pick Dora bouquets of black-eyed Susans. I wanted to point it out to her, to say how lonely I felt now. I knew I was being dishonest by not telling Dora about Hart. Why should I let myself become part of a conspiracy? Sooner or later she'd find out. How long did my mother think she could hide it? I was trying to broach the subject in the gentlest way possible when she turned to me. "They toss me around like an old apple." Only she said "epple." "They toss me around like an old epple."

I believe that was one of the saddest moments in our lives. What could she have done to deserve such treatment? "Oh, Gramma," was all I could manage to say.

I parked the car on Main Street and we went into Griffith's Drugstore. Old Mr. Griffith, who was always called Old Mr. Griffith, stood behind a waist-high partition dispensing pills. Both he and the inventory on his shelves had shrunk considerably over the years. Dora whispered to me confidentially that he didn't carry her heart medication anymore and my parents had to drive all the way to Gloversville to get it. We sat at the ice-cream counter on red padded stools patched with electrical tape and ordered scoops of chocolate ripple. As Old Mr. Griffith was bent over the canisters digging out the ice cream, Dora leaned closer to me.

"I don't want I should scare you."

"What's wrong?" I said, panic beginning to rise in my gut. If she died from a heart attack, right here, right in front of me, I'd tell everyone Louie had killed her.

"You remember when I used to give you ten cents for ice cream?" she said, pausing for effect. "It's a dollar thirty now."

Neither one of us had the slightest desire to go back home, so we slowly walked along Main Street with our cones, peering into the windows. The "inspirational store" still featured Jesus Christ with his crown of thorns, which, as we headed toward the Laundromat, became a blond angel in a pink robe blessing a happy boy and girl who were playing by the side of a blue brook. I stopped for a moment and swayed, left to right, right to left, left to right, right to left, like I'd done countless times as a kid who'd been intrigued by a religion that sold such things. Jesus Christ. Angel, children. Jesus Christ. Angel, children. "It's a regular miracle," Dora said.

The Deer Head Lounge, which we'd never been to because my parents said that only the *goyim* went there, was doing a brisk business at three in the afternoon, the regulars whooping it up at the bar in a haze of cigarette smoke. At least they were laughing, which was more than I could say for the regulars at our house.

"Hey, Gram, what do you say I take you to the movies tonight?" It didn't matter what was playing, I just wanted to sit in that theater once again with Dora. It may have been the tiniest movie theater in creation. Even as a child, when everything seems big, I thought that. But I can still remember scenes from movies I saw there forty years ago, and pieces of dialogue almost verbatim. And the green-satin-and-black-lace outfit Marilyn Monroe wore in *Bus Stop* when she sang "That Old Black Magic." That was the first time I remember being aware of sex. In that small theater, the power of movies captured me. Like the night we all went to see *The Member of the Wedding* in revival. After the movie, we stood on the sidewalk, eating our ice cream in the warm summer evening, and I made an announcement: from then on, my name was no longer Francine. I was Frankie. My backward inspiration was Julie Harris, who proclaimed to Ethel Waters that she wasn't to be called Frankie anymore, but F. Jasmine. "All people belong to a 'we' except me," Frankie said, and I knew exactly what she meant. She didn't feel like she belonged. She felt like an outsider and it made her angry and mean. Up until that moment I never knew anyone felt like I did.

"The movie theater closed last summer," Dora said. "And even the one in Gloversville is closed down."

Sure enough, the poster window was empty, the glass a target for BB-gun practice. The doors had a thick chain around the handles, clamped with a large padlock.

For years I'd dreamed of coming back when a movie I'd written was on the marquee. I imagined myself walking in unnoticed and unknown, taking an aisle seat toward the front. It wasn't so much seeing my words come to life that I envisioned, it was the moment when I'd turn and look at the faces as they watched the screen. It was the beauty of coming back to the place where I'd seen my first movie, only it would be MY words and MY thoughts that were moving people.

"Why did it have to close?" I asked, although it really wasn't a question so much as an elegy.

"They couldn't make a living anymore. No one wants to pay so much for a movie that's not so good," Dora said, explaining to me what every studio executive knows and fears.

I stayed at the family cottage through the week. On my last day, Louie, whether as an overture of some kind I couldn't tell, took me fishing on the lake, like we used to do in the best of times. Smitty, the next-door neighbor, insisted we borrow his boat. We gathered up Louie's Old Pal tackle box full of rusty lures, but for insurance we stopped at a house in town to buy some live bait. The man of the house remained on the front porch, sitting in his red vinyl re-cliner, looking down over his domain, a yard filled with old washing machines and car parts. He acknowledged us with a nod of the head and a one-fingered wave, as if using his whole hand was too much effort. It was a weekday and he didn't seem to have a regular job, though he didn't seem too worried about it. He was at peace with the world. It was a look you never see in Hollywood, a state of grace which could only be attained by being blessed with low ambition and no natural predators. A cigarette hung from his mouth and he squinted at the smoke as he took the baby from his wife's fleshy arms. She said something and they both laughed. Then she hoisted herself off a folding beach chair, her contour suggesting a fifty-five-gallon oil drum on the move. She shuffled down the steps in her flip-flops and hot-pink shorts.

"I hear they're biting up by the spillway," she said to us.

"Have any night crawlers, dear?" Louie crooned in his sweetest, most ingratiating way. Since he'd lost his business over two decades before, Louie had also let his old friends go. Now he felt most com-fortable with educational inferiors, the economically depressed, peo-ple who weren't a social threat and wouldn't judge him. The missus had put him right at ease. She had a pretty, open face, although she was missing a tooth and her bleached hair was the color of their parched lawn. There was a large scraping bruise on her generous thigh, which looked like she'd slid into home plate. She had to be younger than I and there was no discernible reason for her to be as cheerful as she was. Three of her children were racing around the washing machines throwing stones at each other but she ignored them as she reached right into a coffee can full of moss and hellgrammites, as if it was just a bag of Doritos.

Louie steered us down the lake toward Conklinville in the little outboard boat. I had a particular spot in mind, a secluded cove Dora and I named The Laughing Place after seeing *Tales of Uncle Remus.* I wanted to tell her I'd been back to The Laughing Place, it would make her happy. I pointed toward the cove and shouted to Louie. He cut the motor and it became wonderfully quiet except for the birds and the deep, clean water lapping against the boat. From a distance we might have resembled a photo on a Father's Day card, but on closer inspection you'd have seen the strained expression and hunched shoulders of a woman expecting the boom to be lowered.

I tried to avoid looking at him but it was hard to do sitting knee to knee. Louie had grown a white beard, and with his sea captain's hat and sky-blue eyes, he looked to me like an old salt. Not the house roofer he once was. And, again, I remembered *Town & Country;* the elegant man in the sailing regatta. I thought about that gallant image as I watched Louie, shoulders stooped, glasses dangling from one ear, try to tie the monofilament into a knot. The skin on his face was ruddy and flaking from the L-dopa he took for his Parkinson's and his fingers were too stiff to perform the delicate task. He finally gave up and attempted to talk me through it. I could feel him staring at me as I threaded the slippery line through the hook, around and around, and back through the little loop.

"So what happened?" I knew it was coming and I was almost relieved he'd finally said it. "Between you and Hart?"

"A lot of things." I had no idea what his reaction would be. He was someone who yelled at the top of his lungs if you blew out the candles instead of snuffing them between your licked fingers. Cutting the tomato wedges too big was cause for a snide remark. But now all he did was go into his tackle box and take out a pair of nail clippers.

"It's too bad," he said.

As he struggled to trim the line, I realized the conversation was over. Not that there was ever much give-and-take between us. It was always one-sided; Louie telling you what he didn't like, what you were doing wrong. At least this time he hadn't made me the cause of his misery. Dora bore that burden.

The fish must have felt the tension, or maybe it was they who were laughing, but they weren't biting at The Laughing Place, so we lifted anchor and trolled all the way home. A few times I thought I had a bite, and Louie kindly shut down the engine, but it was just my line dragging on the bottom of the lake. We returned the boat to Smitty's dock and I asked if we should buy him a tank of gas. He pretended not to hear me, as he'd pretend to Smitty we'd hardly used any. And Smitty, who'd known my father for years, would understand and overlook it.

Dora and I took the train back to New York City. We sat side by side and held hands until Poughkeepsie, when we unpacked the lunch my mother had made for us. There were peaches from the farm up the road and wet paper towels in a Baggie for the cleanup. It was Perle's penance. She'd tried to keep the peace with Louie by pushing Dora out of the house, and had salved her conscience with egg-salad sandwiches.

After lunch we played a few hands of kaluki and then Dora's eyes got tired and we put the cards away.

"You look blue, *mamelah*. Maybe you're missing Hart."

I tried to see in her face if she suspected. No. She knew nothing. "Don't worry about me, Gramma. I'm fine. How 'bout you? You miss Grampa?"

"Every day. I knew him since I was sixteen. So that's a lot of years I knew him already."

"How'd you and Grampa meet, anyway?"

She reached into a plastic tote bag that was collapsed on the floor by her feet and brought up her wool and needles. She didn't need her eyes for knitting. "You know sometimes you say you can do this or that . . . as I joke . . . so I did. There was a lot of young people and we were behind the synagogue and I said I could chugalug a bottle beer . . . a bottle, not from a glass."

"Chugalug?" I was surprised she knew the expression. But she misinterpreted and thought I didn't know it.

"To drink it all down in one breath. But I really didn't make it in one breath. I caught a breath while I was drinking but nobody noticed."

"Was Grampa impressed?"

"He must've been because afterward he said, 'Can I take you home?' So, I didn't refuse him. He looked very nice, a good-looking fellow, so we came home and my mother, of course, accepted him and asked him from where he comes and he said 'I'm coming from Vilna.' And my parents asked, 'Who's your folks?' He said, 'The Zuckermans.' And Mama said, 'The Zuckermans? Your mother's name is Yedda?' He said, 'Yeh.' So it turns out that was Mama's girlfriend. That was her girlfriend's son. And that's how we met. And he remained in the family."

"So that was your first and only boyfriend?"

"How many do I need?"

"Were you working then?"

"I worked for the Berkowitz brothers who owned a shirt factory. They were my father's cousins. They used to come many times to visit us, and my mother, she used to make many times on the holidays a dinner."

"How old were you when you first went to work?"

She stopped knitting for a moment while she thought about it. "I think I was already about thirteen when I went to work for the Berkowitz brothers. I'll tell you a story," she said, her face lighting up like I hadn't seen since that first day I'd arrived. "They had a place on Forsyth Street. My father was a cutter there. My sister, Zelda, and myself, we also worked but we worked not at the machine, we worked by hand. And one evening when they were working time and a half, I said to my sister 'I'm going to ask the boss for an increase.' We were making three dollars a week. I think we used to start at seven o'clock in the morning, twelve o'clock lunch, a half an hour, and six o'clock, if it's not time and a half, we could go home. So I said to my sister, Zelda, 'I'm going to ask for an increase.' She said, 'Don't.' She always called me Big Mouth. Because I think I had more nerve than she had. So I go over to one of the bosses and I asked for an increase. And he said to my father, 'Shlomo! Commere! Commere! Commere!' Papa didn't know what happened. I'm standing there talking, he thought maybe I got hurt or something, so he came over and said, 'What's wrong?' And the Berkowitz brother said, 'Your greenhorn is asking for more money.' So my father started laughing. And the boss says to me, 'How long are you in this country?' And I said to him, 'Do you pay people the value of what they produce, or you pay for the time being in the country?' And he said to my father, 'Oh, she's going to get married before the other children. Because she has nerve.' And he was right because I DID get married before my older sister."

"And did you get the raise?"

"So listen what happened," she said, lightly touching my arm with her warm hand. The old-fashioned diamond wedding ring she wore looked cloudy. When Zucky died, the better diamond, which my grandfather had worn, was appropriated by Aunt Lucille. This one, no doubt, would go to Perle. "I go back and the first thing I said to my sister, 'Do you know what Berkowitz said? That I have nerve and I'm not long enough in the country to come and ask for a raise.' So she said to me, 'You with the big mouth. Maybe they'll fire us.' So come payday, they handed us the envelope and instead of three dollars it's two and a half." She laughed. "They took off fifty cents from the pay. So my sister got a little bit angry at me and she complained to Papa. 'I told her not to ask for a raise.' But anyway, they just played a trick. Because the following week we got our fifty cents what they took off and fifty cents increase. So that's the story."

She let the knitting rest in her lap, leaned back in her seat, and looked out the window at the heavy green trees rushing past. The sky was starting to darken. I wished we were headed right out to California, that we had our own sleeping compartment and I could lie on the top bunk and listen to her stories as the train clackety-jerked across the whole country. When we'd pull into Union Station, we'd get off and put the suitcases in a locker, then I'd take her arm and we'd step outside into the sun and walk to Olvera Street. I imagined her sweet reaction to the shops with little lace children's dresses, the fat white candles, the huaraches, the Mariachi bands, and the carts selling every *chotchke* made in Tijuana.

Then, as if we were actually going, I started worrying about how I would get her across the wide street in front of Union Station. Could I borrow a wheelchair from Amtrak if I left a deposit or my driver's license? Could I take a taxi for such a short ride? Could we just walk slowly, her hand on my arm, and would the cars stop for an old woman? I heard their angry horns honking, the screeching tires as they drove around us. By the time I'd gotten us there, I needed a great big margarita.

"It's going to rain," Dora said, and the next moment a streak of rain hit our window and made a slow, jagged path across the glass. "Are you cold? I have a sweater."

"I'm not cold, are you?"

She shook her head.

"Gramma, why don't you come out to California and live with me?"

"Me zol nit darfen onkumen tsu kinder."

"What does that mean?"

"You should pray that you're not a burden to your children."

"Gramma, you're never a burden to me."

"You mean it?" I could see how much she wanted to come. I'd given her false hope because I loved her, but how could I be responsible for my grandmother? She was eighty-nine years old, although she said that some days she felt like ninety. I had my own life to get straightened out. That meant going back to L.A and finishing the movie script that would not only earn me money, but my rightful place in Hollywood.

"Of course I mean it."

"Better you should ask Hart. An old woman isn't that easy."

Maybe this was the reason Louie didn't want her. He'd gotten tired of taking her to the kosher butcher and the various doctors who kept her going. Maybe it was as obvious as that.

We got off the train at Grand Central and my grandmother's niece Zippy, with the bright red hair, was on the platform waiting to bring

Dora back to Yonkers. Zippy is only a few years younger than Dora and stands about the same height, but she has a bustling, bossy manner I'd always found unnerving. As a girl she was with the Ziegfeld Follies, and although her beauty had disappeared about the same time as vaudeville, she refused to become invisible. If anything, she was more theatrical than ever.

"Your father's a bastard. You know that?" was her opening line. Then she grabbed my grandmother's arm away from mine. "Come on, Dora. You're coming with ME." She commandeered a young man carrying a violin, whom she called "sonny," to help her with the suitcases. He looked a little scared of her and did as he was told. We'd all stepped onto the escalator with our luggage when Zippy turned around, still firmly clutching Dora's arm, and addressed me as if I were in the enemy camp.

"Your grandmother's not a rich woman . . . she and Morris worked hard for every penny they made."

"Zippy," my grandmother said, interrupting her. *"Shveig! Sha!"* And then she said something in Yiddish I understood. *"Ez is a shandeh far di kinder."* It's a shame on the children.

"Why should I be quiet? Let her know what kind of a man her father is." Zippy turned to me again. "And then he has the goddamn nerve to pretend like she's taking up room. I'll spit in his face the next time I see him. You tell him that."

Although I agreed with everything Zippy said, it still made me flinch. It was okay if I criticized him, but I didn't want her calling my father a bastard. I suppose I didn't want to hear independent confirmation of the truth.

We said good-bye on the street in the cool gray drizzle. I felt a deep sadness right in the middle of my chest, only dimly aware of commuters rushing past us in a blur of umbrellas and briefcases. Home seemed very far and there was no one waiting for me. I had a terrible premonition I'd never see Dora again. I thought I was going to cry but I don't think she saw. Zippy was already in the cab haranguing the taxi driver, some dark-eyed Middle Eastern import, who was obviously impatient for Dora to get in. I wanted to scream at him. Instead I kissed Dora and rushed her into the cab. "I love you, Gramma," I said with one eye on the taxi driver. She turned to me, "I love you, too, you have no idea." Then she said what she always said. "Good-bye and good luck to you."

On the ride to Yonkers, Zippy told my grandmother I was getting a divorce.

7

MIRIAM'S HERSHEL

EVEN THE CAT didn't come out to greet me when I returned to the big Spanish house. Ana had left the newspapers and mail piled on a table by the front door and just the idea of sorting through my mail and Hart's made me anxious. An ant trail led to the garbage under the kitchen sink, where a colony was feasting in a 9-Lives turkey-and-giblets can. On the countertop was a note from Ana telling me the washing machine was making a burning smell during the spin cycle. I decided to try my luck in the den.

There were only four messages blinking on my new answering machine. The first was from Hart, saying he thought he must have left his sunglasses in the kitchen when he stopped by to feed the cat. Short, to the point, and very Hart. The second was from my friend Miriam saying she'd bought a beautiful free-range chicken at Mrs. Gooch's and did I want to help sort clothes for the synagogue bazaar and then come for *Shabbes* dinner. My exciting, new social life. When emptiness and loneliness forced me to join the synagogue maybe I'd finally be recognized as a writer—of the annual Temple Follies.

Hart had phoned again reporting his glasses had been retrieved from between his car seats. Still no "How're you doing? How'd it go with Louie and Perle?" I decided not to tell him. The last blink was from Jonathan Prince.

I dialed Jonathan first, hoping he'd say something to make me feel better. Hoping Freyda had gotten me a job. But Jonathan wasn't acting on Freyda's behalf. I was surprised to learn he'd called me on his own.

"You were in the Adirondacks? Lucky you."

"Not really. I was visiting my parents."

"You have crazy parents, too? Every Jew I know is sure their parents are crazy. I actually think there's a certain amount of competitive satisfaction we derive regaling each other with the particulars. You want to tell me the particulars and then I can tell you the particulars?"

"Not particularly."

"Why? What happened?"

I couldn't help reporting my visit in detail, with scathing editorial comments liberally thrown in. That I unburdened myself to a twenty-four-year-old kid I'd met a week ago struck me as a bit odd. But he'd caught me at exactly the right moment.

"How'd you turn out so normal, anyway?" he said when I finished my lamentation.

"Who said I was normal?"

"Those people sound like what Shaw said about parents being not so much examples as warnings. Or that Philip Larkin poem:

> 'They fuck you up, your Mum and Dad.
> They may not mean to, but they do.
> They fill you with the faults they had
> And add some extra, just for you.'

He went on to perfectly recite the rest of the poem without a pause, like a smart schoolboy. I decided at that very moment, despite his Long-Island-Five-Towns-Princely behavior, Jonathan Prince might just be worthwhile after all. I even chided myself for being too judgmental when we'd first met.

The next week I moved out of the house with only my clothes, my computer, my desk chair, Hart's name, and the Mercedes. Jonathan had volunteered to help me and showed up that Saturday morning with two large lattes and muffins from the Zen Bakery. I'd been around long enough to know that when people in the business do something for you, they expect without question something in return. But Jonathan seemed the exception. I obviously wasn't in any position to help him.

Before we started loading up the cars, Jonathan wanted to see the house. He took in each room very carefully, pausing to ask questions about certain pieces of furniture or art, where it was acquired, when we bought it, how old it was. When we got to Hart's writing room on the second floor, he zeroed in on the Oscar. "This is so cool," he said, hoisting it in his hand, feeling its weight, as everybody does. He did a few biceps curls with the statuette and then just cradled it in his palms, caressing the smooth coolness of the gold. Then he took it in his right hand and held it up for me to see. "And I'd especially like to thank my agent, Jonathan Prince, for nurturing my talent, for believing in me all these years, and mostly for being a great negotiator and getting me gross-fucking-points." He returned the Oscar to Hart's bookshelf. "I've just written your acceptance speech."

"Maybe you'd better give it to someone else. I somehow doubt I'm going to be needing it."

"Why CAN'T you win an Academy Award? You're a good enough writer."

"Thanks, but the scripts have to get made first."

"So we'll get them made."

"Unfortunately, Jonathan," I said, trying not to sound too sour and annoyed at his naive confidence, "there's no predicting which scripts are going to get made and which ones won't and sometimes it has nothing to do with how well they're written."

"But there's still no reason you can't be up there making the big bucks like the other writers I read who aren't half as good as you. I obviously haven't been in the business as long as you have but at least I understand a few things, one of which is that those guys out there are idiots. It's all part of my job. When they think I've gotten them enough bagels and made enough restaurant reservations, I get to listen in on their phone calls so I can learn how to become a killer."

"Oh. Is that how it's done."

"How else would you know how to be an agent, unless you're a natural-born asshole? By the way, don't ever say anything about anyone on the phone because you never know who's listening in."

"Now you tell me."

"You've just got to know how to deal with them. There's no heat on you right now. That's the problem. You just do the writing. Give me a good script and leave the hype to me."

I didn't exactly know how Jonathan was going to accomplish this since he wasn't in any position. But I still found myself not wanting to disappoint him.

I was grateful to him for coming over. If Jonathan wasn't there I'm sure I would have fallen into another dark place, but he distracted me, kept everything moving, and got me out of that house. There was none of my usual dithering and barely enough time for a glance good-bye. It took us four trips in two cars, but that was as much as I could handle. I was only moving a mile away, but if I could have camped in my backyard, I would've. I didn't want to get far from the familiar. Didn't want to learn a new supermarket and pharmacist. I was scared of the change. I needed a place that felt like home.

Thank God for Hershel and Miriam. They lived within my restricted geographical zone and had offered to rent me their little back house. I'd met Miriam and Hershel through Hart, but after the separation, when you divide up friends, which you invariably do, they'd been left to me.

They were older, in their early sixties, and had raised their five children with Hershel's income from a very spotty writing career. He used to say he would've been rich if only he hadn't *shtupped* his way out of a standard of living. Their children all went to good colleges, four of them were married now, they liked their jobs, and none of them went to psychiatrists. I guess I was hoping by moving in with them the same would happen for me. That somehow I'd grow up successful and happy.

They knew Hart, so I didn't have to explain why we were separating. Hershel understood the anxiety writing produces, and said numerous times that two writers should never marry because at the end of the day there should be someone to happily mix the martinis. Hershel wasn't a drinker, but Miriam happily made his meals and took care of all the day-to-day things everyone wishes they didn't have to do. In all their married years I don't think Hershel ever once opened a bill or licked a stamp. It's a good thing Miriam was from the old school. A woman who didn't mind. She knew Hershel was a genius and it was her preordained wifely duty to make sure he wrote unmolested and undisturbed.

Hershel and I had an understanding, too. We both knew how it felt to write scripts that didn't get made. But unlike me, Hershel had other irons in the fire: he'd turned himself into a playwright. Unfortunately, his plays were never hits. When Hershel and Miriam were desperate for money, he'd still have to go back to looking for a writing assignment. He'd call one of the old producers he'd worked with in the heyday of live television, when he and his writing were treated with respect. If the old producer's dwindling account at the Hollywood favor bank could still get a meeting at a network or studio, Miriam would invite him for *Shabbes* dinner and buy a center-cut brisket, which she'd cook overnight in a bottle of wine and Lipton onion-soup mix. She'd bake her famous *Shabbes* carrot ring, and top off the enticement with a crème renversée. I'd been invited on more than a couple of those occasions, and after coffee, when Miriam and I were in the kitchen doing the dishes, we'd hear Hershel's genuine high-pitched laughter coming from the next room and know he was amusing himself as he spun his story for his now captive audience. A month or two later, when Hershel had worked out all the details, they'd go in and try to convince some development executive that Hershel was the man for the job.

Some writers are known for their pitches. They may not be able to write but they get hired because they're good salesmen. A good pitch is a performance, a combination entertainment and snow job. As on-screen, you've got five minutes to grab the audience by their throats. But Hershel, who in 1955 had been taken with a *Life* magazine article which had pictured William Faulkner outlining on the whitewashed walls of his workroom, did something in a pitch no one has ever done before or since: he brought a roll of shelf paper with him, and taping it to a door, he'd outline his entire idea in grease pencil, like a professor imparting great wisdom to beginning students.

For a medium that devours product, it's a big mistake to spend too much time agonizing over anything, which Hershel began to do the moment he was hired. Consequently, when he finally finished his script a year later and proclaimed it a work of genius, the executive who'd hired him had invariably been replaced and the new man in charge wasn't interested in any project he couldn't take credit for. Hershel called it writing for the garbage can. Miriam would tell everyone Hershel was too good for television and he'd go back to spending seven days a week in the little paper-strewn office above his garage, slowly writing and rewriting his "little gems" as she called them. Fortunately, they'd bought their house before the real-estate market in Los Angeles had skyrocketed. They were living in the best neighborhood, sitting on a gold mine, in fact, but they couldn't afford the new roof they needed before the winter rains. Hershel and Miriam were counting on my rent money to help them out. That's how I came to live with them. We were both providing a roof over each others' heads.

Jonathan and I pulled into their driveway with the first load and I heard reggae music coming from the house. I knew Miriam was cooking. When she cleans it's Mozart, when she drives it's opera, and recently she'd taken up reggae for cooking. We opened the screen door and stepped inside her long, narrow kitchen (wallpapered by Miriam herself in massive euphoric daisies). She was in a deep V-necked muumuu wiping down her Formica countertops with a sponge, her generous, balloon breasts bobbling with each wipe. She's a short woman with wide hips, very lively dark eyes, and short hair Miss Clairol'd to a purplish shade of brunette. A border of bright white roots framed her tan face. Turquoise-and-yellow fish earrings were darting around her chin.

"What are you making in here?" Jonathan said, taking in a deep breath. "It smells fanTAStic."

"I'm feeding the homeless tonight. I'm sure they get chicken all the time. I'm not bringing them any more chicken. I just put in the *Shabbes* carrot rings, it's something they never get. Everybody goes crazy over it. I made three. Two's plenty. You only need a little piece, it's very rich, like a cake. I'm going to freeze one. They freeze nicely and it'll keep." Although she lived frugally herself, Miriam's generosity in administering to the hopelessly dependent was renowned, her biggest charity case consisting of Hershel. Her face suddenly lit up. "Did I get something great!" She slipped past us into the laundry room. "I went to my favorite thrift shop after school and wait till you see." On the washing machine was a pile of neatly folded clothes.

"Look at this." She held up a royal-blue corduroy dress with two black satin ribbons hanging from the collar. "Four dollars. Do you BELIEVE it? It's a Laura Ashley. It's corduroy. Feel that. It's hardly been worn. Some rich woman buys it and then she gains some weight or her husband says, 'I don't like you in that style,' so she gives it away. I got my whole winter wardrobe for nineteen dollars." In the land of conspicuous consumption, she had, by necessity, become a connoisseur of *shmattes*. She sidled around us and opened the refrigerator. "You look hot. You want some juice?" She took out a can of grapefruit juice.

"No," Jonathan said. "I want some of that *Shabbes* carrot ring."

Bull's-eye in the heart. I hadn't even introduced Jonathan to Miriam but she was already flattered and enchanted. I could see her mother-hen feathers begin to fluff, her mind taking inventory of Jewish hospitality. "Come for *Shabbat* dinner. I'll freeze it in two pieces and then I'll take out half on Friday. I'll stick in some potatoes and we'll have string beans and a nice trout. They have beautiful trout at Gelson's this week and I'll bake a *chollah*." A visit to the Wailing Wall would be next on the agenda.

Jonathan accepted her invitation without hesitation and gave Miriam a warm hug when they were finally introduced. As he put his arms around her, Miriam rolled her eyes up at me and stuck out her tongue in a cartoon gesture of ecstasy. It didn't take very much to turn Miriam from the Wife of Abraham into the Wife of Bath. "Ooohh, I can see why you like him," she said to me in a way that left no doubt about her meaning. "You can bring him over ANY-time."

"I'll see you Friday. We'll break *chollah* together," Jonathan said.

"I can't WAIT," she said and she went back to wiping down her counters, as if the immeasurable weight of her duty could be relieved only briefly, lest she let Hershel's genius share the pedestal.

As I led Jonathan out the back door, we saw Hershel, in his batik kimono, sitting in a patio chair Hart and I had given them years before. Some of the webbing was broken and Hershel sat low and stooped, making him look like an old Talmudic scholar. He held some crisp typed pages in his hand but he was staring off into space, slowly rocking his body in a way that reminded me of my grandfather. Zucky would whisper his prayers in Hebrew as he swayed backward and forward with his worn black prayer book. When I was a child I would quietly enter his bedroom as he was *davening* and stand next to him. I asked him once what he was saying. He told me he was thanking God for returning his soul, which God had been looking after during the night. I knew Hershel wasn't so much worried about the state of his soul as he was the state of his play. But he was praying nonetheless. *Dear God, make it a hit. Let it go to Broadway.*

"Hey, Hershel. This is Jonathan."

Hershel put on his glasses and turned to us with a dreamy slowness. With his wild hair and untrimmed beard, it looked as if he never bothered with mirrors anymore. "I've been going over my notes all week. I'm exhausted. But I wrote one brilliant line today." He let out a big sigh and then he half-roused himself. "So. Jonathan," he said, using his droll voice. "What do YOU do?"

"Me?" Jonathan said, as if he was a little embarrassed being asked the question by a luminary such as Hershel. "I'm what you'd call a lowly-literary-agent-trainee. But Frankie says you write plays. When I was in college I actually tried to write a play. It was a lesson in humility. It was embarrassing. I couldn't figure out how to get people on and off the stage. Just a slight problem."

"Ah," Hershel said. Jonathan had stirred him from his torpor. "You've just hit upon the very thing neophytes don't understand: exits and entrances. There are no FADE INs and CUT TOs on the stage." This wasn't just bombast. Hershel, if anything, knew what made good, dramatic writing. He just couldn't apply it to his own work in any kind of commercial way.

"NOW you tell me," Jonathan said with charming weariness. "I think of all the writing forms, plays are the most exacting. And the most maddening. So, can you talk about your new play or would you rather not?"

Such deference. Such worshipful acknowledgment of Hershel's craft. Hershel never needed an excuse to expound on his writing, all he needed was an audience, and Jonathan had thoughtfully provided himself. Hershel was as taken with Jonathan as Miriam had been, and it pleased me. Jonathan being there that day made him an important, good part of my new life and I wanted to share him with Hershel and Miriam. He was just the kind of smart, *haimisher* Jewish kid I knew they'd like.

I left Jonathan listening raptly to Hershel's lecture on Chekhov while I went to inspect my new living quarters behind the garage. From the moment I stepped through the front door I was overwhelmed with something I never expected: a sense of relief. I didn't at all feel the knot in the pit of my stomach or sadness at my condition. I felt free. Not only from my possessions but from my marriage. Hershel and Miriam's two oldest girls had lived here during high school and the place still looked like a teenage clubhouse, which fit perfectly my state of mind. Those two small rooms made me instantly buoyant with happiness. As Jonathan came behind me, I could have turned and kissed him.

"Is this great, or what?" Jonathan said, looking around. "I love it. I may have to move in here with you. It's like really good off-campus housing. All you're missing is a few joints lying around in ashtrays and a straw Chianti bottle with melted wax." Jonathan picked up a blue glass vase which still had a little masking tape on the underside marked twenty-five cents. "This is kind of cute."

He helped me set up a table as my writing desk, near the window so I could look out on to the garden. Other than that, I left everything the same, except for adding some old family photographs. My mother had gotten them down from a box on the top shelf of Dora's closet. Even the photographs smelled of mothballs, just like everything from that summer house, and I felt a tender, transient melancholy every time I inhaled them. I had no idea who most of the people in the pictures were but I loved looking at their faces, especially the women, with their thick, dark hair piled on top of their heads. I did recognize my grandparents' wedding picture and an occasional great-uncle or aunt who had pinched my cheek at family gatherings, but in these studio portraits they were upright and solemn, the women in high-collared blouses and cameo pins. The men in gloves and bowler hats. They were trying to look like prosperous Americans, not the poor Jewish immigrants they were.

There was one photograph, though, which didn't fit in with the others: a husband and wife right out of the *shtetl*. She in a long black dress with her thick-fingered peasant hand fisted in her lap and the hint of a mustache across her upper lip. He had a graying unkempt beard, a black threadbare coat, and a glassy shell-shocked look in his eyes. He rather resembled Hershel after a tortured day of writing. And the woman could have been Miriam, without the pizzazz and purple hair. The bottom of the photo said *Cabinet Portraits Brooklyn New York* in writing meant to resemble Cyrillic.

"That is some gorgeous couple," Jonathan said, looking at the photo over my shoulder. "I hope, for your sake, they're not REAL close relatives. They look like Grant Wood's *Polish Gothic*. Or a poster in the back room hanging just under the Nazi flag where they're cranking out 'Jews drink Christian children's blood for breakfast' pamphlets. I'm starting to worry that maybe you're taking this ancestor worship business just a little too far, *tsatskeleh*."

I was putting the picture on my desk, when I caught sight of Miriam sunbathing nude on the chaise. She'd finished her chores and was working the crossword puzzle in the newspaper.

"Nice view," I said to her through the open window. "You know, Jonathan's still here."

Miriam's not the least bit self-conscious about her body and couldn't even muster up the modesty to put on her towel when a meter man once blundered into the yard. "What do I care?" she said to me, not even looking up. "Jonathan's young enough to be my son." I took Jonathan by the hand and led him out the door, along the side of the garage and into town, where I bought him lunch and told him he could go home.

"Just wait till I inform Freyda I have to leave early to go to a *Shabbes* dinner. This is going to generate some interesting buzz. A screening she'd understand, but *Shabbes*? Who knows? Maybe I'll become a born-again Jew," he said as he drove away.

Miriam scrimped on everything except those Friday-night dinners. It was the one night of the week she set the table with the good dishes (Methodist Church Rummage Sale), got the wineglasses (Bel Air estate sale) from the breakfront (Optimists Club sale-a-thon), and put the brass *Shabbes* candlesticks (synagogue bazaar) on the table. Only on Fridays did Hershel stop writing early and not return to his workroom right after dinner.

On the Sabbath, their home was a haven for foreign visitors, divorcées, widows, orphans, lost souls, Jews and gentiles alike. Everyone at the table might not know each other but we were almost all showbiz veterans. Sometimes I'd see Hershel's retired agent or a former critic for the *L.A. Times*. Occasionally it was Hershel's old secretary, the story editor on *Lamp Unto My Feet,* Buddy Hackett's publicist, or an ex-head of production at some studio. It was a table full of people whose time in Hollywood had come and gone. Maybe that's another reason Hershel, Miriam, and I embraced Jonathan as we did. Besides the smarts, the charm, the flattery, the quips, quotes, and parlor tricks, he was just starting out. I think we all knew he was going places and maybe, just maybe, he'd bring us along.

Jonathan arrived for supper bearing an inexpensive bottle of Merlot. Miriam (who knows absolutely nothing about wine) put on her reading glasses to examine the label. "Ooohh, nice," she cooed, absolutely delighted with Jonathan. Jonathan caught my eye and I thought I saw a look that said, *You know better, but don't give me away.* But I was as pleased with him as Miriam was.

As it turned out, it was just five of us. Jonathan was seated next to Peggy, Hershel's former secretary, an outgoing, heavy woman with an easy laugh, a pretty face, and thick brown hair worn in a braid into which she often stuck her pen. Hershel was always telling people she was born a couple centuries too late for her "lushness" to be appreciated and he seemed fascinated by her and the kind of men she attracted. Which, in recent years, had been a poetry-writing mailman and a Scottish plumber. Tonight she was dressed in a flowing India-print dress and she and Miriam spent the first five minutes admiring each other's ethnic earrings.

I could see Jonathan was amused by Miriam and tried his best to make her laugh. And she, in turn, *kibitzed* with him as if they'd known each other for years. That evening felt to me like we were all a family. A family who liked each other. Just before sunset, Hershel came down from his office, took a seat at the head of the table, and stepped into the role of wise father.

Miriam took great pride in lighting the candles, saying the prayer, blessing her children in absentia and everyone at the table. Then, as Miriam bustled back and forth between the kitchen and dining room, Hershel poured the wine, recited the *kiddush,* blessed the bread, and tore off pieces of the *chollah* with his long, delicate fingers.

"Peggy," he said, leading off as the evening's moderator. "Tell us how your script is coming."

"Funny you should ask, Hershel. I brought it for you to look at. Again. If you hate it don't tell me, although I know you will." She turned to Jonathan. "Hershel is one of the few writers who actually tells you the truth about your writing. And he's always right." She made a face. "Unfortunately."

"Are you a writer, too?" Jonathan asked. "All these writers. I love it."

"Well. I'm trying to be. You know, I'm like everyone else in this town, writing their spec scripts, hoping to sell it for a small fortune so I can quit my job." Peggy turned to me. "What are you working on, Frankie? At least Frankie gets paid," she said to everyone at the table.

"A spec script." I didn't want to talk about it actually and Peggy wasn't interested anyway.

"Oh, my God. You've joined the legions of amateurs. I just got back from Calistoga last week, and a masseur spent the enTIRE hour and a half he worked on me talking about the script he wants to write. About growing up on a commune in Northern California with hippie parents. He KNOWS his life would make a great movie. I wanted to tell him, 'I came up here to get aWAY from that shit.' And he's already cast it. He sees himself as Sean Penn."

Jonathan spoke up. "The guy behind the counter at my health club, who stamps the parking validations, and who I SWEAR I've said about two words to, sent me his script in the mail with a note saying he'd appreciate my comments. I want to say to him, 'I'd appreciate clean towels.' "

"I've always wanted to go to Calistoga," Miriam mused. "I want to take a mud bath."

"The problem with accepting scripts from amateurs," Hershel said solemnly, "is that they really don't want to find out why it doesn't work. What they want is representation. Professional writers at least know what they're in for." Hershel took a small sip of wine as punctuation and continued his thesis. "Delivering a script that you've labored on is like giving birth to a baby, except that instead of getting screwed in the beginning, you get screwed in the end. When you give your baby up for adoption, you hope it will find loving, nurturing parents, but more often than not, they cut the baby's hand off thinking that they're improving it. And then they'll take just a little snip off the foot and make a cut here and a cut there and 'Let's just take the whole damn arm off, what does it need an arm for, anyway?' What they wind up doing eventually is slowly and painfully killing your baby. Ah. But THEY think it looks better."

Taking his own analogy a little too much to heart, Hershel used to get into his batik kimono and go to bed for two weeks of recuperation when he finished a script, which was longer than Miriam ever allowed herself after giving birth to real babies. But I understood Hershel's self-indulgence, not wanting to face the inevitable expropriation. I was already having symptoms of postpartum malaise and I hadn't even finished my script.

"They can have my baby," Peggy said. "Just give me the money and you can cut its head off."

Hershel laughed. "Maybe you'll turn out to be the successful writer after all."

"All I want is to get an agent. You SEE, Hershel, you're right about amateurs. But you already have an agent, so you don't have to worry."

"You call that an agent?" Miriam said, as if she was referring to her own agent. "He does nothing. The old man was good but this new one he has is a lox."

"Show it to me when you're done," Jonathan said to Peggy. "I'd be happy to read it."

"You would? Oh, bless you. Bless you. And I'll even wash your towels."

"How much does a mud bath cost? It's mud. How much could it cost?" Miriam said, almost answering her own question. Then she stood up from the table. "Who wants more carrot ring?"

"The little oink-oink would," Jonathan said, raising his plate. "As they say on Freyda's French tapes, *Répétez s'il vous plaît: Toute chose est délicieuse*. Unfortunately, I think I've gained about five pounds. Maybe I should join you at synagogue tomorrow and I can JOG over there."

"You should look for someone like him," Miriam advised me, waving after Jonathan as he drove away in his car with a piece of *Shabbes* carrot ring in Saran Wrap. "Too bad he's not older. Or maybe not. The younger ones try harder in bed. With Hershel I have to do all the work. He's a winner, that Jonathan. He's a winner."

HOLIDAYS ON ICE

WHEN THINGS WERE going well I didn't mind staying home all day with my characters. They were good company and I was always surprised at how fast they made the hours fly by. I felt comforted hearing real life just outside my door, the sounds of the neighborhood as I worked; the hums and the buzzes of the lawn mowers, hedge clippers, and leaf blowers. It was a way to stave off the fear of isolation.

Then there were the days when I'd find myself alone in the dark woods of despair. I'd sit lost at my desk hour after hour, typing and deleting, creating and erasing. An excruciating anxiety would blanket me until my eyes got so heavy I'd take a long nap, pretending to myself it was horizontal thinking. I'd awaken groggy and reread my pages from the beginning, hoping to get a new running start. But nothing would come and I'd have the compulsion to get up and look at myself in the bathroom mirror. Over and over I'd study my skin, my eyes, my teeth, my hair. I don't know why. Maybe for company. I didn't dare call anyone or go anywhere. God forbid I had a break-through and I wasn't near my computer when the floodgates opened.

Sometimes in the evening I'd get out and walk to the bluffs to watch the sunset and the car headlights below as they snaked their way up and down Pacific Coast Highway. There was a little bald spot with a bench, where some of the other sunset watchers gathered. It was as close to a communal experience as I got, although I rarely ever spoke to anyone. On the way home, I'd look into all the houses as husbands were returning and lights coming on, smell the aromas of dinners being cooked. I felt like a Peeping Tom of the comfortably ordinary.

I ate by myself and watched television, letting my brain go numb switching channels. When I'd been writing hard and it was cold or I was too tired, I didn't even bother to undress for bed. I'd fall asleep in my turtleneck, roll out of bed, and wear it the next day. I was living the life of a crack addict.

The only person from the outside world I kept in touch with, or I should say who kept in touch with me, was Jonathan Prince. He called almost daily to give me the latest news on Freyda and Marty, to gossip about office happenings and industry hoopla, to find out how the writing was going:

"Freyda and Marty have decided to rent a house in Tuscany in the spring. She just had me order her some Italian tapes so she can practice in her car on the freeways. It's called *Italian 101 to the 405*. I think she wants to learn how to return her food in another language."

"We just got a new cappuccino machine for the kitchen and all the secretaries have to learn how to use it. Now I give good phone AND good foam."

"How's your script coming? Just tell me if you want me to read your pages. Of all the scripts we're waiting for, I have a feeling yours is the one that's going to take off."

Jonathan was getting good at playing the encouraging producer. He was my own personal Hollywood Hotline, my little buddy. My fluffer. With Jonathan by my side, whispering in my ear, I felt smarter, funnier, more confident. He was the perfect mirror to my desired reflection.

I finished my script two days after Thanksgiving. Unfortunately, the printer was at Hart's and I'd never gotten around to buying a new one. Hershel, who was hopelessly unmechanical, understood how frustrating it can be reading a new instruction booklet, setting up a new gizmo. The real reason, which I couldn't confess, was fear.

That printing the script was not the final step to completion, but to failure. But it couldn't be put off any longer. Without thinking it completely through, I phoned Hart and asked if I could come over. Then I started rushing around, trying to get myself presentable. I peeled off my leggings, turtleneck, and sweatshirt and took a hot shower, scrubbing off whiffy nervous writing sweat. I washed my hair, shaved my legs, and put on makeup and cologne. I'd just been sprung from the penitentiary.

It felt strange being a visitor at my own house. Should I ring the bell or use the key? When Hart didn't answer I let myself in, just like I'd done for the past ten years. It was quiet and I stood for a moment in the foyer surveying the living room. A big bouquet of roses and calla lilies sat on the coffee table, no doubt picked by Ana, who still came to clean twice a week. It didn't look as if I were missed at all. The late-afternoon light, coming from the open French doors, threw a golden glow onto the walls. I walked out into the garden. The leathery leaves from the old magnolia tree littered the patio like large petrified potato chips. I'd forgotten how green everything was in my backyard and I just stood there in a daze, feeling like a traveler returning home after a very long trip. Until I heard digging in the rear of the garden, where I found Hart in a hole up to his waist. All around him were boxes of white PVC pipes.

"What are you doing?"

He looked up at me, his jeans and work shirt covered in dirt. "I'm building a Jacuzzi."

"Well, hurry up. I'm stiff."

Hart climbed out of his hole and brushed off his clothes. "I just came back from the hardware store and a woman looked at me and said, 'Whatever you're doing, I hope it's worth it.' " He laughed that hearty laugh of his and I realized how much I'd missed him, how much I'd been trying to tell myself I didn't.

When I'd first met Hart, thirteen years before, he was teaching nineteenth-century literature at UCLA and he invited me to sit in on his lecture, to watch him perform, as it were. I remember picking a spot in the back of the hall, listening to Hart rhapsodize on Flaubert's perfect three-part structure of *Madame Bovary;* the symbols that foreshadowed her doom and the use of irony in Rodolphe's passionate love speech to Emma, spoken at the county fair as the first prize in manure is being awarded. I amused myself imagining what his students would say if they knew we'd just gotten out of bed, and I think I fell in love with Hart right then and there, as he probably hoped I would. I wasn't that much older than the girls in his class and it flattered me to think I was capable of capturing his attention, as it pleased him to think he could interest someone my age. We were a mismatch from the beginning. But Hart lived life as a great big adventure, grabbing at good times anywhere he could. He knew happiness was fleeting and wasn't suspicious of it. I'd been around such worried, fearful Jews all my life Hart was a revelation, my at-tempt to escape the hand-wringing heaviness of it all. Also he's the only person I knew who would build his own Jacuzzi, do all the plumbing, tile it himself, and not make a big deal about it. He was about as un-Jewish as you could get.

While I got the printer going, Hart made us drinks. "To your script," he said. "I'm looking forward to reading it." We clinked glasses and went back outside. Our cat climbed down from the mag-nolia tree and sat purring on my lap.

"Lila's missed you."

The fog had blown in from the ocean and the sun was going down. We watched as the mountains became a Japanese painting, row after row of blues fading to grays fading to mist. It was getting cold but we didn't go inside.

"It was strange not being with you for Thanksgiving," he said.

"Who were you with?"

"Wendy Rubin was having some people over." He said it as off-handedly as he could because he anticipated my reaction. Wendy Rubin considered herself to be THE Hollywood Woman's Writer. No one could write a PMS, orgasm, or shopping joke quite like Wendy. When her projects got approved it was because "they got my humor," the highest compliment Wendy could bestow upon anyone. Being a self-proclaimed expert on humor allowed her to decree what was *Funneee* and what was *UNbelievably unfunny*. Just after Hart and I were married, when I'd answer the phone, she would make the most perfunctory, condescending conversation with me before asking for Hart, who was Funneee. She would leave messages on the answering machine. "Hart Sweet? Are you there? Are you writing and you won't pick up? I've got to talk to you. I'm having a Hart attack. Call me." Is this the kind of message you leave for a wife to hear? She wasn't married at the time and she was too needy for my taste. And Hart, prone to flattery and thinking he can save every unhappy woman, took the bait. In the beginning it led to arguments which I'm sure would have delighted her.

Even after marrying some up-and-coming studio executive eight years her junior, whom she badgers with her brilliance, she continued to call Hart for lunch dates. Although the other calls, the ones that had to do with computer questions and financial advice and rodent removal, eventually tapered off.

"How is old Wendy? She still going to her anger workshops?"

"She and Isaac are having problems."

"You better not take up with her. If you do, I'll be very disappointed in you."

"Don't be ridiculous. Isaac adores her. She just keeps beating him up and he comes back for more. She's a great mystery to him. He hasn't got a creative bone in that soft, scared, limp-dicked body of his and I'm not changing gears that quickly, believe me."

When we finished our drinks, we went up to bed. The smell of martini on his breath, the smell of sun on his skin, it was all familiar and too nice.

I didn't want to be there the next morning when Ana came to clean. She's Mexican and comes from a large family. When I broke it to her that Hart and I were getting a divorce, she'd cried and said she would pray for me. It would only be confusing for her to see me back there again. As it was confusing for me. So I left early and was in Miriam's kitchen by seven-fifteen for our usual morning walk.

"Well," she said when she saw me, her hands on her hips like a scolding housemother. "I just hope you had some good fucking. Do you want some toast? I bought some delicious rye bread at Gelson's. Are you in for a treat."

Being with Hart had me feeling sad, yearning for something more. I'd just left the warm, playful Hart but I also knew the Hart you can't get a hold on. The Hart that slips right through your fingers. The Hart that keeps you hoping. I tried to explain the loss I felt for something that never really was but I wondered how much Miriam understood. Sex, food, marriage, laundry—except for Hershel's writing, everything was given equal weight. Even succor was administered in a practical way. She slapped a plate of hot, buttered rye toast in front of me. It was such a simple thing but it felt so nice to be taken care of.

We were walking out the kitchen door when she called for Little Macho, a half–Jack Russell terrier, half-pug on whom she dotes. Heading down the street, I noticed Miriam was still wearing her apron, the pocket stuffed with a couple of plastic bags that read *Fresh Produce*. Her hair looked a toxic lavender in the bright morning sun. As we passed a house with a moving truck out front, Miriam turned an authoritative eye to a breakfast set that was sitting in the driveway. "Oy, what *dreck*," she said in her best stage whisper, insensitive to the new occupant of the house, who was standing in the garage, and who even if he didn't understand Yiddish couldn't mistake her intonation. I found myself wanting to hide behind a hedge. Miriam was so obliviously Jewish. I had no idea what the neighbors on the quiet, manicured streets thought of her manner, but Miriam wouldn't have cared. It was impossible for her to blend in nor would it have ever occurred to her to try. She was perfectly at home in that short, strong, voluptuous body of hers, and no matter where she was, she carried her world with her. She screamed at Little Macho. "Get back here, you! You stay with me! Keep up! You hear?" As he scampered back to her side, she got down to business.

"You missed all the excitement last night while you were with Hart doing God-knows-what. There's big interest in Hershel's play. Hershel showed it to his agent in London. He called last night because he thinks there maybe could be some interest in the West End."

But before I got the particulars, Little Macho ran onto a lawn where the automatic sprinklers had just turned off and assumed that unmistakable hunchback posture. Miriam yelled, "Don't shit in the wet, doo-doo brain! You couldn't go where there aren't any sprinklers?" She took the Fresh Produce bag out of her apron pocket and boldly traipsed across someone's glistening lawn. Her hand inside the bag, she deftly picked up the offending peanuts in one swift motion, and tying the bag into a knot, she continued walking, the warm plastic beginning to steam up. "But in the MEANtime, there's a producer here who's crazy about it. He thinks Hershel is Chekhov, Ibsen, and Neil Simon all rolled into one. He thinks he can raise the money. He's talking about a New York opening in May. He wants to send the play to Charles Durning. New York. Would that be great? Charles Durning as Hershel's father." She cackled. "It's obviously not perfect casting but it's a name. I just hope he can play old enough. Charles Durning as an old Jew." She laughed again with delight. "I'm not even going to think about it. Tuey Tuey Tuey." She pretended to spit three times to ward off any evil that could befall her for the Charles Durning hubris.

Hart called that afternoon. "Frankie? I read *Ivy and Men.* I loved it. I laughed and you made me cry. I think it's just terrific. You've got some real characters here. I loved Arthur. I think you wove him in and out very nicely. You've got some problems with the structure of act two and you lose him for too long but it's nothing that can't be fixed. Congratulations."

"You mean it? You're not just saying that?" I felt the weight of the world lift from my shoulders. I wanted to call Jonathan and tell him the good news, but Hart was just about to leave the house, so I hurried over to pick up my script. I caught him as he was on his way out. He had turned distant and cool, as if we hadn't just spoken warmly only a few minutes before.

"Good luck with it, kiddo," he said as he threw a pile of button-down shirts into the trunk of his Jaguar. Then he drove away. I stood in the driveway feeling more lonely than if he'd just dropped the script on my doorstep and I'd never seen him. I opened the script. He'd made copious notes in the margins, crossed out whole scenes. It was all done in red pen, and I felt like I'd just gotten back a term paper but didn't quite get the grade I'd hoped for.

I let myself back into the house, found Lila, a couple cans of her food, and left Hart a note telling him I'd borrowed the cat. Then I drove back to my little house, sat at my desk, and watched Lila nose around the corners and into the cupboards. I read Hart's notes more carefully, agreeing with every one of them. There was one more rewrite needed before I could show the script to Freyda and Jonathan.

It took me until just before Christmas. All of Hollywood had been virtually shut down since Thanksgiving but I just had to get the script out of the house. I couldn't stand looking at it a minute longer. Just as I was about to call Jonathan, the phone rang.

"So where's my one-hundred-and-twenty-page Christmas present?"

"I just finished it. It's done."

"Oh, my God. It's a miracle. I feel like we should break out the incense and myrrh. So, when do I get it?"

"As soon as I print out and make you a copy. I was hoping Freyda would read it, too. Where is she?"

"I'm not supposed to tell anyone but she's out doing some last-minute Christmas shopping."

I had to get something for Freyda and it had been plaguing me. Frankly, it's no fun buying something for someone who has so much already but there was no way out of it. Freyda celebrates herself unstintingly and it was an unspoken understanding that you were supposed to celebrate her, too.

"You have any suggestions what to get her?"

"Just get her something stupid but it has to be the right kind of stupid. A rubber ducky is stupid but it's the wrong kind of stupid and she understands the distinction, which escapes most people, including, I confess, me. I found her an old print ad for Fairy Soap. '*Is there a little Fairy in YOUR house?*' You're never going to top that one unless you're Marty, who bought her a Zorro lunch box. Let's see. You can't get her clothes because only Freyda knows how to put together those *shmattes*. You can't get her books because she gets reimbursed for them anyway and she doesn't really consider that to be a REAL present. Hmmm . . . what CAN you get her? You know, for a Jewish girl from the Valley she sure makes a big fucking deal over Christmas presents. Go to Montana Avenue. I'm sure you'll find something stupid in one of those overpriced antique stores."

I took Jonathan's advice. After searching up and down the street for something appropriately outré, I finally bought a Bakelite Scotty-dog pin with rhinestone eyes and a tam-o'shanter, which cost much more than I'd wanted to spend. I returned home to a message from Jonathan. Freyda could meet for breakfast the next morning and he couldn't wait to get the script.

I arrived at the Beverly Hills Hotel, my script and Freyda's Christmas present in hand. I gave my car keys to the valet, then saw Freyda moving toward the hotel doors. She was Annie Oakley Wyatt Earp in hand-tooled boots and suede leather skirt with a child's sheriff badge glinting from her pearl-button shirt. But instead of an old muzzle loader, she was brandishing a large blue shopping bag from Tiffany's. I caught up with her in the lobby.

"I'm crazed," she said. "We're leaving for Hawaii tomorrow and I still have about a hundred things to get done. I can't wait to just be on that PLANE already. How ARE you? I can't believe you finished your script. I can't wait to read it. Is this it?"

I handed her my script and her Christmas present. She reached into the Tiffany bag and brought out a book-shaped package that, unfortunately, was not wrapped in Tiffany blue. The little robin's-egg gift box was for the hostess, who showed us to a large booth in the Polo Lounge, right next to none other than Jerry Slotnick. Jerry appeared to be in the same tennis clothes as the last time I'd seen him. He was sitting alone with the *L.A. Times,* his hand down the front of his shirt.

"Con-grat-u-LAAA-tions," Freyda said to him by way of a salutation. "When do you start shooting?"

He looked up from his paper but didn't seem surprised to see her. They probably met here so often, it was like coming down to breakfast in their bathrobes. "They want it for a summer release. I told Scotty he's fuckin' out of his mind. I got two writers working nonstop and every day I'm getting new notes for revisions. They don't leave you alone over there. And they're so fuckin' cheap. They want stars but they're not willing to pay anything. Every day I'm on the phone screaming at someone. The Beverly Hills Hotel is the only place I can have breakfast in peace. What's Marty up to?"

"If he doesn't decide on a project soon I'm going to kill myself."

"I'm gonna call him. You know Eric Farley? Young writer with a lotta heat on him right now. He just finished something for me which is dynamite. You guys going to be here over the holidays?"

"We're leaving for Hawaii tomorrow."

"I'm gonna messenger the script to him today. What's with that *shtunk?*"

"Uh. Please."

"Tell him this script can make him a rich man and THEN he can retire."

The goddess of fortune must run Hollywood. A routine rotation of her wheel could put you in the right restaurant at the right time, and depending on who was at the next table, your whole life could change. Freyda had known this when she said Jerry Slotnick would be a good person for me to meet, only for some reason she kept failing to introduce us. Freyda turned back to me when the waitress came with coffee. A few minutes later Jerry Slotnick said he had to get to the studio and departed unceremoniously, barely giving me a glance. I felt invisible, which normally I don't mind. I'm happy being the observer. But on this particular morning his dismissive glance carried an unmistakable message. Loser. Freyda didn't introduce me because I had no good credits to explain who I was. Basically, I was nobody until my script was bought or made. When I'd handed it over to her, I realized everything was out of my control. My life was now dependent on people like Jerry Slotnick. It was a sickening thought.

After breakfast, I got back in my car already feeling the letdown. I decided to open up my Christmas present at the first red light. It didn't cheer me up too much to see that Freyda had given me a *New Yorker* date book, and she'd neglected to remove the business card another agent had slipped into the month of January when he'd sent it to her. *Dear Freyda. Another year, another deal. Love, Leon.* Ana said she could use the calendar when, on my way home, I stopped by Hart's to drop off a copy of my script. Hart had already left to go skiing in Deer Valley and wouldn't be back until after the new year. I was desperate for positive feedback.

Like all good Jews, Hershel and Miriam looked on Christmas Eve as the night they could get into the big, popular holiday movies without having to wait on line. They'd invited me along but I didn't want to always be a third wheel. Though without a script to work on, without anything to make me obsessed and self-absorbed, I had no idea how to occupy my time. I'd lost my sense of purpose and was wandering around like a Border collie without its sheep. It's not like I had the right to a full-on Christmas depression because, after all, it wasn't even my holiday. When I was with Hart I'd tried to make the perfect Christmas as I'd always imagined it. I cooked the goose crispy-golden-brown, made a rich, warm persimmon pudding, decorated the tree with tiny white lights and cranberries strung on thread, and served nutmeg-spiced eggnog in an old, sparkling pressed-glass punch bowl. But I felt like an impostor, filching someone else's tradition. Jews, as hard as we try, can never be entirely comfortable celebrating Christmas. Even if we tell ourselves it's become just a seasonal holiday redesigned by merchants to promote the economy, we know in our hearts we're crashing Jesus Christ's birthday extravaganza. Still, I didn't want to be doing laundry on Christmas Eve. I was just gathering the whites, thinking about everyone else skiing or snorkeling in the warm waters of Hawaii, when the phone rang.

"Wow. I just finished reading your script. The whole relationship thing with her cousin was great and then that ending just blew me away. I have to tell you I didn't see it coming."

I loved this kid Jonathan. "Where are you?" Now I could get through the holidays. I could hear busy noise in the background.

"LAX. This is a fucking madhouse here, all these Christians trying to get home before Santa comes down the chimney." He was shouting into the phone as if I was the one surrounded by noise and not he. "I'm on my way home to see Ruthie and Harold for some holiday family fun."

"I presume by that tone that you're referring to your parents."

"Of course. You want me to stop by your old neighborhood? Go by your old high school or anything? Tell them you made good?"

"Not particularly."

"Wait a second," he said, and I heard an announcement in the background. "They're boarding my plane. This is where you really want that small child and a wheelchair."

"It's so nice of you to call me from the airport."

"I just wanted to tell you that if I ran a studio I'd buy this in a heartbeat."

"Well, I hope you get to run a studio soon."

"Have you heard from Freyda?"

"Not yet."

"Oh, well. I'm sure she'll get around to it. One of these days."

"Jonathan. I'm really grateful for your call."

"Hey. Let's get together with Hershel and Miriam when I get back. I miss them."

I wished him happy holidays and we hung up.

A week and a half later Freyda finally called.

"I loved it, now turn left here and go to the end of the block and make another right." She was in her limo on the way back from the airport. "The only thing that worries me is that maybe your script is a little TOO sensitive. Now bear left and at the stop sign make a right."

"What do you mean by too sensitive? What's too sensitive?" I heard a defensiveness in my voice and so could she. She backed off.

"It's a character piece. It's very dependent on casting. But I loved it. Okay, we're the fourth house from the end of the block with the black gate on the right. I've got to go. I'll call you as soon as I have a chance to breathe."

Jonathan distributed the script to the other agents in the office. Every day Freyda didn't call with news was another opportunity to worry what would happen if no one liked the script. I decided I'd give her one week to get back to me. A day before the deadline, Jonathan beat her to it. "The word's coming in that the other agents like your script. I knew they would and I think even Freyda's finished reading it."

"Freyda read it in Hawaii."

"Oh, really?"

"What do you mean? Are you telling me she didn't?"

"Okay," he said, his tone getting rather confidential, "you didn't hear this from me, but I've seen Freyda get on a plane with a script IN HAND and lose it by the time she's landed. Don't ask me how this is possible. All I know is Freyda will do ANYTHING not to be the first one to read a script because she doesn't know how to feel about anything until someone tells her. She's one of the most insecure people I've ever met in my life. When I asked her how she liked your script all she could do was speak in generalities. She was more interested in what I thought. Whatever you do, don't tell her I told you this."

"Of course not," I said. Was it possible Freyda had called me without ever reading the script? Recalling our conversation, she hadn't spoken about any particulars. I knew Freyda was political, always weighing the consequences, always playing to the most important person in the room. But I accepted that as the way she did her job. She'd never handle the really big writers or be an important agent because she was unwilling to alienate anyone with more power than she. That didn't matter because she'd always been so protective of me, so encouraging. Even though her opinions were oh-so-carefully ventured and never actually lofted into anything but the prevailing winds, I understood. Like everyone else in Hollywood, Freyda didn't want to be associated with losers. But I never realized she might just be a coward, with no faith or conviction in her own tastes. Not until Jonathan pointed it out to me.

"I'm going to call you," Jonathan said, "just as soon as I can co-ordinate everyone's schedule and set up a meeting. So be prepared."

"It sounds ominous."

"You never know."

SPEAKING OF VASELINE

1990

BY THE END of January, everyone's schedule had been juggled, shifted, shuffled, reworked, and finally pinned down. An hour was cleared, a meeting set up so I could meet the team of agents who were going to strategize the selling of my script.

Freyda was on the phone at the appointed hour, so at Jonathan's suggestion, I took myself down to the conference room and introduced myself to Paul Fisher and Nicole Kahn, the two new agents Freyda thought were so terrific. Instead of trying to cultivate relationships with every studio, network, and cable network, the agency was divided into "specialty teams." Paul and Nicole covered a different territory than Freyda and were here because they had relationships with the players at THEIR studios, knew what kind of material THEIR studios were looking for.

"Frankie Jordan," Paul repeated after I'd introduced myself. "Any relation to Hart Jordan?"

"Wife," I said, not wanting to go into details.

"What a talent. Really. Say hi to him for me, will you? Tell him we met at the DGA Awards a couple years ago. I was with ICM at the time."

"Sure," I said, knowing that Hart wouldn't give a rat's ass, even if I told him.

"Were you there, too?" he asked, suddenly realizing why he was here.

"Yes."

"THAT'S why you look so familiar," he said, lying. I wasn't offended because I didn't remember him either. A lot of people I don't know come up and introduce themselves to Hart at these events. Unless they're really nice or really rude, they tend to quickly melt from consciousness, just like we wives. I studied Paul Fisher carefully, trying to fix him in my mind for the next time we met: tall and slender, long nose, slightly effeminate manner. He reminded me of a Christmas-card photo I'd seen in my vet's office, of a silky-furred saluki lounging on some pillows. (*May the coming year bring you puppy love and dog days!!!*) Even the way Paul looked around and seemed to sniff the air made him appear aloof and delicate. Paul Saluki, I said to myself a few times. Nicole Dachshund had red-brown hair, and true to the breed, she barged into the room on stubby little legs and beat a hasty path for the food.

"Did you ever see a Jew try to make a decision without food?" She helped herself to the fruit platter just as Shelley, her assistant, brought in a basket of muffins, bagels, and a bowl of microwave popcorn. Taking some of everything, Nicole plopped herself into a chair, kicked off her shoes, and put her fat, pedicured feet up on the chair next to me. "I think Frankie should sit at the head of the table and Paul, sit over there. Freyda, whenever she shows up, can sit here."

As we were taking our assigned seats, Jonathan entered the room with a tray of beverages.

"Freyda will be right in. She's stuck on the phone, what a surprise." He put his tray on the table and handed us our drinks. "This is yours," he said to Paul, holding out a cappuccino.

"If you don't make it as an agent, Jonathan, I can always hire you as a houseboy." Paul's tone could have been construed as world-weary or whiny but definitely not convivial. I felt protective of Jonathan and looked over to see his reaction, but his face betrayed no emotion.

"If I don't make it as an agent," he said, like the most reasonable man alive, "it's probably because I've figured out it's a job for idiots."

"Ooh. Touchy touchy. Maybe you'd be happier working somewhere else."

"No doubt I would."

"Well, please don't let me stop you."

"Don't worry. You're not."

"Boys, boys," Nicole said. "Pass me the popcorn please, Paul darling," and as the food was being sent her way, Jonathan and Shelley walked out of the room. Paul Saluki looked for a moment like he'd had his leash rudely yanked, though he recovered almost immediately.

"Didn't we have any breakfast this morning?" Paul said as he handed Nicole a napkin. Hollywood is filled with soft men and hard women and Paul and Nicole were perfect specimens. Their theatrical bitchiness obviously hadn't bothered Freyda but Jonathan was more discerning. I couldn't wait to talk with him after the meeting. He'd fill me in on them in a way Freyda never could.

Freyda entered, a little breathless, wearing a bright yellow Mexican felt jacket with donkey and sombrero appliqués. In one ear she wore a saguaro cactus, and dangling from the other, a red-hot chili pepper. "Hola."

"Very south of the border today, aren't we?" Nicole said.

Freyda sat next to Paul and took a bunch of grapes and half a dry bagel.

"It's important for you to know that we work as a team here," Paul said to me.

"Why don't you tell her first that we loved the script, darling?"

"I was getting to that, darling."

"Well, it's important to say, darling."

Paul turned to me. "We loved the script."

"We thought it was fabulous."

"Thank you," I said.

Nicole turned to me. "I loved the scene where they talk about sex on the cafeteria line."

Freyda opened the script and started thumbing through it. "How about the scene where she dates the star football player everyone wants to go out with and he gets drunk at a fraternity party and starts running around with her head underneath his arm like he's going out for a pass. Did that really happen?"

"It was one of my better dates."

"Well, it was hysterical. I can just see it."

Paul joined in. "I loved the scene where the most popular kid in high school keeps doing Señor Wences. 'Difficult for you, easy for me.' "

"You're showing your age, darling."

"I watched *Ed Sullivan*. I remember the Beatles' first night on *Ed Sullivan*. I remember Elvis. OH GOD I MISS ED SULLIVAN!" He threw his head onto the table.

"Poor Paul." Nicole patted his hand and then reached for a muffin. "Will you PLEASE stop me from eating?" She pushed the basket across the table. "Will you put this down at the other end of the table. I don't want to look at food."

"You're obsessing, darling."

"If your thighs looked like mine, you'd obsess, too." Nicole picked up the phone and buzzed her secretary. "Shelley, can I have a Diet Coke, please."

"Don't mind us," Paul said to me.

I smiled, hoping that they couldn't read my mind. I could tell Freyda wanted to get in on their merry palaver but they'd obviously honed their routine in those bumper-to-bumper rides out to Burbank.

"Okay, children. Down to business," she said. "I think this is a special script and we've got to proceed very carefully."

"In other words," Paul said to me, "how are we going to sell this motherfucker?"

"I don't think we should go wide. I think we should explore one avenue and, if that doesn't work out, explore another." Freyda had given her cautious advice.

"I'm a very strong advocate of that in certain situations," Nicole said. "But we've got to figure out how to describe it first. How do you describe it?" They all turned to me.

"It's basically a love story that deals with forty years in the life of a woman named Ivy and all the men who have come and gone.

The one person who's always been there for her, loved her uncon-
ditionally, who puts up with all of her craziness, insecurities, and
anger, is her gay cousin, Arthur, who dies at the end."

"Not exactly your high-concept Jeff Katzenberg script," Paul said.

"But a *tour de théâtre* for the actors, darling."

"Okay," Paul said. "So its main characters are a woman and a
homosexual. And the two actors have to age from eighteen to forty.
Who do you see in it?"

"When I was writing it I saw Holly Hunter."

"Holly Hunter's character in *Broadcast News* was great," Freyda
said.

"Holly Hunter would be fabulous," Nicole said. "But she's not
exactly box office. What else has she been in that's made money?"

"The problem I have with Holly Hunter is I just can't imagine
wanting to fuck her. Although I loved *Broadcast News,*" Paul said.

"And by the way, darling, it was the best Albert Brooks has ever
been."

"That phone scene . . . 'Wouldn't it be great if NEEDY were attractive?' . . . UH, I love that scene. I *KVELL* over that scene."

"Or Debra Winger," I said.

Freyda joined the fray. "She's box-office poison but that's not to
say that something wouldn't change."

"Goldie has her own production company, and they're desperate
for material," Nicole said.

"She's not right for it," I said. "I don't see her in this role."

"It's a discussion," Paul said. "Anything can be a discussion, right?
If they love it, we can talk."

"She's too old," Freyda said. "She can't play eighteen."

"So they'll Vaseline the lens," Paul said.

"Speaking of Vaseline, darling, I heard on very good authority that
someone we all know and love is a pillow biter. And I have this on
very good authority."

"Who now?" Paul said wearily.

"Should we name names? Seth Sobelman at HBO."

"Who said he was gay?" Freyda said.

"My tileman, Julio, swears he saw Seth Sobelman in some bar in

West Hollywood propositioning a boy toy wearing leather and a lovely little tongue stud. SUCH an attractive look."

I had no idea who they were talking about but I had to ask anyway. "How would your tileman know Seth Sobelman?"

"He did Seth's bathroom in Malibu. AND he saw them walk out together."

"Maybe Seth Sobelman is bi," Paul said. "But he's not gay."

"Just watch your rear," Nicole said.

I made a mental note not to give Nicole any ammunition she could use against me.

"Okay, Roy Cohn, thank you for that *Outweek* update," Paul said, and then turned to Freyda. "If I were pitching it to a studio I'd categorize it as a cross between *Beaches* and *Same Time Next Year,* God forbid it doesn't resemble another movie, right?"

"*Beaches* wasn't exactly my favorite movie," I said.

"It doesn't matter. It made money."

"The book was much better than the movie," Nicole added, "although I didn't mind the movie. I got into their relationship."

"It's a coming-of-age story about a woman," Freyda said. "And we haven't really seen that. But it's also a buddy picture, too, really. The buddy just happens to be gay."

"I would REALLY stay away from the gay aspect of it," Paul said. "You don't want to scare people into thinking it's an AIDS movie."

"Of course, AIDS is never mentioned," I reminded them.

"But it's a specter."

"Well, of course, it shows how his death affects a heterosexual. But there's no death scene or illness scene. The movie jumps ahead and we don't even know he's dead at first. Only during the course of the scene do we come to learn that Arthur died, and, of course, it must have been AIDS but the overriding emotion is 'What a waste.' And the audience should miss him as much as Ivy does because he was handsome and smart and kind and funny. And in the end, through his death, his final gift to her is his old college roommate, who comes back for the memorial party and we know that he and Ivy will finally get together." I felt myself getting passionate about my own story.

"Well, you're going to have to fess up that he's GAY, darling. I mean, Tom Cruise isn't going to play him."

"Okay," Paul said to her. "So the point is, do we give this to a fag or a woman producer?"

"Why not both? Why not Judi Golden and Joel Dweck?" Nicole turned to me. "Known to us in the biz as Golden Dweck productions. A most unfortunate *nom d'alliance*."

"Perfect," Freyda said.

"Obviously their relatives weren't standing in the same line at Ellis Island," Paul said to me. "Or it would have been Golden Dawn productions."

"I can just see their logo before the movie starts," Nicole said. "Darkness. And as the sun begins to rise up over the mountain, the world is suddenly bathed in the golden light of GOLDEN DAWN PRODUCTIONS. It's almost as good as TriStar with the galloping horse sprouting wings. Their logo could have been BEAUTIFUL if only they'd been on the same line."

"The reason I wrote this on spec," I said, wanting to get the conversation back to business, "is that it's very important to me I have some say in how it gets made. I really want to find someone who sees it as I see it. Because if it's not done well, it could really be bad and I've been through that before."

"The most important thing right now is to sell it," Paul said. "We can fight those creative battles later."

"Joel is directing his first movie and I hear it's supposed to be fabulous," Nicole said.

"That's Ian Mandel's script," Freyda said. "I put that deal together."

"Good," Paul said. "Then you call them." The huddle broke and the script was now in play.

When Freyda and I got back to her office, Jonathan handed her a long list of calls. Then she turned to me and said, "Aren't Nicole and Paul terrific?" Freyda was obviously smitten and wasn't looking for a truthful response.

"They seem like quite a duo."

"Get Ed Rice back for me. Then Sondra Berman. And then call

Judi Golden's office and get her number in Louisiana," she said, looking at me.

"I should go," I said, and after we kissed good-bye I stopped by Jonathan's desk.

"So what did you think of Nichols and May?" he said. "Did you ever have to spend time in a room with two people who are less funny? Boy, do they need a writer."

"Obviously Paul likes you, too."

"What a power dork that guy is. I know more about agenting than he does and I just started."

"You think he's ineffectual?"

Jonathan made a dismissive face. "He's a *putz*. With his triple decaf espresso and his milk heated to one hundred and seventy degrees. Like I have a fucking thermometer. And Nicole Kahn. Each week she has a new expression that she tries out. 'I'm a very strong advocate of . . .' That's her expression this week. And 'I've got a gut feeling about this one. You've got to go with your inkling.' Right, Nicole. But don't worry about it. I'll keep an eye on what's really going on."

His other phone rang but before he picked it up he validated my parking ticket and said good-bye. "I'm on your case," he said as I walked out of his cubicle.

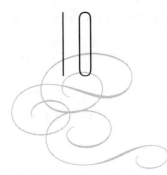

WHAT TAKES THEM SO LONG?

PRODUCERS ARE LIKE feudal lords exercising *droit du seigneur;* they all want to have first crack at a promising virgin script. And like the poor young maiden, once a producer gets hold of a script, spreads its pages, and tosses it aside, it's never as valuable again. Even the agents begin to lose confidence and interest after the first rejection. There was nothing I could do but hope. I should have used the time to start another project, but I was out of ideas and couldn't seem to concentrate. Freyda put me up for a rewrite that didn't pan out and mainly I just hung around the house reading and waiting.

"I've developed a meaningful telephonic relationship with Judi and Joel's reader, who told me she gave the script very good coverage." Once again, it was Jonathan who phoned with the updates. "She's sent the script to Judi and Joel in Louisiana. But so far she hasn't been able to get them to read it because they're still shooting. I keep telling her that other people want to get their hands on it and we're not waiting for them forever. If I were Freyda I'd be on the phone screaming to Louisiana but I can only do so much from my humble position."

A month went by. I was grateful Jonathan kept trying to promote the script but the delay could only mean one thing. No one felt the script had heat. Finally, I got up the courage to call Freyda, who put me on a three-way with Paul Saluki and Nicole Dachshund.

"So what's the status with the script?" I asked, trying to sound upbeat.

"According to Judi's secretary, it's in her satchel," Freyda replied.

"Does that mean it's actually getting closer to her night table?"

"Who KNOWS? I keep trying to goose them, but they've just finished their movie and they're exhausted. But I told them about the plot and they seem very interested. The reader liked it. She gave it positive coverage is my understanding."

"Who's her reader?" Paul asked.

"Some bimbo who used to work as a secretary to what's-his-name," Nicole said.

"I don't think Katie's a bimbo," Freyda said.

"No, she's a rocket scientist. Excuuuse me."

"Do you think we should move on?" I asked.

"Definitely not," Freyda said. "The fuse is lit, and if we don't hear from them in a few days, I'll give them a call TELLING them we're moving on, but they're very excited to have first look."

While I was sitting at home waiting for Judi and Joel, everyone else I knew was busy driving their kids to play dates or tai chi chuan. One by one, I'd lost my girlfriends when they'd joined the Great and Holy Mother Club.

My life had taken a strange turn and I began to ponder for the millionth time the meaning of it all. Hart used to say happiness was very elusive for me and he was right. I was always looking at other people's lives, trying to figure out a way to be. I envied those who knew motherhood was their calling, who said their lives really began when they had children. To be honest, the idea of being responsible for making a totally dependent person happy scared the hell out of me. I was too selfish to spend my life sacrificing for someone who'd only take it for granted. All those childhood rituals you have to go through year after year: Halloween costumes and Christmas pageants and Saturdays wasted buying presents for other people's children and attending birthday parties. I imagined myself being forced to stand around holding a "Happy Birthday" paper plate with a slice of frosted cake, pretending to be interested in talking percentiles with other mothers whom I didn't particularly like and who said, "Isn't that darling?" much too often. No one I knew ever just played pin-the-tail-on-the-donkey anymore or musical chairs or handed out plastic baskets as party favors, filled with jelly beans and Hershey's Kisses. Instead they hired magicians and clowns who made balloons into animals and did nontoxic face painting. They rented trampolines for the front yard and drove sport utility vehicles filled with shouting, jaded children to miniature golf courses or Disneyland. Then these mothers complained to me they never had time for themselves anymore. They were always exhausted. And they weren't trying to write for a living. I imagined my life would begin when my screenplay got produced.

That made me think about calling Louie and Perle, who were hovering in the wings, waiting for me to present them a new part. But I had nothing to offer. I wanted to talk with Dora but she never stayed on the phone too long because she was afraid my father would get jealous. Every time the phone rang I hoped it would be the call I was waiting for and not them. But I knew I was pushing my luck.

"Well, heLOW."

There was no mistaking the meaning of Perle's intonation, which was meant to convey that I was a bad person for not calling.

"Hi, Mom, what's up?" It had the immediate effect of making me want to hang up.

"What's up is I thought we'd HEAR from you."

"There's not really much going on."

"What's happening with your screenplay?"

"I'm still waiting to hear."

"What TAKES them so long?"

"People are busy."

"Is anyone interested in BUYING it?"

"That's what I'm waiting to hear. But very few scripts get bought, Mom. I may only get a job out of it. If that."

"There's nothing wrong with a job."

"That's true."

"Did they PAY you to write this one?"

"I wrote it on spec. I told you."

"How's Hart, do you ever hear from him?"

"Not in a while."

"We saw his movie on television. I taped it. When Eleanor Fuchs and her son come over we're going to watch it. I'm just going to serve coffee and cake. I have a low-fat cheesecake I make that's just delicious. I make it with the low-fat cream cheese and sour cream. Did Eleanor get FAT. Tsuh, she's as big as a house. I almost didn't recognize her."

"Really?" There was a pause and I was trying to figure out why I felt so angry when she suddenly changed her tone of voice.

"Gramma isn't doing that well. We've put her into a nursing home." I couldn't believe what I was hearing.

"A NURSING home? She always said she NEVER wanted to go into a nursing home. She said she hoped she DIED before she went into one of those places."

"Her legs gave out and it was honestly too much for me. But we got her into a Jewish nursing home and we visit her every day. And they serve a lovely lunch there. We take her down to the dining room. They have soup and usually chicken and some vegetables. No salads though. I asked them, 'Why don't you serve fresh salads?' and they said it sticks to their dentures. Gramma never had trouble with her dentures. And those were supposed to be temporary ones. They were made by Uncle Abe. When I brought Gramma to Dr. Dryer— you remember him; he had a practice in Rockville Centre—he said to me, 'There's nothing wrong with these dentures. I've never seen dentures that fit so well.' But the GUMS are all discolored, I told him. They were made in rubber back then and they had turned color and he said 'I can make her new dentures but they'll never fit as well as these.' The food's a little bland at the nursing home, so we bring our own salt. But the people who work there are SO STUPID. HONESTLY. Lucille brought over the white afghan that Gramma made and can you BELIEVE they WASHED it? It looks like a HANDKERCHIEF now. That was PURE wool, and the work-manship on it, you don't see that anymore. Now you go to buy yarn and it's all acrylic. I can't even FIND wool yarn in Florida. Poor Shayna. She's home alone all day and she's such a good dog that she holds it in, but the second we're home, she RUNS outside to do her business. Sometimes it's right by the front door. And she NEVER used to do that. Here, talk to your father. Louie! LOUIE! Pick up the phone. It's Frankie. FRANKIE!"

Then my father picked up the extension phone but I could barely hear him because their phones didn't quite work in tandem. He sounded angry, as usual.

"Hi, Dad. How are you feeling?"

"My back is hurting me again. The doctor wants me to go to the pain clinic but these SOBs are just interested in money. They put me in physical therapy and it got worse."

"When we're not at the nursing home he comes home and gets right into bed. That's the only way he can get comfortable."

"Why don't you try swimming?" This was the same conversation we had year after year. I was always trying to get my parents to go swimming.

"It's too long a walk to the pool," my mother answered for him. "And it's so EMPTY there, you can go to the pool and you're the only ones there."

"Good. You can do laps." I don't know why I pursued it.

"They don't heat the pool in the winter because they're trying to save money. Even so, our assessment just went up."

"Do you speak to your sister? She's in New York. She thinks she may have her apartment rented." It sounded like my father was talking from the bottom of a pit.

"Good," I said.

"Do you speak to your brother?"

"I can barely hear you."

My mother interceded again. "Marsha and the boys said they may fly down here for Passover. Jay's working on a big case in New York, so they'll stay in Tampa with her aunt. But I'll invite them all here for dinner. Maybe you can think about coming."

"This is getting expensive, Perle," my father said. "You know, you can call US every once in a while, TOO." Then they hung up and I realized I'd forgotten to get Dora's number at the nursing home. But I couldn't bring myself to call them back. I should've gotten right on a plane but that would entail dealing with Louie and Perle at the other end. For a second I entertained the notion of asking Hart to come with me. But even if we were still together he'd be too busy. If only I were too busy. Busy was the greatest excuse for not doing what you had no intention of doing anyway. Money was another good excuse, as was illness. I had no excuse except fear, which wasn't any kind of an excuse at all. I was afraid of seeing her in that nursing home, afraid I'd be saying good-bye to her forever. The funny thing is, Dora's the one person who would've understood. I sat at my desk and watched a fly that had gotten caught between the glass and the screen. It kept crashing into the mesh and then washing its hands over and over again, like a trapped person with a guilt complex. I picked up the phone to call my parents back but there was no dial tone.

"Hello?" I said.

"Are you sitting down?" Freyda said. "Judi and Joel loved the script."

"They want to meet with you," Nicole said.

"I have a good feeling about this," Paul said.

"I'll call you back as soon as I can set up a meeting," Freyda said.

I hung up the phone and it rang again immediately.

"About fucking time." It was Jonathan, who had been listening in.

DEVIATED SEPTUM, MY FOOT

IT WAS LATE February and winter had finally begun. My meeting with Judi Golden and Joel Dweck was set to be in their offices, at the studio, in the Valley, a distance to drive in torrential rain. It was long past the usual rush hour and I wondered who the people on the road were and why they didn't just stay home. They couldn't ALL be out trying to sell their screenplays. As my car waded through rivers of water on Sunset Boulevard, I prayed the weather wasn't an omen. I was nervous about the meeting, running late because the right lane was closed due to flooding and the rain just kept on coming. The traffic bulletin on the radio reported Pacific Coast Highway was closed northbound due to a mud slide. A big rig and a motor home had collided on the 10, there was a flash-flood warning for the desert, and on Ventura Boulevard cars were getting swept away like a ride at Universal Studios. As with Miriam and her Charles Durning hubris, I hoped God wouldn't snatch away my life now that happiness seemed just down the road.

I got onto the 405 and drove in the slow lane with both hands on the wheel, ready to swerve to the shoulder to avoid a multicar pileup. The truck in front of me threw sheets of water onto my car and my

wipers smeared months of L.A. sunshine across my windshield, reminding me I should've gotten my blades changed. I'd meant to fill
up the car but didn't dare get out of traffic, and now the tank was
dropping below a quarter. My eye went from the gas gauge to the
clock to the road to the gas gauge to the clock to the road, as if I
could control their descent. I hadn't been able to eat anything and
my stomach was churning.

I pulled onto the studio lot and the guard at the entrance opened
up his kiosk. He had a white tissue hanging out of one nostril. He
found my name on his clipboard, reluctantly stuck his arm into the
rain, handed me a soggy temporary pass to put on my dashboard, and
directed me to Little Red Wagon Productions.

Judi Golden's secretary was in the outer office humming to himself
as he cut a brown-edged frond from a fishtail palm tree that just
brushed the ceiling. He was obese as an avocado, with light blue eyes
and fine, thinning, reddish golden hair like a baby. As I stepped into
the office still dripping water from my raincoat and umbrella, he
turned around, scissors in hand.

"Oh, ma word, you MADE it," he said in a drawling twang. "I
mean isn't it just the WORST out there? Of course, where I come
from we get tornadoes, so I shouldn't complain about a little rain.
This here's nothing. Trust me."

He was wearing a high-school letterman's sweater with his name,
Sparky, embroidered in yellow thread onto the dark blue wool. I
asked and he explained it really WAS his name because his mother
had thought he was a little spark plug from the moment he was born
and that he didn't actually PLAY any sports but that he WAS a
cheerleader. He wore his jeans riding right across his little tummy
and his leather sneakers were still bright white. I complimented him
on how neat the office looked. Even the teas were all fanned out in
a little wicker basket.

"I just can't live in mess," he said, and I immediately wanted to
take him home and have him organize my entire life. "If I seem
frazzled you'll have to excuse me. I had such a traumatic morning
I'm still recovering." It was said with his delicate hand resting on his
heart. He wore an antique gold ring on his pinkie with a tiny diamond and two little rubies set into the band. He hadn't seemed

frazzled to me at all. In fact, he was a little like a tranquilizer. There was something very comforting about his fussiness. I felt myself lulled by his drawl.

"What happened?" I asked, thinking his supposed trauma was weather-related.

"I had to take Hermione into the vet for her leukemia booster. Oh, ma God." He handed me a framed photo of his cat, a brown-and-white long-haired domestic who looked like a well-fed raccoon. "She was reduced from fifteen dollars to nine-ninety-five when I bought her twelve years ago and it was the best bargain I ever got. But I MEAN. It really takes two people to get Hermione into her carrying case and I live alone, boo hoo, but the vet, Dr. Peterson? Right on Lankershim here, who's an absolute doll, said that cats are afraid of falling headfirst and will always put out their paws to break the fall. So I'M supposed to set the case up on end and put Hermione in headfirst and SHE'S supposed to just slip right in like she's diving into water. Right. So I do as he says, and as soon as she sees where she's headed, she splays out her front paws and wraps her claws around the metal grid that's the side of her cage and her back claws are digging into my wrists. Look at what she did to me. She drew blood." He pushed back his sweater and showed me the neat ribbons of red claw marks. "But you know what made me stop was the sound. I mean, it was just this yowl, poor thing. It was pure animal fear and it just broke ma heart. So I finally let her go and found an old towel and wrapped her in it, in this rain mind you, and got her out to the car and let her loose, which is what I should have done in the first place. And, of course, she found her way under my seat and sat on the car pedals, which makes driving a little weird, with a cat sitting right on your feet. I brushed her this morning but all this fur started drifting up from beneath the dashboard and floated in the air around my head. I had fur up my nose, fur on my pants, fur in my eyes. NEVER wear your good sweater when you're dealing with a mad cat. She practically ruined it. It took me hours with my crochet hook to get out all the little pulls. By the way, if you're hungry we just had the snack lady come? And she brought all kinds of goodies but I shouldn't be eating any of them but I can recommend the peanut butter pretzels or the chocolate-chip cookies and I just put up a new pot of coffee and help yourself to anything in the fridge."

By the time Sparky had finished relating his morning, we were like old friends listening to the cricket frogs and swapping yarns on the front-porch rockers. Rainstorms, sick cats, ruined sweaters, money worries . . . who all cares? With his homey chatter, a pot of coffee brewing, and a plate of cookies sitting right on the watercooler, Sparky almost made me forget why I was there. His unedited presentation reminded me of Miriam. They were both aberrations— willing to deal with the huge ambitions of others, seemingly content to remain in service themselves. Miriam had found her job as Hershel's handmaiden and Sparky was lucky to have found his own wifely niche. In what other business could he have survived? Even the fashion industry would expect someone more tasteful, svelte, and professional at the front desk. Hollywood not only attracts, but embraces the otherwise unemployable.

With Sparky as my guide, I surveyed all the sparkling glass food canisters, which were labeled and alphabetically displayed on a shelf above the refrigerator. It occurred to me, as I reached into a glass canister and extracted a strip of beef jerky, just how many enterprises had grown up around the movie industry. Snack ladies, film suppliers, casting departments, editors, the guards at the gate, the Java Bus, the towel man who delivers fresh towels to executive bathrooms, tour guides, wardrobe departments, projectionists, even the masseuse on the lot who charged a dollar a minute for an at-your-desk-neck rub. An entire ecosystem, all dependent on one thing for its survival: a writer going into a room and creating something. You'd think the writer would be at the top of the food chain. And yet, if the snack lady failed to show up on a rainy day, I'm sure she'd be missed a lot more than any screenwriter.

"Judi Golden's office." Sparky stood with his little watering can and tucked the phone receiver under his soft white chin as he continued to water and prune. "Well, HI YOU. When are y'all gonna come down and have lunch with her? You have to see my new figure. I lost ten pounds. I look like a god. She's on the phone. I'll tell her you're on." Then the other phone rang and he answered it, too, and buzzed Judi. "Henri Faroli on three, Valerie on one, and Frankie Jordan is here." A third line rang. "Wouldn't you know it?" he said like a harried homemaker. "Val, can she call you back? She's just swamped. Thank you, luv." He finally turned back to me. "She's on the phone but you can go in."

Judi Golden had Henri Faroli on the speakerphone, her hands free to Windex an enormous glass desk. She waved me in with some paper towels and I felt a nervous energy that seemed to pulsate right across the room. She was wearing black leggings and a long black cashmere sweater that emphasized her skinny little body. Around her neck she had a rope of pearls and a long heavy gold chain with a watch. On another long chain was a locket. Her large black Chanel purse hung on the back of her chair. Another black leather bag bulging with scripts was on the floor. She held her pearls and chains against her sweater with one hand as she leaned across the desk to wipe away the dust. "Henri, I've got to make this quick. I'm in a meeting with a writer but I've been trying to reach you and you're never there and I hate that."

"I'm out shopping for yoooou," he said, sounding like he was trying to placate a child.

She turned to me. "Just sit anywhere. The whole office is being redone." She had a fast, staccato way of talking, which was relaxing as being around someone dribbling a basketball in the house. She wasn't much in the looks department, as my father would say, although she definitely did as much as she could with herself. Her hair was light brown and precision-cut into a chin-length bob with feathery bangs that just covered her eyebrows. I'd heard a story about Judi before I met her, supposedly told to my friend by Judi herself. When she was in high school, Judi had driven her car down to Palm Springs for the weekend with her boyfriend. Only she hated her nose so much that she would never let him see her profile. Even behind the wheel, she'd kept her face turned right for the entire ride. Since then, she'd acquired a small, button nose in the style we always referred to in my family as "The Dr. Diamond nose." Dr. Diamond being the premier nosejob doctor where I grew up, who seemed to have perfected only one style of nose. My cousin Jackie made her fiancé,

Marshal the tax attorney, go to Dr. Diamond before the wedding. Although she told everyone that Marshal had a condition which made it hard for him to breathe, my mother knew better. "Deviated septum my foot," she said after she'd seen the results of the surgery, which had the effect of making Marshal and Jackie look just like brother and sister. Alas, the sins of the parents are visited upon the children, and their two girls, Madison and Cosette, have the noses their parents left in the operating room. Knowing Jackie, I'm sure she already has the girls booked for their day under the knife, which in certain circles has become something akin to a rite of passage.

Fortunately my family escaped all that. To this day my mother will say to me, "From where did you get that nose, from where?" because my nose is small and turned up and it's never been tampered with. She is proud of my nose. "That's not a JEWISH nose," she says. "You look like an Irish *shiksa* with that face," and I always hoped when I was little that if the Nazis came, with my blue eyes and my dark hair and my *shiksa* nose, maybe a nice Catholic family would hide me in their secret annex.

Judi tore off a few more sheets of paper towel, moved over to the glass coffee table, and gave it a few squirts as she continued to talk across the room into the speakerphone to Henri Faroli.

"Alan didn't like the chair. He wants it to look more masculine. Maybe leather. But distressed leather. Old leather. Ralph Lauren leather. We were at Ralph Lauren last weekend. We saw the chair. Maybe not that style but the leather. It's on the first floor. You know the main room when you walk in? It's the first room to the right. It's the chair with the little wheels, just opposite the belts. With the nail heads. Did you see *A Room with a View?*"

"Yes. I looooved it." It was a nasal, mushy voice and I couldn't picture anyone but Liberace at his white piano on the other end of the line.

"Do you remember the scene where Maggie Smith goes to the vicar's house and there are two leather club chairs in front of the fireplace and Denholm Elliott is in one of them?" *Squirt. Squirt. Squirt.* "THAT'S the chair Alan wants."

"You want it to look distressed?"

"I can't explain it. It's just comfortable. It looks like it's BEEN there. Rent the movie. That's the look I want. The goatskin was nice but it didn't look old."

"I just saw a chair at Rose Tarlow. It was wooonderful."

I couldn't believe I'd driven through a tsunami so I could listen to Judi Golden discuss goatskin and nail heads with her decorator on a speakerphone. I was actually impressed that she could be so completely unconcerned with my opinion of her. I could have been just one more piece of unwanted furniture in her office. I started to get a heady feeling, as if I could float out of my body and see myself from above. I felt pity and impatience for that mute person sitting there, forced to be nice, just because she hoped Judi Golden would think her script was good enough to produce.

"Can I SEE it? Can you get it to the house on memo?"

"I'll get you a Polaroid. What did you think about the trims for the dining room pillows? Did you like the braid or the fringe or the ribbon?"

"What do YOU think?"

"I think the braid could look looovely but I love the feel of the fringe but I think the ribbon is the most unusuuual."

"I don't know. I have to think about it. I've got a writer here. It's not a good time. Do you think we should go with the straight sage or the radicchio-and-sage braid. I mean, which one would pick up the rug better?"

"We'll have to look at it together."

"I'm in a meeting with a writer. Call me in an hour. Okay? Arright? I'm going to be here. I'm going to be expecting your call."

"I'll call you at twelve-thirty."

"I'm not going out to lunch until I hear from you. And go over to Ralph Lauren and look at that chair. I have to tell Alan. Because he wants the library DONE."

"Things take time."

"Explain that to Alan. And I cut out a picture of a mudroom I want you to see. It's in last October's *Architectural Digest*. It's in Connecticut. Find it and we'll talk."

On her gleaming glass desk, I could see a page torn out of the magazine with the referenced mudroom. I tilted my head in order to see it better. It was a whitewashed room with a slate floor, a potting table, flats of flowers, drying herbs hanging from a hat rack, and a neat row of riding boots and Wellingtons. An old mackintosh on a peg behind a wicker chair and a collection of walking sticks completed the set piece. Yes. Exactly the kind of room one needs in Beverly Hills. A yellow Post-it, in what I assumed was Judi's handwriting, said *Hats?*

Judi made sure the phone was disconnected then turned to me as she continued to Windex her coffee table.

"I'm spending a fortune. He's supposed to be good. They said he was good but he might have to go. I have to be able to work with someone, I'm a very collaborative person. They have to be on my wavelength. I don't know if he gets it. I mean, I've cut out pictures and everything. I loved your script, by the way. I flipped. It's very uncommercial. But that's me. I take chances." She yelled into the other room. "Sparky, get Joel in the editing room and call Katie in here."

I wondered how Sparky could put up with her.

"Will do," he said, soft as peppermint. Then he walked into her office and karate-chopped the silk pillows that were sitting on her sofa until they all had a neat identical indentation right in the center. "Is everyone okay in the drinks department?"

"I need a Diet Coke. My energy is flagging." Then she turned back to me. "Do you believe this office? It's so cold. I don't know who would decorate a room so cold. The glass shows every speck of dust. Everything's going. I'm starting over from scratch. I told them, you better give me a good-sized budget to redecorate this room because I'm not working in this office. It's too cold."

"You're doing your house AND your office at the same time?" I said with appropriate awe. "My God. They should erect a statue of you in the Pacific Design Center."

Judi took to the idea right away. "I should be holding a big bolt of cloth maybe and have my foot up on an ottoman. And maybe I should have six or seven decorators groveling at my feet. And they're each offering me accessories."

"It sounds like it has religious overtones. The Gift of the Magi."

"No. It's the Homage to the Jewish Princess," she said, and I knew how clever Judi was for calling herself that before anyone else had a chance. "Actually, it's a nightmare. It's way too much to keep track of and we just got back from six grueling months in Louisiana. But the picture's going to be great. I mean, I had to hold Joel's hand through every shot but it's going to be great. I'll invite you to a screening. I'll make sure you're on the list. Sparky," she yelled into the other room. "Put Frankie Jordan down on the screening list."

I found myself acting very calm and talking very precisely, probably to compensate for her manic pinball energy. I could see that with Judi anything could become a crisis. She created friction so she could ricochet from one drama to another, eventually resolve the situation, and then complain about what she had to go through. It's what made her feel vital. She was an arsonist putting out her own fires.

Sparky entered pouring a Diet Coke with Katie right behind him holding my script and a Styrofoam cup filled with recently reconstituted noodle soup. It was so steamy she couldn't drink it but she didn't dare put it down on the coffee table, lest it get seasoned with Windex.

"I loved your script," she said. "I loved the characters. And you have a real fan in Jonathan Prince. That guy did not stop calling me. What's he like, I'm just curious."

"Tenacious, apparently."

"Well, I wouldn't want to have him working against me, that's for sure." She was soft-spoken, very feminine, and certainly didn't deserve to be labeled a bimbo by Nicole Dachshund.

Joel Dweck entered the room in a barn jacket, jeans, and urban hiking boots. "*Oy vay iz mir,* she's cleaning again. We're all suffering from secondhand Windex. Will you put that away? The *shvartzeh* comes tomorrow." Sparky took Joel's coat and dripping umbrella away before they had a chance to mess up Judi's rug. Joel took off his red-framed glasses and wiped them off on his denim work shirt. He was the kind of fag that fag hags love. They know their way around, they pick up checks, they like women, but don't want to dress like one. He turned to me. "She's a *baleboosteh,* it's in the genes."

I could see everyone adapted their behavior around Judi, cosseted and humored her. No one ever altered their behavior to fit my needs and I always wondered how these kinds of women got away with it.

Joel's secretary, a timid, young Chinese woman named Mai Lei, transferred her calls to Sparky and came in to take notes. We talked about casting possibilities and Judi said she thought Julia Roberts could be good but didn't know if she had the depth. Joel said if we were going that way he preferred Meg Ryan because when she smiles you want to root for her, but thought that Michelle Pfeiffer could do no wrong. But what we really needed was a young Sally Fields. Demi Moore was mentioned because she could play the young Ivy but Judi doubted she could play the older Ivy and wondered if she could do comedy. Mai Lei dutifully copied down the names of the actresses. Then Judi asked if we had seen Demi and Bruce's house in *Architectural Digest* and said it had persuaded her to go dark with her floors.

We were in the courting stage and I was still being wooed and flattered. I was pleased they liked the script as much as they said they did. It made me want to like them, too. It was a nice position to be in, to sit back and have Joel and Judi sell themselves to me, because it doesn't happen often. They knew at this point I could still bring the script to another producer, so Judi let it be known they were hot at the moment, and that the feature they'd just finished shooting already had good buzz, that "if this studio doesn't bite we have other studio executives who'd love to be in business with us." They assured me they got behind "their" writers one hundred percent and supported them through the process. Then Joel said the magic words. "You might make more money putting it up on the auction block, but with us at least you know we'll protect your script and make one hell of a good movie."

Judi got up only once, to take the call from Henri Faroli, who'd slogged his way through the rain to the Ralph Lauren store in Beverly Hills to look at the chair. I could only hear Judi's end of the conversation, but from what I gathered, he felt he could have his person make the chair up cheaper. Or else that's what Judi wanted him to do. They discussed smooth versus tufted and nail heads versus no nail heads and then she returned to the conversation group without apology. During the course of our meeting Judi changed her hairstyle three times. First she went into her purse to take out a barrette and pulled her hair off of her face. Then she went back to her purse, found a scrunchie, and made her hair into a little bun at the nape of her neck. Just before the meeting was over, I looked over and saw that she had pulled her bun out and had put sunglasses on top of her head.

But my eyes kept returning to Katie, because she was tall and long-waisted with white straight teeth. She sipped her soup in a dainty way and ate the noodles with a plastic fork, twirling them neatly around the tines. Oh, I could see exactly why Nicole Dachshund would brand her a bimbo. It's the Ugly Girl Syndrome. You have to be careful of the ugly girls because they're usually smart and filled with self-loathing, in spite of the clothes and therapist and money. The ugly girls push themselves to become a success so they can show everybody. They define themselves by what displeases them and make themselves superior by criticizing, and early on, they develop a bitter humor which they turn against any attractive woman who's threatening to them. Since they can't attack their looks, they attack their taste and their intelligence. Judi, to her credit, seemed oblivious to Katie's demure beauty.

When we said good-bye, both Judi and Joel kissed me. We were now best of friends.

AND THE WINNER IS

"IT'S YOUR AGENT calling." Like Nixon, Freyda often referred to herself in the third person. She'd awakened me from a deep sleep and I wasn't anywhere near ready to surface. The rain hadn't let up and it had taken me almost two hours to get home from the studio. When I'd walked in my door I felt so heavy and drugged I couldn't think of anything but climbing into bed and shutting out the world. Now I looked at the clock on the night table and realized I'd only been asleep for fifteen minutes. "Judi LOVES you. She said you two had a great meeting."

"I think she's crazy."

"But Joel's nice. I mean, he's a little in-your-face but I hear their new movie is supposed to be great."

"That's the rumor they keep spreading around."

"Ian Mandel's script was very atmospheric. Oh, shit. Hold on."

She was gone, replaced by music sounding like an ice-cream truck, playing the same, simple tune over and over again. From experience, I placed the phone down, found the newspaper, and got back into bed. The rain pelted the roof and overflowed the gutter like a small waterfall, splattering the flagstone patio outside my window. A distant ambulance siren was warning cars out of its way. I felt safe from danger being in my bed, underneath a warm feather comforter. After about five minutes I heard Jonathan's voice coming from my pillow.

"She's still on the phone. You want us to call you back?"

I picked up the receiver. "Tell her to call me back when she can stay off the other phone."

"I spoke to Katie. She said they're excited about the script. What does she look like? Is she pretty, is she cute, is it worth meeting her?"

"What am I, running reconnaissance for your romantic life?"

"I don't want to waste my time with her if she's a dog."

"She's not a dog, believe me. Actually she's beautiful."

"So who's this doctor idiot she's seeing?"

"You obviously have had more personal conversations with her than I have."

"I'm making nice. It's part of the business. I'm giving her love advice."

"LOVE advice?"

"She confides in me. She tells me her problems and I give her solutions."

"Well, when you're done with her, you can start on me."

"What's your problem? You shouldn't have any problems. Not a lovely girl like you," he said, his voice mockingly sweet.

"Thank you, Aunt Iris."

Freyda picked up the phone with Paul and Nicole patched in. "To be continued," Jonathan said before he went off to get another call.

"Congratulations," Paul said. "I hear you had a great meeting with Judi and Joel."

"I hear they thought the script was fabulous."

"They want to take it to the studio as soon as we've completed the negotiations with their company," Freyda said. "I'm going to tell them that you want an executive-producing credit and adjusted gross."

"Maybe we should give it to another producer just to get a reaction. I'm not too sure about Judi."

"Judi's a little excessive," Paul said. "We all know that. She's the Marie Antoinette of Burbank, but she mothers a project along and she's gotten some impossible ones off the ground."

"Of course it doesn't hurt that her father could probably buy the whole studio, darling."

"True, but that only works in our favor. If we start shopping it to other producers and no one wants to take a chance on it, then we can't go back to them and we're screwed. It's your first time up to bat," Paul said, "and you've scored a base hit. Why change teams in the middle of an inning?" Why was it that men like Paul, probably the last ones picked for any team, were the ones who used the sports metaphors? "I think this could be a home run."

I hung up and I wasn't tired anymore. I was elated. For a long time I'd been avoiding people, even my dentist, because I didn't want to have to explain myself when someone asked what I was working on. But now I had something to say. Someone wanted to do my script. Judi and Joel had made me legitimate again. I leaned back on my pillows and composed my Oscar acceptance speech. I thanked Hart for putting up with all my endless rewrites. I thanked Judi and Joel for taking the chance on a script that was different, and I thanked the members of the Academy for giving me the reassurance that it was possible to tell a quiet story and have it deliver a loud message. After I called Hart, I made an appointment to have my teeth cleaned.

For the rest of March I caught up on everything I'd been putting off. I spoke to my parents, bought new underwear, had my car tuned, new heels put on my worn-down shoes, my hair cut, went to the gynecologist, the dermatologist, and the mammogram clinic. By the time negotiations ground to a halt in April, I felt almost organized. At stake was how much of their back end Judi and Joel were willing to share with me. Since the studios almost never give a percentage of the gross profit to writers, and since no one ever sees net profit, it was up to Judi and Joel to show good faith and give me something, "a little taste." At least, according to Freyda, who called me on her way to Two Bunch Palms.

"Do you believe—*chozzers*? I'm asking—a fucking half a point."

"How many points do they have?"

"I don't know their deal with the studio but I'm sure they have—. We're dividing up—in the sky anyway, but it's the—of the—"

"WE HAVE A TERRIBLE CONNECTION, FREYDA," I shouted. "YOU'RE FADING OUT."

She came back at me talking even louder. "I'M DEALING WITH NORMAN DIETZ, THEIR LAWYER—TOTAL PRICK. ARE YOU—ACADEMY AWARDS PARTY?"

"OF COURSE I'M COMING."

"WE'RE—AT FIVE."

The closer it got to the day of the Academy Awards the more I didn't want to go, especially alone. But I was obligated. I was just hoping it wasn't one of those parties where you had to put a dollar in a kitty and mark your ballot and everyone talks at the TV, trying to outdo each other making witty comments. This was the first time Freyda and Marty were officially entertaining, so I had no idea what to expect.

For ten years they'd gone to everyone else's dinner parties, including mine, but never reciprocated. Marty and Freyda had originally rented a furnished house in the flats of Beverly Hills, but it had "bad traffic flow," so they were waiting to buy a house before inviting anyone over. Over the years she'd collected large white buffet plates and hand-painted Italian buffet plates and handblown wineglasses and colorful napkins in various and assorted patterns. Her kitchen drawers bulged with napkin rings. The woven wheat napkin rings for Thanksgiving, the pink watermelon napkin rings for the Fourth of July, and the fish napkin rings for the phantom bouillabaisse dinner she never served, because they could never find the right house in which to entertain. They looked at every kind of house and Freyda always had a flyer with a photo of the latest property they were interested in, but Marty was so indecisive that the price of real estate doubled and they couldn't afford what they wanted. They finally bought at the top of the market, a house in Hancock Park that, according to Freyda, would have been an easy three million if it were in Beverly Hills.

Freyda told me when they moved in they still couldn't entertain because there wasn't a powder room. Actually, I knew there was because I snuck a peek at it once. But the pink wallpaper featured poodles combing their hair and looking in hand mirrors and Freyda kept the door closed so no one could see. After a few years Freyda made Marty interview decorators but he couldn't decide which one to use. Finally Freyda put her foot down and informed Marty, and the rest of Hollywood, that if he didn't redo the powder room and buy a sofa, she was leaving him. It seemed to me as good a reason as any. Their marriage was based mainly on eating and traveling, and Freyda didn't need Marty because she was a pro on her own. Freyda called his bluff and moved out to the Bel Air Hotel. At six hundred and fifty dollars a night, Marty figured out pretty quickly that he was making a financially imprudent decision and bought the sofa. For two years they'd been redoing their house and Academy Award night was the unveiling. For Freyda, there was a lot riding on this party and I knew she was beyond nervous.

The invitation included a little Xeroxed map, but it wasn't hard to find. It was still light out as I made my way east on Beverly Boulevard. I turned out of traffic into Hancock Park and saw a silver Porsche racing up the street in front of me. I had the feeling we were going to the same place. I followed at a discreet distance through the hushed, shady streets right to Freyda and Marty's house, taking my time parking so I could see who it was I was tailing. Ian Mandel, whom I'd last pretended not to see at my agent's, got out of the car with a girl who looked from a distance to be about twelve. It was a cool evening and I was in a turtleneck and blazer. Ian's girlfriend was wearing a sleeveless black crushed-velvet peasant dress with a lace-up bodice and black leather lace-up ankle boots that made her look like she'd stepped right out of *Les Misérables*. I waited until they were inside before I got out of the car because I didn't want to pretend I didn't recognize him. Not that I relished talking to him either.

Hancock Park is one of the genteel old neighborhoods built before the advent of smog and crime and freeways. They were the in-town homes to the very wealthy who rented little shacks in the beach communities as summer getaways. Now, of course, only the brave or foolish walk the streets here after dark without their Doberman and stun gun. And those little beach shacks are worth a fortune. Hart always said most people like California best when it reminds them of someplace else, and Hancock Park, except for the occasional palm tree, reminded me of some of the wealthier towns on the North Shore of Long Island.

The house was a large brick Georgian Colonial set back from the street behind high wrought-iron gates. I skirted around the cars parked on the circular brick driveway, past two old sycamore trees with mottled gray bark and fuzzy green leaves that were just starting to make a comeback. The landscape lighting had been turned on, waiting for the sun to disappear. The tiny white lights strung in the flowering pear trees gave the house the feel of a resort hotel, something I'm sure Freyda could appreciate.

Four massive Doric columns flanked a mahogany front door. I stood on the wide brick steps for a moment and admired the pots of perfect white impatiens and begonias. There were beds of pink hibiscus and New Zealand ferns, lily of the Nile and azaleas that looked perfectly happy. White gardenias were blooming early and scented the air with the heady smell of prom night. A sensation of privilege swept over me, a feeling verging on elegance.

And then Dora came to mind. I tried to imagine what she would have made of all this. Even Hart's house, which wasn't on such a grand scale, had overwhelmed her. The first time she took a shower, Hart had showed her how to turn on the various nozzles and sprays. When she emerged from the bathroom with a sheepish look we asked her how she enjoyed it. "To tell you the truth," she said, "I was more nervous than wet." Now she was in a nursing home where strangers stole the body lotion and the large-faced watch I'd sent her. She had nothing of value she could call her own. But I knew she wouldn't complain, she'd expected very little in life. We'd arranged so she could call me every Sunday morning from the home and the operators always said, "I have a collect call from Gramma. Will you accept the charges?" That was her luxury; talking to me for as long as she liked without Louie glaring at her. That's what I was thinking when I rang the doorbell.

The front door was manned by a butler in a tuxedo who offered to take my jacket and my drink order. I kept the jacket, took him up on the drink, and as he disappeared in the direction of the kitchen, I looked through to the living room, where people were gathered around a giant TV. Most of the men were dressed in jeans and I briefly wondered at what point the help started looking better than the guests. The tuxedoed man came back with a glass of white wine and I found Freyda standing at the bottom of the stairs with a small group of people clustered around her, looking like a docent at Monticello. The five-fifteen tour was about to begin.

Ian Mandel and I, standing next to each other, were forced into mutual recognition and I got a kiss on the cheek. He introduced me to his girlfriend, Portia, and I made a stupid comment to the effect that it's not every man who has a car and a girlfriend with the same name. He made some noise like "puh," which was about all it deserved and Portia had no response at all. She didn't have to. She was beautiful, with golden-brown pupils ringed in black and perfect little child's teeth that looked like white corn kernels. Her light brown hair, streaked with blond, was pulled straight back into a softly twisted bun at the nape of her neck. Little wisps of hair framed her face. I shook her small, icy hand, wondering how Ian ever got a girl like this, when I realized he must wonder the same thing. Ian now had everything he couldn't get in high school. He'd finally won, even though the game was long over. But like a lot of men I know, Ian couldn't stop playing. I presumed Portia was an actress because no one else wears a dress like that on a cold night. Without any trouble, I caught sight of her shapely little white breasts. You'd think Ian might say to her before they left the house, "Hon, I think people can look right down the front of that dress and see your nipples." But I guess Ian must find it gratifying to find other men admiring what only he possesses.

Holding our glasses of California Chardonnay, we followed Freyda up the grand staircase. "This is that Byron Chardonnay," Ian said to Portia. "Remember? The *Wine Spectator* gave it a ninety-one. It's supposed to have a nice finish with overtones of citrus and oak. You're going to like this."

She took a little sip, then raised her eyebrows and looked at her glass as if still unconvinced.

"I told you," he said to her. "This Chardonnay really kicks butt." Then he turned to me. "So what are you working on?" I knew he wanted me to ask him the same thing so he could mention that he had a movie coming out. I recognized his cockiness, knowing he was on the brink of success.

I told him Judi and Joel wanted to produce my script. "How did you like working with them?" I added, to let him know I was aware of his good fortune.

"UH . . ." There was a pause for effect while he took in a big, weary breath and let it out. Then he sort of laughed. "Huh-huh-huh."

"That good?"

"No, really it was fine. Actually it was great. I love Judi. I really do. Fuha."

"Ian thinks she's a cunt." Little-waif Portia had spoken.

"I said she was cunt-LIKE," he said to me, and smiled. I realized he actually had a very nice smile. "We had one unbelievable fight and we got past it."

"Was this an original script?"

"They optioned some book but I threw the whole thing out and started from scratch."

"So were their ideas any good?"

"I've heard worse. Have you seen Judi's house? I hear they have an unbelievable house." He was trying to change the subject. The movie was going to be a hit and he didn't want to bad-mouth anyone. What was the point? Good for him. He was being an adult.

"I haven't seen it. What about Joel?"

"UH . . ." Another dramatic pause and deep weary breath. These questions seemed to be exhausting him. "You mean Mrs. *Haime-sheh*?"

"Who calls him that?"

"The actors love him. He's great to them. He kisses their ass. He lets them improvise. You know."

Portia threw him an annoyed look. "Why shouldn't he be great to them, Ian? As an actor you're putting yourself in his hands. You're trusting him."

"Portia's an actress," he said to me, looking like a proud father.

"It's not DONE yet," Freyda said as we entered the master bedroom. "The curtains are going to be in a natural linen and the lighting fixtures are still being made, but at least you can get the IDEA. Marty wants to electrify the curtains so we can control them from the bed."

The house was coordinated in beiges and whites, but unlike some decorated houses, it still maintained vestiges of the personal. It looked like a place where someone actually lived. Without children. Freyda and Marty were both rambunctious collectors and everything was now professionally displayed on shelves, in nooks or on walls with recessed lighting targeted just so. Even the Yankee baseball cap Marty wore during his directorial debut was beautifully mounted in a Plexiglas box, giving it relic status, like the Buddha's tooth.

Freyda narrated her way through the two master baths and into her room-size closet while I found myself cornered in the bedroom by Lydia Schultz and Sinclair Wood. Lydia, who has an acute case of the Ugly Girl Syndrome, was brought up in Beverly Hills. Sinclair was middle-class Atlanta, but as a couple they are somehow perfectly suited. Sinclair is fond of saying his family didn't like Jews until they met Lydia and then they REALLY didn't like Jews. They write and produce sitcoms that are just about as funny, but the ratings are good, or good enough to keep them on the air, and they were the first of our crowd to make the cover of *House & Garden*. Which, I know, is one of the reasons why Marty had been so reluctant to commit to a sofa. He was afraid they'd tell him he'd gotten the wrong one.

Lydia and Freyda have known each other since college and the two couples used to take vacations together, until Lydia surprised everyone and got pregnant with Graham, whose birth was conveniently timed with TV-season hiatus. Lydia was the kind of woman who hated children and would never allow them into her house, but when she became a mother every woman without a child was suspect. I never understood how anyone could spend two minutes with them, much less priceless vacation time.

"Do you believe they waited ten years to decorate and this is the best they could come up with?" she said on cue. "I mean, it looks like a Kreiss showroom. It probably IS Kreiss. They probably have the entire Kreiss COLLECTION right here in this house. I don't know why they didn't use Henri Faroli. I told them to use him but asshole Marty was probably too cheap."

It was the second time I'd heard the name Henri Faroli. He was in the air, part of the Hollywood-style Zeitgeist. People have become as obsessed with decorating as they used to be about sex, and Henri

Faroli, who knew how to procure whatever fantasies his clients demanded, seemed to have become the Madame of the Moment. "Did you see the kitchen?" Lydia went on.

"Not yet."

"It's like a fucking granite quarry in there," Sinclair said.

"It's so Valley. And they've got TWO Sub-Zeros. Who are we kidding? Like Marty is really going to start entertaining." Lydia was wearing a beautiful Art Nouveau necklace of seed pearls and fire opals and I wanted to rip it off of her neck because she didn't deserve it.

"We saw Hart in Deer Valley," Sinclair said. "He got grayer. What did you do to him?"

"Nothing he didn't do to me," I said. I felt like a dog with its hackles up. One more sniff in an indelicate place and I'd have to be restrained.

"Who was he with?" Sinclair asked me.

"She looked like a teenager," Lydia said. "They keep getting younger and younger."

"That was his daughter," I replied, and I could see that Lydia was genuinely disappointed.

"Is that the one you had all the trouble with?" she asked, putting me on the defensive again.

"She's fine," I lied. "That was just a stage."

The beeper beeped on Sinclair's belt, and when he picked up the phone to call their nanny I made my escape. Walking down the stairs I thought of their poor son. Maybe if he could be taken away from them right away, there would be some hope.

When I returned to the living room, new people had arrived and were examining Marty's collection of old toy trucks like polite gallery goers. I copped the last endive stuffed with salmon pâté from a girl holding aloft a silver serving tray. A buffet was being laid on the dining-room table. I stood in the living room eating my hors d'oeuvre over my napkin, realizing how lonely I was out in company. I thought I'd been missing something, but now that I was here I didn't know what to say to anyone. I was wishing I could come down with a dramatic case of hives so I could go home and be alone, when Jonathan Prince entered the room. I waved my endive and we made our way toward each other like long-lost relatives.

"Thank god YOU'RE here," he said, kissing me on the cheek. I felt a sudden and genuine warmth for Jonathan, knowing he would get me through the evening. He was carrying a box wrapped with gold paper and a bow. "I bought Freyda and Marty a bottle of champagne for finally almost finishing their house. 'Now it still needs WORK,' he said, parroting Freyda's mantra, 'and we still have to put in the gold bidet, but at least you can get an IDEA.' " Then he stopped and said to me, "I really like the way you look tonight. You look lovely." And I, known far and wide for accepting compliments gracefully, said, "Well, that's probably because I'm holding my stomach in," and he replied, "Well, whatever you're doing, it definitely has an effect. I mean it." Then he did something very odd. He softly took a lock of my hair and put it behind my ear. It was an unexpected gesture, almost intimate, and I wondered if he was flirting with me. I was a little out of practice myself. As we talked, I watched his eyes blink in rapid little bursts behind his glasses. I couldn't exactly tell what color they were, some kind of brown or hazel. He seemed to be very at ease except for those eyes. I hadn't noticed his blinking before and wondered if somehow I was making him nervous. If he was attracted to me and I just hadn't realized it.

We both spotted Freyda in the entry hall having a small tiff with Marty. All I could overhear was chicken wings, garbage, and plumber, and I presumed the help had put a no-no down the brand-new disposal. I was about to head the other way but Jonathan locked his arm around my waist and steered us right into the squall.

"Congratulations, the house looks great," he said, kissing Freyda on the cheek. "When's the first sleep-over?" He knew just how to calm the waters.

"What's THIS?" Marty said. "A PRESENT?"

"It's just for you and Freyda. It's not meant for public consumption. It's for the two of you to drink at your leisure without any interruption." He handed the wrapped gift to Freyda.

"Uch," Marty said. "Does that mean I have to have SEX with her?"

"You don't HAVE to," Jonathan said. "You can give me a call and I'll be happy to oblige."

"Thank-You-Jonathan," Freyda said, looking at Marty pointedly. "You just made my night."

"NOW I see why you hired him. So he can't type. What difference does it make?" Marty was getting into his buoyant company mood. The hell with the garbage disposal.

"Should I open this now?" Freyda said.

"Did you ever see Freyda wait to open a present? What is it? What is it?" Marty hung over her shoulder as she opened the box.

It held a bottle of Perrier Jouet and two champagne flutes, all nestled in its own satin-lined box. Jonathan was like the kid coming home from college making nice with his parents' friends. The kind of kid who feels comfortable around middle-aged successful people. The kind of kid who is middle-aged.

"Come see the kitchen and then I'll take you on a quick tour of the house," she said to him. I should have gone to see the kitchen with them but I didn't make my move fast enough and Marty and I were left alone with each other.

"Do you believe that?" he said to me. "That was an expensive gift for a secretary. That probably cost him something."

"I'll bet it did."

"What do you think that costs?"

"I have no idea."

We both realized we'd run out of conversation. Jerry Slotnick saved the day. He came over to us holding beef sate on a bamboo skewer. I didn't want to be the one to tell him he'd dripped peanut sauce on his blue silk shirt. Before the evening was over, there would be a stain on the new living room sofa, I was sure of it.

"I don't believe it. You finally got the fuckin' house done."

"Jerry!" Marty was fully animated now as he threw up his hands in greeting.

"Jesus Christ. How can you pay for all this if you never work? It's a good thing you got a wife who brings in money." He turned to me. "This is the only man I know who can turn a Go Project into a development deal." Jerry had no idea we had actually almost met twice before. Marty changed the subject.

"Where's Yoshi?" he said, referring to the elusive Japanese wife.

"Abby has the measles. She had to stay home with her."

"You're KIDDING? We got all this FOOD."

Marty introduced me as Frankie Jordan who used to be married to Hart Jordan and Jerry said, "Talented writer. Very talented. Not a bad director either." Then he turned back to Marty.

"Did you read that script I sent you? This is a very talented writing team. They just sold something to Castle Rock. Everyone's very high on them."

"I'll read it this week."

"I'm gonna call you on Friday."

"What are you *hockin'* me for?"

"So you can write off this fuckin' party, that's why."

Freyda announced that dinner was served.

Jonathan and I met up again on the buffet line when he handed me a buffet plate and napkin in a carved duck napkin ring. We found a seat next to each other in the media room, in front of a large-screen television and watched my favorite part, the Arrival of the Dresses.

"The TV is going to be built-in," Freyda announced. "We're just waiting for our carpenter."

"Thank God. We were worried," Sinclair said, and Lydia laughed wickedly. Portia sat next to Sinclair, her plate prudently arranged with a few lettuce leaves and a small scoop of tabbouleh. I saw Sinclair glance down the front of her dress. And I saw that Ian also saw Sinclair glance down the front of her dress. And I saw Jonathan watching Ian watching Sinclair. Jonathan bumped my knee, leaned in close and whispered, "Are you catching this great show?" Then the real show began.

If you're not nominated or representing someone who is, or if it's not politically advantageous for you to be seen there, you don't want to attend the Academy Awards. No one over twenty-five wants to get into formal dress at three in the afternoon, hit a traffic jam of limousines, and run the gauntlet of star watchers to sit in a theater and celebrate someone else's victory. There was an infectious infestivity that evening because every writer, director, producer, and actor in that room had fallen short and we knew it. The All-Stars were out there on the playing field scoring points, and we on the bench could only watch with envy.

The only one who seemed to be genuinely enjoying himself was

Jonathan. During the commercials, when people got up for seconds or dessert, he worked the room, introducing himself to people with whom he'd previously only spoken over the phone. He was good at it. He was friendly in just the right kind of way. When he looked at you, he really focused in on what you were saying. And he didn't seem to be trying to impress. When I was his age, I was always worried what people were thinking of me. That's one of the good things about getting old; you realize it doesn't matter. For a moment I actually found myself attracted to Jonathan and had to remind myself that I was fifteen years his senior. But I had drunk enough wine to think, So what?

When the awards were over, everyone left en masse, driving off in various directions in an L.A. diaspora. Freyda and Marty looked exhausted, and anyone passing on the street at that moment would have thought the house was owned by the man in the tuxedo who stood by the door and wished us all a good night. Jonathan walked me to my car and kissed me primly on the cheek. "Hey, thanks for being my date," he said, squeezing my hand. I thanked him back, he waited until my car started, and I drove away.

I had no trouble spotting Ian's car again on Sunset as we both headed home. It was late and traffic was light as he slowed his Porsche down to a crawl. Then I realized what he was doing. The poster for his movie was looming up over the strip on a large lighted billboard. Ian was cruising past it as slowly as he dared, savoring his moment. Unfortunately there was a small typo. The billboard read: WRITTEN BY JAN MANDELL. Ian's Porsche gunned past me with an angry change of gears and the last thing I saw were his taillights disappearing into the west.

13

SO MUCH HAPPINESS

HART WAS PAYING my rent and I'd been using my savings for expenses, but May arrived and I was getting very nervous. It'd been months since my last phone call from Joel Dweck and Judi Golden. Once negotiations on the sale of my script started, we were at war, and the enemy doesn't fraternize.

"I finished the script five months ago," I reminded Freyda. "What can you still be negotiating? I need money."

"I keep waiting for their lawyer to call me back. They're not moving. They're not budging. They don't want to give you more than a quarter of a point."

"So then take it."

"Okay. Fine. But it's an insulting offer."

"So then tell them to screw it and let's give it to another producer."

There was a silence on the other end of the phone. I presume Freyda felt I was abusing her by this outburst.

"Freyda? Any thoughts? Comments?"

"You want us to start all OVER again?"

"What do Paul and Nicole think?"

"They think Judi and Joel are being assholes."

Later that day the holy trinity called.

"I just got off the phone with a friend of mine"—it was Nicole—"who said she heard my client had written a script called *Ivy and Men* and that the studio was considering it. And that HER friend who works at the studio in casting had read it."

"What does that mean?" I asked. I knew it didn't sound good.

"It means," Paul said, "that Judi and Joel have leaked the script and are showing it to the studio on the sly to see how much interest there really is before they conclude their deal with you."

"I asked them not to show it to anybody," Freyda said. "I specifically said it was for their eyes only. That no one else had seen it and that they were getting first look."

"You can bet that it's Xeroxed all over town by now," Paul said.

"It's probably a Movie of the Week by now," Nicole said.

"Fortunately it's not high-concept enough to rip off but I still think it was an amazing abuse of confidence," Freyda added.

"She wouldn't tell me who it was who read the script," Nicole said. "I tried to find out but she wouldn't say. But she knew I was really afflicted."

"Don't you mean affronted?" Paul said.

"I can say afflicted. I'm afflicted by it."

"It sounds like it's given you cancer." They were having a conversation with themselves and I was listening, all the paranoia rising in my gut.

"So what should we do?" Freyda said.

"What can we do?" Paul said. "It happens all the time."

"Are they allowed to show my script like that? Without consulting me?" I finally asked. Hart would know what to do. He was the one I wanted to talk to.

"Of course not," Paul said. "It's like giving them a free option."

"Fuckheads," Nicole threw in.

"You think I should call the Writers Guild? Report that they're shopping it around without my permission?"

"First of all we'll never prove it and second of all you'll queer the deal," Paul said. "We'll just play it out."

"How do we do that?"

"Let them know that we heard. They'll deny it of course, but at least they'll know that we know."

So, after I got Hart's advice, that's just what my agents did. Judi and Joel expressed shock and outrage and said if they found out someone in their company had Xeroxed the script and showed it, whoever it was would be fired. Then the matter was dropped and the deal with their production company concluded within the week. I would get a quarter of a point, exactly what they'd offered me from the start, and if the script got made I'd be an executive producer, a nominal feature credit they give to anybody who needs paying off.

Joel was the first one to break the silence. He called as soon as the deal memo was sent.

"*Mazel tov.* We're in business. Do you believe those *gonif* lawyers?" he said as if they weren't his *gonif* lawyers. "But I think you're going to be a very wealthy woman. The studio wants to take a look at your script as soon as possible, so I'm going to send it over today, if it's okay with you." He paused to let me know he considered us partners now and that he wasn't the one involved with the leaked script.

"Fine," I said.

"Lance Topping, whom I have a very good relationship with, is flying to New York tonight and I want him to read it on the plane. He was the one who bought my film and I think we have the best shot with him. He's very close to Cantrowitz, and if Lance likes it, we're in. If I were you I'd put the champagne on ice."

It was a weekend full of anticipation and dread. I just wanted to get out of the Westside and drive down to Chinatown to smell something different. I was tired of white people. I wanted to go rummaging around the little shops filled with teas and incense and meat cleavers and the medicine shops with jars of unidentified floating objects. I wanted to forgo forks and remind myself there was a whole world which functioned very nicely without Hollywood. But Miriam, who usually accompanied me on foreign adventures, was making the rounds of garage sales in the neighborhood and Hershel, a prodigious consumer of dim sum, had taken to praying with the Lubavitchers. I wound up meeting my friend Daphne for lunch at a restaurant only five blocks from home.

I got there on time and sat outside next to a fountain in the small patio restaurant. At the next table, drinking mango iced teas, were a couple of real-estate ladies having a meaningful exchange about title companies. I went ahead and ordered because Daphne had a four-year-old and a sixteen-month-old, and it took military strategy just to get them out of the house.

Daphne appeared as I was finishing my lunch. She was pushing a stroller with both kids inside and a diaper bag hung over the handle-bars. She had a beatific look on her face and the placid manner of a Christian martyr. Or she was suffering from sleep deprivation and was just too tired to react.

Little Molly, the older one, was adorned in her pink crinoline tutu with a pink bridal veil and pink ballet slippers and pink lipstick. She carried a clear plastic wand with colored sparkles suspended inside which she kept waving around Matthew's head as if she wanted him to disappear. Her other hand clutched a box of Tree Top apple juice with a straw inside. She calls me "Fwankie," which I find endearing, and I call her Molly Wally, but my repertoire with kids is limited. I can only take them for a few minutes before I want to make them disappear and move on to adult fare.

"Watch your wand, Molly. Don't poke Matthew. I'm sorry," Daphne said, turning to me. "Just as we were walking out the door, Matthew did a great big poop."

Daphne and I really had nothing in common. I met her through her husband, William, who did a score for a Movie of the Week I rewrote. Unlike most of my other friends, she'd constructed a gentle life around family, friends, and make-your-own-pizza parties and she was totally unaffected by Hollywood. She didn't complain about it, didn't worry about it, wasn't obsessed with the quality of her life or with getting out of the business. She had no idea what my life was like and I didn't try to explain it to her because she wouldn't un-derstand. The only battles she knew were the ones between her two children, and then she was in full control because she could predict and shape any outcome. It's amazing to me but I'd never heard her say anything bad about anybody, which really got on my nerves. Sometimes I wanted to yell at her, "THAT'S NOT THE WAY LIFE

IS!" Every time I was with her I felt she was that mealymouthed Melanie to my bitchy Scarlett.

Daphne and William were the only couple I knew who gave pot luck parties. Their sofa bed in the living room was called the jumping couch. In the backyard was a big hammock usually filled with neighborhood children. There was a playpen for Matthew that wasn't put away when company came, and baby gates you had to climb over on your way to the bathroom. The toilet had a child seat attached to it so Molly didn't drown. Their walls were covered with Molly's drawings, the floors were booby-trapped with toys, there was usually a box of baby wipes wherever you wanted to sit down, and a mouse named Steve lived on the kitchen dryer. It wasn't a house to impress dinner guests on Academy Award night.

Daphne parked Matthew in the stroller with me, and Molly followed her inside the restaurant to order. Matthew had Cheez-Its on his face and an extremely unappealing cable of green snot coming out of his nose. I took a Kleenex from my purse and wiped away the whole mess, mostly because I didn't want to have to look at it anymore. When he started to fuss, I made the mistake of lifting him out of his stroller. He headed straight for the fountain. I held on to the back of his pants as he tried to fall in. Then he lost interest in the fountain and I chased him around as he headed for the street or the parking lot or the orchids in front of the flower shop. I finally realized I was the adult and could put him back into his stroller. Only then did he seem to remember that his mother was gone and he let out a cry to chill the soul. We both turned to the restaurant as Daphne appeared and I don't know who was more relieved to see her. Matthew's nose started running again, and when she started to feed him a very soft banana, I had to get out of there. I explained I was expecting a call and went home, so glad to be alone.

Monday passed without a word from Joel or Judi, which I knew wasn't a good sign. On Tuesday Joel called me.

"Well, it's not great news," he said. My heart sank.

"What did he say?"

"Lance isn't as enthusiastic as we are. He doesn't see it as a movie."

"What does he see it as? A car?"

"I was really surprised by his reaction. I really thought he'd like it."

I didn't know how to respond. I knew from experience that if anyone shows a moment's uncertainty along the way, it will only add kindling to the smoldering mountain of insecurity. If I let them know I'd lost confidence in my work, I was as good as dead. I was looking at a little Japanese antique chest that sat on my desk for paper clips and pens. It was my birthday present to myself. I was forty years old. Miriam was giving me a small party that night and I'd been hoping for good news, as a sign that everything would be all right. That my life wasn't a total waste.

"He just feels like it's not the kind of picture Cantrowitz is looking for right now."

"Oh, well," I said in my most nonchalant manner. "If he doesn't like it, we'll bring it someplace else."

"The thing I have to say about Lance is, he's usually right on. That's the thing that worries me. He thought the ending was a downer. He said he really wanted to feel exhilarated, but he didn't."

He was dragging me to the bottom again and I had to fight for air.

"Exhilaration wasn't what I was aiming for. The ending is more sweet irony. With maybe a little catharsis thrown in for good measure. But it's certainly not a downer."

"He didn't hate it. He kept me on the phone for twenty minutes telling me that he appreciates the quality of your writing. I asked him if it was worth a meeting. Let's hear what his objections are. Let's see if we can reassure him."

"So what did he say?"

"He said he'd talk to Cantrowitz about it."

"How's Judi?" I asked. She had been curiously absent during these delicate proceedings.

"Judi's here. You want to talk to her?"

I really didn't and I was mad at myself for even bringing her up. "No, that's okay, I'm sure she's busy."

"No, wait a second. Here she is."

"Do you believe that fucker?" she said, grabbing the phone away from Joel. "I mean, this is the idiot that passed on *Rain Man*. The guy has zero taste in my opinion. He kisses Cantrowitz's ass, that's why he's there. We just brought in our movie under budget and on time and it's going to be a big picture for them, which they desperately need by the way, and that fucker still doesn't trust us. We're calling him right now and setting up a meeting for all three of us. If that's what it's going to take, then that's what it's going to take."

When I hung up with Judi, I actually felt a little better. She was a vicious majorette running up and down the field clobbering everyone with her baton, but as long as she was on your team, she was okay.

I knew I should call Freyda and tell her what'd transpired but then I'd have to speak with Jonathan, give him the bad news. I needed time to recover. I didn't want to speak to anyone. Then the phone rang and I picked it up, which goes to show you should trust your instincts.

"Happy birthday."

"Thanks, Mom, how you doing?" I looked at my watch. It was two o'clock, which meant it was five o'clock back east and the rates had just gone down.

"We're doing fine. What are you doing for your birthday?"

"Miriam's giving me a little party."

"That's nice. Did you hear from Hart?"

"I haven't heard from him yet." And I didn't expect to. Hart was always forgetting my birthday even when we were together.

"How's your script? Are they casting it yet?"

"Nooo. They don't cast it until they decide to make it."

"I thought you said they liked it."

"I said the producers liked it. It still has to get over many hurdles before it's made."

"What should we send you?"

"Don't send me anything. I don't need anything."

"I have to send you SOMEthing for your birthday."

"Don't worry about it. Really."

"I'm not WORRIED about it, I just thought it would be nice to send you something. We have so many things that I've never even unpacked when we moved here. I have so much JUNK in the closets that every time I start to clean it out, I get dizzy and I have to sit down. I've been so DIZZY today that I had to sit down twice. And

I had that pain in my chest again. Dr. Zeidy wants me to take a stress test and do an ultrasound on my carotid artery. He's not ruling out heart condition but he thinks it could be my gallbladder. You know those dessert plates with the roses painted on them? Those are all hand-painted. They were a wedding present to Gramma. They're Rosenthal china. There used to be eight of them, but when we moved here, the movers just THREW the box in the back of the moving truck. They were wrapped in bubble paper and I had it marked 'Fragile,' but when we got here and I opened the box, I saw that the plates were in pieces. Now there are four. Would you like them?"

"No, really, I'm fine. Why don't you keep them?"

"Darling, we have so much STUFF. This is a small place. I don't have ROOM for all the stuff we have. You know, it's been almost a year since we've seen you. Any chance that you'd come up to the country this summer?"

"I don't think so. I really have to stay around here and work."

"All that work, it would be nice to have something to show for it."

I quickly changed the subject. "How's Aunt Iris and Uncle Irv?"

"She's had a lot of company lately. Sheila and David came down for two weeks and she invited us over and served turkey and *kugel*. It was so HOT that day, who could EAT such a big meal? I had a little piece of the *kugel* and one slice of the white meat. I would have been happy with just a cold salad. But you know Iris. She loves to entertain. And before you're even done, she's cleaning up the dishes. Your father wants to wish you happy birthday. He's already in bed. Louie. Louie, pick up the phone. It's Frankie."

My father picked up the phone.

"Happy birthday." He sounded old.

"Thanks, Dad. How you feeling?"

"Not too good. The doctor wants me to have an operation. They want to fuse my disks."

"Why don't you get a second opinion?"

"This WAS the second opinion."

"Did I tell you we gave Shayna away?" Perle said.

"You gave Shayna away?" I couldn't believe what I was hearing.

"We met a nurse at the nursing home and she wanted to get a dog for her children but she didn't want a puppy that she'd have to house-train and that would eat up all the furniture. And we weren't home enough. So we gave her Shayna."

"How could you just give your dog away to a stranger?"

"We gave away our children," she said in her victim's voice. "Why shouldn't we give away our dog?"

"That's a lovely analogy," I said, feeling myself getting very weary.

"Anyway, have a happy happy birthday."

"And many more," my father said, and then we hung up. I lay on my bed for a while and then roused myself and looked in the mirror and played around with the skin on my face, seeing what I'd look like with a face-lift. Then I fed Lila and went over to my desk and looked at the flower arrangement Freyda sent that morning. A note she'd dictated to the florist read, *Dear Frank E. Have A Happy One. Love Your Agent.* Then the phone rang again.

"Happy birthday." It was my favorite aunt, Iris.

"Hey, I hear you made an amazing *kugel.* I hear it was the talk of Century Village."

"Who told you?"

"I heard it on the news." She laughed. She was always good for a laugh.

"You spoke to your mother."

"I just got off the phone with them."

"Sheila and David came down and you know me, I like to enter-tain. I enjoy the company. Your mother tells me you sold a script."

"It's not exactly sold yet. There are just some people who were interested in it." What was wrong with my mother?

"I'll bet it's a comedy. You were always very funny as a little girl. You always made us laugh. Uncle Irv still remembers when he took you out on the boat and you couldn't have been more than six and you said to him, 'Damn the torpedoes, Uncle Irv. Full speed ahead.' He got such a kick out of that."

"I loved coming to see you and Uncle Irv," I said, and really meant it. Iris made me chicken coated with mayonnaise and cornflakes, which I thought was the best thing going, and Irv sometimes let me steer the boat. Staying at their summer house was a relaxing, carefree vacation, which I needed a lot more at forty than I did at six.

"We went to a *bris* today. You remember Uncle Irv's brother Jake?"

"I don't remember him."

"You were too young to remember. He lived in the house behind us at the lake. You were just a little girl when he died. It was at his daughter's house. They used to live on the Island near you but they sold their place for some good money and bought a house in Pompano Beach. She had sixty-two people to the *bris* but you didn't even know they were there, that's how big their place is. Her husband has drugstores with ten people in each store, so I think he does okay. His sister had breast cancer though. She was only forty years old, just your age when she was diagnosed. She was there with her two girls and with the chemo and everything else they did, they still don't know if she's out of the woods. She's a brilliant girl, too. It's just a shame. I hear your father's not that well. He may have to have some kind of an operation."

"For his back."

"I just hope they know what they're doing. We know someone who never recovered from a back operation. They were worse off after they had it than if they never had it in the first place. And this was supposed to be a good doctor. Let us know when your movie is coming out. What's the name of it?"

"*Closed for Renovations,*" I said as a joke.

"Okay. We're going to look for it. Uncle Irv sends his love. He had to go out to one of his men's club meetings but I didn't want to miss you on your birthday. We love you."

"I love you, too, Aunt Iris."

"I hope we get to see one another before it's too late."

I decided to let my answering machine pick up the rest of my birthday calls. There was only so much happiness I could take.

If I could have called off my party, I would. At six-thirty I was in the kitchen helping Miriam when the doorbell rang. It was too early for the guests to start arriving and we both expected it to be someone selling something. When I opened the door, I was surprised to see Jonathan Prince.

"Happy birthday," he said, handing me a bottle of Cordon Rouge. It wasn't wrapped, but it was cold and wet and just out of the supermarket refrigerator, which was good enough for me. "I thought you might need some cheering up."

"Why? Just because I'm forty? And alone? And unemployed?"

"I heard. Joel called Freyda and told her about Lance."

"It was nice of her to call me," I said, knowing I sounded petulant. It'd slipped out before I could control my tone of voice.

"Freyda left early to go to a screening. I'm sure she'll call you tomorrow. So I left early, too. I just had to get out of there. I was meeting some friends for dinner in Santa Monica and I thought I'd drop this off." Jonathan seemed a little down himself.

We went into the kitchen and he perked up a bit when he saw Miriam bent over her counter chopping rosemary and garlic. I asked Miriam if she wanted to join us in a glass of champagne.

"What are you making?" Jonathan asked. "It always smells so good in here."

"Look at this lamb," she said, her eyes melting with love as if it were a small baby. "It cost me a left lung but what a beautiful piece of meat." Miriam declined the offer of champagne but insisted we get the good glasses from the heavy dark breakfront in the dining room.

Jonathan and I sat next to each other on the white living room couch. Unlike the rest of the house, a cluttered mix of hand-me-downs and curbside finds, the living room was almost austere. Where every other room showed that five children had passed through on their way to adulthood, and hadn't bothered to wash their hands much while getting there, the living room had been turned into the front parlor, neat and clean and void of personality. Miriam, herself, had just finished painting those very same walls Pompeian red, a color she had seen at the Getty Museum and that "brought out the Hummels," and the room still smelled of fresh paint. Her prized collection had started with a wedding present of *Boy with Toothache* and had blossomed to thirty-three pieces her children and friends had given her for various birthdays and once when she broke her foot. Tacked down with florist's clay and devoutly dusted, they were arranged on the mantel, the coffee table, and in two shadow boxes hung on the walls. The Hummels were the only German product she allowed herself to own.

"This smells like my new apartment," Jonathan said. "It's owned by these two gay guys. They like me, so they keep coming over to do things. I'm probably the only tenant whose landlord polishes his mail slot."

"What do they expect in exchange?" I asked.

"Just their rent, I hope," he said as he took the champagne bottle and solemnly unwound the wire from around the cork. Jonathan pulled out his shirttail and wrapped it around the top of the bottle so the cork wouldn't go flying across the room. He opened it with a neat little pop and poured some into my glass, knowing just when to let the foam subside. I had a feeling this little ritual was forestalling something he wanted to tell me.

"I don't think I have it in me to be an agent," he finally said, handing me my glass. My heart sank. Jonathan was my only true advocate at the agency and now he'd be leaving Freyda, like all the others.

"Well, that probably says something for you as a human being. What happened?"

"Nothing. That's the problem. Agent trainee," he said derisively. "You know what that means? It means that I get to call a messenger when Gloria Bersoff needs a nursing bra. God bless her and the little tyke."

"I thought you worked strictly for Freyda."

"They had me floating for a while so I could find out how the agency worked. The thing is, I know how it works, I'm just tired of working there. I realized that, okay, what's the best thing I could be there? A partner? Big fucking deal. Or I'd open up my own agency? Is that the way I want to spend the rest of my life? I might as well kill myself now." The way he eagerly took his first sip of champagne, I knew his death wasn't imminent. He put the bottle down on the glass coffee table right between *Puppy Love* and *Little Fiddler*.

"What did you expect being an agent was going to be?"

"I don't know. I guess I wanted to work with writers. I thought it would be fun."

"That was your first mistake. Who do you know who's a 'fun' writer?"

"I think writers are the most interesting people in Hollywood."

"They're also, collectively, the most defensive people on the planet."

"You know what I mean. Let them try to make a movie without a script."

"What are you talking about? They do it all the time."

"Oh well," he said. "Why am I burdening you with my life on your birthday? Happy birthday."

We clinked glasses.

"So what does it feel like to be forty?" he asked me, straight-faced.

"It feels the same." The truth is, I didn't know how to feel. Forty is some kind of mossy stone marker along the path of life. By the time you're forty, if something significant is going to happen, it usually has. I wanted time to just slow down so I could catch up.

"I just meant, does it feel grown up?"

"First of all, I feel like I'm thirty-four and I've felt like that for the past six years. And as far as feeling grown up, no, I don't feel grown up. I don't know when you start to feel grown up."

"Well, I'm glad to know it's not just me."

"How old are you? Twenty-four? Give me a break."

"I'm twenty-five and I still don't know what I'm doing with my life."

"Gee, that must be tough."

"Why are you being sarcastic?"

"Jonathan, I don't know what I'm doing with my life."

"You're a writer," he said, and it sounded so definite.

"If this script doesn't sell, I'm a nothing."

"One person turns you down and you're a nothing?"

"You can't write in a vacuum. I need some kind of official acceptance, don't you see? Otherwise I'm just like every other idiot who thinks they have this really great idea, and if they only had the time, they'd turn it into a really great script. What they don't get is that ideas are like Kleenex. I have a million of them. Ideas aren't the hard part. It's the writing that's hard."

"What else would you do if you didn't write?"

"That's just it. I know there must be another way to live but I can't seem to kick the habit. Writing is the only way I can put my life into any kind of order. And the thing is, I really love movies. Every once in a while I'll see a movie like *Manhattan* or *All the President's Men* or *Chinatown* or *All About Eve* and I'll get transported and excited all over again and remember why I wanted to be a part of it in the first place. Movies are what made me want to tell stories. It's a compulsion with me. I'm like one of those addicted laboratory mice who keep pushing the drug lever. I keep writing because getting a movie made, actually telling my own story, is the high I'm waiting for. And I've invested so many years and endured so much anguish I can't just walk away. If I walk away, I want to walk away a winner. I'm stuck in the Vietnam Syndrome. Do you even remember Vietnam?"

"I saw *Platoon*. Does that count?"

I could feel the champagne starting to take effect or I wouldn't have used the word *anguish*. It's not a word you use with a person who doesn't write screenplays.

"Anyway," he said, "I haven't worked in the business for that long but one thing I've observed is that it can turn on a dime. One minute you're shit, the next minute you're gold. You have time," he said.

"Then so do you."

"Tell it to Ruthie and Harold. I'm already the black sheep of the family."

"What exactly do they mean by black sheep?"

"Oh, you know. I come from one of those Jewish overachieving families where my father is a doctor and my older sister is a doctor and I'm out here doing *bupkis*. Maybe I should have stayed at Harvard and gone to law school." Then he leaned back and yawned as if the whole subject bored him. "So what should I do with my life?"

"What are you passionate about? What are you good at?"

"I don't know. I guess I'm still looking. I'll find it. One of these days." Then he put down his empty glass. "Thanks for the talk," he said. "I guess I just wanted to be with someone older tonight. No offense."

I was glad he'd stopped by. I was feeling more philosophical about the evening. I'd unloaded on Jonathan and he'd said all the right things, except for the "someone older" part. But I think he thought I'd take it as a compliment. As I was saying good-bye, Miriam came out of the kitchen and said it was no problem to set an extra place. Jonathan had actually put me in an awkward spot. I hadn't told Freyda I was having a party because this wasn't Marty's crowd. There weren't enough important people coming and I didn't want to worry all evening that he was being underamused. But her feelings would be hurt if she found out she'd been excluded. Jonathan promised he wouldn't say anything to her, canceled his previous dinner engagement, and accepted Miriam's invitation. Once again, he made the perfect guest. He listened to Hershel go on about his play, talked with Daphne about her children and with William about composing film scores. He discussed restaurants and politics and movie stars with my TV-producer-friend Ilene, and tennis and compost heaps with her husband, Phil. And with Joyce and Richard, who were not in the business, he debated public schools versus private schools for their son Jordan. He even helped Miriam with the dishes.

Jonathan was the last one to leave that night, and when I walked him to the door he said, "This really cheered me up. The whole evening was great. Thanks." Then he took my face in his hands and kissed me. It was a light kiss on the lips, but he lingered just a little too long.

Miriam called out from the kitchen, as if she could see through walls. "What's going ON in there?" It was the same thing I was wondering myself.

"Nothing, Mom," Jonathan said innocently, breaking off the kiss. He walked out the door and turned back to me with that smile. "I can see why you like living here. If you ever want a roommate, give me a call."

EVERYONE'S A CRITIC

I WALKED INTO the offices of Little Red Wagon Productions expecting to be enveloped by Judi's pervasive hysteria, but the door to her office was closed. Sparky was behind his desk, hands on hips as he critically considered Mai Lei, who stood stiffly in front of him.

"Turn," he said to Mai Lei. "Turn, turn, turn." He made a little circle with his finger as Mai Lei did a self-conscious pirouette. "Now, don't you think she'd look better with a short haircut, a bob like what's-her-name, the silent-movie actress with the great haircut who turned her back on Hollywood and then went off to live in Rochester or some such place?" This was addressed to me. Without any pre-amble, I'd been recruited to be part of the fashion consultation.

"Louise Brooks."

"Right. Because I think it would frame her face better. And she has the kind of hair that could take a bob." He got up from behind his desk and walked toward Mai Lei. I could see Sparky was rushing to embrace the summer in his seersucker shorts, short-sleeved shirt, navy-blue bow tie, and white, white sneakers. In the five months since I'd last seen him, he'd put back the ten pounds he'd lost and then some. He was all moon-faced smiles, plump as a steamed dump-

ling stuffed with savories. He looked like some cheery, beaming con-
coction that would be floating above the Macy's Thanksgiving Day
Parade. A small plate of chocolate chip cookies sat on his desk. He
lifted Mai Lei's hair so we could see the effect.

"I'm gonna go shopping with you one day after work. You're
gonna be my personal summer project."

"Really?" she said in the shyest, meekest little voice. "Gee,
thanks."

Then Sparky picked up the phone and buzzed Judi to tell her I'd
arrived.

Judi was sitting behind a fruitwood desk looking into her Chanel
compact, putting on her Chanel lipstick. She was still dressed all in
black, only she'd switched fabrics from cashmere to linen. On her
head was a straw boater with black grosgrain trim.

"You've changed your hair and you've changed the decor," I said,
demonstrating my acute powers of observation. Judi's hair was now
a shoulder-length flip and her office an apartment in the sixteenth
arrondissement. A beautiful flowered 1930s Oriental area rug had
been laid over the gray industrial carpeting and an enormous armoire
with six mirrored doors took up almost an entire wall. It was filled
with scripts, VCR and TV equipment. The armchairs were olive
velvet and the two down sofas were covered in a cream damask.
Everything was subtle and overstuffed, the complete opposite of Judi.
Henri Faroli had done a remarkable job. Behind her desk was a
framed poster for their upcoming movie. Two old California plein
air paintings were hung above the sofa.

"Don't you love it? I worked very hard on this office but I'm very
happy with the results. It looks romantic, doesn't it? I wanted Vic-
toria's Secret without the underwear models. Sit on the sofa."

I sank right into the feathery softness. I could see Sparky had already punched down her tapestry pillows. "Comfy," I said. I didn't
know exactly what Judi had done to deserve an office like this. It
seemed highly disproportionate to her achievements.

"Did you get your invitation for the screening?"

"I just got it." Maybe their movie was great, and she was a producer, after all. God, I hoped so.

"You better RSVP quick because it's filling up."

Then her intercom buzzed. "What!" Her tone of voice had changed alarmingly. It was now pure exasperation. Some cloud had drifted in and I could feel a storm brewing in the air. "Sparky! Please!" she said. "I've got to keep track of a million little fucking things! I'm exuding minutiae from every pore! You take care of it! You're a bright person! You can handle it! I can't deal with this right now!" and she slammed down the phone. "I don't believe this," she said to no one in particular. "Where is Joel? He's supposed to be here." She shot up from her chair and opened her office door. I could see Sparky giving the Charles Chip lady his order for office snacks.

"All I wanted to TELL you," he said to Judi, "is that they've come out with fat-free-yogurt-covered raisins and did you want me to order any."

"What do I give a fuck what you order? I was up until three o'clock in the morning last night in the editing room trying to recut this goddamn thing! And I'll probably have to be there again tonight! Okay? Understand?"

"Chocolate or vanilla?"

"Jesus Christ! Nobody takes this thing seriously around here except me. My cock is in the ringer. It's only my fucking life and reputation that's on the line here, that's all." She was Camille with a nasty mouth. I looked to see how the Charles Chip lady was reacting to all of this but she was a stone. She'd probably seen it all before.

I remembered Joel had mentioned they were sneak-previewing the movie. The only thing I could presume was that it hadn't gone as well as anticipated and they were in a panic. "Previews?" I asked.

"Fucking Lance has the preview out in fucking Downey, wherever the fuck that is. It's four fucking freeways away, I couldn't find it if my life depended on it, with a preview audience of total fucking morons. I mean, I stood out in the lobby when they were turning in their comment cards and you never saw such poor white trash. And THESE are the people who are judging MY MOVIE?"

"There must be more than one focus group," but Joel entered the office looking a little piqued and she didn't answer.

"You want to call Lance and tell him we're all here?" Joel said to Sparky. Then he turned to me. "I should have listened to my mother and gone into business with my father, the housecoat king."

"How's it going?" I was hoping for a more sanguine response. If the preview cards had influenced the studio's attitude toward Judi and Joel, there was no reason for this meeting. We were going to fail for sure.

"It's going great, compared to Auschwitz."

Judi, Joel, and I trudged up the stairs to Lance Topping's office because Judi, who usually took the elevator, announced she'd been sitting too much in the editing room and needed the exercise. I kept hoping her endorphins would kick in but she complained the whole way. I have no idea why Judi didn't leave her boater hat, her purse, and her large black Filofax back in her office, but she lugged them all. She looked like she was going off to meet the girls for lunch at Bistro Gardens.

We ascended to the third floor and the atmosphere transformed. The upper floor was all business, isolated and removed, even in decor, from the nuts and bolts of moviemaking. The first two floors had movie posters and stills on the walls, it looked like a movie studio. The third floor had blue-chip institutional art . . . Jasper Johns and Ed Ruscha. The first two floors were writers running down to the basement for microwave popcorn, directors casting actors, and producers sweating deals. The third floor was hushed and corporate, as if the very carpet under our feet deadened creativity.

Scott Cantrowitz wasn't known around town for his subtlety, either in his personal relationships or in the movies he approved for the studio he ran. But the few times I'd met him, I knew that he didn't pretend to be anything other than what he was: a bullet train aiming right for your head. Lance Topping I couldn't pin down. When we walked into his office, he was leaning back in his chair with his argyle-stocking feet up on his desk. He appeared mid-thirties, dressed conservatively in a greenish-gray suit and horn-rim glasses. He had thick, reddish-blond hair and pale skin a little flushed in patches. The kind of skin that gets pink with drink or exercise. Or stress. Definitely the wrong skin type for his profession. "Hey, GUY," he boomed at Joel as he got up and padded toward us in his socks. "So how's it GOing?" Before Joel could answer, Lance turned to Judi. "GREAT HAT. Where'd you buy it? My wife loves hats, too. Well, come on IN, you GUYS." His voice was big, pointlessly emphatic. Like a politician speaking from the back of a flatbed truck, trying to enliven his meager audience without having to actually engage with any of them. Lance wasn't interested in this get-together. He was just doing his job, humoring Judi and Joel before he delivered the speech he knew they weren't going to like. When he turned to me I tried to appear relaxed and friendly, but when we shook hands, my ice-cold hand betrayed me. This was the man who didn't think my script was a movie and was about to tell me so.

Lance had come from publishing in New York and the story was that Cantrowitz had sat next to him on a plane, purely by chance. They had a five-hour conversation and he was installed as Cantrowitz's aide-de-camp the next week. He had no experience in movies, but Cantrowitz had personally trained him.

I'd been worried about Judi's overwrought mood, but the moment she crossed the threshold into his office she, too, was transformed. She became almost charming.

"Are these adorable children or what?" she said to me as she picked up a silver frame on Lance's desk and thrust it in front of my face. Her finger pointed to the blond wife, a Brooks-Brothers-blazer-Bally-loafers-single-strand-of-pearls-Junior-League type, and the two daughters, who looked to be about five and seven. "Whitney, Anabelle, and Miranda. This is like the perfect WASP family."

They looked familiar but I couldn't tell why. Joel grabbed the photo out of Judi's hand. "You probably met her at cotillion, right?"

"Close," Lance said. "Our families summered at Martha's Vineyard and I met her at the beach."

"Which beach?" Joel said. "Squibnocket? Lucy Vincent? Menemsha?"

"It was a private beach," Lance replied. "In Chilmark."

"Windy Gates?" Joel said, showing that he was up on his Vineyard geography.

"You know the Vineyard?"

"UH. Are you kidding? Beetlebung Corner? I LOVE the Vineyard."

I really hoped this wasn't going to be one of those "forget-the-Hamptons, they're-so-crowded, so-ruined" conversations, but Judi skipped strategically right over vacation spots and went for those children again.

"So when do you want to lend me your children for the weekend?"

"You don't know what you're getting into," Lance replied.

"Tanta Judi," Joel said to her, then turned to Lance. "Just make sure if you lend them to her for the weekend, you have a shrink appointment lined up for them early Monday morning."

"You think I'm that neurotic?" she asked him.

"Oy. Do I have to answer that?"

They were doing their *shtick* for Lance to ease into our meeting. Fortunately, before they started exchanging recipes for *matzoh* balls, his development people Bruce and Jona came in with their requisite yellow legal pads and we all moved over to a black leather sofa that wound around three walls. His secretary brought us drinks and we settled down to business.

"So," Lance said as if we hadn't already gone through enough pleasantries, "here we all are. How is everyone?" This must be what country clubs are like, I thought.

"I hear you had problems with my script," I said, just to get the meeting going. Judi shot me a look and Joel jumped right in.

"Don't forget, nothing's written in blood. We're here to discuss. But before we get started I have to say that I've never read another script like this. You always see men and their sexual adventures. You never see it from a woman's side and that's what I responded to when I read the script."

"The gay aspect worries me. Who are we going to get who wants to play gay? And then I guess we're supposed to presume that what's-his-name"—he opened the script and quickly glanced down—"Arthur died of AIDS at the end, although I think that part of it was handled very nicely. What major actor wants to die of AIDS? I think we're really limiting our pool of actors here. Not to mention that it's just been done in *Longtime Companion*."

"I haven't seen *Longtime Companion* yet, is it any good?" Judi asked him.

"I haven't seen it yet either but I know what it's about and it's about AIDS."

"Fuck the AIDS thing," Joel said. "I don't want to make an AIDS movie. *Longtime Companion* is low budget anyway. It's a very small movie which happens to be good but it's targeted to a small audience. And there aren't too many laughs in it, trust me. No one wants to sit through another movie about AIDS and gays. Least of all Frankie. Am I right?" he said, turning to me.

"That's not what the movie's about," I said. "It's about a relationship that stands the test of time. It's about the different stages in life that we've all gone through and it's about looking for love. It's about coming to terms with a big loss and finally growing up."

"Right," Joel said to Lance. "So if it bothers you he has AIDS, we can change it to a car accident. Or cancer. The point is, he dies and she loved him."

"We can't change it to cancer," I said. "That takes all the guts out of it."

"I mean, she wrote a comedy," Judi said as if I wasn't in the room. "Basically it's a dramatic comedy. And then if you can make them laugh and then pull the rug out from under them when the character you really like dies of AIDS and you don't have a big obvious death-bed scene, I think you've done something. I think you're talking Academy Awards. You know what I think?"

Lance interrupted. "I didn't like the denouement. There's something about the denouement that bothers me."

"Can you be more specific?" I asked him.

"They go back up to the country, they have to sell the house, it goes full circle. That part I like. But is she going to be happy? Are we leaving on an upbeat note or have we sat through two hours with a down character? Is there any kind of an arc here?"

"She leaves with her first love. He comes back into her life. She turns into Arthur at the end. She says exactly the same words that he said in the beginning. I think we presume that something profound has happened and he's passed his gift for life on to her in some way."

Lance sighed. He put his hands behind his head and leaned back into the sofa. I found myself looking at the soles of his socks, which were up on the coffee table. His toes were waving at me.

"Maybe the problem I have is with her character all the way through. Arthur is funny, although the gay aspect worries me, but you're going to want the audience to root for her. I just don't know if she's rootable, for lack of a better word. You have to want to follow her adventures. She has to be appealing. I don't know. I gave the script to my wife, Whitney, to read and she said, 'I just don't know people like this.'" And then I realized why his wife and children looked familiar. While I was growing older in the lobby of my agent's office, I'd seen them playing croquet in *Town & Country*.

"What Scotty's looking for isn't just a home run," Lance said, explaining why he was going to pass on my movie, "we're looking for out of the ballpark." On cue, Scott Cantrowitz walked into the dugout. No one was expecting him and I could see everyone in the room, including myself, shift into a higher gear. Scott threw himself into a chair, took a handful of pretzels from the table, and put his feet up. In spite of the pose, there was nothing relaxed about him. His foot never stopped moving and he drummed the arms of his chair with the fingers of both hands.

"So how's the picture coming?"

"It's great, Scotty," Joel said. "We've already taken out seven minutes."

"Those preview cards are a killer, aren't they? Those people show no mercy."

"Hey," Judi said, "they see things we don't. We're too close to it."

"Scotty, do you know Frankie Jordan?" Lance asked him.

"Hi, Scott, nice to see you again." I've learned to say "again" just in case they don't remember.

"How you doing? I hear you wrote an interesting script."

"We were just talking about it," Lance said.

"You want us to take a chance on it?" Cantrowitz said, turning to Judi and Joel. "We'll do it, only don't give me a downer. I hate downers."

"It's not going to be a downer. Do I ever give you downers?" Joel said.

"So make the deal," Cantrowitz said, and then he got up and walked out of the room.

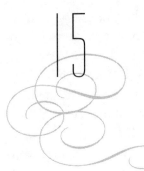

ZYDECO HEADACHE

AN ACQUAINTANCE OF mine went to a party where two comedians from *Saturday Night Live* were talking about how they were going to make a million dollars each for appearing in a thirty-second commercial during the Super Bowl. A sitcom actor with his own show was listening to all this and suddenly became very depressed. "I can't believe they're making a million dollars for ONE commercial," he said to my friend. "It takes me TEN WEEKS to make a million dollars." Which only goes to prove that if you want to feel successful in Hollywood, don't read the trades or talk to anyone else about THEIR deals. Because I had no idea what other people were making, I was happy. Freyda had gotten the studio to include my script in an overall deal. They'd agreed to employ me for two years with an option on the third. Jonathan was right. Things in Hollywood can turn on a dime.

During negotiations with the studio, Judi and Joel disappeared from my life again. All their energy was consumed in overseeing the ad campaign for their movie, which was opening in July. The screening was held at the Academy. I invited Miriam, who hardly ever passes up a free movie, because I wanted her to see Judi and Joel. Hershel hadn't left the house in weeks and had no interest in coming because he was busy revising his play. Since my script had sold, my relationship with Hershel wasn't quite as close as it used to be. His congratulations had been cursory. There was new sarcasm now whenever he talked about Hollywood, always a little put-down that I pretended not to notice. Hershel and I had both been standing at the door of the frat party peering in, only now someone had actually asked me to dance. *"I can't believe you'd want to GO to that party,"* was what my studious, less-popular roommate was saying to me. But it was the only party in town and we both knew it.

For Miriam, the evening started out on a high note. "Look at THIS," she said, jamming on her brakes in order to snag a premium parking space on Wilshire Boulevard right in front of the Academy. "And it's after seven so we don't even have to feed the meter!"

We crossed the street and headed for the black mirrored-glass structure where I could already see a former agent and a few other people I wanted to avoid. That was one of the reasons I didn't go to screenings. I preferred to pay for my entertainment and leave when the movie was over. Not when you've been personally invited. Judi and Joel were expecting me to stick around and tell them how much I loved their movie. They were expecting everyone invited to tell them how much they loved it. A true word is rarely spoken at an industry screening. But this time I wasn't too worried about having to lie. According to Judi, they'd gone in and done some drastic cutting, tightened it up, and lost twenty minutes. Word of mouth had it Joel had turned out a dark, stylish mystery.

Judi warned me to get there early because they were overbooked, and indeed, a large crowd was already swarming around the lobby. I stepped up to a blond handling *A* through *M* and gave her my last name. She ran one perfectly French-manicured nail down the master list and then looked up at me and said, "Hart?"

"No, that's my husband. I'm listed separately. Frankie." Miriam gave me a look that said, *What's Hart doing here?* I craned my neck to try to find myself on the list. Although he hadn't been checked off yet, I saw Hart had himself down for two.

"He bringing someone?" Miriam asked. I shrugged. It was just a matter of time before we found ourselves at the same function with other people, except my other person was Miriam.

"I don't see you," the blond girl said, looking at me suspiciously.

Miriam took charge. "Here. Let me see that list." She grabbed the list before the girl could stop her. It's the teacher's aide in her. She's used to dealing with six-year-olds who won't stay in their seats and she has perfected what Hershel calls her "look," which you don't cross if you know what's good for you.

"Oh, ma God, we're really fillin' up," Sparky said. "You better go in and find yourself a good seat." He had appeared behind Miriam, tactfully taken the list from her hand, and returned it to the blond girl. Then he turned back to Miriam. "I love your beads. Where did you FIND them?" Miriam was wearing a V-neck turquoise cotton gauze dress that she'd picked up in her thrift shop for two dollars and fifty cents, and she'd talked them down to two dollars because the seam was loose in a few places. Her turquoise, crystal, and silver-coin necklace lay on her tan skin right between her cleavage. It was one of the few things Miriam bought for herself which hadn't been previously owned and she was proud of those beads.

"Aren't these beads great?" she said to Sparky, looking down at her own chest in admiration. "A woman at the synagogue makes them out of doodads and bibelots she finds around. Each one is unique."

He picked up her necklace and fingered it between his soft, delicate fingers. "I just LOVE the design."

"She's very talented. Her husband was a school principal who had a heart attack and died two days before retirement."

"You're kidding?" Sparky said. I didn't know where this was leading but it didn't seem to bother Sparky.

"Two days away from full retirement and the bastards didn't want to give his benefits to his widow. She had to hire a lawyer and sue them. Do you believe it?"

"That is so rotten," Sparky said. "After all the good years he put in."

"She was so depressed she lost a hundred pounds. She just wouldn't eat. We were all really worried about her. Out of the clear blue he drops dead. But she always liked beads and she just took this up as a hobby and now she sells them for a nice price. Every time she travels she picks up more things and she's got herself a nice little business going. And she looks terrific and found a new boyfriend she said she can really open up to."

"I think maybe we should find our seats," I said, wanting to cut this biography short.

"I'll see you after," Sparky said to us.

"Oh, I like him," Miriam said as we were climbing the stairs to the theater. "Who is he?" Since every conversation with Sparky begins in the middle, introductions had seemed superfluous. I filled her in.

"Why are fags so much fun?" she said. "Regular men are such pills. I mean, Hershel is always working. He won't go anywhere. I can never get him to do anything. Find me a nice fag friend."

Most of the center aisle seats were taken, if not by actual people then by jackets and purses. Miriam and I sat off to the side and scanned the rows looking for familiar faces. Looking for Hart and his date.

I spotted Ian Mandel in the cordoned-off section, standing in the aisle, talking to a man I didn't recognize. Ian was trying his mightiest to look unfazed and laid-back. The sleeves of his white linen jacket were pushed up to his elbow and his vintage Hawaiian shirt could have come right out of Freyda's office. But Ian was too wound up to be cool. This was his movie we were about to see and he was flying high, his face a little sweaty from the excitement. He kept bobbing his head in rapid agreement with whatever his conversational partner was saying. Portia was the relaxed one. Her slim white arm was draped across the back of the empty seat next to her. Even from across the room, I could spot her breast peeking out from the armhole of her suede vest. On the other side of her sat two people who could only have been Ian's parents. His mother was turned around in her seat watching who came in. Every once in a while she would nudge her husband, lean in and put her hand over her mouth, and then he would turn and look, too.

I knew without introduction, when I saw Eleanor, that she was Judi's mother. The familial resemblance was irrefutable, even though there was nothing remotely maternal about her. Eleanor had the same pale, tight skin as her daughter, the same flattering shade of Chanel lipstick, and the same nose. Only now that Eleanor was growing older, her nose had become too small for her face and she was starting to resemble a very stylish mummy. She was exercised to a size four and her hair was colored a lighter shade than Judi's, but the bangs were identical. Both were dressed in black pants and black sweaters. Eleanor had a black Gucci backpack. Judi had her big black Chanel purse. Judi had her necklaces, Eleanor had her stack of bracelets, and I'm sure they made the same clinking sound as they walked across the room. They were the Jewish Judds.

I expected a more formidable person, after hearing Judi describe her husband, Alan, but men with red hair and freckles never appear too awe-inspiring. He was standing stooped in the aisle talking with the female lead of his wife's movie, a girlish woman who looked as good in person as she did on-screen. One arm was hugging his chest and his other hand was pulling at his beard. He looked like he was wincing in pain. Either he had terrible gastritis or else he realized that at the end of the evening, he would have to say good-bye to that vision of beauty he was talking to, get in the car, and drive home with Judi.

Just before the lights dimmed, I saw Jonathan slip in with Shelley, Nicole Kahn's secretary, presumably using their bosses' invites. Even though these screening passes are marked "absolutely nontransferable," nobody pays attention and they're traded like baseball cards. The house was pretty full and I wondered if they were going to be able to sit together, but then a hand went up and someone who'd been saving them seats waved them over. I was beginning to see Jonathan left nothing to chance.

Joel stepped out in front of the crimson curtain covering the screen. The black, red, and gray color of his wardrobe had been taken, I don't think coincidentally, right from the theater's Art Deco palette, and he looked like some tasteful accessory that had been plunked down center stage. On either side of the stage stand two colossal Oscars who, like golden pagan gods, preside over the worshipful. They made Joel look rather small and insignificant as he stood for a moment and surveyed his audience. "God, I can't believe we're finally HERE," he said in mock exhaustion, and there were claps and whistles in appreciation. "Anyway, there's not one person out there that didn't give it their all. I don't know about blood but there was definitely sweat and tears with an emphasis on the sweat. And those of you who've been to Louisiana in August know what I mean." More laughter and hoots. "There are so many people I want to thank for helping me lose my virginity. But you all know who you are, so what can I say? Enjoy the movie. It was a labor of love and a collaboration between many, many people. And finally, Judi wants me to thank you all for coming and to tell you she finally found her contact lens." There was more laughter. Miriam looked at me and rolled her eyes. "In-jokes," she said.

When the credits began, everybody clapped and whistled as the names came up on the screen. My eyes kept returning to Ian, who clapped enthusiastically except when his own name came on, and then he modestly refrained, turning to watch Portia.

It always amazes me how many scripts there are floating around Hollywood and how few are good and then how few of these scripts actually ever get made. You'd think the cream would rise to the top. You'd think with all the people who want to get into movies the talent would finally win out. I sat in my seat watching the movie unfold, and tried to figure out why Joel had wanted to make this particular script. The studio, of course, must have thought it would make money because that's their only criterion. But I had no idea what spoke to Joel and Judi, unless they just didn't know the difference between good and bad, which made me extremely anxious. For my taste, it wasn't enough of a mystery or love story to sustain anyone's interest, and I think the people of Downey were probably being too kind when they returned their preview cards. The characters were all stock types you'd pull out of your character closet and hang in the script. The score was loud and intrusive, trying, I guess, to make up for the lack of real drama. And then there was the requisite love ballad thrown in that would be released as a single. Even the sex was ho-hum. All it had was a manufactured Southern ambience smothered on like heavy barbecue sauce—probably because Joel came from Great Neck and it wasn't exactly as if he was going home again. The only mystery about the movie was why it ever got made.

Miriam, who's not much on subtlety, sighed audibly a few times and a few times she said, "Come ON." I didn't acknowledge her. I kept hoping it would get better but it never did. Everyone stayed seated until the Dolby Stereo credit and copyright infringement warning rolled by and then the lights came on and Miriam said "Stiiink-o," just a little too loud.

The hard part was yet to come. I hadn't a clue what to say to Judi and Joel. I'm a terrible liar and I hoped I wouldn't have to say anything. There'd be so many people at the party maybe they wouldn't even know if I was there. I just wanted to sneak out but Miriam said she was starving and needed to eat. People in the aisles were already gathering around Judi and Joel, congratulating them. As Miriam and I got caught in the bottleneck, I saw a pudgy man wearing a red wide-striped shirt and a blue polka-dot bow tie with an oatmeal cotton sweater thrown around his shoulders. His salt-and-pepper hair was combed forward over his brow in the style of Julius Caesar or a five-year-old boy and his contact lenses were turquoise blue, a color so extraordinary that it's usually only seen on tropical butterfly wings or advertisements of Caribbean beach resorts. The vintage brown-and-white saddle shoes on his feet didn't go with the big-boy mustache or the diamond-stud earring, but it was the glistening spittle in the puppet lines of his mouth that was most disconcerting. He looked like he'd been thrown together for maximum laughs from a Mr. Potato Head kit. "Brava, Lady Judith. Brava," he said, clapping one hand into the other palm and I knew from the voice that it had to be Henri Faroli. When she turned around, there was such a barrage of effusive greetings between them that I couldn't tell whether Judi felt more important by showing off Henri as her decorator, or Henri felt more important by showing off Judi as his client. In any event, his being there made them both look good, which was really the whole point.

"I need a drink," I said to Miriam. I didn't want to talk to anyone until I'd had an iced Stolichnaya to wipe out the metallic fear I felt in my mouth.

I made a beeline over to a bar that had been set up in the lobby. I tried to hide in the crowd, keeping an eye out for Joel and Judi as I also scanned the faces for Hart and his date. The only person I wanted to talk to was Jonathan Prince. I needed his acid take on the movie.

But the first person I encountered was Gail Sylver, whom I'd worked with years earlier when she was an executive at Lorimar. She was standing with her business partner, Nancy Bliss, a former executive at ABC. They were both very diplomatic and knew exactly what to say in awkward situations. They'd be excellent buffers in case Judi and Joel appeared. Gail's the kind of fortyish woman that other woman always puzzle over, as to why she's never been married. If I wanted to venture a guess I'd say it was because she enjoyed staying home on Friday nights straightening out her closet, spacing the matching hangers until they were all perfectly equidistant. Or because she was an exfoliating fool, with masks, grains, scrubs, and a special lip treatment that necessitated using an old toothbrush and Vaseline. It could have been a hygienic reason, because she'd put white wall-to-wall carpet in her bathroom and would probably have a heart attack if any man used the toilet standing up. Nonetheless, she's a real woman's woman who got fixed up by her girlfriends more than anyone I've ever met and somehow had that knack of keeping almost every man she'd ever dated as her friend, probably because she was smart enough not to sleep with them. Gail was at the screening because Nancy's husband was the studio publicist. Being a professional best friend, Gail was invited along. I introduced them to Miriam and then Gail said to me, "So? You look exactly the same. What are you working on?"

I had to confess that Judi and Joel were now my producers.

"What did you think of the movie?" she said with a glance over her shoulder, keeping her voice low and neutral. She wasn't going to reveal her opinion until she was sure we were on the same side, which is probably one of the reasons she was a successful executive.

"It felt like it was written by committee," I said.

"They just shoehorned in that relationship," Gail admitted. "I mean, I didn't feel any chemistry between them at all, did you?"

"No way," Miriam said.

"They probably got them cheap," Gail said. "You know Cantrowitz. Get 'em while they're down. Get 'em while they're cheap."

"I can just hear the note meeting. 'Give us sexual tension. The characters need to have sexual tension.' Am I right?" Nancy said, turning to Gail.

"And what was with all the *shvitzing*?" Gail said. "I mean, everybody in the movie looked like they had baby oil sprayed all over them. I know it's the South and it's hot but . . . ."

"It's supposed to show passion when they're screwing," Miriam elucidated for all of us.

"It's like, no one in that whole town has ever heard of airconditioning?"

"Whoever wrote it sure doesn't know how to write women," Miriam added, shaking her head in disgust.

"Well, you know Ian Mandel was fired off of it and it was totally rewritten by Heller and Weiss," Gail said.

"You're kidding? I know Ian and he never mentioned that he'd been taken off the movie." But why hadn't Freyda told me?

"He obviously hoped it was going to be a better movie than it was," Gail said. "There was a big fight about the credits. Judi and Joel told Heller and Weiss they'd get credit. It went into arbitration and Ian finally got sole screenplay credit but there was a lot of bad feeling. I actually saw them here. I was surprised. They were sitting way in the back."

We all started looking around for Heller and Weiss, although I don't know why, because only Gail knew what they looked like. But I swear, I spotted them right off, skulking in the corner. They were both slightly built, wearing wire-rim glasses. At first glance it was hard to tell them apart. It's not that they were physically so much alike; one of them was dark and taller than the other, who was blond. But the two of them affected an air of young, modest, gifted screenwriters. They appeared rather self-conscious as they stood together in their black leather jackets and jeans, casing the crowd for whom they hated most. I pointed them out.

"Look at those *pishers,* no wonder they don't know how to write women," Miriam said, sounding too much like Hershel. "The only women they know are from other movies. If I were them I'd take the money and run."

"I can't believe Judi and Joel promised them a credit," I said to Gail.

"I'm sure what they meant was that the studio would recom-MEND them for credit and Heller and Weiss took them literally."

"My husband's in the business," Miriam said. "He always says that one of the most degrading aspects of writing is fighting over a piece of shit."

"But when the piece of shit goes to CAble and you start getting those reSIDuals . . ." Gail said in a singsong voice. "The next residual check, I'm getting liposuction and I'm upgrading my computer. In that order." Then she turned to me. "How did you get away with it? No hips, no thighs. You don't have any of the Jewish genes. It's bad enough I have to work with Nancy, who's five-nine without an ounce of fat. But YOU I expect more from."

"Oh, please," Nancy said. "There's fat. Believe me. I just wish they could take it from HERE," she said, pointing to her nonexistent rear, "and put it HERE." She pointed to her fine hollow cheeks.

"There's a woman doctor I just read about in *Allure,* at the hair-dresser's of course, where else do you read *Allure,* and she's supposed to be THE ONE for fat injections. You know what her secret is? She kneads the fat. You're supposed to knead it once you inject it under the skin and what do men know about kneading? Unfortu-nately she's in New York or she'd be kneading me right now."

"I saw a woman in temple on Rosh Hashanah," Miriam said, "and from behind she had the most perfect little figure. In a knit suit yet, and I'm thinking to myself, who could this possibly be? Everyone around her has these big broad beams and she has this tiny little tush, and when she turns around, I see it's Beth Jacobs. A CONVERT!"

"Of course! What then?" Gail said.

"So I said to her, you may be Jewish but you don't have any of the Jewish genes."

"Oh . . . is that funny," Nancy, the token *shiksa,* said.

"I was fine up until about two years ago," Gail said, refolding the sleeves back on her blouse that she had just folded perfectly a minute before. "I was a size six. And then I'm driving to work in my car and 'Moon River' comes on the radio and I burst into tears. I came into the office and I said to Nancy, you wouldn't believe what just hap-pened. 'Moon River' came on the radio and I burst into tears. I'm in menopause."

"That's too funny. 'Moon River' comes on and she's in meno-pause," Nancy said, with her charming habit of echolalia that made her seem so agreeable.

"And it wasn't even Audrey HEPBURN singing, it was Andy WILLIAMS!"

"Andy Williams, is that funny."

I spotted Hart across the room. Actually, I heard his laugh first and whip-panned to catch him standing at the bar. My heart was pound-ing. The first thing I thought was, I hope I look good. A group of people were standing around him and he was holding court. I saw a tall woman with long red hair standing next to him. I couldn't tell whether she was his disciple or his date, but when he handed her a glass of wine and I saw the way her hand touched his, I knew. What was the protocol? Was I supposed to go up boldly and introduce myself? Or wave to him coolly from across the room? He caught my eye and I lost all bearings. I waved to him and smiled and he lifted his martini with an olive AND a twist and saluted me with his glass in return. The redhead turned to check me out. I quickly averted my look to Gail and Nancy, but they were already conversing with someone new. And Miriam was standing on a buffet line telling the catering staff exactly how much popcorn shrimp, jambalaya, Creole okra, and corn bread she wanted. If I hadn't had something happen-ing in my life, it would have been intolerable seeing Hart with some-one else. He was still the most interesting man I knew, and the smartest. And it was painful to know I'd spent so many years with this person and that I was so quickly replaceable. But in some very small way, it was also a relief. Hart and I had reached that stage in a marriage where he saved his considerable charm for other people. It didn't matter how many times I'd heard the same stories. He always played for a larger audience.

"You in line?" It was Ian's father standing behind me, in a powder-blue short-sleeved shirt and matching pants. He was much smaller than Ian and he had a white mustache and blue eyes. His bald head was filled with large freckles. He looked like about six million Jews from Florida.

"No. Go ahead of me."

"I'll get behind you, what's the big deal? I'll get you a plate. Here."

He handed me a plate and I was standing in line whether I wanted to or not.

"My son wrote this movie you just saw."

"Congratulations. You must be very proud."

"We just flew in from New York to see this. We just arrived today. You know what time it is for me right now?" He looked at his watch. "It's one-fifteen in the morning. I keep my watch on New York time." He showed me in case I didn't believe him. "My wife, she went to the ladies' room, she wouldn't have missed this for anything. So what do you do? You in the business, too?" I knew he was going to ask me that.

"I'm a writer. So where in New York are you from?" I guided the conversation away from my profession, because the next question from him was going to be, "What have you written that I've heard of?" I hate going through this with strangers. If they say they liked what you've written and you hated it, what can you say? If you detect that they didn't like what you've written and you happen to agree with them, what can you say? And if they've never heard of it, there's nothing to say. It's very embarrassing not to have anything out there that you really feel proud of.

"You know New York?" he asked me. "You know Queens Boulevard?"

"The Turnpike Deli."

"You Jewish?" I could see him relax. He was among his own. We had pastrami and pogroms in common. "I run a wedding-dress shop right on Queens Boulevard. Magic Moments it's called. Wedding dresses, bridesmaids, flower girls. Whatever. We'll custom-order."

"So how's business these days? You must have just gotten done with the June weddings." The redhead whispered something in Hart's ear. He threw back his head and laughed. Could she be THAT funny?

"Business is good. People are getting married in white again. In the sixties, with all the hippies, only the Puerto Ricans were getting married in style. I had a slump. I almost went bankrupt. Now big weddings are back. My wife says to me, reTIRE already. What do you need the aggravation?" I began to imagine Hart married to the redhead. She was young enough, of course she'd want children. How would I cope if he had a baby with her? "There she is. Estelle," Ian's father called out. His wife was standing in the middle of the room looking lost. "Estelle."

"Where did you GO?" she said as she joined us on line. "I said I'd be right out."

"I TOLD you I'd be standing in the food line."

"I was looking EVERYwhere for you. You couldn't wait for me?"

"You didn't LISTEN to me. I SAID—I'll MEET you by the FOOD."

As Ian's parents argued on, I spotted Judi and Joel coming down the stairs making their grand entrance. Ian Mandel, his parents forgotten, was sticking close to the power, hoping, I suppose, to lap up any spillover attention. Judi was carrying her Filofax, Sparky was at her heels, and Henri Faroli was pulling up the rear of the court procession.

"Hart's here." Miriam appeared at my side holding her plate and pointing her chin in Hart's direction.

"I saw." I grabbed some food and we moved out of the line into a more private corner.

"Who's the redhead?"

"I have no idea."

"Is he *shtupping* her?"

"You want me to find out for you?"

"I just thought maybe you knew. Maybe he told you. He looks good. He's got that nice carriage. Hershel is all bent over from writing in that terrible chair. It's really a kitchen chair is all it is. He really should get something with lumbar support. You want me to go over and say hi to him? Check her out?"

"If you want."

"My friend FRANKIE is cuter than THAT old redhead ANY day." It was said in the most loving way but I wondered if Miriam had any idea how far her voice carried. Everything she said was belted out like Ethel Merman doing "Everything's Coming Up Roses" from the stage of the Broadway Theater for the benefit of the back row.

"Thanks, Miriam."

"AnyTIME, my darling angel. The food's not bad. It's a little greasy."

Then I saw Jonathan and Shelley making their way through the crowd toward us. The first thing Jonathan did was hug Miriam. "I'm still telling people about that lamb you made."

"Oh, that lamb!" she said, almost swooning.

"Why didn't anyone bother to tell me that Ian had been fired off of the movie?" I said before I could edit myself. It shot out like an accusation. Jonathan and Shelley looked at each other.

"I didn't know he was," Jonathan said.

"If you have to be fired off of a movie, this would be a great one to be fired off of," Shelley said.

I was starting to get a headache and wanted to leave. I didn't want to see Hart with his girlfriend or Judi and Joel or my ex-agent or Ian Mandel and Portia. I looked around for Miriam, who had slipped off again. She was at the dessert table, talking with a writer friend of Hershel's about Hershel's play, which Charles Durning's agent didn't want to let him do because it paid nothing. By the snippets of her conversation, I knew she was recounting the play's whole history, which I'd heard too many times. As she conversed with him, she was taking chocolate truffles, wrapping them in a napkin, and secreting them into her secondhand Le Sportsac shoulder bag.

Jonathan seemed to read my mind. "Shelley and I are getting out of here. We're going to grab a bite to eat. You want to join us?"

"Yes. We don't feel like sticking around congratulating someone on their bad movie," Shelley said, as only a twenty-five-year-old would say, and I cringed knowing Ian's parents were standing in the vicinity. But the zydeco band had struck up a number and even Miriam was drowned out by the accordion and washboard.

"I don't have my own car. I came with Miriam."

"She can come if she wants," Jonathan said.

"She won't want to. It's getting past her bedtime."

"Then I can drive you home."

"It's a little out of your way, isn't it?"

He was very close and I could feel his breath on my neck as he whispered, "For you? Never."

PEYCHAUD'S BITTERS

SHELLEY TRIED TO follow us in her own car, but Jonathan drove much too fast and left her behind when he sped through a yellow light. When I pointed out he'd lost Shelley, he glanced in his rearview mirror but didn't slow down.

"She knows where we're going."

"Where ARE we going?"

He named a restaurant in Beverly Hills that was rather pricey, especially on a secretary's paycheck.

"I hear it has a great bar," Jonathan said. "I thought we should check it out. There's nothing like a good, solid drink to cheer you up after a lousy movie. Freyda was smart to have bailed out of THAT screening. Poor Frankie." He reached over and began to lightly massage the back of my neck. As soon as he touched me I felt delicious chills pass through my body and I could hardly keep my eyes open. My head began to loll forward like a drunkard. "After waiting for Judi and Joel all those months, it turns out they haven't got a clue. Maybe it'll do okay at the box office, though. The one thing you have going for you is that the studio's not going to alienate Judi Golden. Her father's too rich and knows too many people. Just don't let Joel direct *Ivy and Men*. I'm begging you," he said, putting his hand back on the steering wheel.

As I opened my eyes I looked out my side window and saw Shelley had caught up and was looking at Jonathan and me. I felt a little foolish, as if she'd caught us at something. It occurred to me that maybe I was intruding on their evening together. But Jonathan was the one person who understood the situation and I wanted to be with him, even if it meant being the unwelcome chaperon.

The restaurant was curiously situated in the bottom of an office building, in a mostly quiet residential neighborhood of older apartment houses. During the day it was a bustling, clubby place, frequented by agents, lawyers, and stockbrokers, and when we walked in that night, it appeared some of them never left. Jonathan quickly assessed the room and requested a table with a good vantage point that was just opening up.

While we waited for our table, Jonathan, Shelley, and I headed for the bar, a black marble expanse with halogen spots beamed down from the ceiling. A couple of women at the bar were looking at their glittering diamond rings in the hot light and I noticed that my own diamond wedding ring looked especially bright. I'd kept wearing it even after the separation. I felt safe from male attention as long as I had it on. But after seeing Hart with someone else, I faced the fact that no one was making any moves on me anyway, and that it might as well go in the false bottom of a Campbell's tomato-soup can where Miriam hid her emergency earthquake money. The bar was almost full, but Jonathan asked someone if he would move over a seat, and Shelley and I sat together next to a spectacular flower arrangement with spiky, fragrant white tuberoses and red torch ginger. It was the kind of overblown bouquet you'd see in the lobby of an expensive hotel. Suddenly I was in an unfamiliar city and then I realized how long it'd been since I'd been out to a nice restaurant. Of course it felt strange.

"What can I get you folks?" the bartender said as he wiped some water from the shiny black marble.

"Do you have Peychaud's bitters?" Jonathan asked him.

"We have Angostura."

"They're totally different. It's not a substitute."

"I've never even HEARD of it, quite frankly. Peychaud's," he repeated, feigning interest. "How do you spell that?"

Jonathan wrote it out for him on a cocktail napkin. "You can order it from New Orleans, where it's made. This is a good bar. I'm surprised you don't have it on hand."

"What kind of a drink do you make with it?"

"Some people use it in Rob Roys but I was hoping to have a Sazerac this evening."

Shelley turned around in her seat and looked back at him. "Why don't you order something a little esoteric?"

"That's a new one on me," the bartender said. "This is a real drink?" And without invitation, Jonathan proceeded to tell him how it was made.

"Two teaspoons Pernod, one cube sugar, three dashes Peychaud's, one teaspoon water, and two and a half ounces of bourbon. First concocted by Leon Lamothe, a bartender in New Orleans in the mid-nineteenth century."

Shelley and I regarded each other like two indulgent parents dealing with their precocious, slightly obnoxious child, and the bartender looked at the cocktail napkin again. "Peychaud's. Hmm. And what's the name of that drink again?"

As Jonathan was on the verge of giving him another napkin with Sazerac spelled out, we were called to our table. Once seated, he decided to have an easy gin and tonic. Our waitress was annoyed before she even took the drink orders. Something had probably happened before we'd gotten there, but we weren't privy to the event, just the effect it had on her. It was a snooty demeanor that let us know she really didn't belong in this position, that she was slumming. Shelley took an instant dislike to her. "I love the attitude . . . 'What do you think I am, your waitress? You want a drink? Get it yourself.' Someone should tell her she's not beautiful enough to behave as badly as she does."

"Oh, but she is," Jonathan said. It was obvious Jonathan was attracted to her. He had actually tried to charm her but she was adamant about remaining in a bad mood.

"Do you think she's beautiful?" Shelley turned to me, wanting another woman's opinion.

"Yes, but she looks like big trouble."

"As far as I'm concerned," Shelley said with good humor, "all she is, is another willowy-pig-faced-actress type. I can't tell her from any of the other girls who Rollerblade at the beach on Saturday. There are so many of those girls in L.A., it's positively disgusting. You know who I think was REALLY beautiful. Ava Gardner. Or Nastassja Kinski. I mean, they're at least DIFFerent looking."

"She has great lips," Jonathan said. "They're very full. I love girls with full lips . . . and dark eyebrows. I love expressive eyebrows."

"God, you sound like a Maybelline commercial," Shelley said, but finally conceded. "Okay. So she's beautiful. So big fucking deal. She thinks it sucks being a waitress? She should work for Nicole Kahn." She slapped her hand over her mouth and looked around as if someone might have overheard her. "Oops. I forget. N.K. The walls have ears."

Our provocative waitress returned without our drinks and dropped a menu and wine list in front of us before she spun and exited stage left. Jonathan was right. She did have great lips. Shelley picked up the wine list, leafed through it, and called after her. " 'Can we have coverage on this?' "

" 'Darling,' " Jonathan added.

" 'And can we have some bread, darling. Oh God. Stop me before I eat again.' " Then she turned to me. "We love Nicole. I probably shouldn't be telling you this."

"I already told her," Jonathan said. "She's one of us."

"Oh, good. Then you know Nicole's a laugh a minute. 'She wrote a FABulous spec *Roseanne*. She wrote a FABulous *Full House*.' But here's the best one. She's on the phone talking with her girlfriend about someone who's just had a baby and she says, I swear to God, she says, 'She was seven METERS dilated.' You know, like, a grown man could walk out of her."

"How about Paul Fisher?" Jonathan said. "That is one stupid Jew. I'm surprised they even allow him into *shul* on the High Holy Days."

"Oh please," Shelley said. "The problem with all these Jewish guys is that they really want to be their wives—tall and blond."

"How about Freyda?" I asked, curious what her take was.

"Freyda's nice," Shelley said. "I mean, for an agent. You know, we adjust our human being criteria a little bit here for agents. I think Freyda's nice, don't you?" She turned to Jonathan.

Jonathan took a piece of bread and slowly buttered it. "Nice?" he said. "Nice, let me see. Would that be how I'd describe Freyda. More like tragically insecure. More like one who suffers from chronic peripateticism. More like a globe-girdling touristic bore. More like a transmigratory jaywalker. Freyda consumes events like a glutton but nothing sticks to her ribs. It's all excreted out like yesterday's undigested food."

"Jonathan," Shelley said in a voice heavy with appreciation.

Jonathan shrugged off her compliment. "Where's that fucking waitress with our drinks?"

There was something very appealing about Shelley. She wasn't very tall and she was just a little overweight, but she had very smart blue-gray eyes, and the kind of imperfect features that made her much more interesting looking than the women she probably compared herself to. I'm sure she had no idea how attractive she was. Women like Shelley know they can't get men like Jonathan with just their looks, which is why they're so pleasing to be around. She was an L.A. geisha girl, catering to Jonathan, trying to entertain him with her barbed observations. She was reassuring him that they were both in the same predicament, that their bullshit detectors were calibrated in sync. When Jonathan excused himself and got up, Shelley followed him with her eyes. I couldn't tell if they were sleeping together. I hoped that they were, for Jonathan's sake.

"Did you meet Jonathan at the agency?" I asked.

"I met him in Boston in a bookstore actually. I went to B.U., and then after graduation I moved out here and he wanted to get into the business but didn't know where to start, so I found him his job. Now I think he holds it against me."

"So what's he going to do next?"

"You know Jonathan. Mr. Social. He'll make out okay whatever he does. He has that kind of personality. In college we all gave each other Indian names? And his was Keeps In Touch. He'd go home for Easter vacation and you'd get a postcard from him two days later. I met him once for dinner in New York with his parents. If you think Jonathan's a social lubricant you should meet his mother. His parents are very small, like two little matching salt-and-pepper shakers and his mother never stops talking. 'Eat this, try that, go here, go there' and his father's a big music lover and can tell you all about Verdi's life IN DETAIL. I mean, they were perfectly nice but it's like you need a long nap after spending an hour with them. They're very intense. I could tell they were disappointed I didn't go to Harvard. It probably just kills them that Jonathan never got his diploma."

"What do you mean?"

"He stopped going to classes his senior year. It's like he lost interest."

"You're kidding? He never graduated?"

"Not officially. I mean, Jonathan's obviously bright, and if you say you went to Harvard, people just presume you graduated, right? So it's like, why bother actually doing it? Typical Jonathan," she said, as if it made him more interesting. And in a way, it did.

Jonathan came back to the table looking triumphant. A chastened waiter with a bottle of champagne was following him. Our beautiful waitress had been banished.

"Sorry for the delay," the waiter said to us as he put out the glasses. "Orman would like you to enjoy some champagne while you look over the menu." He showed Jonathan the label.

"That's very nice of him," Jonathan said graciously. "But you know, before you open that, the last time I was here I had the Veuve Clicquot."

"Would you prefer that?"

"Yes, and while you're at it, we could use some assorted appetizers. We've been kept waiting for so long, we're all famished."

"What's all this about?" I said after the waiter had gone off to do Jonathan's bidding.

"You're getting to see a real Jew in action."

"We thought you were just going to the bathroom," Shelley said. "We had no idea you were going off to pray."

But before Jonathan could explain, we saw a man heading toward our table, his face a mask of concern and solicitousness, aimed right at Jonathan.

"Is everything being take care of? Is Randy getting you your champagne?"

"Yes, thank you, Orman."

"And again, I apologize."

"You know, normally," Jonathan said, "I would have just let it go because I know the service in this place is usually impeccable. But as I explained, I just came from a screening at the Academy with two of my colleagues and we left a perfectly wonderful party there because we needed a good quiet place in which to discuss some business matters. Since I recommended this place very highly, I feel a certain responsibility to my guests . . ." I knew he was doing this for our benefit and it embarrassed me.

"Of course."

". . . and I just wanted to let you know that the unfortunate woman who passes as a waitress isn't representing your restaurant the way it deserves to be represented."

"I'm glad you said something to me."

"We've done nothing to provoke her. She's obviously having a PMS day and we're the unfortunate recipients of this hormonal disaster."

"You know, as much as you try to get good help," he said, confiding in us all, "sometimes someone just slips through who isn't . . ."

"I understand," Jonathan said. "And as I said, I love this place and I was just a little surprised. And while you're at it, Orman, you might ask the bartender to get in some Peychaud's bitters."

"Jesus, what you won't do to get those ridiculous bitters," Shelley said to him after the manager had walked away, looking at the cocktail napkin Jonathan had written out for him. "I'm going to get you a case for your birthday. How's that?" But Jonathan didn't answer her.

"I think I got the waitress fired," he said. "By the time I'm done here tonight, we're going to get the whole dinner for free. Just watch me."

"Jonathan. You're shameless," I said, appalled but intrigued by how he had managed to parlay an annoying slight into some kind of personal victory. This wasn't the frustrated little agent trainee. This wasn't my pal Jonathan who'd mastered trench comradery, the we're-all-in-this-crazy-mess-together Jonathan. What I witnessed in that restaurant was a transformation. Jonathan Prince had turned into the commanding officer, treating everyone as his inferiors and doing it very, very skillfully.

Sure enough, when Jonathan asked for the bill at the end of the evening, the waiter said it had all been taken care of. Jonathan left a fifty-dollar tip, which he put into the waiter's hand as we were heading for the door. The odd thing is, it wound up costing Jonathan much more than if we'd just each paid for our dinners, which consisted of three salads.

"Thank you, Mr. Prince," Orman said, hurrying over to say good-bye to us. "I hope everything was okay, and once again, we apologize."

"Everything was fine. But, you know, I'm coming back here on Friday at eight and I'd like to have the same table again. I wonder, can that be arranged now or should I have my secretary call you?"

"I can take care of that right now."

"You're coming BACK here?" I said to Jonathan after the manager had gone off to reserve his table. I don't think I quite hid my disapproval.

"Are you kidding? Of COURSE he is," Shelley said. "Orman's his new best friend. They're like this." She crossed her fingers in front of my face. "Or this." She turned one hand into an O and thrust a forefinger into it, leaving no room for interpretation.

"How dare you, madam, the impudence," Jonathan said, waving away her obscene gesture. "If it wasn't for me, we'd all still be waiting for our drinks. You should thank me for saving you from that slut-of-a-waitress."

"What ever happened to the 'full lips' and 'expressive brows'?"

Jonathan ignored her. "Actually, the only reason I did it," he said, turning to me, "was I just wanted to show Frankie I know how to get things done."

17

ANDY HARDY COUNTRY

THERE AREN'T TOO many times in my life I remember being really thrilled. I was thrilled when my sixth-grade teacher, a very handsome, divorced fallen Mormon, took me for a ride in his new white Corvette with custom cherry-red side panels. He brought me to a pool club he was managing, where my sister was the lifeguard. I was thrilled when he bought me a golden heart on a golden chain, which I wore until it turned my neck green. I realized only fifteen years later that he was after my sister, who looked a lot like Gina Lollobrigida.

The second time I felt the thrill was when Dr. Kildare came into my drab junior high school life. I was actually embarrassed to watch him with anyone, lest they suspect the depth of my feelings. I wanted to watch him alone, in my own room, on my own black-and-white TV with the metal clothes hanger Louie had fashioned into rabbit ears. I fantasized about having an epileptic seizure, like Yvette Mimieux, who fell off her coffee table right into his arms as she was demonstrating her surfing moves. When a critic described Richard Chamberlain as having a profile you might find on a bar of lady's hand soap, I was personally wounded. What's so wrong with that? I thought.

In high school I was thrilled twice. Once was when Fred Ferris, who was elected Most Musical, Wittiest, and Most Popular, asked me to go to Jones Beach with him. I was thrilled until I realized why he wasn't elected Most Likely to Succeed. The second time was when I opened up a letter addressed to me and read that I'd been elected to the Honor Society and the PTA was awarding me fifty dollars to go toward college textbooks. There was no one home I could share the news with and in a very modulated voice I yelled "Yippee" and scared the parakeet.

I was thrilled in college whenever I saw my first boyfriend, Peter Katz. I remember absolutely every detail of our first date. We went to a restaurant on Sunrise Highway with sawdust on the floor, I was in a new black double-knit sleeveless culotte dress that Perle had brought home from the wholesale warehouse where she went to work after Louie lost his business, and we ordered whiskey sours in a pitcher with cherries swaying gently on the bottom.

I was only half a person when I wasn't with Peter. When he picked me up at my dorm on Friday nights, and we drove away from the small, muddy state college and entered his big Ivy League brick-edificed world, I felt like my life, which had been on hold for the week, began again. When we had to say good-bye on Sunday nights, I cried and smoked Kool cigarettes, which made me nauseous, and in general carried on like Madama Butterfly. That is the exquisite thrill and pain of first love, which you never quite feel again.

But I was REALLY thrilled the first morning I officially drove onto the studio lot to go to my own office. I'd gotten there early because of my air-conditioning problem, and as I walked into my outer office, I found Suzie Piccioni, the studio temp assigned to me, on the phone. Actually, I smelled her before I saw her. She had ladled Oscar de la Renta perfume on herself and wherever she roamed, a redolent contrail followed. She'd already put "The Far Side" calendar and the photographs of her three cats on her desk and was drinking a mug of Swiss Miss Hot Cocoa Mix with her raisin bagel. Without introduction, she put her hand over the mouthpiece of the receiver.

"My mother in New Jersey. She just had a bunionectomy. It's no joke. I just hope you never have to go through what she just went through." I nodded. "By the way, I stopped at Smart & Final and picked up three boxes of cocoa. You have to sign the receipt for petty cash." She handed me a receipt and went back to the phone. "Ma, I gotta go. The woman I work for just walked in." Then she grabbed a tissue from a large box and blew her nose.

"It's fine," I said. "Take your time. I have nothing for you to do right now." She took me at my word and she spent the next thirty minutes talking with her mother about hammer toes and orthotics. I went into my office and sat at my desk and read the card on a gift basket. *Welcome to the team.* One of Scott Cantrowitz's cards was stuck under the clear wrapping. Gift baskets carry special significance in Hollywood and you learn to read their contents like tea leaves. Baskets come down from on high, bestowed by your superiors as rewards, bribes, and thank-yous. They are edible PR. I know a TV producer who knew his contract wasn't going to be renewed by what he found inside his basket: Chee·tos, ginger ale, and Gummy Bears. I've also seen gift baskets of champagne, caviar, cheeses, strawberries, and wines, presented in a large wicker picnic hamper, delivered for someone's birthday. My own gift basket that day was filled with brownies, cookies, and muffins from Miss Grace Lemon Cake Company. It fell right into a respectable zone of gift baskets for a writer such as myself. After I'd consumed a couple of very rich brownies, I opened up all of my desk drawers, which Suzie had kindly filled with notepads, legal pads, and Pilot Razorpoint pens.

I had no idea what to do with Suzie, never having had a secretary before. I told Freyda, when she was negotiating my deal, that I didn't need one, but she assured me I did. "Everyone has a secretary," she said. "Why would you not want a secretary?"

"What will they do? Watch me write?"

"They'll answer the phone and do the crap that you don't want to do. A good secretary is indispensable."

The phone did ring a few times that day and Suzie answered it. The first call was from a woman who wanted to drop off a three-ring binder filled with possible poster choices for my walls. Three selections were allowed. I let Suzie pick the one for the outer office.

"Which do you like better?" she said, leaning against the doorjamb to my office and thumbing through the notebook. "A *Sunday Afternoon on the Island of La Grande Jatte,* I love that one, or *Starry Night,* which I can't believe they didn't think was good when he did it, you know what I'm saying? It's so famous now. Can you imagine if you bought it back then? What it would be worth today? I'd never have to work again. Although I like Gauguin, too. I'd love to go to Tahiti. I love HOT. I don't even mind Palm Springs in the summer. I love not wearing too many clothes. That's probably because I'm from back East. I'm sorry. I don't miss the seasons. If I get back for Christmas it's enough. I like to look at the store windows on Fifth Avenue and see my nieces and nephews and then I'm ready to come home, you know what I'm saying? The Matisses aren't bad either. The *Harmony in Red.* That's from the Hermitage Museum in LENINGRAD? LENINGRAD'S sending us stuff now?" Then she blew her nose.

"You have a cold?"

"I'm allergic to cats. Do you believe it? They sleep on my pillow, they sleep on my head. What am I supposed to do with them? Kick them off the bed?"

"I'll bet you and Sparky are friends."

"You know Hermione had a urinary-tract thing? It cost him five hundred bucks. I tell you, I should have been a vet. Those guys make the money, you know what I'm saying?"

Suzie was not one of those indispensable secretaries Freyda had mentioned. Like a lot of other people working on the lot, Suzie wasn't particularly interested in movies. The only place she liked being, besides the studio store, was the casting department. And that was only because she'd worked there briefly and had thrown herself into the drama of dating actors. For all she added to a project, Suzie might just as well have been working at an automotive plant. But it still didn't stop her from having a definite opinion about movies, because it's axiomatic that everyone in Hollywood is a critic.

After waffling back and forth between Gauguin and Degas and conferring with the secretary in the next office and asking the Sparkletts man who came in wheeling water what HE thought, she finally settled on Renoir's *Luncheon of the Boating Party.* I picked out a couple of moody Edward Hoppers, one for over my tweedy sofa and the other to be hung over the light oak credenza. Decorating choices completed, Suzie and I both went back to our respective offices to wait for something to happen. I asked her to please shut the door.

The second call I got was from Freyda. "I'm calling on behalf of Jonathan, who I'm not talking to right now."

"What's the problem?"

"He wants to leave me and go work for you. Do you have a good secretary yet? Who answered the phone?"

"Someone the studio assigned me."

"He hates it here."

"I don't hate it here," I heard him say. "Anyway, I love YOU and that's the important thing."

"He hates it here. He's intellectually bored. He doesn't want to be an agent. He wants to move on."

"Don't dramatize," Jonathan chimed in. "Jesus, you're worse than my mother."

"I'm not letting him go until I have a really good replacement."

"If he's bored with you, he's certainly going to be bored with me."

"She says you're going to be bored with her, too. Is that my other line? Go get the phone," she instructed him. "Jonathan is intelligent," she said back to me, when he was presumably no longer at her side. "At least meet with him."

"I know Jonathan quite well. I don't have to meet with him."

"He wants to get into a studio situation. I told him he's not going to be happy with you either but that's what he wants. Is that for me? I've got to take this call. Think about it. Wait a second. Jonathan wants to speak to you." Freyda got off the line and Jonathan picked up.

"Do you believe her? She makes it sound like I just murdered someone."

"She's fine."

"I've just come to the end of my line here. I know I don't have to explain it to you. You of all people."

"The thing is, I don't know if working for me is exactly a promotion."

"I don't care. Maybe I can work on my own stuff while I'm sitting there fielding your phone calls. I have absolutely no time to write here."

"I didn't know you were writing."

"I didn't want to tell you because I know the attitude you have toward people who say they want to be writers—but yes, I'm trying. I'm sure it's shit, but I'm trying."

"Knock knock." I looked up. Suzie had stuck her head through my door. "Sorry to interrupt you but do you mind if I take lunch now? I just got my period. I can't believe it. No wonder I've been such a bitch lately. I thought it was next week. I'm so pissed. I want to go to the health-food store and get some evening-primrose oil. And an Advil. Do you want me to forward the calls?"

I told her not to worry about it. After she left I said to Jonathan, "If you want the job, it's yours."

"I love you."

"I don't know anything about salary. I have no idea what they pay secretaries."

"It couldn't be any worse than here. I'll work my way up to your assistant/reader-cum-development boy. I just want to get out of this fucking place."

"What about Shelley?"

"What about her?"

"I hope she doesn't feel you're deserting her."

"Of COURSE, I'm deserting her. And if Shelley was smart, she'd desert, too. I gotta go. I have to call the restaurant and tell them Freyda's on her way."

I hung up and looked at my watch. Twenty after twelve and I didn't know what I was going to do for lunch. I just didn't feel like sitting in the commissary all by myself and didn't want to eat at my desk. The whole thing felt like the first day of junior high school when I didn't know who had the same lunch period. If Jonathan was working for me I could have lunch with a friend. There was always Ian Mandel.

I wasn't sure what frame of mind I'd find Ian in. His movie had opened to generally tepid reviews. The *L.A. Times* had described it as "a so-so thriller besotted by atmosphere." *The New York Times* said the clues were as heavy as anvils and Siskel and Ebert gave it two thumbs down. But I guess someone was going to see his movie, because when I walked into his office, he was nailing a framed page from Variety right next to the Richard Diebenkorn poster. The movie had opened wide and had grossed $6.9 million the first weekend. Not out of the ballpark, nothing to write home about, but an honorable number for a movie with no special effects showing on a nonholiday weekend.

"Nice box office," I said.

He muttered something that sounded like "Yeaha fuh ha. Portia framed this for me."

"That's great. So how does it feel to have a hit movie?"

"It better be a hit. Fuha. We just bought a house in Topanga Canyon. We're in escrow. I don't want to tell you what my mortgage payments are going to be. Chuh."

"What are you doing for lunch? Anything?"

He yelled into the other room. "Did you leave a drive on for Paul and Nicole?"

"For twelve-thirty," his secretary yelled back.

"Did you make a lunch reservation?"

"For twelve forty-five."

"Lunch with the agents?" I said.

"Hey, you know. Gotta keep 'em happy."

I took a seat by myself in the commissary, ordered the Chinese chicken salad, thumbed through the newspaper, and realized that maybe my life hadn't changed that much after all. I saw Heller and Weiss sitting across from each other, their heads bent over a script they were working on. They were both wearing black leather jackets, but they weren't the same jackets they'd worn to the screening. These were soft, summer-weight jackets, more like second skins. Probably just the thing to ward off a chill from the over-air-conditioned offices. I wondered how Ian was managing to avoid them. Jonathan had told me Heller and Weiss were looking to change agents and had met with Freyda. They'd mentioned Ian's movie as one of their uncredited rewrites and had bad-mouthed his script. Even though Freyda represented Ian, she'd agreed to take them on. It's no wonder there's no writers' community in Hollywood.

After lunch, I took myself on a walk around the backlot. I found

myself in New York strolling past a pawnshop and an Italian restaurant hidden behind red-checkered curtains and vacant brown-
stones with empty front stoops. New York has never looked this
clean. There were some old black cars parked at the curb but the
only life I saw was a security guard who glided past me in a golf
cart. I lost him on the dusty streets of the Old West and found
him again in the American Town as I sat in the white bandstand
on the village green. Then I walked up the steps of town hall and
down again past the deserted movie theater, and into the shady
streets of friendly wooden homes with their white picket fences. I
could've been standing on a street in the Midwest or the Deep
South or even upstate New York, where I'd stood many times. But
these houses had no old washing machines and car parts in the front
yards. Or obese women. Or unemployed men on welfare lounging
on their porches. There were no gutters that needed replacing, nor
was there one screen door that showed evidence of a dog who'd
lunged at a cat sitting on the other side. This was a perfect, safe,
tranquil town, an image of America created for the movies by Jews
who wished life could really be like that. *Shtetls,* pogroms, thugs,
bloodbaths, Nazis, ghettos, Cossacks . . . they'd all been left far behind. These neatly painted houses, with the comforting creak of
front-porch swings, had taken on almost mythic proportions. It was
a place none of us would ever find. A world where goodness tri-
umphed over evil. That was the magic of Hollywood.

I leaned against a tree, across the street from a white house with
green trim, and watched a feral cat. It was on the front porch, eating
some kibble that someone, probably Suzie, had left in an I Can't
Believe It's Not Butter! container. When I approached, it gave me a
nervous look and scampered underneath the house with its tail
cocked. I went up the front porch steps, almost expecting to apologize in case the owner came outside to see who this stranger was.
The front window was open and a white lace curtain was lifted by
the breeze. When I peeked through the window it was a shock to
see the scaffolding and lighting rigs. It all looked so real, I'd half-
expected to find a life going on inside. Or at least a sofa with an
afghan of different-colored squares thrown over it, and an oil lamp
sitting on a doily-covered dark oak table. Faded mallard-duck wall-

paper in the dining room and, over the red painted drop-leaf desk, a framed certificate for trees that had been planted in Israel. I'd wanted it to look like Dora's house. I sat on the porch swing and rocked gently. It was July, hot and smoggy, but the trees made the street bearable and at least the rustling of the leaves was real. I felt a profound sense of peace. There was no place else I wanted to be at that moment.

"God. Is this fucking Andy Hardy country or what? Do you beLIEVE this place?" It was Paul Saluki and Nicole Dachshund sniffing their way down the quiet street toward my little house. Like the cat, I wanted to disappear under the porch.

"I feel like having lemonade or sarsaparilla or something." Nicole stepped right into the cat kibble, scattering it across the porch. "Shit. Do you believe what I just did?"

"We can't take Nicole anyplace."

"Kitty, kitty."

"It's hiding," I said.

"So?" Paul asked. "How does it feel to be on the lot? We stopped by your office and met your secretary."

"She's just a temp. Jonathan Prince is going to be my secretary."

"OUR little Jonathan? Does Freyda know?"

"It's with her blessings."

"Just as I teach them how I like my cappuccino, they leave."

"Kitty, kitty."

"Will you leave that poor cat alone?" Paul said.

"Did you tell her that we stopped by to see Joel and Judi, darling?"

"I was getting to that. We stopped by to see Joel and Judi. You should call them. They want to set up a meeting with you next week to talk about the script."

"God. I could just stay here all day," Nicole said. "Who wants to go back to work?"

NO JEWS, NO DUST

"AN OVERALL NOTE." Joel was sitting back in his leather chair with cowboy fringe hanging from the arms. He had his cowboy boots up on a Navajo blanket that was thrown across the ottoman. It was just Joel and me. Their box-office grosses had fallen off fifty percent and Judi was in New York with one of the stars, shepherding him through some morning talk shows.

"Lance thinks we should make Ivy more likable and I tend to agree with him. I don't want her to come across as too neurotic and insecure. I know you made it funny but we still want to root for her." We hadn't discussed the script since our meeting with Lance and Cantrowitz many months ago and I sensed immediately what had happened. Joel was no longer sitting on a hit. He needed to ally himself with Lance Topping, who'd never been a fan of my script. He was going to cave in to whatever it was he thought Lance wanted. I warned myself to stay calm.

"Annie Hall was neurotic and insecure."

"*Annie Hall* also had Woody Allen writing and directing and Diane Keaton acting."

"I'm saying . . . it all depends on how she's played. What if Annie

Hall was played by Liza Minnelli directed by Richard Benjamin? Or Candy Bergen directed by Blake Edwards or Frank Marshall? I think if she's underplayed and played vulnerable then she's likable. She has to have somewhere to go. Arthur has to pick her up when she's down. It's what their relationship is based upon. If she's strong and he's strong then what's the story? What's the relationship?"

"Just take a look at it. I think there may be places where you can tone her down."

"Like where?" I waited, pen in hand, ready to write down everything he said. Script meetings are about give-and-take. I wanted to appear cooperative.

"There's a couple places in the first few scenes," he said.

We both opened our scripts.

FADE IN:

EXT. GEORGE WASHINGTON BRIDGE—DAY

It's summer 1958. The ROSES' car, loaded down with luggage, heads over the bridge toward a sign...UPSTATE NEW YORK.

> IVY AND DANIEL'S VOICES
> (singing)
> John Jacob Jingle-Heimer Smith!
> Ya da da da da da da . . .
> John Jacob Jingle-Heimer Smith
> His name is my name, too . . .

INT. CAR/TRAVELING SHOT—CONTINUOUS

IVY (10) sits in the backseat with her brother DANIEL (15), a wise guy. Ivy has long, skinny legs sticking out of her shorts. She wears her hair in a ponytail but she's combed the front to cover her forehead, hiding behind her bangs.

HARRY, Ivy's father, drives as her mother, JANETTE, rummages through a gigantic ice chest on the seat next to her.

> IVY AND DANIEL
>
> Whenever we go out!
> The people always shout!
> There goes John Jacob Jingle-Heimer Smith!
> Ya da da da da da da da . . .

> JANETTE
>
> Who wants a snic snack? Daniel? How about a nice ripe peach?

> DANIEL
>
> What else do you have?

> JANETTE
>
> Chicken, salami, hard-boiled eggs, Mallomars, cherries, grapes, bananas . . . Ivy, you haven't had a banana in a long time. Why don't you have a banana?

She thrusts a banana into the backseat.

> IVY
>
> Because I hate bananas.

> HARRY
> (*in his rearview mirror*)
> Did you ever see those shrunken heads, Ivy? That's what you're beginning to look like.

Ivy makes a face. She's heard it about a hundred times.

> HARRY
>
> And get your hair out of your eyes. You look like a beatnik.

> DANIEL
>
> A beatnik with a shrunken head.
>
> JANETTE
>
> Dr. Frankel told Aunt Esther that she should eat a banana every day.
>
> IVY
> *(quietly)*
> Well, goody for her.
>
> HARRY
>
> Talk louder!
> *(to Janette)*
> She talks in my bum ear! I can't hear what she says!
>
> JANETTE
>
> Talk into your father's good ear.
>
> IVY
>
> Well, good for her!
>
> HARRY
>
> And you better stop being so moody if you know what's good for you!

"First of all, let's change the names of everyone, shall we? Rose. Frankel. Aunt Esther. We don't have to make it SO Jewish. I mean, we're talking yieddle dieddle Philip Roth here."

I knew those names were going to be trouble, so it didn't surprise me when Joel brought it up. But if I could give in on some of the easy points like names, then I could possibly get to retain what was really important to me. If they could be drawn in and involved in minor script decisions, they would begin to look at the script as their creation. They would try to nurture it.

"What would you like to name them?"

"I don't know. Just something that doesn't scream Jew. You know Scotty's policy. No Jews. No dust."

"No dust?"

"He hates westerns. He says there's absolutely no way to ever do an original western ever again. It's all been done. And Ivy IS a moody little kid. Why does she have to be so moody?"

"She's moody because they're insensitive to her. She's not moody with Arthur because he understands her."

"We want her to be lovable. Cute. Funny. Make her responses funny instead of moody. You'll accomplish the same thing. Let's go to page five, interior dining room."

INT. DINING ROOM—DAY—A FEW WEEKS LATER

The family is gathered around the table, very engrossed in eating dinner.

> HARRY
> You should learn to play the accordion!

> DANIEL
> I hate the accordion.

> HARRY
> It's a beautiful instrument!

> DANIEL
> Yeah. For Lawrence Welk.

> JANETTE
> The tomatoes are so beautiful. Aren't these beautiful tomatoes? Fifteen cents a pound.

> UNCLE HERMAN
> The corn is so sweet you don't even need butter.

> JANETTE
> Twelve for a dollar.

HARRY

Abe Levin's son learned to play the accordion
and now he's playing FUNCTIONS!

GRAMMA

Who wants more brisket? Ivy? You hardly ate
anything.

IVY

I'm full.

HARRY

Did you ever see those shrunken heads, Ivy?
That's what you're beginning to look like.

ARTHUR

I think shrunken heads are cute.

DANIEL

What's cute about them?

HERMAN

Maybe I'll have another piece.

As he reaches over to the meat platter, Aunt Harriet SLAPS his
hand away.

AUNT HARRIET

Herman. You've had enough.

Harry gives Herman a look of contempt for taking this behavior
from his wife. Arthur and Ivy catch the look.

"Let's have them eating different food, okay? I mean, *Gottenyu!*
They're eating brisket? Where's the *shmaltz* on rye bread? How come
they're not eating *gefilte* fish? I'm surprised you don't have them kiss
the *mezuzah* when they walk in the front door. They should have an
Adlai Stevenson bumper sticker on their car."

"I'll change it to hamburgers. Okay? Is that generic enough for you?"

"Neil Simon's characters are Jewish but they don't necessarily walk around eating brisket."

"Can they be Jewish or can't they be Jewish?"

"Fake it. They don't have to be anything."

"How about High Episcopalian. They could be drinking martinis by the lake."

"Make them no religion. Why do they have to have a religion?"

"Because most people do and it frames their beliefs."

"You think people in the Midwest know from these people? Some of them still think Jews have horns. You think the South understands Jews? I just had a Teamster in Louisiana who was driving me around and he starts telling me the reason Jews have to suffer is that we killed his savior. What am I supposed to do? Give him a lecture on history or tolerance or sensitivity? This is the idiot who came up to me on the set the first day of shooting and starts screaming in my face, 'THERE'S NO LUNCHEON MEAT ON THE CRAFT SER-VICE TABLE!' I wanted to say to him, 'What do you think my job is around here?' But can I fire him? Of course not, I'll have the whole union after me, they'll shut down my picture. If I'm lucky they'll only poke holes in my tires. If I'm unlucky they'll poke holes in my head. But that's okay because I'm a Jew and I was meant to suffer because I killed Jesus Christ. I just heard it on the radio, some call-in Christian station, not two weeks ago when I was driving back from Las Vegas. Some subliterate redneck starts talking about how someone Jew'd him down. I couldn't believe my ears, they're spout-ing anti-Semitism right on the radio. There are people out there who think we run the media and the banks and create worldwide con-spiracies in our spare time. There are all these neo-Nazi right-wingers who think the Holocaust never happened. Or wish it would happen again. You think these people want to watch a movie about a bunch of Jews running around *kvetching*? This won't play east of Fairfax. If one character is Jewish, that's okay. But every single character?"

"It's not every character. The Sweeneys aren't Jewish. May who runs the soda fountain isn't Jewish. And once it cuts to high school there's hardly a Jew in sight. Fred isn't Jewish. In college, her first boyfriend isn't Jewish. Grady, the guy who owns the waterbed store, he isn't Jewish. It's just that she is. I don't make a big deal over it. It's just her background."

"Ivy is Jewish. Arthur is Jewish. You telling me that Uncle Herman in the rug and linoleum business isn't Jewish? Most of these scenes are just incidental to the story anyway."

"What are you saying?"

"You're going to have to really cut the beginning. The way it's written now, you're not going to have the actress who plays the adult Ivy come on until"—he thumbed through the script—"page eighTEEN? Whew, I didn't remember the opening as being this long. If I give this to a Michelle Pfeiffer or a Demi Moore, and she sees that she doesn't come on until twenty minutes into the movie, she's not even going to READ the script. And the audience isn't going to want to wait that long for her either. This whole first part where they're kids should just be a quick introduction to their characters and BOOM, you're outta there."

"Joel, the beginning isn't just a bunch of random scenes." I was beginning to feel queasy. I was getting the urge to smother Joel with his Navajo blanket. "It's an integral part of the story. It's the beginning of her whole disappointment with men. Her father, her uncle Herman, and even Patrick Sweeney, the kid next door. If you don't meet Patrick up front, it means nothing at the end when we find out that he never returned from Vietnam."

"It's too much. He's not a main character. It's a little bit of commentary thrown in about who we sent over to Vietnam, but it's way off story. It's too novelistic."

"There's a whole part with Patrick on the golf course calling her Poison Ivy and Arthur defending her honor."

"You show him at dinner sticking up for her with the shrunken-head thing. How many times do we have to see it? You've got to lose some of these scenes." I was beginning to feel bile brewing in the pit of my stomach.

"This is going to be very hard to cut. Everything plays off of everything else."

"In *Beaches* how long does it take to set it up? You see them on the beach as little kids and BOOM, you've got Bette Midler and what's-her-face as adults. You know, you should rent *Beaches* and see how they did it."

"I've seen *Beaches,* thank you."

"Look, let me tell you something. My movie is going into the toilet and you want to know why? Because I tried to make it real. I tried to make it noir. People don't want noir. They want froth that doesn't make them think too hard. I learned my lesson. It's a very painful lesson but a valuable one."

NOIR? I wanted to scream at him. It was just pretentious and boring. That's why no one is going to see your movie. Because you can't direct and you know nothing about what makes a good script. Instead I got up and made myself some tea.

Joel and I continued picking apart the first eighteen pages that morning, going back and forth and arguing, both trying to control our tempers. When I returned to my office at lunchtime, Jonathan was there waiting for me. I threw myself into his desk chair and he massaged my shoulders like a trainer and his fighter in between bloody rounds. Much to my satisfaction, he talked about the script as if he had a personal stake in it. "I can't believe Lance doesn't think she's sympathetic. He just doesn't get it. What a dim bulb that guy is. Doesn't he realize why she's like that? That's the whole point of her character. It's what Arthur sees right through. You're going to take away all the humor if you bland her down. It's amazing, isn't it? I mean, here you've given them something original and they immediately want to turn it into something familiar. You've written *Cinema Paradiso* and they want to turn it into *Beaches.*" Jonathan said things that, out of modesty, I could never have said myself. "By the way, I was talking to Cantrowitz's secretary and she says if Joel's movie doesn't pick up at the box office this weekend, it'll probably be pulled from the theaters." I was sure that hiring Jonathan was the best move I ever made.

Jonathan had fixed up the office and finagled someone down the hall into giving us their cornstalk plants. Jonathan bought flowers with his own money because he knew how much I liked them. He changed the Degas poster into Rousseau's *The Dream*. And if I had pillows I've no doubt he would have plumped them up and karate-chopped them down. Freyda was right after all. A good secretary is indispensable.

I was trying to figure out how I was going to address the script notes and gloating over Joel's sliding movie grosses, when Ian Mandel lumbered through the door. He'd begun stopping by my office when he realized his movie was not going to make him the next Joe Ezterhas. Ian had put on some weight, which sat in a billowy pillowy paunch right over his belt. From the look on his face, he was under some stress. I wondered if he'd just heard the news about his movie being pulled.

"You free for lunch?" he asked, not acknowledging Jonathan. Although Jonathan and I were planning on having lunch together, I knew that Ian needed to talk to someone. And the truth was, I wanted to talk to him, too. We had an enemy in common now and nothing forges a friendship faster than feeling screwed by the same person. Jonathan would find another lunch companion. He knew everyone on the hall, where they came from, their credits, who their agents were, long before I did. Within a week of coming on the lot, Jonathan had a retinue of single women stopping by his desk to chat, including Suzie, whose job he had taken. I had to keep my door closed if I wanted to get any work done. As I left the office with Ian, Jonathan was already on the phone, setting up a new lunch date.

Ian and I decided to go off the lot to a Mexican restaurant. The hostess sat us in a booth, next to a table filled with women office workers who kept toasting the birthday girl with slushy margaritas. They all seemed to be genuinely fond of one another and I thought, How strange it is that no one really wishes each other well in Hollywood. Just as I was thinking that to myself, Ian illustrated my thought out loud.

"I can't wait to see Judi and Joel fail. I just hope they fail really big."

"Why would you want that?"

"I didn't tell you this, but I was fired off my movie and it was extensively rewritten."

"You're kidding," I said, feigning ignorance.

"I told them the rewrite sucked. I had it out with Judi. I went to the mat with her. She deserves everything she's going to get."

"But your name's on the script."

"You're telling me. Fucking Heller and Weiss. The little *yeshiva buchers*. They actually wanted credit. They actually thought they saved the script. This was one of the best scripts of my career before they got their hands on it." He shook his head in disbelief and stuffed another ten or twelve tortilla chips into his mouth. "I'll tell you what they should be getting credit for. They should be signing their names to the bottom of supermarket bags. What really gets me is that Lance Topping actually thinks they're good writers. That's what gets me. He thinks they're this young new hot team. He's just offered them an overall." I was hoping Ian never saw the gift basket they were going to get.

Judi and Joel, Heller and Weiss, they were part of the unforgivably successful in Hollywood who prosper and thrive for no fathomable reason, and Ian was taking it all too personally. But he'd gotten it off his chest. His reputation as a writer was safe, at least with me. I'd heard it many times before—the Hollywood Hymn: Take the Credit and Place the Blame. I didn't judge Ian because I understood it. Then, of course, I told him my tale of woe and we decided to order a small pitcher of margaritas and another basket of chips. By the time lunch was over, Ian and I were as fond of each other as the ladies at the next table.

Judi came home a few days later, and Joel left for his annual week-long stint as a volunteer fireman on Fire Island, where he'd summered as a kid. Trying to picture Joel as a fireman taxed the imagination and I can only hope the residents of Kismet are careful with their barbecue lighter fluid the last week in August. My script meeting with Judi went just about the same as with Joel.

"Why can't they be Italian? Make them Italian."

"I don't want to make them Italian. Hollywood always tries to change Jews to Italians."

"Because people like to watch Italians. People loved *Moonstruck*. I'd rather have a neurotic Italian Ivy than a neurotic Jewish Ivy. Make her Italian. That will solve the whole problem." Judi went into her purse, took out her brush, and began restyling her hair.

"So where do you picture them going for the summers? Still up-state New York?"

"I don't know. The Jersey Shore. Find out where middle-class Italians went for the summer."

"I don't know the Jersey Shore. I don't know middle-class Italians."

"Go rent *Moonstruck* and see how John Patrick Shanley handled it." Judi got up from her desk and headed across the room toward her reflection in the mirrored armoire.

"I can't copy from another writer, Judi. Can I? Then it wouldn't be very original, would it?"

"So make it UP. I don't know the Jersey Shore EITHER but it's a BEACH. They have a house near the BEACH." She was beginning to treat me like I was an idiot. Like I was the snack lady. Or Sparky.

"Why the Jersey Shore?"

"I didn't say it HAD to be the Jersey Shore. It's just a sugGEStion. I just don't want it to read like the CATskills." She looked at herself in the mirror and posed, actually posed as if she was alone, pursing and pouting her lips like a sixties cartoonish sex kitten.

"It's not the Catskills. I'm not writing about the Borscht Belt. It's the Adirondacks. There's a big difference." What would Judi know about it? She had no frame of reference. She would never understand the sweet peace of sitting in a rocking chair on the front porch during a summer thunderstorm. Or fishing on the lake at sunrise when mist floats just above the water and your fingers are too cold and stiff to let out the line. Judi could only truly be at home, she could only relax, as far as she was capable of relaxing, in Beverly Hills and certain parts of West L.A. The rest of the world she perceived as vaguely threatening and hostile. Judi's survival technique was to keep reassuring herself that other people were stupid. I tried to imagine her coping in the Corn Belt or hiking the Himalayas or even attending a wedding in Bellflower, only thirty miles away. Outside of her little fiefdom, Judi would be regarded as dangerously bizarre. "Listen, Judi, I thought you liked this script the way it was. Now all of a sudden you and Joel want to change it drastically."

"It's not drastic. I KNOW from drastic, beLIEVE me. The story is still the same. I'm just trying to put it in a miLIEU that's a little more INteresting."

"Says who?"

"Says the people in Downey. You think I ever want to go through THAT again? I had a great movie. Those fuckers upstairs made us change it. If Joel and Lance hadn't caved in to their changes it could have been a hit. Now I'm SMARTer. I'm anticipating the notes. I want to give them what they want before they ask for it. At least then, I'M the one making the choices, not THEM."

"You're already anticipating test-audience results?"

"I know Scotty. He won't green-light the script as is. It's not his kind of movie. I'm trying to get this movie MADE. It's not going to do either one of us any good sitting on a shelf, is it?"

That was the part I couldn't argue with.

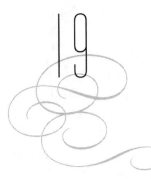

19

THE MONKEY CAN
DO ANYTHING

DESPITE A SATURATION campaign of print and TV ads, radio spots, the gamut of talk-show appearances, and mobile billboards featuring their two sultry stars plastered on the sides of buses, Judi and Joel's movie wasn't bringing in an audience. After three weeks it had grossed only nine million against the eighty million they'd spent on production, promotion, and advertising. It was no surprise to anyone when it was no longer playing in a theater near you. The surprise was Cantrowitz had immediately given Judi and Joel a new script to produce. It wasn't an idea they'd come up with or a script they'd found themselves, nor was it something they'd put into development and nurtured along. It was plunked right into their lap, a script the studio had bought in turnaround, with a star already attached. They had a firm start date only twelve weeks away. The script was going through a two-week rewrite by Heller and Weiss, who were getting paid double what I made for my original script. Judi and Joel were being given the equivalent of a big house fully furnished and landscaped with maybe a couple leaky faucets to fix, but otherwise in move-in condition. People on the lot, mainly Ian Mandel, muttered how Judi and Joel had to be the "two luckiest Jews in Hollywood."

After my meeting with Judi and Joel I'd done one quick rewrite on my script, addressing some of their easier notes, and was waiting to hear from them. But they never got around to reading the changes before they left to do their bonus movie. My script had been spurned for another and whether I could ever entice them again, lure them back, excite their interest, or whether they'd grown tired of it for good was what was waking me up at four in the morning.

"The love affair with a script is all too fleeting," Hershel said to me one evening after I'd voiced concern. "It's obviously been replaced by a new, more exciting amour. You got paid for it. At least that's something. You have your health insurance for the next year."

"This happens all the time," Freyda reassured me. "They're just putting it on the back burner for a while, and when they get done with their other movie, we'll get them going on it again. I'll give Lance a call."

"What does Lance know about anything?" Jonathan said. "I'll go out to lunch with his assistant, Emily Ginsburg, and tell her what a terrific script it is. The more Lance hears it from other people, the more he'll start believing it himself." I put my faith in Jonathan.

Studios don't pay writers to sit around and do nothing. Judi and Joel hadn't been gone a week before Lance Topping's office called to set up a pitch meeting.

"So I understand we're putting *Ivy and Men* on the back burner for a while," Lance said as he stretched back in his chair, kicked off his shoes, and began putting his toes through their exercise routine. "Well, in the meantime, let's see if we can get you started on another project." Lance was sitting tall now and opening up a manila folder that revealed five sheets of crisp white paper. We were meeting in one of the conference rooms on the third floor; Lance, Emily Ginsburg, and two note takers who reminded me of those little birds who follow hippos around. I had my yellow legal pad, ready to jot down story ideas. Emily Ginsburg spread out her notes on the long teak table, but Lance kept his pages close, the edges carefully aligned, still in their folder. He studied the words and then looked up at me as if he were about to reveal the contents of a Top-Secret document. "A remake of *Roman Holiday*. Lady Di goes to Vancouver on official business and meets Andy Garcia."

Emily cut in. "She escapes all the ladies-in-waiting and all the attendants and gets to be a regular person for a day."

Lance finished it off. "They fall in love, but at the end, she has to go back to being a princess."

"It's really hard to remake a classic like that," I said, not committing either way.

"Well, that's why it doesn't have to be a newspaper reporter," Lance said. "It's going to be shot in BC, so she could even meet a Mountie. Who saves her from distress. Of course he has no idea who she is and she's immediately attracted to him, but he's a commoner, so of course nothing can happen."

"It should just be totally romantic," Emily said. "I just think it could be a really great idea."

What Emily didn't have in brains, she certainly made up for in enthusiasm. I thought about Andy Garcia as a member of the Royal Canadian Mounted Police. "Interesting."

"The Woman on the Fifteenth Floor."

I looked at Lance, waiting for more explanation.

"We don't know what happens, we just love the title."

"So it's really up for grabs."

"We see it as kind of a mystery," Emily said.

"It's definitely not a comedy," Lance added.

"I think it sounds very mysterious," Emily said.

"I mean, if you came up with a great comedy idea for it, we'd hear it," Lance said, "but basically we saw it as a noirish kind of *Body Heat*."

"Uh-huh. Okay, let me think about that one." I knew the studio would never make it. Judi and Joel had killed film noir. At least until another studio did it successfully, which would resurrect the genre like a phoenix.

"Humphrey the Humpback Whale." I had the get-me-out-of-here look on my face and hoped it wasn't as obvious to them as it felt to me. "Remember the whale who got stuck in the channel and they tried to get him out to sea?"

"Yes?"

"Kids' movie. G-rated. It could be fun."

"Could be." I jotted it down because they were all looking at me.

"The Treasure." A group of kids find some old buried treasure and go off to fulfill their fantasies."

"This one could go anywhere," Emily said. "That's what I love about this idea. I mean, it just appeals to every kid's fantasy of what would I do if I found a million dollars."

"Where does the money come from?" I asked, stalling for time, pretending to be interested.

"Could be an old bank job, could be buried pirates' treasure that they come upon in Martha's Vineyard," Lance said. "They could be on vacation with their parents in Egypt and they stumble across an old tomb."

"So it's basically a kids' movie. Steven Spielbergish."

"Exactly."

"Okay, let me think about that one," I said, envisioning the shopping-mall scene they would inevitably make me put in. Lance turned back to his list.

"Hey. Here's one that needs a quick rewrite. This one could be satirical and sophisticated, it just needs the right writer to see what it's about. This one has terrific potential." I waited. "I don't know if I can do this justice." He turned to Emily. "You know, we should get Isaac on the speakerphone and he can tell her about it. Ask Jona to see if Isaac Green is in his office."

Emily picked up the phone. "Jona, would you see if Isaac Green is in his office? Or have his secretary find out where he is and patch him in here."

Hollywood is really too incestuous, which might explain why so many crazy things have to be borne. Isaac Green was married to Wendy Rubin. Hart had been to their house for Thanksgiving. I wondered if their marriage was still in trouble. If she was still after Hart, still leaving him those "Hart Sweet" phone messages. I'd never met Isaac and just couldn't imagine what kind of man would be married to Wendy. What kind of man would put up with her? Even Hart, who'd once been flattered by her attention, had grown weary of her. As I was going through these ruminations the phone rang and Emily picked up.

"It's Isaac," she said, putting him on the speaker.

"Isaac?" Lance shouted in his booming voice. "We're sitting here with Frankie Jordan. I was just about to tell her about your project but I thought maybe you'd want to do it. I didn't know if I could do it justice."

"Frankie?"

"Hi."

"We just saw Hart the other night, is that a small world or what?"

"Too small."

"He says you're a terrific writer and I should read your stuff."

"He's just trying to keep the alimony down." I don't know why I was making jokes with him. Hart and I had never even discussed alimony. We just weren't ready yet.

"I think you're going to love this project. Did they tell you anything?" He didn't bother to disguise that he was eating something, which sounded like a bagel. It seemed to be a comment on how I fit into his life. I wondered if anyone else was as annoyed by the chewy, doughy, masticating noise as I was.

"Nothing."

"We were waiting for YOU," Lance yelled in my ear. Between Lance and Miriam I was going to go deaf.

"You ready?"

"Ready." I leaned forward in my chair toward the phone in the center of the table.

"*Wall Street* but instead of Michael Douglas and insider trading, we have a chimp who can pick stocks. It's about greed. It's about New York and big-time money. It's about a young idealistic kid who loves Wall Street and gets caught up in the game, but he needs the chimp to pick the stocks."

"I presume it's a broad comedy," I said.

"Not broad. It should have real bite. This isn't a kids' movie. Don't think of it in terms of kids. That's the mistake the first writers made. This one should have sophisticated wit, definitely for grown-ups. It's *Wall Street* with a chimp. Think of Michael J. Fox. This kid never went to Harvard Business School like all the hotshots around him. He's working his way through some community college but he'll do anything to get ahead, anything to get on top, and we love him for it. And, by the way, I've met the chimp. The monkey can do anything. He should be written as a real character, not as a monkey. If you're interested, I'll set you up with the monkey and his trainer. When he came to the studio he had a whole crowd gathered around him on the lawn outside. He wears Bermuda shorts. I mean, it goes to prove that people love watching monkeys."

Lance turned to Emily. "Why don't you get her the script." Then he turned toward the speakerphone and raised his voice a couple hundred decibels. "WE'RE GOING TO LET FRANKIE READ THE SCRIPT AND THEN WE'LL TALK."

"Good idea."

Emily turned to one of the little birds. "Send a script of *Swinging on a Star* down to Frankie Jordan's office."

"Frankie?"

"Yes, Isaac?"

"I'm looking forward to talking with you. Just keep in mind when you read it, that the script isn't there yet. The first writers totally missed the boat. There's a lot of opportunity for real satire that they just didn't get. Wendy thinks it could be terrific."

Knowing Wendy, I think what she meant was that the script BETTER be terrific. Since she'd married him, Isaac had gone from a studio executive with a steady paycheck to being an independent producer, which meant he wouldn't be bringing home much bacon unless he started getting things produced.

We all said our good-byes to Isaac and his bagel and I was already trying to figure out how to tell him I didn't want to do his rewrite when Lance went back to his list. "LIFE as in *Life* magazine."

I don't know why but it intrigued me immediately. "What about it?"

"Romantic comedy. A reporter and a photographer go out on a story together. Margaret Bourke-White and Jack Nicholson."

"I wish I was around when *Life* magazine was big," Emily said. "It was probably so much fun to get it every week."

"I kind of like that one," I said. "It sounds like it could be a look back to an age of innocence."

"A bit of nostalgia for the good old days of America," Lance said. "That was my take exactly."

"I like that one," I said again.

Lance went through the rest of the ideas but LIFE was the only one that interested me.

"Let me set you up with Jerry Slotnick." My luck. Another Jerome Slotnick production. It's not as if *Humphrey the Humpback Whale* wouldn't have suited him just the same. Basically, he was a pushcart peddler who hawked his wares up and down the street and it made no difference to him who bought what. I could already imagine him cornering Marty at some party and jamming the LIFE script down his throat. "We'll get you two together and see what you can come up with. Emily, remind me to call Jerry Slotnick."

When I got back to my office, Jonathan wasn't there. He'd left me a note indicating he was down in Mai Lei's office. They were both trying to write scripts and sometimes they'd get together and discuss their work, exchange pages, and critique each other's scenes. Mai Lei's screenwriting teacher had told her to do a profile on each of her characters, so Jonathan, too, had been dutifully sitting at his desk creating character bios.

I went into my office, closed the door, and turned on my computer. The LIFE concept had actually come to me when I was walking down the stairwell from my meeting. It was a story about three people: a young cub reporter who's eager to experience life, a jaded photographer who thinks he's seen everything in life, and a beautiful innocent showgirl who's seen nothing of life. They all meet in Las Vegas while waiting for the first publicized testing of the atom bomb to go off and they create their own heat. I remembered reading that there was a delay in the testing due to weather conditions and that the media was holed up in one of the hotels on the strip for two weeks. They couldn't stray too far because at any hour, day or night, the announcement could come that the bomb had gotten clearance. Dropped on a typical American town that had been constructed out in the desert, complete with Mommy mannequins in kitchens and Daddy mannequins reading their newspapers in easy chairs in the living rooms. I vaguely remembered seeing photos of it in *Life* magazine at the time it happened. I would show how television would eventually steal all the thunder, publicizing the event before *Life* hit the newsstands. It was actually the beginning of the end for *Life* magazine and the beginning of TV as we know it.

I'd gotten excited about the possibilities of setting a fictional story behind real events. Typing as fast as I could, the thoughts flying out of my head onto the screen, and then I saw the red light on my phone blinking and blinking. Jonathan hadn't bothered to forward the calls and I had a momentary flash of annoyance because about half of the time the calls were for Jonathan and I wound up being his secretary. But it was just Emily Ginsburg telling me Jerry Slotnick was out of town, tied up with another project for the foreseeable future, and the more they thought about it the more they wanted me to do the monkey rewrite.

"Just do it," Freyda advised. "Who knows? It's so stupid it just might get made."

Isaac Green was a very unhealthy-looking specimen. With his young, chubby face and deep purple shadows under his hooded eyes, he looked like some abused child that an astute social worker would remove from his home environment immediately. All I could think was he'd become this exhausted trying to garner his wife's approval. He seemed at times panic-stricken, nervous, unhappy yet aggressive, and I didn't know whether to pat him on the back and reassure him everything would be all right or run from him as fast as I could.

"I've set you up with the monkey and his trainer," Isaac said. He was perspiring and mopped his brow with the sleeve of his shirt. "I want you to see what I'm talking about. I want you to get as excited about this project as I am."

"Oh, boy," Jonathan said with his customary sarcasm when I invited him to come along and watch the chimp do his routine. "I've never met a real star before. At last I'm going to get a taste of why Hollywood beckons and fascinates."

"Charley," Isaac said to the chimpanzee, "I'd like you to meet Frankie Jordan. Frankie Jordan, this is Charley who is an aMAZing chimpanzee."

Every actor has a lucky audition outfit and the ape was no exception. "You see? Bermuda shorts," Isaac said to Jonathan and me as we stood on the grass near the commissary and watched the ape go through his paces. Charley attracted a small following as Isaac had predicted. "You see? What did I tell you?" Isaac said as he looked around at the crowd. "People love monkeys."

But despite what Isaac had boasted about the chimp's abilities, when it came right down to it the handler could only get him to do five things: clap his hands, blow a Bronx cheer, do a kiss, a smile, and a screech. Isaac was a little wary of Charley and prissily backed away when the chimp went to put his finger in Isaac's ear.

"Whoa, big fella. Whoa, there, Charlie." But the chimp was insistent.

"He must like you," the trainer said. "He wants to groom you."

Isaac looked disgusted by the notion. But he tried to play along like a good sport, even when the ape's fingers went for his hair.

"Whoa, big fella. Nice shorts you're wearing. Whoa. Okaaay. Not the hair."

"I wonder who he knows," Jonathan said after we'd left Isaac and the chimp and were headed back to my office. "He's got to know someone, because no one in their right mind would give him twenty million dollars to go make a movie. He obviously didn't fuck anyone, so I'm sure his father must know someone. He's got to have connections. If you're Isaac Green, you don't just come out to Hollywood and become a producer. Whoa, big fella. I guarantee you, he's a payback for something."

The rewrite took me the rest of the summer and I hated getting up in the morning. Especially since I knew Wendy Rubin was reading every page. She called me one day at work just to give me a little pep talk, which sounded suspiciously familiar.

"The first writers entirely missed the boat. They left out all the satire. It should be *Wall Street* with a chimp. The humor should be sophisticated. They wrote it like a cartoon, which was UNbelievably unfunny. The trick is to write the monkey as a real character."

Isaac insisted I turn in pages as I finished them, to make sure the tone was right. A lot of revisions go into a script before it's ready to be seen, but Isaac was adamant. I let Jonathan read the first twenty-five pages, which to my great satisfaction made him laugh, and then he hand-delivered them to Isaac's office. We both waited. Isaac called me at home on a Saturday, his voice deeply distressed.

"I . . . I . . . I don't know what to say. You missed the boat. You missed the boat comPLETEly. What am I supposed to do? I thought you understood we wanted bite. We've got to get together. We've got to meet in person and go over this." He took in a deep, deep breath and let out a sigh of despair. "I'm supposed to be leaving town tomorrow and I have Michael J. Fox's agent just WAITING. I have no idea what to tell him." Another hopeless sigh. "What are you doing now? What are you doing RIGHT now?"

"I'm talking to you."

"Very funny. Look. Can I come over and we'll talk this out in person? Because I have to tell you, I just don't have the confidence you can do this." Why was it that Isaac was beginning to sound more and more like Wendy? She had married him when she was thirty-nine, a desperate age for a woman, and now she was stuck trying to make him into something. It must have been hard on them both.

Isaac could barely make his eyes meet mine when I let him in. He sank down on the sofa, a beaten man, his perspiring forehead going right into one hand. My apparently worthless script scenes were in his lap, and as he slowly reread the pages to himself, the wet rings under his armpits seemed to spread and darken. I sat at my desk, for lack of anywhere else to sit, and went through some notes pretending to look writerly as I waited for enlightenment. After a few deep, deep sighs Isaac finally looked up, although not directly at me. His gaze grazed my shoulder and continued right out the window.

"Wendy and I are supposed to be leaving for Puerto Vallarta for a week. Do you want me to cancel the trip? Do you want me to stay here and I'll go over every page with you, scene by scene? Wendy will kill me. She's had the reservations for six months. My marriage is going to be in deep trouble. But do you want me to stay home? Is that what you want? Because if that's what you need, I'll do it."

"I don't want to be responsible for the breakup of your marriage. Maybe if you could try and explain what tone you're looking for . . ."

"Don't concentrate on the humor. Just TRY and get the story down. Don't even THINK about the humor. We know an unemployed comedy writer and I can get him to punch it up when you're through."

"What don't you like about it? Or give me an example of what you'd like to see."

He sighed. He picked up a pen. He flipped through some pages in the script. He shook his head. He ran his fingers through his hair and rubbed his bruised-looking eyes. "Okay, here. Michael J. Fox in the car with the chimp. You missed a big opportunity here. He should tell Charley to put on his seat belt. You've got to remember that the monkey is a character. He's got to say to Charley, 'We're not going anywhere until you put on your seat belt.' And maybe the monkey gives him some lip and he says: 'You want this banana, pal?' or 'Put on your seat belt or you're not watching *Wall Street Week.*' Do you understand what I'm getting at? For instance, when he invites the girl home for dinner, you didn't explore all the possibilities."

"Like what?"

"Maybe he's trying to make her spaghetti and the spaghetti's going all over the place and the whole kitchen's a big mess and there's sauce everywhere and Charley keeps getting in the way. And he says to the monkey 'Get out of here,' and Charley goes into the living room and starts watching *Wall Street Week,* and when he disagrees with what they're saying, he starts jumping up and down and he throws the onion dip at Rukeyser. You changed that whole scene. And you left out the idea that every time we see Michael J. Fox's boss, he has pink around his mouth from drinking Pepto-Bismol. Why did you take THAT out? That WORKED."

"I thought you said you wanted this to be sophisticated."

A BIG hopeless sigh. "Do you want me to stay home? It's only taken us a year to get the reservations at this villa. It's the one time of the year we get to go down there but I'll cancel it and stay here and we'll work on the script line by line if that's what you want."

Only Jonathan could appreciate this. Only Jonathan knew how to assess the situation and portray it the way I wanted him to. I phoned him just after Isaac left.

"Are you kidding me? There's no way that guy would ever stay home and work with you. Because then if his wife didn't like the script, she'd blame him. This way, he's out of the country and he can blame you. By the way, I know his secretary. She told me some good stuff you'll love. Apparently, they have a lovely tradition of going down to Puerto Vallarta once a year to do Ecstasy. That's why it's so important that they take this vacation. So they can gaze into each other's eyes for a week and try to forget why they married each other. I guarantee you, there's a connection somewhere. His parents know someone in Hollywood. This guy did not get to be a producer on his own."

When I turned in my final rewrite, it was never acknowledged by Isaac or Wendy or anyone at the studio. It mercifully vanished into the ether. The only one who seemed to appreciate it was Jonathan, who said it was the first chimpanzee movie he would actually consider seeing.

THE RIGHT MATCH

OCTOBER CAME AND Miriam took time off from school to visit her daughter in the East and watch the leaves change. She left Hershel nine days' worth of frozen stew and plenty of bean-and-barley soup so he wouldn't have to worry about food. So he could just write. But when she was gone, to my surprise, Hershel asked if he could take up our morning walk.

Unlike Miriam, whose little legs worked double time to keep up with mine, Hershel was a slow, preoccupied walker. Where Miriam flew out the door in her apron, Hershel dressed cautiously in layers and wore a watch cap in case he got an early-morning chill. His beard tucked into his chest and his hands clenched behind his back, Hershel bent his head into an imaginary wind and told me he was starting another play. It was about a forty-year-old woman in L.A. who leaves her successful husband and has to start her life with men over again. He wanted to pick my brain.

Unfortunately, I was bad subject matter. I was sending out negative signals to men. I didn't elicit responses from them anymore. Sexually I'd shut down and they sensed it. Miriam the sex expert said I could be ignited again by the right match but I wasn't interested in dating.

They'd tried casually introducing me to a brother of a friend. "You might like Marvin," Miriam said. "I mean, he's no Hart, but he's very intelligent. He's a mathematician who teaches at Princeton."

Miriam and Hershel invited Marvin to their Sukkot dinner, a sort of Jewish Thanksgiving. It was given in their backyard underneath a shelter fashioned from a few two-by-fours with a palm-frond roof. The structure looked like the framing of a tiny house, and was designed to be assembled in a matter of minutes, each piece slipping into place like Lincoln Logs. But Hershel took to the challenge as if he were building the Great Pyramids. His soft hands protected by canvas work gloves, he carried out the two-by-fours from the garage with a great deal of grunting and sweating and swearing. When the hammer came out and his shirt came off, exposing his milk-white skin to the sun, Miriam and I sang "Let My People Go" and watched him from the kitchen window, betting on how long before his back twinged and we'd end up finishing the job. Miriam gave him ten minutes, I gave him fifteen. It was clear after five minutes Hershel never would have made it with the pharaoh.

Miriam put on the palm fronds and I attached bananas, oranges, and apples to little strings and hung them from the roof. Hershel sat exhausted in the slack-webbed Brown Jordan chair and critiqued my work. "That banana can be on a little longer string. Too many orange clusters, you might want to put an apple in there to break up the color." It was the only time Hershel ever got to play producer.

Marvin arrived with his sister and Miriam told them I'd hung all the fruit myself. It's the kind of information even a happy person would have a hard time responding to, but poor Marvin was at a complete loss for words. He was so withdrawn he could hardly speak, much less compliment me on my swinging fruit. They sat us next to each other and Hershel led the proceedings with scholarly dash, recounting the forty years we wandered in the desert, and how, tired and hungry, the Jews built temporary huts under the stars, praying that one day they would have a real home. He reminded us that when the harvest came in, they sat in their shelters without walls and thanked God for his bounty, just as we were doing this very night. But even as Hershel steeped us in Jewish lore, I could see him watch-

ing Marvin and me, wanting something to happen. But Marvin dom-
inated the listening for the entire evening. After dinner, we both
helped Miriam clear the table and Hershel followed us into the
kitchen on the pretext of getting more wine. In the breast pocket of
his shirt was a pen and the small spiral pad he kept to record bits of
thought and dialogue before they could escape. Marvin and I scraped
food into the garbage, Hershel hovering close.

"Miriam says you're a screenwriter."

"Yes, I am."

"That must be fun."

"Not really."

"I know the feeling. I feel like I've done my best work as a mathematician. I really don't see what the point is anymore."

"He's taken a leave of absence to get some treatment," Miriam
whispered to me. "They think he may have whaddaya-call-it with
the light . . . SAD syndrome. But he's on pills now and he sits in
front of a special lightbulb for a few hours every day and his sister
says he's doing a lot better."

He committed suicide less than a week later. Despite "the tragic
waste of a life," Hershel said he couldn't have asked for a more dramatic event and happily went up to his room to make more notes
for his play.

"It's a good thing he didn't ask you out," Jonathan said when I
told him what had happened. "Just imagine. You would've been his
last date, and knowing you, you would've always wondered what
you'd said to make him kill himself."

A lesser disaster occurred that Hershel might have stolen, but I never
told him. I was at my office working when Jonathan buzzed me.

"Do you want to speak to Shepard Blum?"

It had been years since I'd seen Shepard. I'd mentioned him to
Freyda a while back at our lunch and wondered if she'd been agenting
on my behalf. I picked up the phone all cheery-voiced.

"Hi, Shepard."

"This is Denise, his secretary. Can you hold for Shepard? He's just
finishing up another call."

I cleaned out my purse of old tissues and wondered why he'd be calling. A television pilot he wanted me to write. It was only logical. How thrilling to feel needed.

"Hey."

"Hey, Shepard. How you doing?"

"I'm doing great and you're doing really great, I hear. I bumped into Freyda last night and she said you sold a feature. Congratulations."

"You know features. They just take forever to get going, but thanks." I didn't tell him about the monkey rewrite. I didn't tell him my producers had abandoned me.

"She also told me that you split up with your husband, which was really great news because, you know, besides really liking to work with you, I always wanted to fuck you."

"I had no idea. You were always the perfect gentleman." In some other places this could conceivably be construed as sexual harassment. In Hollywood it passes for charm. Poor Shepard was one of those men who can't help themselves. He was always making stupid sexual comments and innuendos and trying to sleep with young production assistants. I never took him seriously, nor did any woman over the age of twenty.

Once you sleep with someone in Hollywood, there are absolutely no secrets. Size, technique, favorite positions, orifice preference, turn-on words—it all goes out on the AP wires. But it's not just the women who talk. Men talk plenty. There's a director who named a very famous actor who's fond of saying, "Once you fuck a woman up the ass, you own her." The director not only shared this aphorism but went on to describe his own adventures. Which entailed having sex with a very famous actress, whom he named, in a lifeguard stand on Zuma Beach, when they were driving home from Big Sur and got so hot they couldn't stand it. I am the recipient of all kinds of tidbits. I should probably be a stringer for the *National Enquirer*. Before I'd even shaken Shepard's hand, I knew what he liked to say in the heat of passion: "Whose pussy is this?" he whispers, and his beloved of the moment is supposed to answer, "Your pussy." That, and more, I heard while standing by the craft service table on location in Vancouver, reported to me by a woman who'd once slept with him.

If Shepard only knew that the women he wooed not only sized him up but broadcast it internationally, he might've been a lot more private with his privates.

"Why don't you marry me and between what you'll get from Hart and my residuals, I'll never have to work again."

"I think you might get into trouble with all that time on your hands." I didn't want to be having this conversation. "So what do you really want, Shepard?"

"That's what I love about you, Jordan. That direct ball-busting style." That was Shepard's way of flirting. Making you feel like some powerful, sexual, she-devil bitch. It must have worked with some women.

"Isn't that your other phone?"

"You know, I've missed you. I miss those little barbs." I went back to cleaning out my purse. "You want to know why I called you? I want to ask you out. Like a date, Jordan."

I'd misjudged my own worth as a writer, let myself become excited and flattered, and felt stupid for having done so. But then a date with Shepard might be good practice. I could easily handle him and it was nice to have some man notice me again. Also, I was curious. I agreed to meet at his house for a drink before we went out to dinner.

The house was hidden from the street by a tall hedge of pink and white oleander. As soon as I pulled into the driveway, I understood why he wanted me to see him in his domain. His house was large, modern, and tasteful, especially for a producer who basically had no taste. A manservant answered the door and I stepped into about an acre of light maple floor finished smooth as amber. For probably the second time in my life, I was sorry I didn't tap-dance. I waited in the living room, which had an expansive view of the city, a very respectable collection of pre-Columbian art, and a few California regional watercolors in an Ash Can School style. Shepard seemed more attractive by the second.

I'd examined everything twice when Shepard finally appeared from the direction of the kitchen wing, a fragrant pipe protruding from under his mustache and, by his side, a fat golden retriever with hip dysplasia trying to get traction on the floor. People who worked for Shepard told me tales of his hair-trigger temper, the childish tantrums, the Jekyll and Hyde personality. But I'd seen only his mellow, Perry Como persona. The cardigan and slippers had been updated to a Missoni sweater and tasseled loafers with no socks. It made me miss Hart all the more and the comfort of being with someone who didn't think about clothes more than I did. It made me miss his jeans and rugby shirts and old sneakers. But once I got over that, I was glad to see Shepard. Sometimes it's fun being around rich people in a tranquil, beautiful, well-ordered setting. I felt cocooned and safe. For a little while I even got distracted enough to forget about *Ivy and Men*. It smelled like something was cooking. Shepard revealed with great delight that his cook had arranged a complete dinner, which only required us turning on the oven, heating up the rice, and tossing the salad. "We're baching it tonight. Francesca makes a terrific canard à l'orange. I hope you like canard à l'orange."

After the manservant finished washing Shepard's cars he was off for the evening and Shepard and I were alone. Without too much difficulty, he persuaded me to have a very dry Sapphire gin martini, ostensibly because he wanted to try out the Art Deco silver martini shaker he'd just bought at auction. It worked like a charm. After three or four cold silvery sips, I could feel myself sliding into silly grins, and I told myself to be careful. Shepard was not my type and the Hollywood census poll said he wasn't good in bed anyway. Also, I had to drive home responsibly and finding my way out of Bel Air in the dark would take a sober head. When we finished our first drink on the terrace, I followed Shepard inside like a happy puppy and we proceeded to the living room.

"I'll show you something," he said, "and I don't show this to everybody. But you're special, Jordan."

He moved aside a small armchair and stepped on a button concealed underneath the Persian carpet. A mirrored wall panel clicked open and slowly revolved around to reveal a small, temperature-controlled wine room. "For when the Nazis come."

I had exactly the same thought and smiled at how Jews are always on red alert, sniffing out any perceived threat with heightened senses.

"Besides, I don't want those Nazi bastards getting any of it." I pictured an army of Nazis in black boots banging down his front door, vicious German shepherds snarling and straining at their leashes, the poor golden retriever scrambling on the glossy amber floor, and Shepard locked in his secret wine room silently screaming, "You'll never get the Bordeaux!"

It was a lot of house for one person, but Shepard had somehow created a purpose, however gratuitous, for each room. He had a game room with a billiard table for smoking cigars after dinner. An exercise room filled with dazzling white equipment, though unfortunately, he didn't look like he used it much. A library media room with suede sofas and a bar that presented a single-malt tour of the Scottish Highland. There was a formal dining room "for large catered affairs" and a sunroom that Shepard called the "moon room" for more intimate dining. And there was the small, round pine table set in front of the kitchen fireplace, all arranged for "a cozy little dinner chez Blum." Shepard's bedroom was a dark-walled masculine affair, and his closet a showplace of meticulous organization. You'd have to hire a full-time sweater folder just to keep up with it. In every room, you got to know a little more about Shepard: I like big towels. I like deep bathtubs. I like watching TV in the bathroom. I like having different places to eat. I like coming home, taking a swim and a steam. I like getting massaged by the fire. One thing about Shepard, he knew what he liked. I was actually amazed at what I saw. Most single heterosexual males don't know you can live like this.

By the time we made our way back to the kitchen I was sick of martinis and overhungry. I could tell I was drunk because when his cat jumped up on the counter, I said, "Whose pussy is this?"

"It's mine. Whose do you think it is?" Which is exactly what I would've said and I couldn't stop myself from laughing at my own private joke.

"What's so funny?"

"Nothing. Ignore me." I was biting the inside of my cheek.

"You know, Jordan," he said, putting the rice with toasted pine nuts into the microwave, "I'm thinking of getting married."

"Who's the lucky girl?"

"I don't know yet, that's the problem. The thing is, I love women. I love a variety of women but this whole AIDS thing is a drag. Women don't hop into bed anymore like they used to."

"I don't know if there's room in your life for a woman. I don't know where she'd fit in. You even have all your dish patterns. What would there be left for her to do? You've taken up all the closet space. Where would she put her clothes?"

"You could have the downstairs closet."

"Thanks, Shepard, it's a lovely offer." Actually we both knew it wasn't. When a woman reaches her forties, she has no use for this kind of man. She wants a man to function like a good appliance. To be completely dependable.

"Okay, you don't have to marry me. If only you'd come over and sleep with me every once in a while, my life would be perfect."

Shepard was right, his life at that moment was almost perfect. He had the beautiful house, the Cuban cigar for after dinner, the girl who is slightly tipsy but won't mess up the evening with sex, and the duck that was perfectly crisp and glistening. I needed protein immediately. I wanted to push him out of the way, grab a knife, and start carving. But Shepard liked presentation. First he showed me what it looked like in the pan, then he drew the duck up to his nose to inhale, twirled around to let me have a smell, and in so doing, met with an unfortunate patch of duck grease that he had dribbled onto the maple floor in just the wrong spot. Shepard's feet went out from under him so quickly that the duck was propelled out of the dish, flew over his head, and went skidding across the kitchen floor like a hockey puck. Shepard was on his back, his forehead dripping bright red, and a fragrant grease stain down the whole front of his sweater, ruining it forever. I grabbed a dish towel, wet it with water, and knelt on the floor next to him, mopping up his blood. It was going to need stitches.

The manservant had thoughtlessly blocked my car with Shepard's Mercedes, probably because there was no room in the garage with his Land Cruiser and BMW Roadster.

"That fucker! That stupid goddamn son-of-a-bitch dumb fucker can't even figure out where to park a car, dumb fucker!" Shepard stood in the driveway with his bloody dish towel and screamed into the night air. His ranting and raving was psychotically out of proportion to the offense and all I wanted to do was get away fast. But I was stuck with him. "Asshole! What a fucking ASShole!" The only other option was to try to calm Shepard. I quickly volunteered to move the car, but he handed me his keys as if I was also in his employ. "You drive my car."

When I opened the driver's side, I saw what I first thought was a pillow, sitting on the black leather upholstery. But it wasn't a pillow exactly, because it had a curious hole in the center. It was a doughnut pillow. Shepard tried to toss it in back before I realized what it was for, but he wasn't quite fast enough. Neither one of us alluded to it, and it sat quietly on the floor behind the driver's seat. It might as well have been swinging from the rearview mirror. My bladder was bursting with Sapphire gin and my head was spinning with the same and the winding streets of Bel Air never seemed so treacherous.

While Shepard gave his vital statistics to admitting personnel, I found a ladies' room, which was a great relief, and a vending machine that dispensed stale peanut-butter crackers. I took my dinner back to the emergency waiting room, and while Shepard was getting stitched back together, I sobered up reading an old *National Geographic* and *Modern Maturity,* which can sober anyone up. By the time we returned to Shepard's house it was after eleven. We both thought about the duck. I'd put it back into the pan before we left but the cat had jumped up on the counter and eaten his fill. What remained had lost most of its appeal. I guess I had, too, because I never heard from Shepard again. Hershel would've loved it.

My professional life was stuck in the mire of Hollywood politics and my personal life had been derailed by a duck. Only Jonathan made things seem like they were moving along smoothly. All summer he'd come up with new things to do and places to go; dim sum in Monterey Park, a play in Hollywood, a drive up to Santa Barbara for lunch on a Sunday, a new restaurant in Pasadena. He got the tickets, he made the restaurant reservations, he'd RSVP to the screenings, he did the driving. He made it so easy for me I couldn't say no. Nor did I want to.

When autumn came we began staying home and discovered a kind of comforting domesticity. I'd had my fill of frozen entrées and restaurant food. The cool weather had awakened a latent desire to cook hearty stews and chicken with olives and fish soups with rouille. We were one of those couples in the supermarket who chatter back and forth to each other, Jonathan cheerfully playing the role of uxorious husband. "Which wine do you think we should get, darling, the Merlot or Cabernet? Does my angel want Gorgonzola in her salad? And what's your heart's desire for dessert, my sweet?" We acted like intimates but without the burden of feeling responsible for each other's happiness. We never blamed the other for our own bad moods. In a way, it was the perfect marriage.

One Saturday night in November we were sitting in my little living room, the wind blowing cold and dry, rattling the palm fronds just outside the door. It was one of those perfect nights to be staying home. We'd spent five or six Saturday nights like this, renting movies I knew Jonathan should see. *A Face in the Crowd, To Kill a Mockingbird, Dog Day Afternoon, East of Eden, Chinatown, Great Expectations.* Jonathan was lounging on my sofa as he finished a second portion of boeuf Bourguignon and watched *The Wizard of Oz,* which to my amazement and dismay was another movie Jonathan had never seen. He wanted to be a screenwriter, yet it appeared he had no real interest in movies.

I've seen *The Wizard of Oz* too many times to count but that night the movie struck me as being even more poignant than usual, the ending not quite happy. Dorothy wakes up back in Kansas but nothing in her life has changed. In a week or two, when Auntie Em gets impatient with her, Elmira Gulch has come with animal control to put Toto to sleep, and Dorothy realizes she sees life differently from everyone she knows, she'll again be dreaming of a land where her troubles melt like lemon drops. I told Jonathan that originally the powers that be wanted to leave out the song "Somewhere Over the Rainbow" because they thought it slowed the movie down. "Isn't that just perfect?" he said. Then he changed the subject. "This is so great not to always be eating in restaurants. I get really tired of the singles scene."

"Yeah. Me, too."

"You could date if you wanted to." He began to massage the back of my neck, which he knew put me into a limp, dreamy state.

"Don't want to."

"Why not?"

" 'Cause."

"I do. I'm thinking of asking Katie out. What do you think?"

"With or without her boyfriend?"

"She's never going to marry him. She just doesn't know it yet. If she married him that would be such a huge mistake."

"Why not ask someone who's not seeing someone?"

"Like who?"

"Blaire Spector." Jerry Slotnick had moved to the lot and Blaire, his development girl, was one of Jonathan's pals who hung around my office.

"Blaire's just a friend. I don't want to go out with her. She's too fucking neurotic."

"Shelley."

"Shelley?"

"I like Shelley."

"I like Shelley, too, but it doesn't mean I want to go out with her. The problem with Shelley is, she's like every Jewish girl I grew up with. They're all afraid of being too cold or too hot or too tired or too hungry or too full." His voice was whining as he said this, presumably imitating all those unfortunate girls. "They're afraid of *shvitzing* too much or *schlepping* too long and they won't swim in lakes because the bottom could be slimy and they don't like the ocean because there could be an undertow. They only feel safe in their bathtubs because nothing can get at them." As Jonathan was cataloging his distaste for Jewish woman I thought how much it sounded like Jonathan himself. Jonathan wouldn't even tighten the nut on a loose toilet seat, much less dirty his hands changing a tire or pulling a weed. But I suppose it's true that most of us are attracted to people who make up for our own deficiencies. "And they want to discuss FEELINGS. An evening with Shelley inevitably turns to Shelley's feelings, which I don't particularly find that fascinating. Shelley says she wants something different in life but ultimately she'll settle for the NICE Jewish boy and the NICE house and the NICE kids and she'll give the beautiful bar mitzvah, even though now she swears she won't. She'll vote for the liberal candidate and have her in-laws over every Passover. She'll set a beautiful table. I know exactly how Shelley's life is going to turn out, better than Shelley does. There are no surprises in Shelley. None." He took his hand away from my neck, our session abruptly over. I lifted my head and opened my eyes.

"Of course there's always you. I just have a feeling you're full of surprises."

"So you want surprises?"

"Of course, who doesn't? The chase is what's exciting. If there's no chase what fun is it?"

"Eventually you're going to get what you want and then what?"

"Tell you what. I'll let you know if it happens."

MR. AND MRS. SCHADENFREUDE

JUDI AND JOEL were back on the lot doing postproduction on the movie Cantrowitz had gifted them but curiously we never ran into each other. Freyda reported they were "deep into the editing process" and it wasn't the right time to approach them about *Ivy and Men*. But she HAD spoken with Jerry Slotnick, who was ready to hear my *Life* magazine story pitch. He phoned me one morning at the studio, a day before our scheduled meeting. The line was full of static, so I knew he wasn't sitting at his desk.

"How's traffic?"

"Traffic, what traffic? I'm calling from my horse."

"Your HORSE?"

"It's my daughter's horse. What do I know about horses? I'm from Brooklyn, we don't know from wildlife. I sit on the thing like a sack of potatoes and walk it around the property. I'm up in Santa Barbara and I can't come down tomorrow for our meeting. Bob Stern is sending me some architectural plans and I have to go over them with the contractor. You want to come up and we'll talk here? We can meet in the late morning and then I'll take you to lunch."

Ninety miles seemed like a long way to drive, not to mention the ninety miles home. Especially since Jerry's office was right down the hall from me. But I said yes and he gave me directions and told me to come around eleven.

I woke up the next day cursing myself for being such a pleaser. I'd forgotten when I told Jerry I'd drive all the way up to Santa Barbara that morning, I had to drive all the way down to Long Beach that evening for the opening of Hershel's play. I'd be spending most of the day sitting in a car.

I couldn't stop stewing about this as I drove up the coast. All through Malibu and Trancas and Thornhill Broome Beach I was shaking my head in disgust, telling myself I was old enough to say no. Maybe if the sun had been out things wouldn't have felt so bleak, but the sky was colorless and low, indistinguishable from the endless ocean. Just before Oxnard, it turned dark and began to rain. I started to resent Jerry Slotnick, who would never have sent his wife out on rain-slicked roads in an old car without antilock brakes. I was still in a foul mood as I turned inland and drove a straight shot through flat, rich farmland smelling almost delightfully of sulfur. It was miles of organization, all the rows planted so neatly, the green lettuce giving way to red-leafed lettuce becoming square acres of onions and then fragrant celery. Out in the fields the workers were stooped, dressed in their yellow slickers that popped against the leaden gloom. "And you think you have troubles," I said to myself out loud.

I got onto the freeway, which looped back again to the coast, past Rincon Point, where a school of black neoprene surfers were out in the cold gray ocean straddling their boards. And then the road narrowed to an old four-lane highway with a divider of cypress, oaks, and eucalyptus. Citrus orchards dotted the foothills on my right and on my left the ocean pounded the empty beach. The rain had become just a mist, and by the time I got off at my exit and followed the directions up the road toward the mountains, it stopped. A woman on a horse was slowly picking her way down the road toward me and I wondered, What kind of a woman gets to live up here and ride her horse in the middle of the morning in no particular hurry? A bright sun peeked through charcoal clouds and the top of the mountains were lost in the darkness. But everything else, the trees and foliage and flowers, was brilliant in the light, as if their colors had been taken straight from the paint tube without diluting them. The grass glowed almost chartreuse. The pavement was shiny black lacquer, clean and wet, and then I saw a rainbow and followed it right to Jerry Slotnick's house.

I stopped in front of his gates, which were old and impressive enough for me to think of Manderley, the imposing estate I'd seen dozens of times on the *Million Dollar Movie* reruns of *Rebecca*. Only instead of the handsome, mysterious, and tortured Maxim De Winter waiting for me at the end of the drive, I'd find Jerry Slotnick, who was only tortured. He'd given me his code in case he wasn't around to hear the intercom, and when I punched in the numbers, the tall, black iron gates slowly parted.

A gardener was raking the gravel driveway and waved as I drove slowly past, my tires crunching up the long narrow road lined with gray olive trees. I parked in front of a four-car garage. The doors were open and Jerry's burgundy convertible Jaguar was parked on the polished terrazzo floor. No oil spots here. No cobwebs, old paint cans, dirty shovels, or half-used bags of Bandini fertilizer. This garage looked like a new-car showroom.

The house itself was a low, Spanish hacienda, with attention paid to authentic detail. But it looked like an expensive remodel, just a little too big and pristine. An ancient bougainvillea, its boa constrictor trunk wrapped around the wooden beam of the deep front portal, became a bright, magenta awning. A three-tiered stone fountain provided the soothing splash of water and from somewhere came the whinnying of a horse. Jerry Slotnick, producer and *patrón*, was nowhere to be found. The door to the service porch was standing open and I entered with the obligatory, "Hello?"

"In here."

I followed the voice through a large Mexican-tiled kitchen, where a maid was polishing plant leaves with milk dipped in cotton balls. We acknowledged each other and she said, "Mr. Jerry is in the dining room."

Mr. Jerry was in his tennis shorts, studying architectural plans, which covered a long refectory table waxed a warm dark brown. His wispy ponytail was gone and he'd grown a beard, which improved his appearance a thousand times, although he'd never be mistaken for a diplomat. Jerry was on his portable phone, telling someone on the other end what to do, his hand slipped underneath his polo shirt where he was absentmindedly pulling on his chest hair. I stepped out to the back portal to let him have his privacy. Over the treetops was a view of the ocean right out to the oil platforms. The Channel Islands looked so clear and close, they appeared only a canoe ride away. Blue sky and white billowy clouds had replaced the old sky and it felt like a whole new day. I wondered if the illusive Mrs. Slotnick felt sad when she'd have to head back to L.A. I already anticipated feeling that way.

"You want some coffee?" Jerry called out, and I stepped back inside the house, realizing he was off the phone.

"No thanks, I'm fine."

"I'm having two outbuildings built and they're starting construction tomorrow. That's why I gotta be here. You leave workmen alone, something's gonna get fucked up. I was just on the phone to the contractor."

I bent over the plans and he pointed out where the guest house/ changing room and office were going to be on the property. "Right down there, by the pool." I looked outside and saw two people by the pool, a woman and a boy. Large houses always seem to have platoons of gardeners and maintenance people and guests drifting in and out. The more house the less privacy. Then I turned back to the renderings and saw the architect's name printed in neat block lettering.

"Bob Stern, your architect, is Robert A. M. Stern?"

"He better fucking well be. He's costing me enough," Jerry said, and then suggested we go out to the patio where we could talk without the vacuum cleaner.

Jerry scooted in the heavy wrought-iron patio chair, knocking into the table, spilling some of his coffee into the saucer. He abandoned the saucer and set the dripping cup on a pristine white script, which was piled with other scripts on the round glass table. As he drank, he left a series of brown rings across the covers of them all, Shawn Hively's *Blind Justice* included.

"What's this?" I asked, pointing to Hively's script, ever anxious to find out what successful writers are working on.

"Terrific writer. Young kid. Just out of USC. Wrote a great script for me about a blind karate master. One of the best pitches I've ever heard. I took it to Cantrowitz, who went crazy over it and bought it in two seconds. This is gonna make *The Karate Kid* and Bruce Lee and Steven Seagal look like a piece of shit." After that one, my LIFE idea seemed pretty tame and I was sorry I'd asked. It wasn't the greatest lead-in but I had no choice, so I sat there on the beautiful patio and told Jerry my story idea.

Jerry was attentive, pulling his chest hair as he listened, making acknowledgments. "Yeah, yeah, uh-huh, uh-huh, I got it, okay . . ." When I was done, he nodded his head, mulling it over. "So the girl's a showgirl. That's good. I never liked that Margaret Bourke-White idea. Too much khaki. When you were talking, I kept thinking Marilyn Monroe. It's the fifties. Who's her role model? Marilyn. All those blonds wanted to be Marilyn back then. She's beautiful and she's innocent and the guys are competing for her, which adds some good tension. One's established and famous, the other young and sort of in awe of the photographer, I like that. I just don't want it to be too heavy about the government thing, about the bomb going off too close to civilization and the fallout because I think that's another movie altogether. But I like the relationships. It's good. It's very castable."

Meeting over. My troubles hadn't exactly melted away like lemon drops but at least Jerry hadn't added to them. I had no idea how Jerry would respond to the story and I realized that's why I was so annoyed at him on my drive up; because I'd anticipated having to justify and defend. Jerry had spent seven minutes with me as producer and now I was free to spend the next six months alone as writer. Time for lunch. Jerry had the same idea.

"I made a reservation at a restaurant just down the street here. My sister and her kid are out from New York for a few days. I thought they could join us. Otherwise they have nothing to do."

"Of course," I said, surprised he'd asked my permission.

Flo sat on a patio chair in her black walking shorts and black opaque stockings looking anything but poolside. Jerry and I made our way across the lawn and she looked up as if she'd finally spotted the crosstown bus she'd been waiting for, only it was too crowded to get a seat. A solid, dumpy woman, she regarded us through over-sized, overdesigned eyeglasses with arms that looped up from the bottom of the frame. Her dark hair was clipped like a poodle, a solid mass of curls on top of her head and a closely shaved neck. Her mouth was set in a look of permanent discontent. When she saw us approaching she pulled her blazer closed to hide her stomach. Her pudgy son was lying on a chaise doing his homework. From the moment we were introduced I knew why I'd been invited. Jerry did not want to be alone with his sister.

"Everything was WET," Flo said, making it sound like something Jerry should fix. "I had to wipe everything down. This weather's so CRAZY here. You never know WHAT it's going to do."

"You know, you can turn on the Jacuzzi if you want. You and Maurice could go in the Jacuzzi if it's too cold to use the pool."

"I'm not goin' in there," Maurice said, as if Jerry had suggested he enter a snake-infested swamp. "Bernie Skinoff."

"Bernie Skinoff?" Jerry said, looking at Maurice and then at me. "Who's Bernie Skinoff?"

Maurice sighed, summoning up all the patience he had in his ten-year-old body. "You can Burn-Your-Skin-Awwwf." Jerry disregarded his nephew's sarcasm and changed the subject.

"You hungry? You ready for lunch?"

"Maurice, are you hungry?" Flo asked her son.

He shrugged. "I guess so."

"Good," Jerry said as if nothing was amiss. "So let's eat."

We all piled into the convertible Jaguar. Flo volunteered to sit in the back with her son, although the moment she got back there, she was sorry. "You'd think in a luxury car like this they'd give you some legroom. You practically need a CRANE to get in and out of this thing." Like a rebuke, she held her hands on her little poodle curls to keep them from blowing in the wind. I felt a comfort with them that put me on edge. There was something much too familiar about Jerry and his family. Sitting in the front and feeling guilty about my legroom, I turned around in my seat and asked Flo how she was enjoying California, which, she informed me, was way too big. "Jerry had his assistant take us to Disneyland. It took Blaire, how long did it take Blaire, Jerry?" He ignored her and she went right on talking.

"I don't know how long it took her. We hit traffic and it just took us forever to get there, is all I know. At one point the traffic was just stopped. Totally stopped. I don't know how you people do it. Everything is so far away. At home, I want to go shopping, everything's in the neighborhood. Or I take a subway. All this driving isn't for me." Then she went on to say how she could never move here because she'd miss Loehmann's. "I have a girl who puts things aside for me. They even let me return." It was strange to think Jerry's life had been saved by a salesgirl he'd never met.

As soon as she mentioned her shopping haunt I knew why I found Flo so off-putting. She was Francine Fingerman. She was Shelley and Blaire and all the other Jewish girls Jonathan had spoken of with fearful derision. She was one of the reasons Jerry had married the invisible Japanese wife.

I caught Jerry's irritated look as he sat behind the wheel of his Jaguar, and had a disturbing realization. We were more alike than I'd believed possible. He was doing whatever he could to escape; the house in Oz, the expensive architect, the horse, the wife. Flo was an unrelenting reminder of what he'd tried to leave behind. I would've married a quiet Japanese woman, too, if I'd been Flo's brother. As it was, I'd married Hart, for much the same reasons. To get as far away as I could from the hand-wringing heaviness of it all.

Maurice clumped his way toward the restaurant and I had the urge to reach out and straighten up his hunched shoulders. Suggest he spend the summer at one of those "Lose Weight . . . You Bet I Did!" camps advertised in the back of *The New York Times Magazine*. The first thing he did when we sat down was knock over the little glass cruet of olive oil and rosemary sitting on our table.

"Watch it," Jerry said to him. "You almost got it all over the place."

"You think I did it on PURPose?"

"He didn't do it on PURpose," Flo said to her brother, as annoyed at him as he'd been at Maurice.

"I didn't say he did it on purpose, I just said to be careful," Jerry said, backing down. Fortunately the waiter interrupted us with three menus.

"Where's MY menu?" Maurice demanded of him. The waiter was

young, probably a college boy, who didn't reckon on having to deal with the likes of Maurice or Flo to work his way through school.

"Can he have his own menu PLEASE?" Flo said, as if trying to remain civilized in a world of heathens.

I could feel Jerry's tension. "He can have my menu," he said, giving Maurice the coveted item. "I know what I'm having."

The waiter left with our drink order and Flo turned to her brother, not willing to let it pass.

"He's a grown-up person. He should have his own menu."

"What's the big deal? You think he wanted to slight Maurice on purpose? Maybe he just forgot to bring four menus."

"How do you forGET to bring four menus? It's not like we're a whole table. We're FOUR PEOPLE sitting here."

"I don't want to look at someone else's menu," Maurice said. "I should have my own. He shoulda known that."

"I wonder what the risotto of the day is," I mused out loud.

Flo then began the negotiation with Maurice about what he should eat. "Try the fish, you eat pasta all the time, you need some protein."

"I hate fish."

"You don't hate fish. You like sole, the way I do it at home. With the almonds. You like tuna salad."

"Yeah, but that's TUNA fish," he said, as if it didn't come out of the same ocean.

"SO? This is FRESH tuna fish. It's a good fish. If you don't want the fish, get the spaghetti with meat sauce." I glanced at Jerry and could see the pain in his face. I was starting to get pretty tense myself. When Maurice knocked over his glass of Coke I expected something to blow but Jerry calmly and slowly handed his napkin to Maurice.

"Don't look at him like that," Flo snapped as she soaked up the table with her own napkin.

"Did I look at him? Did I look at him any special way?" Jerry turned to me for confirmation that his sister was crazy. "I'm handing over my napkin to him. What more can I do? What do you have such a bug up your ass for?"

"You know, Jerry, I don't care how rich you are. I don't care how much of a big man you are or who you know. I don't like you talking to me like that."

"What are you talking about 'who I know?' Who do I know?"

"You know who you know. You're always putting us down. You think you're so superior. You treat us like we're nothing. Like we're your inferiors you can walk all over."

"I flew you and Maurice out here. I put you up at my house. I'm building you a guest house. How am I treating you badly? Explain it to me. Please."

"You're not just building the guest house for us," Maurice said. "You're going to have other guests there, too."

"Maurice, you're a kid," Jerry shot back. "I don't want to hear from you right now. Shut up, okay?"

"Don't talk to Maurice like that. You see? You see? You have no respect for our feelings." She grabbed her purse and stood up from the table. "Let's go, Maurice."

"Where are you going?" Jerry asked, still trying to sound patient.

"I'm going home. I'm going to call about a flight out of here."

"How are you going to get to the airport?"

Don't look at me, I thought. But Flo and Maurice never answered him. They were out the door of the restaurant grabbing for each other's hand.

"Do you believe them? Do you believe them?" Jerry said to me. "Her *gonif* husband leaves her and the kid with nothing and I buy them a condominium and send them money every month and she actually begrudges me. Never have I gotten a genuine or heartfelt thank-you from that woman."

"Maybe she feels bad being dependent on you," I said.

"Well, I feel bad she's dependent on me, too, believe me. But what am I supposed to do? She hates me for being successful. Like she doesn't benefit from it. You know what I call Maurice? The BoyMan. Because she treats him like her little husband. Does he act like a kid to you? Except for spilling everything, that kid's forty years old. The two of them are miserable Jews. And you want to know something? I'm going to wind up sending that kid to college. That's the beauty of it."

"Maybe she feels she doesn't fit into your life because it's too nice for them. Maybe she feels diminished and threatened by it." I don't know why I was defending Flo.

"Can I tell you something? They would rather be in Brooklyn right now. They would rather complain and feel miserable than sit here and have a good time. Because she's only comfortable around misery. Give her someone with colitis or shingles and she's there in a second. She loves cancer. A car accident or root canal really gets her happy. But give her a beautiful house and a beautiful day and a good restaurant and she and that kid start looking for something to be miserable about. They accuse me of acting superior but they only feel superior when they're martyred. There's no winning with people like that," Jerry said, as if he was trying to convince himself not to feel guilty. "There's just no winning." Then he asked for the check, although we'd hardly touched our food.

Flo and Maurice hadn't gotten too far from the restaurant and for lack of sidewalks were walking in the road. Jerry pulled over just ahead of them and I got out of the car and slid into the miniature backseat. When Flo and Maurice walked up alongside the car I could see that they were both crying.

"Will you get in the car already," Jerry said to her as gently as he could.

"We're fine."

"You don't have to walk. Just get in the car and I'll drive you back."

"Jerry, we're walking. Maurice and I are walking."

"I don't know why you want to walk," Jerry said, but it was obvious he wasn't going to get anywhere with them and the two of us drove home. I stayed in the back and Jerry chauffeured, which might've looked a little odd to anyone who didn't know the history of that lunch or how hard it was to extricate oneself from that seat.

I said good-bye to Jerry in his driveway and he apologized for subjecting me to family shit. I told him not to worry about it. I realized I liked Jerry. He was graceless but with a good heart, though I didn't want to spend one more second around him.

I got into my car as fast as I could and, heading down the driveway, saw Flo and Maurice. I waved to them and smiled as if nothing had transpired and she waved back and smiled at me. She'd probably already composed the story she'd tell her girlfriends. Just as I was already composing the story I'd tell Jonathan.

By the time I drove home, Maurice and Flo were just another bump in the day I'd left behind. There was still one more event to get through before I could climb into my little bed and close the curtains on the world.

"I made dinner reservations at a Greek restaurant in Long Beach that's supposed to be great," Jonathan said when I called him at the office. "I made them at six so we'll have plenty of time to get to the play by eight. I figure we can always go out with Hershel and Miriam to the Queen Mary for a drink afterward."

"I think there's supposed to be a little party afterward." I already pictured myself leaving the party early.

Hershel was dressed up in his only suit, the one he wore to weddings, bar mitzvahs, all his openings, and funerals. He'd gotten his hair cut and his beard trimmed, like a successful playwright who'd be going to Sardi's after the performance. Miriam was wearing a black dress, black boots, and her beads. Her cheeks were two pink circles of rouge, like a marionette. She had four trays of lemon bars and brownies she'd baked for the party, and Jonathan helped carry them into the theater from her car and put them on folding tables in the basement rec room. None of Hershel's children could make it, which was why I was glad Jonathan had come. Only Hershel's father, Abe, showed up. Miriam had driven down to Leisure World earlier that day to get him and his girlfriend.

Hershel wasn't particularly close with his father, who looked dapper in his vest and tweed sport jacket. Abe had made his living as a diamond cutter in New York and was a critical, tyrannical parent. But now that he'd grown old, his feistiness and independence made for good material and an "Abe character" began appearing in Hershel's plays.

Abe's girlfriend, Minna, sparkled in a blue sequined sweater Miriam couldn't stop admiring. She was a little woman with fine, apricot-colored hair, curled, teased, and sprayed into a nimbus, and bright pink lipstick, most of which was on her teeth.

"I can't wait to see Hershel's play," she said to Miriam.

"It's so good. I only hope the actors are worthy of the material. Hershel said the female lead keeps wanting to change his lines. Can you imagine? Doing that to a playwright?" Hershel, who was telling someone else the exact same thing, had overheard.

"It's a brilliant play," he said as if he were reviewing someone else's material. "The lines are like poetry. You don't change poetry."

"Of course not," Jonathan, standing at my side, added. "That's the whole point of being playwright. Your words are sacred."

Miriam put her hands firmly and squarely on Jonathan's cheeks like a mother blessing her child. "Oy, what a *ziskeit* this boy is."

Then Hershel disappeared into the theater to talk with the director and we all took our seats. Miriam was pleased to see a full house and seemed surprised at how many temple members were there, as if she herself hadn't goaded everyone into coming.

The play was called *Vilna Redux* and dealt with the aftermath of the death of Abe's second wife and his move down to Leisure World after his cataract surgery and his pacemaker implant. He fought the move every step of the way because he didn't want to be with a bunch of old people. Finally his granddaughter, writing her Ph.D. thesis and needing a free place to live, decided to move in with him.

Abe and his granddaughter become established in their different routines and learn to stay out of each other's way. However, when the granddaughter meets Minna in the laundry room, the two women get to talking and the granddaughter decides it's time her grandfather has a date. She tries to become the matchmaker but Abe keeps insisting he's not interested in any more women. When the granddaughter goes away for a week, Minna stops by his place with one of the granddaughter's socks, which had been left clinging to the side of the dryer. Abe invites Minna into his apartment. Minna lights the Sabbath candles for him, and when they start to talk, they find out that they both come from Vilna. They reminisce about the old country, she cooks him a nice meal, they sing an old Yiddish song, and they go to bed together. End of act one.

Act two. They can't get enough of each other. Every night Minna is at the apartment. When they find out the granddaughter has cut her vacation short and is on her way home, they run around his apartment hiding her Mevacor and her nightgown and her face cream and her nitroglycerin patches so the granddaughter doesn't find out what they've been up to. Of course, part of it is the joy of having illicit sex after all these years, and they both want to keep up the pretension that nothing is going on, to prolong the excitement. It wasn't Chekhov, but it was sweet, touching, and gently wry. The audience seemed to like it. Although I couldn't vouch for the BoyMan, I was pretty sure the play would have even appealed to Flo. Abe and Minna got a huge kick out of seeing their lives portrayed on the stage, as did Miriam, who cackled the whole way through. After it was over, when we were all standing around the rec room eating Miriam's desserts, Minna announced to Jonathan and me, like an old star who doesn't want to get off the stage, that she wanted us to know what REALLY happened. "Hershel's only telling half the truth. He makes out like I'm some kind of a floozy, although I did give Abe a nice dinner that first night, as I remember, but it was mostly leftovers I had in the refrigerator, and we went back to eat it in my place." Hershel and Miriam were beaming with all the accolades, and after Miriam told me for the third time how funny the play was, it was time to go home.

Not until we got in the car did Jonathan volunteer his opinion.

"Well, THAT was like a not-too-good episode of *The Golden Girls.*"

"That's all you think it was?" I felt the criticism was a little harsh. I was also taken aback because I thought Jonathan liked the play. He'd laughed in all the right places and after it was over he'd stayed talking to Hershel as the others came by to congratulate him. But I realized Jonathan felt nothing toward Hershel's characters. I didn't know if it was a generational difference or just something in Jonathan.

"I kept hearing about how brilliant this play was going to be. Competent, maybe, but that's about it. The problem with Hershel is he doesn't have any commercial instincts. He writes to a very limited audience. I can see why he never became a great screenwriter. I mean, who is this play going to appeal to? Everyone in Leisure World, a few temple members, and the Hadassah ladies. Who wants to watch a play about two old Jews having sex except maybe two old Jews having sex? I'm afraid it's pretty forgettable."

He was right about the play's appeal . . . it closed after three weekends. All the work Hershel had done, the time he'd spent, and the endless rewrites had netted seven hundred and fifty dollars. Jonathan knew Hershel was the failure we all hoped he wasn't. Only it didn't seem to dampen Hershel's enthusiasm for himself. Or alter Miriam's opinion of him. But, as Minna would say, Jonathan was only telling half the truth. Maybe some of the audience thought Hershel's play forgettable. But, like his recitation of "Casey at the Bat," Jonathan managed to remember it quite well.

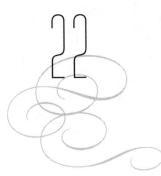

AND TO ALL
A GOOD NIGHT

"FRANKIE SPANKY."

I looked up from my computer. Jonathan stood in the doorway of my office as if he wasn't sure he should interrupt. We only saw each other at work now. The movie and dinner evenings at my place had stopped when I'd begun writing the LIFE script. Jerry was anxious to get it before Cantrowitz lost interest and I was anxious to finish it before Jerry lost interest.

"Can it wait?"

He rolled his eyes in mock exasperation. "Will you get that script done already? How am I supposed to pull this thing off on my own?" It was a question that demanded another question.

"What 'thing'?"

"I've decided to give a Christmas party." He came into my room and made himself comfortable on the sofa, forcing me to turn around and face him. "I want it to be like an old-fashioned New England Christmas. You know, with eggnog and one of those cute chocolate Yule logs for dessert. I need you to help me shop for Christmas-tree ornaments and come up with a great menu and the right wine and tell me where I should go to get all this stuff. I figure we can leave campus over lunch period today and still be back here before the bell."

Jonathan earned a modest salary and he wasn't ashamed to admit his parents still sent him money every month. How else could he afford the pretty pastel Ralph Lauren shirts and the dinners at good restaurants? I knew Jonathan wasn't exactly hurting but he couldn't be extravagant with this party either. "You're welcome to just borrow my Christmas-tree ornaments. They're nice ones and I'm not going to use them and Hart isn't using them and that will save you money right there."

"I should get my own Christmas ornaments. I mean, this is my first tree. And I don't want any fucking filler icicles either. I want it to look like a really homey old-fashioned you-put-your-ornaments-in-a-box-in-the-attic-and-you-drag-them-out-every-year kind of a Christmas tree."

Off we went to Pier 1. We decided he should start out with a couple dozen shiny red apples and then we found some reproduction antique glass ornaments from Germany in a Christmas-tree shop. The ones he liked were rather expensive and it all added up to a tidy sum, but Jonathan insisted he'd have them for the rest of his life. In the Pottery Barn I threw some cinnamon pinecone potpourri into his basket and he grabbed some squat red candles. At Sav-On, he bought strings of tiny white lights and red-and-green paper napkins. Instead of writing, I found myself creating the menu and shopping list for him. Instead of doing research on my script, I researched Honey-baked Hams. This party was Jonathan's big show and before I knew it I'd become his lowly production assistant.

Jonathan spent days composing the fifty-five invitations, each one with a personal note geared to the level of the invitee: *Hope you can make it. Love to see you again. Hey, you big piece of shit—get your ass over to my party,* and so on.

Freyda was the first to decline. She told him she had a previous engagement, but I knew Freyda was covering for Marty, who would never have gone to some secretary's apartment for a party. Ian Mandel's secretary called to say Ian wasn't going to make it (for much the same reason I suspected) although she would be there. Jonathan got a few more declines and I have to say I was beginning to worry he'd reached a little high. In addition, Jonathan had made out a B-list, hoping to catch some of the big fish along with the little. I still didn't understand what he thought he might gain, but he seemed unafraid of being rebuffed.

Surprisingly, Hershel and Miriam were an A, the only time they'd ever been considered so in Hollywood. Jonathan must've thought they had some cachet because Hershel's play had gotten a good notice in the L.A. Times, which Jonathan had cut out and mailed to Hershel with a congratulatory note. Heller and Weiss were A-writers at the studio, so they were also on Jonathan's A-list. I was an A because I was his boss and Katie was an A because she was unattainable. The B-list was Mai Lei and Sparky and Suzi Piccioni and Blaire Spector and the other assistants, secretaries, and development girls.

The week after invitations went out twenty-eight people said they were definitely coming. I suspected there would be more who were holding out to see if a better offer came. Jonathan revised his list with checks and little reminders to follow up with phone calls and by the second week in December we were ordering the ham. I took him to Trader Joe's and bought the wine and pâtés and nonfat bean dip with chips and goat cheese, which I told him to marinate in olive oil and herbs. I gave him his Christmas present early, a big serving platter, and told him I'd be happy to help him set up before the party, but Jonathan said it wasn't necessary. I'd never been to his apartment and imagined wine in plastic cups and everyone jockeying for position on the floor with paper plates of food balanced on their laps.

West Hollywood is a mixed neighborhood of Spanish thick-walled apartments from the twenties and thirties and trashy paper-thin condos from the sixties and seventies. Miriam drove their Mazda and Hershel held on his lap a *Shabbes* carrot ring in a bundt pan. The other carrot ring was at his feet and she kept reminding him not to step in it. I sat in the backseat with the hummus and crudités platter and we all squinted out the window trying to find the address.

"Someone else is having a party," Miriam said when she saw the valet parking sign in front of Jonathan's apartment complex. "They're going to take up all the good spaces. Maybe I'll let you out here so you can bring in the food." Which is what she did, stopping the car in the middle of the street. The valet came jogging over.

"We're not going to YOUR party," Miriam said to him, putting down her window as Hershel and I were climbing out of the car, blocking traffic in both directions.

"This is for the Jonathan Prince party," the valet said as if he'd been explaining it all evening.

Miriam was delighted. "He got valet parking? I don't have to look for a place to park in this *feckuckteh* neighborhood?"

"No, ma'am."

"Valet parking. Do you BELIEVE he got valet parking?" She laughed as if one of her kids had made good. "I wonder what that cost him. But it's a good idea. Who wants to go *schlepping* around this neighborhood looking for a place to park?"

I had a different reaction. As we walked up the steps into the courtyard of Jonathan's apartment, I realized I was bothered by his extravagance. This generous gesture wasn't meant to save his guests the trouble of parking a few blocks away. It was meant to distinguish himself. Jonathan was throwing a party people would talk about. He might not have attracted the right people this year but this was just a setup for next Christmas and all the Christmas parties to come.

Jonathan lived in one of the older, nicer buildings on the block, six duplex apartments opening onto a long courtyard filled with giant bird of paradise. Unlike the other tenants, who'd decorated with wreaths and foil-wrapped red poinsettias right from the grocery store, Jonathan's doorway had a large urn with a sculptural bare white birch branch wrapped in tiny white lights. It looked like something lifted out of a display window at Saks Fifth Avenue. The front door was open, waiting for the guests. White poinsettias in clay pots filled an entryway table on which a paisley shawl had been thrown.

Miriam, Hershel, and I stepped into the living room, which was already crowded with revelers. There was one L-shaped sofa against the wall and the rest of the apartment was taken up with four round tables for ten, set with white linen, tall silver candlesticks, and tall white candles. At each place setting was a small gift wrapped in crimson tissue paper, tied with a silver cord. A dozen votive candles stood on the white plaster mantelpiece of the nonworking fireplace and more candles were placed on each step of the dark-stained oak stairs leading to the second floor. The effect was dramatic and startling. So much for a homey Christmas.

Miriam, Hershel, and I stood in the room holding our offerings like bemused Magi.

"Wow," Miriam said. "This kid has style."

"No one celebrates Christmas as beautifully as a Jew," Hershel said with the sarcasm he reserved for Jews who celebrate Christmas.

"I can't believe he pulled this together himself." Besides the corn-stalk plant in the office and the flowers stuck in a cheap vase, I'd never seen Jonathan show much interest in decor.

"I couldn't see Noah giving a party like this, ever." Noah, their son, was roughly Jonathan's age, but acted it. "Could you, Hershel?"

"I couldn't see YOU giving a party like this."

The coveted tree Jonathan had finally attained stood by the fireplace wrapped with large raffia bows. Instead of the string of lights, there were little tin candleholders with white unlit candles. We walked up to the tree for a closer inspection, but I couldn't find any of the ornaments Jonathan and I had bought together. Hanging from the branches were dried pomegranates and pinecones and tiny stalks of wheat.

A stocky man wearing turquoise contacts and a beige sweater wrapped around his shoulders minced his way toward us, an official party-greeter smile on his mustachioed face. So, it wasn't Jonathan with the style after all. It was Henri Faroli.

"Is that hummus? Wooonderful. I smell the garlic already." He lifted the platter from my hands and the limp arms of the sweater hugging his neck got right in the dip, garlic and all.

"Mine needs to be heated all the way through before it's served," Miriam instructed, without giving thought to who he might be.

"Just give it to Rufina in the kitchen and tell her what you want her to do." Henri the hostess. How Jonathan had seduced him into decorating his apartment for the party I could only surmise. It crossed my mind that maybe Jonathan was gay or that Henri Faroli hoped so, but then I spotted Jonathan with Katie and I understood this show was partly for her. She'd brought the male version of herself, a square-jawed blond chap who was over six feet tall. He was holding a cup of eggnog and was nodding very seriously at something Jonathan was saying. Jonathan had his work cut out, I thought.

Hershel and Miriam headed for the kitchen and I followed Henri as he wove his way through the guests toward the dining room, where a white linen table was set up with hors d'oeuvres.

"Let's just put it right here next to the pâtés." He rearranged the tabletop and put my platter where it would look the prettiest.

"So how do you know Jonathan?" I asked, couching extreme curiosity in the all-purpose party icebreaker.

"He's the tenant of some dear friends of mine. Reese and Charles. They own this marvelous building, although they should be publicly flayed for planting those begonias in the courtyard. One of these days I'm going to come over with a couple gallons of motor oil."

"The apartment looks great. I love the Christmas tree."

"With a little help from his friends."

"How so?"

"When I saw how he was going to desecrate his tree, I went home and dragged out some things from the back of my closet." His voice was affectedly delicate and simperingly sweet, which missed the mark of cultured grande dame and made him seem instead like a prunish old maid. My eyes were drawn to his mouth and the sprinkling of poppy seeds in his jumbled teeth. I had obviously caught him prematurely sampling the strudel. His two cocker spaniels with raffia bows around their necks had caught him, too. They were wiggling their stubby little tails as they jumped up and down, checking out the hors d'oeuvres.

"Do Mr. Darcy and Lady Mudpaw want a G.G.C.?"

"G.G.C.?"

"Good Girl Cookie." Then he spread the marinated goat cheese onto sesame-studded heart-shaped water crackers and I walked away, glad something I'd done for Jonathan wasn't going to waste.

"Isn't this cool?" Jonathan appeared as I was pouring wine into a rented stemmed glass. "Did you see I got help in the kitchen? She works as a maid for my landlords. Is that cool or what?"

"Very cool."

"The tables look great, don't they? The candlesticks are from the

Pottery Barn. We saw them there but you didn't think to tell me to buy them. This gay friend of my landlords told me to get them. They weren't even that expensive."

It wasn't the words that were so curious, it was the intonation. It came out as if I'd disappointed Jonathan, let him down. Jonathan had gotten someone much better to help him and didn't mind letting me know. Before I could respond he went on.

"How 'bout the tree? Doesn't it look professional? Henri, the faggot-decorator candlestick guy, thought the ornaments you helped me pick out were way too ordinary. And he HATED the red candles and pinecone potpourri you wanted me to use. The ONLY scent is bitter orange. My landlord calls him Mrs. Billy Baldwin. He set the tables, too. He told me to keep everything all white. 'All white is soooo elegant,' " he said, imitating Henri Faroli. "That's why it's good to hire a professional."

"Did you HIRE him?" I asked, not bothering to remind Jonathan that he, not me, had picked out the red candles.

"Are you kidding? Of course not. He probably had nothing to do tonight. I think he's kind of lonely. Did you check out the spittly drool in the corners of his mouth? The guy's really weird. Even my landlords think he's weird. He kind of attached himself to me. You're going to have to stay late to make sure he leaves. Maybe I should introduce him to Sparky."

"I wouldn't do that. I like Sparky."

"Henri Faroli would probably like Sparky, too. Excuse me," he said. "I guess I'd better do my Noel Coward routine and go charm my guests."

I stood looking at Henri Faroli's perfect Christmas tree, annoyed beyond reason. No matter how I tried, I couldn't seem to get a grip on life. What I craved—success, recognition, satisfaction—was out of my control, dependent on other people's whims. Yet Jonathan, this kid, had a way of getting exactly what he wanted. Jonathan had replaced me without a second thought. Henri may have thought he was responsible for the evening. But he, like me, was only an un-witting gofer.

While Jonathan took care of the guests, I could see Henri Faroli dealing with the less aesthetic aspects of entertaining; keeping track of the time, making sure hors d'oeuvres didn't extend into the dinner hour, picking up errant olives from the floor. At precisely eight o'clock Henri Faroli lit the candles on the Christmas tree and the room spontaneously hushed, as if we were all observing a holy ritual. Then Jonathan announced dinner was served.

Our table, the A-table, was closest to the tree, and consisted of Hershel and Miriam, Heller and Weiss, their dates, Katie and her boyfriend, me, and, of course, Jonathan. Miriam picked up the little crimson-wrapped gift. "What's this?" I half-noticed she'd come to the table with a damp dish towel draped over one shoulder, but it looked so natural for her it didn't strike me as odd.

"It's just a little gift for everyone," Jonathan said.

Weiss picked up the present and shook it. "How'd you know my size?"

"A gift," Miriam cooed, enchanted by the notion that someone would actually buy her a gift.

Then we all opened our little packages. Jonathan had given each person at the party a Christmas ornament, the ones he said he was going to keep forever. The A-table got the German ornaments, the B-tables got the apples.

"It's just a little something," Jonathan said, and Miriam, the infidel, turned to me with her golden glass Santa and rolled her eyes as if to say, *I'm a JEW. What am I supposed to do with THIS?* Then she whispered she'd give it to Mrs. Dickson, the teacher in whose classroom she worked. That decided, she quickly wrapped the Santa in tissue paper and hid it in her purse, like it was a crucifix with all the trimmings.

"Does everyone at the table know everyone?" Jonathan asked. "Let me see. Frankie, of course, is the most important person here because she actually employs me."

"You actually hired this dude?" Heller asked.

"Hey, I'm a great assistant, right?" He turned to me.

"The best," I said, playing along.

"And Hershel is a fantastic playwright who just had a play produced that the *L.A. Times* gave rave reviews." It wasn't exactly a rave and it was only one small review but who was going to quibble with Jonathan's panegyric? Certainly not Hershel or Miriam.

"It's a hit in Finland," Miriam announced. "We just heard from Hershel's agent. They love it over there. It's actually making money."

I could see Hershel was seething at her remark but I couldn't figure out why. Miriam was insensitive to his reaction and oblivious to anything except Lady Mudpaw, who had two paws in her lap, heading for a third.

"Miriam is an amazing gourmet cook and she's the one who brought this," Jonathan said, pointing to the *Shabbes* carrot ring. Miriam wasn't a gourmet cook. She cooked a nice potato and nice peas and a nice roast chicken.

"This is SO GOOD," Katie said, and Heller and Weiss's dates both agreed.

"It's easy. I'll give you the recipe," Miriam said. "And it freezes beautifully."

"I'd love the recipe."

"And Katie gives great script coverage and finds properties for Judi Golden and Joel Dweck to produce. And Chet is a doctor."

"What kind of doctor?" Miriam asked.

"I'm specializing in plastic surgery. I'm doing my residency at UCLA."

"You're a good person to know. Let's keep in touch," Heller's date said, and as the table guffawed, Katie turned her serene blue eyes on Chet, reached over, and gently took his hand. I gave Jonathan zero chance of winning Katie away. Jonathan quickly redirected any further attention Chet might receive by continuing his introductions over the laughter. Heller's date was an "amazing assistant producer" on a local news show and Weiss's date was a "terrific, talented actress" who was also writing a "really funny" screenplay.

"And lastly but not leastly Heller and Weiss, we don't actually know their first names, but they are very hip screenwriters who use a lot of words like 'dude' in their screenplays."

"Because, DUDE, Cantrowitz thinks every kid talks that way, DUDE," Heller said, defending his writing. Then he turned to Hershel. "Writing plays must be so satisfying. Although, I mean, I actually don't know what I'd DO with my life if I didn't have to keep on getting notes from studio executives and keep on rewriting. I'd have too much time on my hands. I'd probably have to take up wood-working or surfing or something."

"You rewrote that Southern movie," Miriam said, remembering where she'd seen them before. I held my breath, hoping she wouldn't let slip what she'd thought of it. But like the smart dudes they were, they beat her to it.

"We don't talk about that," Weiss said.

"We don't fess up to that," Heller said.

"It was just a quick dialogue polish," Weiss added. "It didn't help much unfortunately. The script had major story problems."

"It was like trying to rebuild a rickety house on a sinking foundation. That script needed to be torn down and totally reconstructed from scratch," Heller concluded, as if he'd rehearsed it a hundred times.

Ian Mandel was mighty smart to have declined Jonathan's party. But that's the danger of Hollywood: no place is safe. Wherever you go, there's always someone you don't want to see.

"The trouble with writing scripts," Hershel said in his quiet, professorial elder-statesman voice, which made everyone at the table lean in to listen, "is that the writer is treated with such contempt by the powers that be that they begin to see their own work as contemptible. They lose respect for their craft because no one else has respect for it."

"It's so true," Heller said. I loved Heller and Weiss. Two mediocre writers at best, complaining their work wasn't recognized or appreciated. Get more than one screenwriter in a room and invariably they'll start tabulating the inequities that have befallen them.

"Yeah," Weiss said, "but look who we're looking to get respect from. I mean, who gives a shit what these guys say about your work? When they start approving is when I start to worry."

"Not quite true," Hershel said. "Every writer wants approval. We write to please the unpleasable parent. Producers know this instinctually. You are the child, they are the adult. They're the ones who talk to the studio heads because you're too emotional and juvenile to deal with your own work. They know what's best for you. And they'll keep you rewriting indefinitely because they know how to do it. That is how they justify their job."

"I wouldn't mind rewriting," Weiss said, "if I knew the script was getting better."

"You're trying to write a serious, emotional script and they want you to put in *shtick*," Heller added.

"Ah, yes." Hershel sighed. "What other art form can so convincingly tell a tragedy with a happy ending?"

I'd heard Hershel's lecture on this particular subject before, many times actually, so I knew exactly where he was headed. But the table seemed fascinated by his thoughts. Except for Jonathan, who was much more fascinated by Katie. The success of the evening would be gauged by her reaction. We were all ornaments who'd been invited to make Jonathan look good. And we were all trying hard to live up to his expectations.

"Tragedy by its very nature is supposed to have depth, it's supposed to make you examine your soul. It's supposed to have a character with a fatal flaw who brings upon the unthinkable, which excites pity and terror and eventually gives us, the audience, moral insight. But the problem is, Jews know the heaviness, they know that life is really like that. Who wants to watch more of it? Ah. But if you can tweak their soul just a little and then let them off the hook, you've got popular entertainment. We can walk away feeling good. In Hollywood movies everyone is redeemed."

Weiss's date, the actress writing the script, spoke up. "So, what's wrong with going to the movies to feel good? Like you said, I could feel bad without having to pay for it. Maybe tragedy doesn't belong in movies. I'd rather see *Pretty Woman* than *The Last Temptation of Christ* any day."

"Talk about a downer," Weiss said. "I haven't seen *Last Temptation* yet but I hear he gets crucified at the end."

"No, I know what he means," Heller said, really serious now. "It's almost impossible to do a piece where it's not all tied up at the end with some pretty string."

"Here's something to consider," Hershel said. "Are movies art? According to Oscar Wilde, art should never try to be popular. The public should try to make itself artistic. Melville HOPED his books would fail."

"We didn't have to hope," Weiss said, looking at his writing partner. "Our movie failed all by itself."

Miriam turned her gaze toward Hershel in admiration. She was impressed by his memory, enamored of his sagacity. I wondered if she ever detected the bitterness in Hershel's sermons. The justifying of his own failure. He was creating art and we were merely pandering. But tonight Hershel was really hitting his stride. "If Hollywood had made *Hedda Gabler,* Eilert Lövborg wouldn't have accidentally shot himself in the bowel after he thought his manuscript lost. He would have recognized his drinking problem and gone to the Betty Ford Clinic, where he would have met Mademoiselle Diana in group. They would probably have had clandestine sex in the visitors' lounge after hours. The manuscript Hedda stole, the virtual child he created with Mrs. Elvsted, would have been saved from the fire at the last moment. It would have been published and made the *New York Times* best-seller list. Hedda never would have killed herself beautifully with a clean shot through the temple. In Hollywood, people don't do such things. Hedda would outlive them all."

"Because you've got to leave room for the sequel," I said.

"She wasn't really a heroine," Heller said, cracking his knuckles. "I mean, she was an antiheroine. Right?" He looked to us for confirmation.

"What I don't get," Weiss said, not interested in pursuing *Hedda Gabler,* "is how do these guys making the decisions get in power? What qualifications are we talking about here? I mean, Chet has to go to school to be a medical doctor and then he has to do his internship and residency, right?" He turned to Chet.

"And then if there's a specialty there's more work," Chet replied.

"And you know, if you want to be a stockbroker you have to study the market and learn the bullish and bearish shit. And if you want to be a teacher you have to learn how to write on a blackboard and assign eraser-clapping duties, but in Hollywood you can go from a nothing life to a big life overnight. Where else can you do that?"

Hershel nodded his head in agreement. "It's a town of tie salesmen and shoe hustlers, merchandisers, playing in a league that could take them all the way to the top."

"Hershel used to write for the movies but he said the business changed so much," Miriam piped in.

"It used to be Harry and Sam and Jack and Louie," Hershel said. "The new breed is Brandons and Scottys and Lisas. I could work with the old-timers. But I don't understand the new breed."

"You're exactly right," Katie said, glancing at Jonathan. "These people I work for, I have no idea how they got to their positions. I mean, Judi's father is rich and knows people. But Joel, Joel used to be a clothing rep in New York."

"Hollywood is the Jewish Mecca," Hershel said. "All believers come to pay homage to the glamour god of a perfect WASP life that they themselves invented. So many striving to get to God."

"It's from all those old Christmas movies they keep playing over and over again," Jonathan said.

"The Jew invented the gentile standard," Hershel reiterated.

"Well, I wish you wouldn't have," Katie said, "because Christmas at my house is the most uptight event." She'd turned from Chet and was talking directly to Jonathan now. "I mean, you should see my mother, who's uptight to begin with. There's all this expectation laid on Christmas like we're supposed to be this great big happy family, and the truth is no one really wants to be there. No one even likes each other."

"It's always refreshing to hear that you WASPs are unhappy, too," Jonathan said.

"Of course we are, we just don't talk about it as much. There's not a lot of emotion expressed in my house. That's why I like Jews. They talk about EVERYTHING."

"We can't STOP talking about everything," Jonathan said. I was starting to revise my opinion of Jonathan's chances, after all.

"It's all the suffering," I said. "Look at Passover. The Christians are out having Easter-egg hunts and eating chocolate bunnies and ham—"

" 'Nice ham this year, Mom,' " Weiss's date said, interrupting me with the five words from *Annie Hall* that Jews believe sum up gentiles.

"—and the Jews are sitting inside eating horseradish and salt water to remind them of the bitterness and tears their ancestors shed when they were slaves in Egypt."

"Jews need better PR," Heller said. Then he told a joke that was making its way around Hollywood. "A Frenchman goes into a bar and says, 'I'm so thirsty I must have a champagne.' An Englishman goes into a bar and says, 'I'm so thirsty I must have a Guinness.' A Japanese goes into a bar and says, 'I'm so thirsty I must have sake.' And a Jew goes into a bar and says, 'I'm so thirsty I must have diabetes.' "

"HA!" It was one syllable, barked so loud that Miriam scared Lady Mudpaw right off her lap.

"Maybe they should remake *It's a Wonderful Life* as a Hanukkah movie," I said. "They can call it . . . *It's a Life*—"

"Starring Billy Crystal," Jonathan said.

"—Billy Crystal returns home after seeing what this world would be like if he'd never been born, and all his neighbors from Encino have taken up a collection for his failing junk-bond market. Then they all gather 'round the *menorah* eating potato *latkes* and sing 'Draydl, Draydl, Draydl.' "

"Where does the bell come in?" Miriam asked.

Weiss answered her. "The telephone rings saying that he still has his job at Drexel Burnham and Moisha gets his wings."

Miriam screamed with laughter. "Is that funny. No wonder you two are writers," she said to Weiss and me with judgmental approval.

The party was all warmed up. Jonathan's glowing introductions had made everyone feel secure in their position. I forgave Jonathan his blatant climbing and relaxed into the evening. And so did he. The more we ate, drank, and talked, the more winning Jonathan became. Even Hershel, who usually left parties early, stayed until the very end. Only Henri Faroli tried to outlast us, disappearing into the kitchen as the party was breaking up. Hershel, Miriam, and I were sitting around the napkin-strewn table when Jonathan leaned in and confided to us.

"Do you think this is the moment where I'm going to have to tell him I'm not into butt-fucking fags?"

"You want us to come with you as protection?" Miriam asked.

"I THINK I can handle it," Jonathan said, pushing back his chair.

We all watched him disappear into the kitchen. A moment later Henri exited, balancing a stack of platters and bowls. Jonathan preceded him to the front door carrying a plastic bag of garbage.

"Looovely to have met you all."

"Good-bye, Mr. Darcy and Lady Mudpaw," Miriam called out, but Henri and the dogs were already gone. Jonathan closed the door and turned to us with a self-satisfied smile.

"What did you say to get rid of him so fast?" I asked.

"I told him he had poppy seeds in his teeth. 'Poppy seeds are soooo not elegant.' "

"Clever boy," Miriam said, putting on her shawl.

"I'll walk you guys out," Jonathan said. But as soon as we stepped into the cold air he changed his mind. "Hey, Franky Spanky. Would you mind throwing this away?" He offered me the garbage. "The cans are all lined up next to the garage. Bless Reese and Charles for being so textbook anal." Jonathan performed a quick profusion of hugs at the doorstep, and as we headed for the curb, he turned back to his warm apartment.

Miriam got right behind the wheel while Hershel uncharacteristically escorted me to the trash. Six cans were perfectly lined up and painted with the address and apartment number. I pried off the lid of Jonathan's garbage can and an odor of decay escaped. I glanced into the smelly heap and caught sight of white typed pages thrown on top of a supermarket bag with a chicken carcass poking out. The pages were stained with grease. I could tell it was someone's script. And so could Hershel.

"Ah. Another screenplay treated with all the respect it probably deserves. I imagine the Hollywood dump must look like Aspen in winter."

Hershel was chuckling at his own joke as I caught sight of a name, a location, then a line of dialogue. I pulled a limp page out of the trash and knew we weren't looking at just another screenplay. It was the first thirty pages of my LIFE screenplay. I'd given it to Jonathan to read a few days before.

"Anything interesting?" Hershel asked, looking over my shoulder.

"No."

I crumpled the page, threw it in the can, and dropped the garbage bag on top, quickly closing the lid on a dirty secret. What right did I have to be angry? We'd already discussed the pages, did I expect him to keep everything I gave him? Of course not. Were my words so sacred they should never be tossed? Hadn't I thrown other people's scripts in the garbage with just as little thought? So why was I taking it personally?

Miriam headed the car up the hill toward Sunset Boulevard and in a couple blocks we turned onto the Strip.

"What did I go THIS way for?" she said, annoyed at herself and the bumper-to-bumper traffic. As we crawled through the corridor of movie billboards, Miriam craned her neck, looking out the windshield. "Look at this. There's not one movie you want to see." Her remark seemed to remind Hershel of something and he retrieved the small spiral pad from the breast pocket of his shirt.

"What are you writing?" I asked, although I'd already guessed.

"Aspen in winter," he said, laughing again in appreciation.

For the second time that night I forgave Jonathan Prince.

23

ABIE THE FISH MAN

1991

THE FIRST DAY back after the new year began with a call from Hart.

"Hey, kiddo, how's it going? You have a good Christmas?"

"Okay. You?"

"I took the kids skiing. How's *Ivy and Men* coming? You having any fun out of it or are they making your life miserable?"

I know Hart so well, I could tell from his voice that this was just a preamble to some other matter of business.

"By the way," he said, after we had told each other how everyone we knew was doing, "I'm thinking of buying a little ski place up in Park City and I need you to sign a quitclaim deed to the house here. As a matter of fact, I think you should think about getting yourself a lawyer just so we can finally formalize everything."

We had been casual about it, it was true, but it suited me. Formalizing meant it was for real and there was no going back. Formalizing meant his lawyer had warned him about community property and that Hart had probably met someone he liked.

"So, have you met someone you like?"

"There're a couple of women I'm seeing." Then he told me about each one and shared a few anecdotes as if we were old pals. One of them was a wealthy San Francisco socialite who'd been recently divorced from the heir to a plumbing-fixture fortune and whose cat peed on Hart's wool muffler the first time he stayed over at her house. The other woman I was acquainted with, a writer and director who was probably the kind of person he should have been with all along.

I hung up the phone and sat rocking in my desk chair. Just to make myself feel better, I tried to recall all the things I didn't like about Hart. All the incidents in our marriage that proved we weren't right for each other. All the things he'd said over the years which rankled. But I couldn't summon up the bad feelings anymore. Then I remembered something I'd once said to him to describe our marriage: "If there was only half a grapefruit left in the refrigerator, we'd BOTH give it to you." Big deal, I thought. That describes most marriages. The telephone call had left me with that emptiness.

I got up and went into the outer office to make a cup of tea and distract myself with Jonathan. The telephone log lay open on his desk but he wasn't there. I glanced down and saw it had become almost illegible, as if taking messages was too much bother. The daisies were dead in their vase, the water rank and murky green. Spilled sugar dotted the credenza, and when I opened the refrigerator to get milk for my tea, it was way beyond sour.

Two hours later Jonathan stuck his head inside my door.

"I'm baaaaack."

"Where were you and why didn't you forward the calls?"

"I didn't think I was going to be so long. I got hung up."

"I don't think Freyda would put up with that, do you? So why should I?"

"Because you don't need a nursemaid and she does."

"What I need is for someone to stick around and keep the office clean and pick up the phones and help me do research so I can get my work done. I realize it's not the most interesting job, and if you're tired of doing it, let's talk about it and we'll figure something out."

"Mea culpa. I fucked up. Let me take you to lunch." He was holding a printout of the commissary menu for the day. "Look at this," he said, pointing to the special. " 'Prime rib with au juice.' What the fuck do they think 'au juice' is? Although I could go for some blood right now. Let's go get some au juice off the lot."

Jonathan drove us to a dark, windowless, over-air-conditioned steak house with a suit of armor standing beside the hostess station.

"I feel like I've just died and gone to *goyim* heaven," he said as soon as our eyes adjusted to the dark and he saw the golfers at the bar who'd come directly from the links, still clad in lime greens, raspberry sherbets, and canary yellows. "You know why God invented the *goyim*, don't you?"

"Someone has to buy retail." I hated that joke. We didn't have to watch them for very long before it became apparent they all knew each other and were on a first-name basis with the bartender and waitresses, who were bringing them their martinis and Scotches. The help, dressed in neat uniforms with name tags, looked like they'd been working there long enough to have served the Warner brothers and Walt Disney himself. "What do you want to bet those are all Republicans," Jonathan said to me.

"Nothing."

As the hostess led us to our table, Jonathan turned back to watch them. "They all look like they belong, don't they?" I didn't query him about it because the hostess could hear us, but I thought I knew what he meant. He meant they all looked too comfortable in their own skins.

Jonathan, whose diet pyramid is totally upside down, dove into the basket of garlic bread with melted cheese, the steak and potato, and sour cream and butter. He ignored his small dish of wrinkled peas and instead of salad ordered soup, New England clam chowder. All this was washed down with a couple of Diet Pepsis and small talk that Jonathan controlled. Like my phone call from Hart, I had the feeling this luncheon chitchat was leading to something.

"I'm about to do you a big favor. I have a proposition for you."

"What's this?"

"Mai Lei, who's a terrific secretary and assistant, is looking to get out of working with Joel and Judi. She's looking for a genuinely nice person to work for and I recommended you."

"Really? How considerate of you."

"Okay, here's the second part of the deal. I go to work for Judi and Joel."

"What kind of a deal is that?"

"You finally get a good secretary."

"You were never supposed to be a secretary per se. You were supposed to use the time to work on your own script. Whatever happened to that idea?" We both knew it was time he moved on. But now he was starting to annoy me with his deals and big favors.

"I realized that writing scripts is not going to get me where I really want to be, which is producing. I like working with writers, I don't necessarily have to be one. That's why I tried agenting until I saw that you don't really work with writers, you only sell them. Script and story are what interests me. I'm a good analyzer, that's what I enjoy doing. I can find properties for Judi and Joel. That's what I should be doing right now."

"I thought that's what Katie was doing."

"Katie has too much material coming across her desk. She can't deal with all of it. And most of it's shit anyway. While she's reading the script submissions and doing coverage, I can be scouring *Publishers Weekly* and *Kirkus* and reading books and meeting with agents. Judi and Joel have a lot of territory to cover and only one person to do it right now."

Jonathan's talk of "finding" properties and "working" with writers irritated me. He hadn't even changed jobs and already he'd adopted Judi and Joel's proprietary attitude. Writing a script was too hard, yet he imagined himself part of the creative process. "So you think Judi and Joel might need you AND Katie to pick through all the excrement?" I thought Jonathan had cooked this up with Katie and was trying it out on me before he went off to pitch himself to Golden Dweck productions.

"They're ready to take me on, I just wanted to run it past you before I definitely said yes." His eyes were blinking rapidly behind his glasses, fluttering.

"If that's what you want to do I'd never hold you back. It sounds like a fait accompli anyway. But why the intrigue? Why didn't you talk to me about it first?"

"The job just came up. I had no idea they were looking for someone. I haven't been PLOTTING this. You need a mole like me in Judi and Joel's office to remind them how good *Ivy and Men* is so the moment they're done producing their other script they'll go back to yours. And if they don't want to produce it, they can let me produce it."

"Unfortunately, it doesn't work like that. Judi and Joel will produce anything the studio lets them. If the studio thought *Ivy and Men* would be a big commercial hit, they'd make it."

"But I think it can be commercial if it's done right."

"And you think they know how to make it right?"

"They don't but I do. I probably know as much about getting a movie produced as Joel does, and let's not even mention his directing. I may not know as much about Fleet enemas or anal hygiene but I guarantee you I can promote your script better than he ever would."

By the time Jonathan paid the check it was all arranged. Jonathan would work for Little Red Wagon Productions and Mai Lei would come to work for me. He had somehow given me new hope. Now I was counting on Jonathan to champion my script, to keep it alive, to get it made right.

Until he and Mai Lei traded jobs I didn't realize what a bad assistant Jonathan actually was. Now the Rolodex was neatly typed instead of written in his scrawled hand. The calls were put on forward when she went out to lunch, the telephone log was readable, a filing system was set up for research, which Mai Lei got out of both the studio research department and the public library, and my script changes were placed into notebooks, labeled and dated. The refrigerator smelled good again and the cornstalk plant, fed on a regular schedule, started to come back to life. When she wasn't making my life easier, she quietly worked on her own screenplay.

Periodically I'd read her pages and give her suggestions, something Jonathan had been doing until he'd gotten too busy with his new job. Her story was about a baker from Brooklyn who's married to a beautiful woman. The baker loves opera and loves his wife. Every Saturday night he and his beautiful wife go to an Italian restaurant where the customers are encouraged to sing opera. He has a terrible voice but sings with real passion. One night, just before he's about to go on, he discovers his wife in the arms of another man. Enraged and then heartbroken, he stands up and, with all eyes on him, begins to sing "Vesti la giubba" from *Pagliacci*. His voice starts quietly, a little off-key, but just as the clown is moved to tears by his wife's unfaithfulness, so, too, is our hero. As his heart is breaking, God kisses his vocal cords and he miraculously finishes the aria singing like Pavarotti.

Word gets out and people begin to come from all over Brooklyn to hear him sing. The little Italian restaurant has people lined up out the door. No one can explain it, least of all our hero. All he knows is that he's miserable without his wife but he sounds like an angel when he sings.

Soon he's discovered by someone from the Metropolitan Opera and his simple life changes. As he becomes famous, world-renowned, his life begins to mirror the operas he's singing. There's an ill-fated romance with a jealous, tempestuous soprano who plays Tosca, and a fling with a high-priced call girl like Violetta in *La Traviata*. Finally our hero meets a pretty, poor girl, who, like Mimi in *La Bohème,* has cold hands and a nasty cough. He begins to fall for this woman who loves him for his soul, not for his fame. But the moment he realizes he's hopelessly in love and can't live without her, he loses his voice in the middle of a performance. He walks off the stage leaving the audience in an uproar. His career abruptly over, he goes back to being a baker in Brooklyn. The last time we see him he's singing off-key at the little Italian restaurant where his true love is now a waitress.

It was an original idea. Very small but sweet and charming. The problem wasn't the idea, it was the execution. Mai Lei was so sheltered and naive that she had absolutely no ear for dialogue. Everyone sounded too polite. Everyone sounded Chinese. Mai Lei was never going to make it in Hollywood. Women like Mai Lei can never learn the hustle. But I couldn't tell her.

For the first few weeks after he'd left, Jonathan would occasionally poke his head in my office to say hello. Then a month went by when I hardly saw him. We were drifting apart, which was inevitable, especially in Hollywood, where friends change with agendas. But one rainy day in March, Mai Lei buzzed to say Jonathan was in the outer office wanting to speak with me.

"You've got to come to this dinner party. Katie's mother, the bitch of all time, is giving Katie a birthday party and I want you to be my date."

"Why do you need a date?"

"Because Katie's just broken up with the Aryan Nazi God and hasn't told her mother yet that she's dating a shortish Jew in show business."

"So I'm the beard."

"If you want to be gross about it."

"When are you going to break it to Katie's mother that you've dumped me and you're now seeing her daughter?"

"I haven't even met her. Right now she thinks we just work together. First I have to win her over. Katie's mother was a New York Talbot."

"Is this supposed to mean something to me?"

"They're a very wealthy family who owned hundreds of acres in Connecticut. They have a school and some roads named after them and her great-great-grandfather was a captain who fought in the Civil War. Aren't you curious to meet her?"

"Not particularly."

"I have no one to bring but you," he said simply.

"Don't be ridiculous. You know a million people."

"But no one appropriate. Who do you think I can take? Blaire? Suzi? Shelley? That's a prescription for disaster. You're the only one I know who can handle the situation."

Katie's mother, Nan, lived in Pasadena. It seemed as if Jonathan was driving me to a land far from Southern California. We were entering a comfortable, upscale, conservative, Midwestern city. It was dark when we arrived, adding to the mystery. Her ranch-style house was modest compared with the neighborhood, but well tended. Jonathan picked up the big brass knocker and let it drop a couple of times, which set off a round of yapping on the other side of the door.

Nan opened the door and a chocolate toy poodle slipped past her and crowded around our legs. "Don't worry, he's friendly," she said. Even if he wasn't he wouldn't have made much of an impact.

"Well," Nan said, looking at Jonathan through icy blue eyes. "YOU must be Jonathan. And you are . . . ?" I had bent down to pet the dog and now looked up at her. She wasn't as tall as Katie or as pretty, although I could see a resemblance in the eyes. She had a crisp, cool manner that, fortunately, her daughter hadn't inherited.

"Frankie Jordan," I said, grateful for the neutral sound of my name. Nan didn't strike me as having a lot of friends of the Fingerman persuasion. It occurred to me that that's what Jonathan had meant by appropriate. When appropriate, I could blend right in.

"Come in and have a drink." She stepped aside and called toward the living room. "Robert dear, our guests are here." She turned back to us. "I've put Robert to work fixing the drinks this evening. Katie will be right back. She's just run to the store for some mixers. I don't know HOW we got so low on mixers." Her chin-length, ash-blond hair was pulled back into a sensible pony and her skin was evenly tan with only a few lines to show for it. Her hands were not the coddled hands of a manicured Beverly Hills matron. Nan's hands looked like they'd done their share of gardening and horse grooming, her nails short and unpolished. Around her neck, lying nicely on her pink cotton blouse, was a spectacular strand of large luminescent pearls for which the Talbots must have sold off a few acres.

"I bought you some Dom Pérignon for the occasion." Jonathan handed her the wrapped bottle. "I hope it's still cold enough."

"How nice. I'm not a champagne drinker, it gives me a headache, but I'm sure Katie will appreciate it."

"Beautiful house," Jonathan said, looking around. "I love your antiques. My mother collects antiques. Her favorite thing is to go into the country and go shopping. She calls it 'treasure hunting.' She's decorated my father's office and waiting room. His patients are always wanting her to do their houses, too, but the problem is she can't bear to part with anything. Your home is quite lovely." This wasn't exactly the *haimisher* Jew I had introduced to Hershel and Miriam. This Jonathan was extremely polite, almost formal, presenting his credentials tastefully; he was the son of a doctor and a mother with discriminating taste, although she refused to share it with anybody, and they had money to spend on good antiques.

Nan seemed unimpressed. "These are hardly treasures," she said, brushing aside his compliment. "It's just what's been in the family for years. It doesn't really look as good in this house as it did in the old house but I've had to downscale." She turned away abruptly and headed into the living room and it was presumed we were to follow.

Robert, the designated bartender, was standing alert and ready at the drink station, a large silver tray with a monogrammed Plexiglas ice bucket and various bottles and decanters at his disposal.

"Hey HEY," he said, walking toward us with an extended hand. "Katie's coming back with the mixers any second. We didn't know we were running low. So what can I get anyone?" He was sporting a double-breasted blue blazer, blue-striped shirt, and paisley ascot. But instead of looking like a David Niven cliché, he looked perfectly wonderful, as if he should never appear in anything else.

I accepted a glass of the champagne. Jonathan wanted a Scotch. It was curious how easily he'd adapted protective coloration. The way he sat carefully on the couch and crossed his legs, showing a bit of paisley sock; how he sipped his drink and made convivial small talk. Even the way he laughed was different, more restrained. No doubt I'd hear his biting take on this evening in the car, on our way back to L.A.

"I want a REAL drink," Nan said as she lit up a cigarette. Robert handed her a vodka on ice and she excused herself to attend to the kitchen. Jonathan asked if he could help, but she firmly declined the offer and disappeared. Jonathan got up abruptly and began examining the bookshelves. He'd obviously concluded Nan's boyfriend was of little import. Out of nervous politeness, I remained seated and made conversation with Robert.

"So, how long did it take you two to get here?"

"It wasn't too bad," I answered, looking to Jonathan for corroboration. "About an hour. We hit Music Center traffic on the Harbor Freeway but then it cleared up."

"Was the traffic bad this time of night?"

"Just at the Music Center."

"Is that right."

He was likable enough, easygoing and thoroughly agreeable. But there was no doubt in my mind who ran the show.

"Nan is a wonderful cook. She loves to entertain. I don't know how she does it but she's a perfectionist. She just loves to entertain.

She and her gal friends had this cooking teacher they got to come over. I'm telling you, they turned out some first-class meals. Get her in that kitchen and she's just as happy as a clam."

Jonathan took a book down from the shelf and thumbed through it. "They've got a first edition of *Catcher in the Rye*," he said to me.

"Nan's ex-husband was . . . is quite a collector."

"Do I hear we're talking about my ex-husband?" Nan said, entering with a tray of stuffed mushrooms and little napkins. She peered at us over half glasses, which made her look like she was taking a dim view of whatever we were saying.

"I was telling them he collects books."

"There are books all over the place. One of these days he's going to have to come over and clean out the damn garage so I can get my car in there without tripping over everything. You've got to eat these mushrooms while they're hot because they're only good while they're hot."

Jonathan, Robert, and I did as we were told.

"These are fantastic," Jonathan said. "What are they stuffed with?"

"Sausage and bread crumbs. I like REAL food. None of these little nuts and berries for me. I don't know how Katie eats like that. Give me bacon for breakfast. And cottage cheese. I aDORE bacon and cottage cheese. And I've never had so much energy in my LIFE. Does she at least eat a good lunch?" She turned to Jonathan.

"She likes salads," Jonathan reported. It was obviously the wrong answer.

"Salads," Nan said dismissively. "Salads don't get you very far. Salads wouldn't get me until two in the afternoon. Eat REAL food. That's what I tell Katie. But I'm only her mother." She obviously understood the rules of life and couldn't understand why others didn't. "So do you work with Katie, too?"

"I'm on the same hall," I replied, not too sure what Katie had told her or who I was supposed to be.

Nan got up as the dog started yapping again. "That must be them." We all looked over in the direction of the front door and conversation stopped when Nan exited the room. "We were afraid you'd gotten lost," Nan said, making it sound more like a criticism than a concern. Taking a couple of plastic supermarket bags from her son, she pointed her children in our direction. "Katie, go in and introduce Talbot to your guests."

There was a languidness about Talbot, a distinct lack of enthusiasm. As if he wasn't all that anxious to meet us or maybe he was reacting to his mother's mandate. Katie entered the room but Talbot fell a few steps behind and seemed to wander in. He was a head taller than Jonathan, athletically built and good-looking, but he'd missed out on his mother and sister's honey coloring. He kept pushing back the straight brown hair that fell into his brown eyes, and the gesture became irritatingly self-conscious almost at once.

"Sorry I couldn't be here when you arrived," Katie said to us.

"Don't be silly," the new, ultrapolite Jonathan replied. "We've all just been enjoying your mother's stuffed mushrooms."

"What can I get everyone?" Robert said, standing up to man the bar. "We have some champagne Jonathan and Frankie brought."

"It was all Jonathan's doing," I said, making sure he received full credit. Jonathan gave me a sidelong glance, an acknowledgment that I was playing my part.

"I'd LOVE some champagne." Katie smiled at Jonathan.

"Talbot? What's your pleasure?"

"God, let me see. I'll have a vodka and tonic even though I know it's a summer drink." He turned to me. "My mother has rules about what drinks fit with what seasons. This is actually a great sacrilege."

"I don't think we have any lime," Robert said, examining the tray as if he still expected to find one hiding behind a bottle.

"I'll live," Talbot said, plopping himself into his mother's chair and taking a mushroom cap. The dog came around with its pointed little snout aimed at the food, sat very still, looked Talbot in the eye, and gave an impatient little woof. Talbot nudged him away with his foot. "Get away. Go into the kitchen. There's the real sucker. She'll give you whatever you want." It wasn't said in a kind way. Talbot was obviously fond of his sister though. They looked close in age and had probably been henpecked through childhood, forging an alliance.

I could see Talbot and Jonathan assessing one another like two banty accountants. Ordinarily, Talbot would be the kind of person Jonathan would challenge or even decimate, if he was in the mood. But tonight he was on best behavior. What kind of brothers-in-law would they make? I wondered. Talbot would routinely whip Jonathan's ass in tennis. But I'd no doubt the competition off the court would be much more underhanded and vicious and in Jonathan's favor.

"The coals look just perfect," Nan said, coming in from the patio. "I'm going to put on the meat."

"Nan makes a wonderful grilled lamb," Robert chimed.

"Robert dear, my glass is in the kitchen."

"You want me to freshen it up?"

"That would be lovely."

His duty never done, Robert tootled off toward the kitchen as if the butler's bell had been rung.

As soon as the grown-ups were out of earshot, Talbot leaned back in his chair and took measure of Jonathan. "I have to say I don't envy you. My mother APPROVED of Chet."

"I told him," Katie said, turning her clear blue eyes on Jonathan. She sat tall, crossed her long legs, and wrapped her hands around her knees. Her movements were feminine, economical, her voice gentle. She was different from every other woman who worked on the studio lot.

"You think I should give him the gathered intelligence on Nan?"

"Talbot. Shut up." It was said very low but not the least bit harshly.

"I don't need any help," Jonathan said, his old confidence returning. "She seems fine. I can handle her. What's the problem?"

"We still have"—Talbot checked his watch—"approximately forty more minutes of cocktails and at least an hour and a half of dinner to get through."

"Open the wine, would you, Robert dear?" Nan called on her way back to the kitchen.

"Which wine?"

She gave a little sigh of impatience. "It's on the TABLE."

"I've got it. It's on the table."

"So what intelligence are you talking about?" Jonathan asked Talbot.

"I thought you said you could handle her."

"Why don't you give him just a tip," I interceded. "I'd be curious to hear it myself."

But before Talbot could reply, Nan returned to the living room and instructed Robert to make us another round. By the time she ordered us in to dinner we were all a little drunk, but it hadn't loosened anybody up. Jonathan especially seemed on edge. None of the old tricks were working.

"Katie tells me you were involved in a literary agency." Nan peered at Jonathan over her glasses. We were still passing lamb and carrots with mint.

"That's where I met Frankie."

"Did you OWN it?"

"It was owned by three partners. I wasn't a partner yet."

Yet? I thought. I wondered what Nan would say if she knew Jonathan was actually a glorified secretary.

"Well, you'd have a lot in common with my ex-husband. You two could talk BOOKS." Even this seemingly innocuous comment came out sounding vaguely disparaging. If Jonathan had picked up on it, I couldn't tell.

"Maybe they'd have a lot more in common than that, wouldn't they, Nan?" There was something in the way Talbot said it that put me on alert. That, and the look Katie gave him.

"I'm sure they would if they got to talking."

Talbot turned to Jonathan. "Did Katie ever tell you about the time our father met one of his long-lost cousins?"

"Talbot, why don't you mind your own business," Katie said, but not in the gentle voice she'd used with him earlier. This was a definite warning.

"This is my business," he said in defiance. Then he turned back to Jonathan. "Anyway, he'd been invited to Dallas to give a paper on something or other and this woman in the lecture hall comes up to him afterward and says, 'We've never met but I'm your long-lost cousin. I'm from the Jewish side of the family.' Then she fills him in on a whole limb of the family tree he knew nothing about. My grandfather, who didn't like Jews all that much, had never bothered to mention that his own mother was Jewish. My father was in total shock. Especially since he'd been brought up to be a very proper WASP, Los Angeles Country Club 'No Jews No shirt No service' and all that. So my father comes home, REELING from the news, and Nan here picks him up at the airport and her first response is, 'I'm just glad my parents are dead so they'll never have to find out.' Isn't that right, Nan?"

I glanced at Nan and, for just a moment, there appeared through the scrim of cool politeness a look of transparent hate directed at Talbot, who had dared to turn an unflattering spotlight on her. Robert, displaying either more smarts or obliviousness than I had given him credit for, picked up his wineglass. "The meat's cooked just perfectly. And I love the potatoes done like this. What is that seasoning I'm tasting? Nutmeg? Now, who'd think to put nutmeg in potatoes except Nan. I'd like to propose a toast to Nan for this great dinner and to Katie on her birthday."

It was the oddest thing. When we all clinked glasses, it was almost as if I had dreamed the whole thing, as if it had never happened. Except for Jonathan I tried to catch his eye but he avoided me. I expected he wouldn't let it pass without so much as a comment. He couldn't. Or a mocking question: why is it better to be dead than to know your daughter married someone of Jewish ancestry? But Jonathan was mum. As was I. Was it my place to ruin his chances with Katie? Or was I just cowardly? I sat there chewing my lamb and an absurd movie flashed before me. *Animal Crackers*.

The evening proceeded like any dinner party where the participants have nothing in common and are glad they don't. Jonathan barely spoke to me but remained cordial and solicitous toward Nan. Even when she told a couple of stories in excruciating detail, one about cleaning out her garage when she moved houses and finding someone to actually come and PAY her for all the old doorknobs and hardware and junk, which she thought was very amusing, and another about taking her dog to the veterinarian to have his teeth cleaned. "Thank GOODness they did the blood test beFORE they gave Milou the anesthetic or the doctor says I could have lost him. His thyroid gland wasn't functioning properly and how was I to know? I noticed that his energy was a little low but I thought it was just because he was getting on toward seven. Now he's on two grains of thyroid a day. One in the morning and one at night and his energy is just fine. But I don't think I'll ever be able to have his teeth cleaned again because I just don't trust the anesthetic. But there's a woman

I heard about who cleans their teeth and who doesn't put them under. You have to bring them to her once a month."

"Is that right," Robert said. "That dog is going to have cleaner teeth than I do."

While we were finishing our after-dinner drinks, Nan went outside to bring in the barbecue tongs. On her return, she walked right into the screen door. She hit it so hard that she ricocheted backward into a rhododendron bush and left a head-and-knee-shaped dent in the screen. We all got out of our seats and went over to see if she was hurt. Her forehead was scraped and bleeding. Robert took her over to the couch and she sat, a little dazed but still doughty.

"I thought it was open, I could have sworn I left the damn door open."

"That could be dangerous," Robert said. "We should put something on that screen door so you can see it better."

"I could have sworn I'd left it open. I feel so ABsolutely ridiculous."

"Damn thing probably looks invisible from the outside. We should put something on the damn thing so you can see it better."

She seemed so human and vulnerable, sitting there with a monogrammed cocktail napkin plastered to her head. I almost wanted to like her. Katie just looked impatient and whispered something to Jonathan I couldn't catch. Jonathan squeezed her hand. The charade that I was Jonathan's date seemed to be over. It didn't matter anymore.

Robert led Nan into her bathroom to attend to her wound, the little dog trotting nervously behind them.

"Anyone for more Rémy?" Talbot said, taking over right where Robert had left off. I motioned with my head to Jonathan that we should go. "Don't worry about Nan," Talbot volunteered, pouring himself another drop of brandy. "She's walked into that screen door before."

Robert returned to the living room a moment later and announced that Nan had decided to go to bed. He then went into the kitchen and started loading up the dishwasher, and Jonathan and I said our good-byes.

"That's an interesting family," I said to Jonathan in the car. "I wonder if they keep a screen-door repairman on retainer." He wouldn't answer me. "How come you didn't say anything?" He knew what I meant.

"There was no point," he said, yawning. He seemed satisfied, as if things couldn't have gone better.

I wanted to talk about the evening, dissect it, find out what Katie had whispered to him. If she had, indeed, warned him about her father's long-lost cousin. But Jonathan turned up the radio to some Milli Vanilli song, precluding further conversation. I let it go. We were both too tired and we'd had too much to drink. When we got to the Santa Monica Freeway and it dumped us off at the ocean, I opened the window and took in the damp clean air, glad to be home. Only then did Jonathan speak.

"Actually, I liked Pasadena. I'll bet you can still buy a pretty big house there for a decent amount."

"Maybe you should just move in with Mrs. Rittenhause."

"Who's that?"

"The Marx brothers. *Animal Crackers.*"

"I take it she lives in a big house."

"And she's having a really grand party and Groucho shows up as Captain Jeffery T. Spaulding, African explorer 'schnorrer,' as he calls himself. He makes his big entrance, carried by black tribesmen, and when he disembarks from his portable throne, he starts to argue about the fare. " 'What? From Africa to here, a dollar eighty-five? I told you not to take me through Australia. It's all chopped up. You should have come right up the Lincoln Boulevard.' "

"That's funny." He wasn't interested but I couldn't let it go.

"You've got to love that Groucho because instead of trying to blend in, he takes everything the aristocracy hates about Jews and immigrants and he throws it right back in their faces. But Mrs. Rittenhause is just too stiff and stupid to notice. Even Groucho's thick, fat, greasy mustache and eyebrows are an affront to polite society."

"You don't say."

"When Chico and Harpo show up they see that one of the guests is this pretentious art dealer named Roscoe W. Chandler. Only they recognize him as a fish-selling immigrant from Czechoslovakia and threaten to expose him by yelling, 'Abie the fish man, Abie the fish man, Abie the fish man.' "

Jonathan gave me a sour look. "Sounds really hysterical."

"You should see it."

Poor Jonathan. He could try to look gentile and try to act gentile, but it wasn't going to make him a gentile. He'd been afraid I was going to give him away, that's why he hadn't been able to look at me all evening. I'd wanted him to be Groucho. But he was only Abie the fish man.

SEAT FILLERS

IT WAS DESCRIBED in the real-estate listing as a "charming doll-house," translated as not having a Sub-Zero, family room, closets, master bath, or any of the requisite amenities grown people are looking for. It did have a sunny, airy bedroom with a tiny room a few steps down that the realtor, who was showing it to me, kept calling "the nursery," calculating, I'm sure, that this was a great selling point for a woman my age. The nursery had one window facing the street and a sloped ceiling you had to watch so you didn't bump your head, perfect for a reading room with bookshelves and a comfy chair. The moment escrow closed, Miriam walked over with a bottle of wine and we sat on the old blue carpet in the nursery, planning where everything would go.

Jonathan surprised me by volunteering his services to help pull up the brown carpeting. But when the time came he didn't show. No phone call, no excuses, no lattes and muffins, no Jonathan.

I began to pull up the rug myself, just as Miriam, trusty Miriam, stopped by on her walk with Little Macho. She saw what had to be done and got to work. I was making a trip out to the garbage with the last plastic sack of nail-studded wooden strips when Jonathan, dressed for dirty work in shorts and an old T-shirt, sauntered in the open front door.

"Wow. Nice house."

Miriam looked up from her bucket of Murphy soap. "Look at these floors we found. Are they gorgeous? She doesn't even have to have them redone. I'm going over to the supermarket right now to rent a buffer. These are going to wax up beautifully."

"I can't believe you guys did this without me. Way to go. Sorry I couldn't make it earlier. The PHONE." He circled his head around as if he were getting rid of all the tension and kinks in his neck. As if he'd worked harder than we had.

Miriam, who's used to hard work, didn't react. Calling to Little Macho, she announced she'd be back in ten minutes with the buffer, and bustled out the door, a woman on a mission.

"Look around," I said to Jonathan, wanting to get rid of him. He was only in the way now. He took himself upstairs and found his way back to the kitchen, where I'd resumed scrubbing out the cabinets.

"This is a great little place," he said, boosting himself onto the countertop. "I've got to get myself a house. Hey, I hear Jerry Slotnick really liked your LIFE script."

"Who told you? Blaire or Suzie?"

"You want me to reveal my secret sources?"

I didn't want to talk about my work. Like Miriam, I felt it was tempting fate to get too excited about a project. But Jerry had liked it and we were waiting to hear from Lance. I tried to put it out of my mind. "How's YOUR work going?"

"I've presented Judi and Joel an idea we're getting a writer on."

"Congratulations. Is this a book you found?"

"It's an original idea, actually."

"Really? Good for you."

"Yeah, everything's going really great."

"You and Katie are good?"

"Yup. We're going to the Hebrew oasis next weekend. It'll be just my luck, I'll probably bump right into Freyda and Marty."

"I presume you're talking about Two Bunch Palms."

"Vut den?"

Despite his derogatory reference, Jonathan was learning to embrace the Hollywood watering place. He and Katie, like others in the business, would bring too many scripts with them. But instead of working, they'd find themselves unwinding in the hot mineral pool, where everyone talks in hushed tones, pretending to be anonymous and laid-back. They'd get outdoor massages under the rustling palms while African music plays softly. They'd revitalize their skin with mud baths and complain on Sunday afternoon, as they drove back to L.A., that the weekend was much too short and they still had all these damn SCRIPTS to read.

"So, what's happening with Judi and Joel?" I'd been busy with my house, waiting for repairmen and painters. I'd been writing at home for a few weeks, finishing up the script for Jerry. I was out of touch.

"You haven't heard? I thought this was the shot heard 'round the world. Judi's pregnant."

"You're kidding?" A thought flashed through my mind. Why her and not me? Then it was gone.

"That's what everyone says but she's very excited about it. It's perfectly Judi. You know how totally obsessive she is. I'm surprised she didn't take out a full-page ad in the trades. Actually I think it'll be very good for Judi and Alan."

"Good for them?"

"Being parents," he said, avoiding the question.

"Has Judi or Joel mentioned *Ivy and Men*?" I hated bringing up my script. I felt like a beggar, as if Jonathan had me under his thumb in some way.

"I've got to talk to them about that. I've got to get them to just sit down and discuss it but they're all over the place right now trying to get their movie out. Don't worry. I'm going to the Academy Awards at Judi's house. I'm going to mention it then."

How did he wangle THAT invitation? I thought.

"They're having a lot of people over," he said, as if he could read my mind. "I'm just one of many."

I could see he was being very guarded with me, strained and polite, like he'd been with Nan. I liked him better as the irreverent, hypercritical, foulmouthed outsider. But he'd found a home in the bosom of Little Red Wagon Productions and was now playing the loyal, albeit overworked, development boy.

"I'd stick around and help," he said, "but I'm so behind in my reading. If I can get away tomorrow, you and Hershel and Miriam feel like driving out to Monterey Park for some dim sum?"

"I'll ask her when she gets back from the supermarket."

"I'll call you tonight and we'll make arrangements." But he never called me and I never called him, which was just as well. I was in my nesting mode and I wanted to spend a Sunday staying home, walking from room to room.

The next morning I went back to work at the studio. I had my own house to come home to, a script Jerry liked, and clean floors. My life felt like it was finally coming together. Until just before lunch when I went to the ladies' room.

I was about to flush when Judi Golden and Wendy Rubin entered all girlish and giggly. Wendy and I hadn't spoken since the monkey rewrite for her abused husband. But I knew she was gloating over my failure to deliver.

"I'm GREAT with kids," Wendy was saying. I recognized the voice right away. Wendy is in love with her own voice. She once told Hart her voice was so playful, she could win people over on the telephone without ever meeting them. "Children love me. I'm like a kid magnet. You should see me at my cousin's house on Passover. All these kids are fighting over who'll get to sit next to me. I know what makes them laugh. I'm surprised they don't call me for play dates."

"I'll set up a play date with you. We can go play at a spa. I really have to get away before the baby comes. Once the baby comes how am I going to get away? I just need to relax. I told Alan, I really have to get away."

"We should just DO it. We should go down to Rancho La Puerta and work on my script down there and get facials and massages and do yoga."

"When they green-lighted your script I told Joel, he better be really nice to me because I can't take this back-to-back production."

My heart sank. Judi and Joel were going to produce Wendy's script over mine. I felt like getting off the toilet, turning around, and throwing up.

"They LOVE me at Rancho La Puerta. I went down there last year and did one of those evenings where you give a talk about screenwriting? I did my whole Hollywood *shtick* and got my week for free."

"How are we going to get in? They're always so booked."

"They keep BEGGING me to come back and do my song and dance."

Of course Jonathan had known about Wendy's script when he'd come to my house. Maybe he'd even brought it to Judi and Joel's attention. I couldn't blame him, after all, that was his job. He knew what I thought of her writing. Was he trying to save my feelings by not telling me? Was that why he'd seemed so careful?

The longer I remained hidden, the harder it was going to be to exit with any grace. I stayed seated with my pants down so my belt buckle wouldn't jingle while Judi took Wendy's place in the stall next to mine.

"What about Joel? He'll be so jealous if we go to Rancho La Puerta without him. Even though all he does is walk around the track smoking his stupid cigar."

"So he'll come, too, and we'll get Isaac and Jonathan and we can get adjoining casitas. Then we can all sit around like five old Jews and complain how gassy the vegetarian food's making us."

Wendy and Judi were in their Rancho La Puerta phase. They'd massage each other's ego until something went wrong with the project. Then it would all turn to bad-mouthing and blame.

I waited thirty seconds after they left, then opened the door and peeked out into the hall, making absolutely certain there wouldn't be an untoward moment.

"Where were you?" Mai Lei said. "Jerry Slotnick's been trying to reach you. He's called twice."

"What's he calling about? Did he say?"

"Just that he's very anxious to talk with you."

"Did he sound like it was good news?" It was the call I'd been looking forward to. Yet I dreaded it.

"He just said, 'Have her call me as soon as she gets in.' "

I slowly entered my office, closed the door, took a deep breath, and dialed.

"Are you sitting down?" Jerry said.

"Yes?"

"Cantrowitz passed. As much as he liked the whole *Life* magazine aspect of it, he said he doesn't want to do any more period pieces. I'm very disappointed."

YOU'RE disappointed? I wanted to scream. What the hell did YOU have to do with it? "If he didn't want any period pieces why did he okay it in the first place?"

"I asked him that. He said it's a new corporate decision. They're too expensive. He's looking for more low-budget movies with unknowns. I gotta take this call."

And Jerry was gone, on to other business.

I hung up the phone and stared out the window, watching Sparky on his way to lunch with Blaire and Suzie. They were all laughing at something, enjoying each other's company, and I began to cry. Now that the script wasn't going to be made, I was sure it was one of the best scripts I'd ever written. This would have been the one that showed them. The more the tears rolled down my cheeks the better the script became.

I was weeping because I'd finally really realized for the last time that my entire adult life had been wasted. I'd chosen a business where you can never feel successful enough because your work and self-esteem could be taken away at any moment. Like all Hollywood writers, I'd been willing to give up authority to anyone who'd have me. Hershel understood the despair and would have been the person to call, but part of him would feel satisfaction in my misfortune. He couldn't help it. I was turning into Hershel. And I couldn't help it either.

If I could only talk to Dora, but she was getting very deaf. She had roaring sounds in her head and it made telephone calls increasingly difficult. I'd never gone to see her because I was always trying to work. For years I'd given up participating in life in order to write about it. I'd sacrificed myself only to be sacrificed. Now I had no more excuses, except seeing her meant dealing with my parents, explaining my failure.

But even as I was crying and hating myself, I knew how laughable it was. If Jerry Slotnick were to call me right then and there and say Cantrowitz had changed his mind—my script had been green-lighted after all—my ego would soar as if propelled by a flaming booster rocket. And that made me feel even worse about myself. I sat at my desk, watching Sparky and Blaire and Suzie disappear into the commissary. I wanted out of Hollywood in the worst way. But where could I go? New York? How would I make a living there? It was too late to change professions. I was stuck. I heard a gentle knock. No doubt it was Mai Lei telling me she was off to lunch. I put on my sunglasses and hoped she wouldn't see from my eyes I'd been crying. She opened the door. "Excuse me for bothering you. Are you busy?"

"What's up?"

She held up two sheets of paper. "I wanted to show you this. Because I don't know what to do about it." It looked like she, too, had been crying. She handed me the pages. I read it through very quickly and then read it through very carefully. It was Mai Lei's idea about the Brooklyn baker who sings at an Italian restaurant, only it had been translated into a Queens garage mechanic who sings at a karaoke bar. Instead of opera it was Frank Sinatra, but the story was essentially the same, beat for beat. At the end of the outline, the author had added his own producer's touch. *I really see this as the perfect comedic vehicle for Nicholas Cage, but in any case it's a good role to attract male leads. It can go anywhere from Tom Hanks to Matthew Broderick depending on availability and budget considerations.*

"What is this?"

"Sparky gave it to me. He doesn't want anybody to know that this came from him because he doesn't want to get into trouble. He got it off of Judi's desk. This is my story. How could Jonathan do that to me? They're already looking for a writer."

This was the original idea Jonathan had told me he'd developed for Judi and Joel.

"The first thing to do is to speak to Jonathan about it and find out what's going on."

"I tried to but he's out to lunch."

"You didn't by any chance register this with the Writers Guild, did you?"

"No. Should I have?"

Not that it mattered. Mai Lei was the perfect victim. She stood at my desk while I put in a call to Judi and Joel's office, hoping to track Jonathan down, but no one was in. I left a message asking Jonathan to call me as soon as he returned. Jonathan was ambitious and lazy but I still couldn't believe he could be so boldly dishonest. I was hoping for an explanation. That somehow he'd forgotten her idea and mistaken it as his own, as authors always plead when accused of plagiarism. But I knew it wasn't possible. That's why he'd been so cautious with me. It had nothing to do with Wendy Rubin, it was all about Mai Lei. At four o'clock I finally walked over to Little Red Wagon Productions.

Jonathan had his own office now, a tiny room filled with shelf after shelf of unproduced scripts Judi and Joel were keeping as writing samples. A copy of *GQ* was lying on the desk. The collared long-sleeved woolen sweater Jonathan wore, with a shirt and tie peeking out from underneath, was probably inspired by his latest reading material. He looked so English schoolboy I wanted to smack him, enlist him in the army, make a man of him. He hung up the phone. "You're on my call sheet," he said. "I've been dealing with agents all day. Oh, God. Do I have a headache." He took some aspirin out of his desk and downed them with a Diet Pepsi.

"Looking for a writer for your project?"

"There are so many bad writers out there you wouldn't believe it. I'm trying to find someone new so I can contain the cost. But it's hard."

"Why don't you suggest Mai Lei to write it?"

"You're kidding, right?"

"Why would I be kidding? It was her idea."

He didn't seem at all surprised when I said that. "The only good ideas in her script are the ones I gave her when we were working together. I practically outlined the whole plot for her. All she had to do was write it."

"How nice of you to make it so easy for her."

"What do you think? I STOLE the idea from Mai Lei?"

"Mai Lei's been working on that script since before you even came to the studio, and for you to just decide to change the borough and the songs is"—I tried to think of a word—"stealing."

"Oh, come on. I can't believe this. Mai Lei's script was going nowhere. I honestly thought she'd abandoned it by now." His eyelids were fluttering rapidly and it finally dawned on me why. Jonathan was lying.

"You were the one who abandoned your script. She actually finished hers."

"Finishing something bad is commendable?"

"No matter what you added to the plot, it was Mai Lei's original idea. You can't just take someone's idea and call it your own. It's just not done."

"What do you mean? It's done all the time. Coppola did it in *Apocalypse Now, West Side Story*'s *Romeo and Juliet*. You telling me *Jaws* was original? All it was, was *Moby-Dick* and *Death in Venice* with a big mechanical shark thrown in to scare everyone."

"*Death in Venice?*"

"Of course. Everyone knows what's going down in Venice but they're hush hush because it's tourist season. I'm not saying that *Jaws* is Thomas Mann or Melville but come on. It sure isn't original."

"It's one thing to borrow inspiration from the classics. It's another thing to borrow from Mai Lei. Do you understand the difference here?"

"Jesus Christ. I don't believe we're having this inane conversation. Would you get off your moral high horse please? I've already spoken to Judi and Joel about it. I said that if anything happens with this project that Mai Lei should get some kind of 'inspired from an idea by' or whatever the fuck the credit is. I'm doing Mai Lei a favor. Mai Lei's not a writer, you know that. At least this way she'll get SOME kind of credit."

I really wanted to believe Jonathan. "You still should have consulted her before you went ahead and wrote it up as your own."

"I was waiting until it was a done deal to tell her. I didn't want to promise her something that was never going to happen. Now, can we get past this, please, because I have some good news for you." My heart jumped.

"What?"

"I think I got you invited to Judi's house for the Academy Awards." He presented it as if he was working on getting me a night in the Lincoln Bedroom.

"You THINK you got me invited?"

"When I mentioned your name she said great, she just has to go over the final list with Alan. I'm sure it's no problem."

"Why would I even WANT to go to Judi's house for the Academy Awards?"

"I'll tell you why. Because if you're not right in front of Judi's nose, she'll forget about you, that's why. If you want to get things done in this town, you've got to put yourself out there. This is a business of personal relationships and you're starting to disappear. That's the trouble with you writers. Everyone else in the business wants klieg lights. You think you can be a forty-watt bulb and people will notice you."

At that very moment I knew I hated Jonathan and I hated myself for having played up to him for the sake of a script. My repulsion was so instantaneous I wondered how I ever could have liked him. I just wanted to get away from him as quickly as possible. "Thanks for the advice," I said, and walked out.

Sparky was miffed at Jonathan for his own reasons. When he saw me abruptly exit Jonathan's office across the hall from his own, he called to me.

"Hi, you. Why don't you come and visit with me." He was sitting at his desk urgently waving me in. "Do you believe him?" Sparky said under his breath. "I mean, have you ever heard of doing anything so rotten? Especially to poor Mai Lei, who wouldn't hurt a fly." And then he spoke louder for the benefit of Jonathan across the hall. "So I haven't seen you. You've been so busy. Mai Lei says you bought a house, lucky you." He resumed talking to me in a whisper. "Not only that, he was only supposed to read scripts on the side. He was still supposed to be a secretary here and all of a sudden I'm having to answer the phones and do my job AND his job. He even asks me to Xerox for him. I'm not going to Xerox for him, I'm sorry, I'm just not. He can just do his own Xeroxing."

I made some sympathetic acknowledgment of the situation and

headed back to my office, creating arguments in my own defense, excuses for having once befriended Jonathan. The truth was, my dislike of him had been slowly building. When you lose a friend, you wonder if it was lack of judgment in the beginning or lack of tolerance in the end. In this case, I'd gotten caught in Jonathan's need to seduce, to win over those who most despised him. I was much too easy. He'd caught me at a vulnerable time in my life. Now he had a contempt for me which he felt for all suckers. I don't know if I felt foolish or duped or just sad at how dangerous relationships are.

I told Mai Lei what Jonathan had said, leaving out, of course, his estimation of her as a writer. Mai Lei told me Jonathan had copied her script onto his own computer so he could help her with it. It would be hard to prove he'd stolen it. If the script ever got made, I promised I'd help her get justice, but I wasn't sure we'd have much of a case.

"Gee. Thanks, Frankie," she said in her meek little way. She was the forty-watt bulb Jonathan had screwed.

Ian Mandel was standing in the commissary in front of an oozing yogurt machine, his eyes fixed on the chocolate banana swirls as they snaked into his cardboard cup. I got in line behind him, two miserable creatures trying to assuage our fear of failure with junk food. Ian's contract was up for renewal and he was worried. Mai Lei heard from his secretary that he'd have to sell his house if he lost his job. I told him what happened, seeking his advice. But he was very unsympathetic to Mai Lei's plight.

"She was stupid. I don't show my scripts to anyone until they're registered."

"Jonathan was her friend. I'm sure she never thought this would happen."

"Puh. Are you kidding me? This is Hollywood. It doesn't matter that you didn't do the work. What matters is that you get the credit and your price goes up and people THINK you did it. Jonathan better not try to fuck with me. It's perfect he'd wind up working for Judi and Joel, two other people I really love." He tossed the empty yogurt cup in the trash and lumbered back toward his office, talking to himself like a homeless person.

Miriam had her own homespun take on the situation. "Friendships in Hollywood have a short shelf life," she said. "They're sweet until they turn to botulism."

I never received that invitation to Judi's house. But about a week later Jerry Slotnick called. "I've got these two tickets to the Academy Awards the studio gave me. I don't know what to do with them. Yoshi's moved up to the house in Santa Barbara because she wants Abby to go to a public school and she doesn't think she can come down here for just a night. You have a dress? You feel like going with me?"

I had the dress. It was the same dress I'd worn the year Hart had won and I hadn't worn it since. But I didn't have the desire to put it on again. "I really hate going to those things, Jerry, but thanks for asking." I could only think he'd been turned down by other women higher up on the list.

"Everyone hates going to those things unless you walk away with a statue, then you feel pretty good for about a day. No question. Winning is better than just sitting there. But I need a date and you're the only one I can think of to ask."

"Why me?"

"I don't socialize in Hollywood as much as you think I do. I'm watching a lot of TV these days. At least I know you."

All week I'd been brooding over what Jonathan had said. That it was a business of relationships and I was starting to disappear.

Jerry picked me up in a white stretch limousine. "I'm sorry," he said. "They were all out of black." It didn't bother the children who lived next door, two girls who'd been sitting in their tree house. They climbed down and walked to the edge of my lawn with their mother and stood a respectful distance from the car. When I emerged from my house with Jerry, the younger girl, a little curly redhead who was about eight, called out to us. "Are you going to the Academy Awards?"

"No, we're going to the prom," Jerry said. "Do you think we'll win for king and queen?"

"You are NOT," her older sister, who must have been around ten, said. "You're going to the Academy Awards. I can tell."

"How can you tell?" Jerry asked her in that voice grown-ups use with children.

"Because you're OLD."

Her mother laughed.

"Oy," Jerry said, stabbing himself in the heart. "That hurts. Even though I'm old, I love your tree house. Maybe you'll invite us up for drinks sometime." He was delighting both little girls. I didn't know their names but I knew that one of them played the piano. I could hear it sometimes when I was reading in bed at night. Her repertoire wasn't very extensive but she practiced a lot, mostly the first few bars of "Für Elise."

"Are you anyone famous?" the younger one asked.

"Not this year," Jerry replied.

We left right after lunch but the line of limousines outside the Shrine was so long we barely made it to our seats before they closed the doors to the auditorium. Not that missing the opening number would have been any great hardship. And not that we would have been missed. You wouldn't know it from watching on television, but during breaks for commercials, a portion of the audience heads for the lobby. Standing against the theater walls, just out of sight of the cameras, are alert, eager people dressed in gowns or tuxedos. They're "seat fillers." They look the part of the invitee, they clap and they laugh at all the appropriate times, but they've never done anything to deserve an invitation. That's what Jonathan is, I thought. He's a seat filler. Only he cleverly keeps moving to better seats.

Jerry and I got up only once. We were spotted almost immediately by Joel Dweck, who was trolling the lobby. "We've got to get together," he said, planting his hand on my arm. "I've just reread your script on the plane back from New York, and I think I know how to fix it." I wondered if Joel had really read the script or if it was said to impress the person he'd been talking to; to emphasize that Joel was a producer on the move and I was one of his writers and he knew how to fix my script.

"I'm available," I said, and continued on to the ladies' room. I'd put myself out there as Jonathan had suggested but it had only led right back to Joel. When I was a safe distance away, I turned back to look at him, to watch him in action. He'd already hooked on to someone else and was standing just a little too close.

By the time the evening was over, Jerry and I had hardly spoken. It was enough just getting there, sitting through the ceremony, trying to eat at the Governors' Ball with waiters rushing to take away our plates, and waiting for Moby-Dick among the sea of black limousines. But once we were cruising along in the car, we were both more relaxed that the night was almost over.

"Thanks again for coming," he said. He was sitting across from me, about fifteen feet away, pouring us some mineral water from the bar. Lighted stars twinkled on the roof over our heads, changing color every few seconds, melting from one color to another as they went through the spectrum of the rainbow. It was hypnotic and I found myself wishing we were driving farther than just home. Jerry slid along one of the black seats and handed me my water. *"L'chayim,"* he said, clinking glasses with me.

We leaned back and enjoyed the light show. "I think this may be Grace Slick's old limo. If you check behind the seats you can probably find some old acid tabs. I used to like that Grace Slick. I thought she was sexy in an acid kind of way. You ever do acid?"

"No. You?"

"Mescaline once. Angel dust once by mistake. Grass was the drug of choice."

"When was the last time you smoked?"

"A few years ago—someone brought a joint over. I hadn't smoked in years. We snuck out to the garage so my daughter wouldn't catch us. We used to hide it from our parents, now I'm hiding it from my kid."

"Was it any good?"

"It was great. I took one smell of the stuff and I was twenty years old. I didn't even have to smoke it and I was high. It brought me right back."

"To what?"

"To a time when everything was ahead of me. When everything felt new. When sex was mysterious and forbidden. Those were the days, huh?" He took his eyes off the stars and looked at me. "By the way, I think Yoshi and I are getting a divorce."

"I'm sorry."

"Yeah. Well. What can you do." He shook his head. "This business is very hard on a marriage. The wife doesn't always have it easy, I know that. And it's doubly hard for Yoshi. She was a professional woman in New York. Here she's just my wife. She hates socializing here because she feels she has no identity. The Academy Awards? Forget it. I should have listened to my parents. I should have married a Jew."

"You really think it would've made any difference?"

"The older I get the more I think you should stick to your own kind."

"You don't think you two can work it out?"

"She wants to move up to Santa Barbara full-time. What am I going to do up there? I mean, it's beautiful with the mountains and the ocean, but do I belong there? There's no tension. There's no stress. I go up there for a weekend and play tennis but that's about all I can take."

"So why can't you two stay together and just go up on weekends?"

"Ultimately it comes down to the fact that we want different things in life. I'm comfortable here. I understand Hollywood."

"What do you understand about it?"

"The whole power and structure thing, it's just a metaphor for the *shtetl,* for the whole Jewish experience. It's the nicest *shtetl* in the world but it's still a *shtetl.* It's got the same *shtetl* mentality. I better get mine while I can because you never know when there's going to be a knock at your door and someone will come and take it all away from you."

"I hate that."

He shrugged. "It may be bad, but I could be living in a Polish ghetto in 1939. What are they going to do to me here? Take away my swimming pool? That's what Yoshi doesn't get. She doesn't get the ups and downs. With the gentiles, they want there to be a reason. The Jews know over and over again that it can happen and not because they've done anything wrong. It's just more of the same *mishegoss* that's been our whole experience. YOU understand the feelings Jews live with. A Jew knows that it's part of the game. To engage in a game where it can all be taken away is second nature to a Jew. And if the studio doesn't take it away, God will. Fires, floods, earthquakes. L.A.'s the perfect place for the Jews."

"But why is it like that? It doesn't HAVE to be like that. Who's making it like that?"

"The power."

"But the power, they're Jews, too. Don't they see it? Why are they such killers? With each other?"

"It's a business. Business is business."

"No. There's something more. I keep meeting the same person over and over again. Where are the heroic men in Hollywood? They write about them, they make movies about them, but they have no such impulses themselves. They're all just out there covering their own asses, running around trying to get the good table, the best hotel room, the right wine, the first-class seat, the big deal, the green light, the huge grosses, the full-page ad in the trades, the credit. Even if they don't deserve the credit they still want it. There's not even any embarrassment about it. They operate under an entirely different moral code, which they all accept. No one's ever surprised by bad behavior in Hollywood."

"You do what you can to survive. It's a tough world out there. There's only room for so many people at the top of the mountain. That's why everyone's always so glad when someone else falls off."

"Maybe if they made better movies there'd be more room on top."

"You know what it takes to make a good movie? You know the hoops you have to jump through? It's a miracle anything good ever gets made in this town. And you think the *goyim* in this business are so honorable? I know plenty of killer *goyim,* believe me."

"So that justifies it?"

"We can't all be Harts, you know. Hart can afford to be relaxed. He looks like his whole *mishpocheh* came over on the *Mayflower.*"

"He's hardly relaxed. He just does it in a different way."

"Maybe it's vulgar to strive but at least it's not dull." He went into the candy dish and took out a butterscotch. Then he put his feet on the seat and looked up at the ceiling twinkling away. "With us, we're just re-creating what we feel comfortable with. It's like unconsciously marrying someone who's like your parent and re-creating your whole childhood all over again. As hard as you try, you can't escape it. Yoshi's more like my mother than I care to admit. She's very disapproving. She's very critical. She's just wrapped in a nicer package."

The car went over a pothole and the water jumped out of my glass onto my gown. Jerry grabbed a napkin from the bar and patted the water away. "It'll be okay," he said. "Fortunately it was just water."

"So if Jews are so obsessed with being Jews, why are they so afraid of portraying themselves on-screen in any realistic way?"

He thought for a moment. "Show business gives you power over the WASP. You reflect back to them like a mirror the WASP culture, and what you present to them, they pay money to see. What they pay money to see is shallow. It's their culture. It's never going to feed the soul. It's the jealousy love/hate thing that the Jews have for the WASPs. The WASPs don't have to be deep. It's the scene in Woody Allen where he stops the two beautiful WASPs on the street and they tell him how shallow they are. They don't feel obliged to suffer. Their God isn't as demanding as our God. He doesn't make you get circumcised, command you to sacrifice your son, and then forbid you to eat spareribs on top of it. And let's face it, WASPs are prettier to watch and they sell more tickets. But if *klezmer* bands suddenly became hot, they'd be making movies about *klezmer* bands."

"But they'd cast it with non-Jews."

"Jews don't feel comfortable showing real Jews because, as my old *bubbe* used to say, a sheep that sticks its neck up above the flock gets it cut off. Besides, no one wants to watch real Jews having sex. Barbra Streisand and Woody Allen in bed together? It's like walking in on your parents. Look at *The Garden of the Finzi-Continis*. Italian Jews. Who does Bertolucci cast? Dominique Sanda. You can't get any more *shiksa* than her. But it worked."

I thought I understood everything about Jerry when I first saw him. I'd understood nothing.

When Jerry walked me to my door he gave me a light kiss on the cheek. "Thanks for listening. It seems like I'm always dumping my family problems on you."

"One day maybe I'll dump my family on you."

"It always easier to take other people's families."

"Not mine." I put my key in the door.

"You like Chinese food? You ever go to Monkee's? There's a place in Venice that has seafood just as good. You feel like going there some night this week? Just as a friend. Just as a person who likes Chinese food."

"Just as a friend."

"Strictly. I just don't feel like being alone these days."

"Being alone is good, Jerry."

"Not in a Chinese restaurant it isn't."

I got up to the nursery, hurried over to the window, and watched the limousine drive away. I sat on my bed and took off my heels and realized that I was actually looking forward to having lotus rice with Jerry Slotnick.

HIKING WITH JEWS

FROM THE DAY I'd confronted him about Mai Lei's script, Jonathan never again stopped by my office. Although he wouldn't acknowledge it outright, the friendship was over. But it wasn't easy avoiding each other on a small studio lot. I was just getting out of my car one morning when a loud *honk honk* made me jump. Jonathan Prince was aiming his car-alarm remote at his brand-new blue-gray BMW convertible. He'd maneuvered himself right into the writers' parking lot only two spaces away from me. Although not as coveted as the executive parking lot, it was still a hell of a lot closer than his old space in the secretaries' lot a block away. I flipped down my sunvisor mirror and brushed my hair, giving Jonathan lead time. I wondered if he would've been as considerate of me.

A few weeks later a black bear was auditioning on a patch of lawn in front of our building. A group of people had gathered around to watch. "Go on. Maul me. Maul me," I heard a man's voice command, and peering between some heads, I saw the bear stand on its hind legs and put its paws around its trainer. There was a moment that looked like a bad fox-trot, where one partner has no ear for the music. Then it was over, the trainer went into a box of doughnuts, pulled out a white powdery confection, and popped it into the bear's mouth.

"You'd think he'd at least give him a bear claw." It was Jonathan. I turned around and found myself face-to-face. "Look who's here. I haven't seen you in a while. How's your house?" He was *schmoozing* me, as if nothing had ever happened.

"How you doing, Jonathan?" I asked, trying keep my manner neutral.

"Oh, you know. Always too much work to do. We should get together though. You should give me a call." The audition was over, the crowd was breaking up, and he was already on the move. "Got to run, I've got a lunch in Studio City." He glanced at his watch, more as a gesture than to actually see the time. "I'm already late."

He sauntered toward the parking lot in no particular hurry, keys in hand, a script under his arm. Whoever he was meeting would wait. Sparky had complained to me that Jonathan was having him call restaurants to say Jonathan Prince was on his way. I half-wondered who his latest conquest was. He seemed so transparent now, I couldn't believe he could fool anyone. I didn't have to wait long to see I was wrong.

"Someone I bumped into said they saw you and Jerry Slotnick together at some function. Are you and Jerry SEEING each other?" Freyda and I were in the exclusive executive dining room. She'd come to the lot on other business and was taking me to lunch. Judi and Joel had been cajoled by Freyda into having me do more revisions on *Ivy and Men,* but we all knew it was just an exercise. Freyda was taking me to lunch so she could do what she did best: be the sympathetic agent.

"We're just friends."

"Are you sure?"

"I don't know. Let me check again."

"I've always liked Jerry. Yoshi was a little tough though. Did you ever meet Yoshi?"

"Never had the pleasure."

"She's terrific, I love her, but she definitely knows what she wants. She wanted Jerry, you know, this rich Jewish husband who would take good care of her. I hear he's giving her the house in Santa

Barbara." It was true. The BoyMan had been prescient. Jerry was going up there every weekend to see Abby and staying in the guest house.

Freyda went into her purse and found a Ziploc bag from which she took a plastic bottle filled with her own salad dressing. She shook it vigorously as we talked. "I can't believe she's already met someone else. I'm sure that just kills Jerry."

"He misses his daughter."

"I love Abby. She looks just like Yoshi, very petite and very cute, but I think her personality is going to be more like Jerry's." She popped the top on the squeeze bottle and dribbled the dressing over her Cobb salad, which had been revamped by Freyda into something resembling no other Cobb salad on the planet. "So how's your re-write coming?"

"Judi and Joel have finally figured out what's wrong with my script."

"I hate to ask."

"It needs jeopardy."

"JEOPARDY? It's a love story between two cousins. What kind of jeopardy are they looking for?"

"They're not cousins anymore. Joel wanted sexual tension."

"So Arthur's not gay anymore?"

"Hell no. He's a REAL man who gets drafted into the Vietnam War but comes home and becomes an architect."

"You're kidding me."

"With his own firm."

"What does Judi know about story?" Freyda said, lowering her voice. "It just drives me crazy."

"Ivy's married now to some war protester but she still loves Arthur."

Freyda sighed as if she couldn't take any more. "You know what you've got to do? You've got to distance yourself from the script. Realize it no longer has anything to do with you. It's just a job, that's all it is."

"I guess I wanted it to be more than just a job. That's why I wanted to be really careful about who I sold it to."

Freyda ignored my innuendo. "You're just tired because you've been working on it for too long. We've got to get you started on another project. I'm meeting with Jonathan Prince at three-thirty to discuss writers. I know he really likes your writing. He's a big fan of yours."

I kept quiet while Freyda rummaged around the salad bowl with her fork. I didn't know what I was going to say until I said it. "Maybe you can explain something to me. Jonathan never made it as an agent. He wasn't even a good secretary. He tried to be a writer but he couldn't finish anything. He wheedled his way into some development job where he now 'finds' properties that agents send to him, or he just steals other people's ideas and passes them off as his own, and you're telling me that you're pitching me to him as a writer? Who the fuck is Jonathan to judge me as a writer and why would I EVER want to work with Joel and Judi again?"

Freyda continued to burrow through her salad looking for hidden crumbs of feta. Nothing I said riled her. She was an inflatable clown with sand feet, popping back up after every punch. "I guess you haven't heard. Jonathan doesn't work for Judi and Joel anymore. He's about to take over Emily Ginsburg's job. He's going to be a creative executive working right under Lance Topping. Cantrowitz is giving Lance his own movie division and my guess is that Lance is probably going to be grooming Jonathan to be his VP, so you're going to have to deal with him sometime. And I happen to like Jonathan. I think he's very smart. And Marty likes him, too. Marty and Jonathan played golf together a few months ago. We all had a great time."

"Where?" I had a feeling I knew.

"We all went to Two Bunch Palms together. Katie is very sweet. While the boys played golf, we got massaged. She doesn't have one spider vein. Her legs are perfectly tan. I hate her."

It was typical Jonathan, lying to me about not wanting to bump into Freyda and Marty in Two Bunch Palms. And it was vintage Freyda and Marty, playing up to Jonathan. Jonathan was now in a position to buy her clients and to send Marty scripts. It behooved them to like Jonathan. If you only knew what Jonathan says about you, I thought.

Fortunately, I was invited to Hershel and Miriam's for *Shabbes* dinner that night, because I needed to tell them what had transpired.

I wanted their reaction, which would be satisfying. It was just the three of us, and Hershel, his attention undivided, listened quietly as I presented all the evidence. Then he pronounced his verdict in that calm, sarcastic voice he used when registering disgust. "There is no justice in Hollywood. Only Hollywood justice." But Miriam didn't have much of a reaction. All she said was, "What a business."

Miriam was uncharacteristically subdued at dinner, too. I knew she was upset because Hershel was working for a producer who was refusing to pay him. Now that the work was done the producer was denying he'd ever agreed with Hershel's agent about a price. Since there was no deal memo, it was Hershel and his agent's word against the producer's. Miriam was getting up and down serving us dinner, not really participating in the conversation. I presumed she was worried about money again.

We were alone in the kitchen doing dishes when she revealed what was really on her mind. She'd been holding it in all evening until Hershel had gone up to his office to write.

"You couldn't have brought up that thing about Jonathan at a worse time."

"What do you mean? Why?"

"It fed right into Hershel's whole feeling about Hollywood. Right before you got here Hershel announced that he's never again going to give his hard work to Hollywood. He's through with the business for good. He wants me to put the house on the market and we'll move to a small place and live on the proceeds while he devotes the rest of his life to writing plays. He accused me of not being supportive."

"What? What's he talking about?"

"Not only that, I embarrassed him at Jonathan's Christmas party in front of a whole table full of people. 'What did I say?' I asked him. 'What could I have possibly done?' Who can remember, it was so long ago? You know what I did? You want to know what I said? I said that his play was a hit in Finland. That's what I did. That was my big sin."

"So? I don't get it."

"So is right. I said it was making money in Finland. I implied that it didn't do well here. I 'undermined' him. Can you imagine? Can you imagine that I'm not supportive? Who typed all of his plays for him? Who goes to the Xerox place? Who stands in line at the post office and mails them out? Who gives the dinners for his agents and reads his plays and tells him how brilliant he is? Who kept the children away so he could write? Who went to all the graduations and did all of the birthday parties by herself when they were growing up because he was always working? Who does all the accounting and pays all the bills because he doesn't want to be bothered? He never wants to know how much money we have because then he won't be able to write. I do all the worrying for the both of us. Sometimes we get down to nothing and I make it stretch. But I shouldn't tell him. And now he's taking away my house from me. For fifteen years he made me move over and over again to different rentals and finally I get a house and he promises me I'll never have to move again. I made all the weddings in the backyard. All the bar mitzvahs. I thought Noah would be married here, too, when the time came. I thought I'd have a house full of grandchildren, where everyone would come for the holidays. But does he care about that? The house doesn't matter to him. The kids don't matter to him. I don't matter to him. All that matters to him are those plays. The selfish bastard."

The Sunday the realtor held an open house, Hershel and I, Miriam and Noah, home from grad school, left before the hordes so Miriam wouldn't have to watch strangers traipsing through her beloved rooms. We decided to take a long hike up Temescal Canyon to Skull Rock. The mountains had turned a beautiful summer golden color but there were still some wildflowers left from the spring. An hour in, we stopped at a waterfall and stood on a little wooden bridge, watching a dog paddling around in the fern-edged pool, biting at his own splashes. Then we began the ascent. Except for an occasional aside, we stopped talking and concentrated on the climb. The farther we got away from the shady canyon, the scrubbier the landscape became. Dust kicked up around our ankles and sweat began to soak the back of Hershel's long-sleeved work shirt. A red-tailed hawk slowly circled high above our heads. I took some sage and rubbed the scented leaves between my fingers thinking how sweet life can sometimes be, when Miriam, who was just ahead of me, turned around.

"Can you imagine doing this if the Nazis were chasing you?"

It was so perfectly Miriam I had to laugh. "It's a beautiful day, the sun is shining, the birds are singing, we have chicken-salad sandwiches for lunch. Enjoy it, you big *meshuggeneh*."

"There's nothing like hiking with Jews," Hershel said. But instead of his usual amusement with her non sequiturs, he sounded impatient.

"Today they'd never have the nerve to deny entry to the S.S. *St. Louis*," she said, referring to the ill-fated boatload of desperate German Jews the United States turned away. "That's why I get so down on these intermarriages where they raise kids who have no feeling for the religion. Who's going to defend us the next time if they don't even know they're Jews?"

But no one wanted to carry this conversation any further, including Miriam, who dropped it to worry about the mayonnaise in the chicken salad, which she thought might spoil in the heat.

When we returned to the house, sweaty, dusty, and tired, the realtor was poised in the living room. There was already an offer. Miriam's legs seemed to give way and she sank to the couch.

Little Macho, sensing something was wrong, clicked across her prized mahogany floors, his black nails like tiny castanets, and jumped right onto Miriam's lap. It was the only time I'd ever seen her allow him near the white couch. The real-estate woman sat next to Miriam and tried to comfort her with soft, ineffectual little pats. "We'll find you a nice house. We will. I promise."

"But never like this. This was my home."

When she began to cry, Hershel, who had watched in silence, walked out of the room.

There were so many things to get rid of it took three garage sales and caused major traffic jams. She sold most of their books to a used bookstore. The heavy breakfront was bought by a used-furniture dealer. Her garage freezer was donated to the synagogue. But everything else went into the rummage pile. Her children's old toys, which she'd been saving for her future grandchildren, were snapped up by gardeners and maids. Towels, linens, and forty ironed damask napkins she used for her massive Passover dinners were put into cardboard boxes and sold in bulk. Forty not-quite-matching wineglasses and the white Passover china she'd bought piece by piece at thrift stores all went. Miriam's collection of glass owls and pigs, gone. Everything Miriam had acquired in garage sales was now dispersed again throughout the city.

Hershel stayed in his writing room. He was trying to finish his new play about the forty-year-old woman who has to seek love all over again, convinced this was his hit. This would be the one that made it to Broadway.

In late September, Judi's water broke in the Design Center's Knoedler Fauchier showroom. Sparky told me she was with Henri Faroli at the time, standing on the sisal carpeting, which I know from experience, doesn't take liquids too well. While Judi called Alan, her obstetrician, and Sparky, Henri Faroli called his wallpaper man, curtain hanger, carpet installer, and furniture delivery service, who'd all been standing by. Judi and Alan had decided they didn't want to know the sex of the baby. The only person Judi's doctor had told was Henri Faroli, who'd worked with Judi to pick out two entirely different color schemes. While Judi was relaxing with her epidural and showing Alan and the nurse a video of her polished rough cut, Henri and the decorating SWAT team were madly putting together the perfect nursery for baby Tess.

A month later I was invited by Judi and Joel to the premier of Wendy Rubin's movie but instead drove to Jerry's house in Malibu. It was Halloween and I wanted to get out of my house before the bell-ringers. Traffic was unusually light on PCH and I was feeling happy and excited for no particular reason. It'd been one of those cloudless days you get in the fall where the sky at the beach is a deep blue and the quality of light makes everything sharp and bright. The air was Santa Ana dry but without the winds and people were beginning to light their fireplaces again. Early-evening walkers lifted their noses to the fragrant smell and took in small, quick sniffs, wondering if the hills were on fire, or if someone was just having a cozy dinner at home. I'd spent the day at my desk with all the windows open, getting rid of bills and medical-insurance forms that had been hanging over my head. I was feeling almost carefree.

Jerry opened the door with his portable phone to his ear. "Dwacula? You're going as Dwacula? How do you know what Dwacula looks like?" He mouthed "Abby" to me as if I couldn't have guessed.

I nodded and headed for the kitchen with Jerry right behind me. I poured myself a glass of wine from a bottle that he'd just opened. He motioned that I should pour him one, too. "Oh, a lot of fake blood, I see." He looked at me as he talked to her, letting me in on their conversation. Jerry had brought four-year-old Abby to the studio one day and she was just about the most perfect child I'd ever met. I could see why Jerry got that look in his eye whenever he spoke to her. "Have Mommy take some pictures of you in your Dwacula costume, will you? Will you tell her to do it? I love you. Call me tomorrow and let me know how your haul was." Jerry clicked off the phone. "Dwacula. What a kid. I'm telling you. I get such *naches* from this kid."

"You sad you're not with her tonight?"

"I'm sad I'm not with her every night. She makes me laugh, what can I say?" He opened up the freezer. "Commere and take a look. I had Suzie go to Trader Joe's and load up on all kinds of shit. Tell me what you want for dinner." He started taking things out from the freezer. "Cheese enchiladas, chicken enchiladas, I don't want Mexican food, do you?" He took out a cardboard box. "PaLAK aLOO?" He read the package. " 'A traditional Indian entrée. A meatless entreé of lightly spiced spinach and potato.' Is she kidding? Is she out of her fucking mind? You got to wonder about Suzie sometimes. Sometimes I worry that she's never going to find someone. I think that's her problem. God, she needs to get laid in the worst way. But who in their right mind would want to have sex with her? She's too hysterical, that Suzie. Palak aloo. She can give it to her cat." He tossed it back in the freezer and took out another entrée. "Look at this cioppino. Look at all the fish they give you. For four ninety-nine that's a lot cheaper than going to Toscana."

I loved that he loved his daughter. I liked that he cared about, albeit in his own way, Suzie Piccioni, my short-lived secretary. He was generous to his sister, he was paying for the BoyMan's braces, he was generous to his ex-wife and generous with me. I'd helped him through his divorce, he'd helped me through my rewrites. Whenever one of us had something to attend where we needed a date, we took the other. Jerry never allowed me to pick up a check and always walked me to the door and gave me a light kiss like the first night. He kept reiterating that it was good we weren't having sex. "There's no pressure," Jerry kept saying. "That's the thing I like about this relationship. No pressure."

While Jerry assembled our dinner, I carved out a pumpkin I'd bought at the YMCA. We found a candle to put in the center and brought it to a small table by the living room window. Jerry turned on the outside spots so we could see the ocean and we settled in with our cioppino.

"You know I've been giving this some thought," Jerry said to me as he poured the last of the wine. "I think we should sleep together."

"When did you figure this out?"

"On my way down from Santa Barbara, right around Neptune's Net. I realized that I'm attracted to you and there's no one else I'd rather be with. And I'm getting tired of being celibate. And who's a safer sex partner than me? I was married, I didn't screw around, and you're practically a nun. We don't even need condoms."

"Well, when you put it like that . . ."

"I'm being honest. Women like honesty, don't they? Suzie's always telling me that men play games. Who has the time for that shit?"

"I thought you didn't want any pressure."

"Now I want it. I want it big time."

"I can't change gears like that. You're my friend. It would ruin everything. Especially if it didn't work out. I think it's a bad idea."

"I don't want to analyze this to death."

"Who's analyzing it to death? We're discussing it."

"Aw, fuck it." He pushed his chair back and stood up. "I've been thinking about this all day. I just need to do this." He pulled me up until I was standing next to him and he kissed me. It was a gentle kiss at first, just grazing my lips, but he held me close, his hands tightening around my waist. Then his hand found its way into my shirt and a feeling swept over me that I thought I'd lost. It had been a long time since anyone had touched me. I was acutely aware of the sensations but felt like I was in a dream. I was pressed against his chest and I felt the warmth of his body, smelled warm wine on his breath. I was just barely conscious of the ocean pounding outside the glass doors and the candle flickering onto the white walls through slit eyes and a jagged-toothed grin. He unzipped my jeans. "You want to know something?" he said when he found what he was looking for. "This is the secret to life right here."

He took my hand and led me upstairs into the bedroom. The maid had been there that day and the white rug still had vacuum tracks. The bed was perfectly made. Jerry threw back the comforter and as we lay back on the bed he unbuttoned my shirt. "This is incredible," I said. "What am I doing here?"

He looked at me in the dim light. "I lied to you, when I said I'd been thinking about this all day. I've been thinking about this for seven months."

At eleven-thirty Jerry slipped on his pants and walked me to my car. It's not that I wanted to leave. Jerry had even offered to go to the supermarket and buy me contact-lens solution. But Freyda had set up a meeting with Jonathan the next morning at nine-thirty that I couldn't cancel. She kept reiterating, over my objections, that Jonathan was anxious to see me and since I was still under contract with the studio I'd better take the meeting. If I stayed with Jerry, I'd have to rush home early and then rush out to the studio. Also, I couldn't remember if I'd left the cat in or out.

"How are you feeling? You okay?" Jerry said as he opened my car door for me.

"I'm good." I had looked at myself in the bathroom mirror when I was getting ready to go. My face was all pink from Jerry's beard and I couldn't stop smiling at myself.

"Yeah. Me, too. You want me to follow you home?"

"It's not necessary."

"Suppose I want to."

"If you want to."

"Let me get my keys."

Neither Jerry nor I got any sleep that night. We were like two starving people who'd discovered there was a restaurant right next door that delivered at all hours. Just before dawn we both finally drifted off and when my alarm radio clicked on at seven-fifteen the last thing either one of us wanted to do was get up. Jerry had a ten o'clock plane to make and he still had to go home and pack. As soon as he'd put on his clothes he was out my door. "I'll call you when I get there. You going to be at the office all day?"

"It depends on how my meeting goes."

"Good luck."

I stood in the doorway and watched his car pull out of my driveway. Then I went back upstairs and took a long, hot, thought-filled bath. Every time I recalled the details of the night, I got a pleasant floating sensation in my stomach, like stopping in a rapidly ascending elevator. I'd managed to put the meeting with Jonathan almost out of my mind. But in the car on the way to the studio I began to doubt myself. Had Jonathan really been that bad? Maybe he was wanting to make amends and that's why he was anxious to see me. Maybe he missed just being friends. If nothing else, Jerry had taught me anything was possible.

GEDDUM A BASKET

SIMON, JONATHAN'S BRITISH secretary, had given me hasty directions to their office, as if instructing one more stupid American. "Proceed down the main hallway and make a right, between the Claes Oldenburg and the Roy Lichtenstein. If you see the Jasper Johns beer cans, you've gone too far."

Jonathan had left behind the cramped, script-filled office when he ascended to the heady realm of the carpeted, hushed third floor. I got to Jonathan's office at exactly nine-thirty but he was in a meeting behind closed doors. Simon was making himself a cup of tea and invited me to join him. "Tea?" he asked, looking at me with arched brows, like I'd shown up at Claridge's in Bermuda shorts. Simon was pasty and pudgy and, judging from a slightly pungent smell, wore rather wrinkled shirts for too many days between launderings. But on the phone he sounded quite proper, almost intimidating, and I'm sure his accent got Jonathan some very good tables. I sat down with my tea and thumbed through the *Hollywood Reporter*. There was a piece in George Christy's column on Judi and Joel's party after the premiere, and sure enough, there was Jonathan. He'd insinuated himself and Katie into a photo, standing very close to Lance Topping and his wife, Whitney. I couldn't believe I'd once suggested to Jonathan that Shelley would be a good match. Jonathan knew exactly what he wanted and short, plump Shelley with her tart comments would not have fit into this pretty picture.

I looked up when the door opened. "Okay, boss. I'm outta here." It was Ian Mandel, exuding his best tough-guy persona for Jonathan Prince. As Ian exited Jonathan's office our eyes met for just a second before Ian looked away. Out of embarrassment or lack of interest I couldn't say. He said good-bye profusely to Simon but barely acknowledged me. We'd come full circle, Ian and I. Jonathan must have gotten him an assignment. His contract had been picked up. He could keep his house for another year.

"Frankie!" Jonathan held out his hand to me in the most ingratiating way. He still had that disconcerting handshake where you couldn't quite get a grip. "You look terrific. You look very relaxed. What'd you do? Just get a massage?"

Was I that transparent? "And how."

"I knew it." He turned to Simon. "Could you get me a Diet Pepsi, and Frankie, what would you like?"

"I'm fine."

"Come in. I can't believe we work on the same lot and I hardly ever see you. So how ARE you? What's happening in your life? How's Hershel and Miriam?"

I followed Jonathan into his office, recognizing the large glass desk as Judi's castoff. I was relieved to see he didn't have a decorating budget. Yet. The only objects allowed to sully the perfect emptiness of his desk were a phone, a yellow legal pad, and a framed photograph of Katie.

"They sold their big house and moved to a little house and Hershel is still writing his plays. He's in London right now talking with his British agent."

"Great. Great. Say hi to them for me, will you?"

I didn't tell him that the move had thrown Miriam and Hershel's marriage into a tailspin. Or that Little Macho was dying in increments and Miriam was spending every spare penny she had on his chemo treatments, trying to keep him alive for another week or two. I didn't tell him that Hershel had talked of staying in England for a year and that he didn't want Miriam coming over because, he told her, he wanted to go to pubs and she had always hated the smoke. I didn't tell him the real reason was that Hershel had a girlfriend named Enid Knuckles, whom Miriam took every opportunity to refer to as the Cockney Cunt. I failed to mention Miriam had found out about it when she opened up the phone bill, which had suggested, due to the frequency of calls, that Enid Knuckles be made part of MCI's friends and family. Nor did I tell him Hershel showed up one day to retrieve the rest of his belongings and, before walking out again for good, left Miriam a Post-it stuck to the refrigerator door that read *M. Happy Hunting. H.*

"I saw Freyda not that long ago," Jonathan said. "She had on her Miss Piggie backpack and her overalls and barnyard pins. All that was missing was the weed stalk in her mouth and the manure on her shoes."

"I heard you and Marty played golf down in Palm Springs."

"If you can call it that. I have a terrible slice. Fucking game drives me nuts." Jonathan was vamping. He'd adopted a third-floor personality, which made him sound just like Lance Topping and the rest.

Simon appeared with Jonathan's soda and set it down on a coaster on the big glass desk. "What would you like me to do about Judi and Joel's movie opening? You want to send them anything?"

"Geddum a basket," Jonathan said, with a dismissive wave of his hand. It was such a perfectly contemptuous gesture that I had to smile, although not with any great mirth. He was only twenty-seven years old and could dispense gift baskets with the best of them. Jonathan had officially arrived.

"So I'm curious why you wanted to see me."

"We've got to get your writing career back on track," Jonathan said, as if he were my caring agent. He remained behind his desk rocking back and forth in his black leather chair. If he felt nervous or awkward being around me, if he recognized any irony, he gave no indication. "I read your original *Ivy and Men* script again and I thought it was pretty good. I'm not sure I agree with all the changes Judi and Joel made, however."

"I don't agree with any of them."

"I can see their point though. They were trying to open it up and make it more accessible. It's a legitimate concern."

"I understand. I just think some of the suggestions were off the top of their heads. I don't think they served the script. There was another way to go if they wanted to open it up." I was trying my best to be diplomatic.

"Well, I've got two pieces of good news for you. I was talking to Lance about this and I think we should go back to the original script."

I couldn't believe it. After all this time Jonathan had finally come through. Why had I mistrusted him so completely? All I wanted to do was make it up to him. Apologize. I wanted to get back to my office and call Miriam to tell her I was mistaken. I wanted to tell Freyda and Jerry and Hart. I wanted to tell the world that Jonathan Prince was a Prince after all. And I wasn't a failure.

"But I still think it could use some changes. Which is my other piece of good news."

I leaned forward waiting for him to tell me they had a director who was interested.

"We're considering Wendy Wasserstein to do the rewrite."

"What?"

"I don't think you can see it clearly anymore. Maybe you're a little written out. I think you need a break from it. Even Freyda says you're tired of it."

"Freyda? Freyda told you I was tired of it? Of COURSE I'm TIRED of it, I've been working on it for three years, but that doesn't mean I want to be rewritten."

"I think you should be very happy. Not everyone gets to be re-written by Wendy Wasserstein."

"This is how you get my career back on track? You fire me off of my own script?"

"You're looking at it too narrowly. With Wendy on board, this thing could actually get made. In the meantime I set up a meeting for you at ten-thirty to meet with my new assistant, who has some ideas she wants to kick around with you. We've got to get you started on another script. Get you working again." Jonathan got up and began to walk me to the door.

"Wendy Wasserstein's actually got a career. She doesn't need to do a rewrite for Judi and Joel. How about asking Arthur Miller? He hasn't worked in a while."

He continued escorting me out. "Believe it or not, I'm trying to do the best I can for you under the circumstances. It's too bad you can't or don't choose to realize it."

"Fuck you, Jonathan. Who are you kidding?"

He paused at his door and stared me down. "You should know, Frankie, you're beginning to get a reputation as a writer who's not easy to work with. Maybe that's why I can't remember the last time I saw anything with your name on it." Then he shouted to Simon, "Get Freyda Wong," and closed the door to his office in my face.

When I got back to my office I called Freyda, too. But it was only ten-fifteen and she hadn't come in yet from her breakfast meeting. Jerry's plane was just taking off and he'd be unreachable for hours. Miriam wasn't home and I didn't want to leave a message on her machine. I started to dial Hart when I realized he wouldn't care. I just wanted to go home. But Simon called asking if I was free for that pitch meeting Jonathan had set up.

Katie had said something about Jonathan a long time ago, that he was very tenacious and you didn't want him working against you. It was true. Jonathan was in a position to ruin my career, what was left of it. I couldn't afford to alienate him further by refusing the meeting. I had fifteen minutes to recover before returning to the third floor.

Simon pointed me to the conference room, which was adjacent to Jonathan's office. Dewey, little blond dewey-eyed Dewey, who'd last appeared behind the receptionist's desk at my agents' office was now presiding at the head of the conference table looking very official in her black gabardine pants suit. I knew when I took my seat next to her that I'd forfeited all self-respect. I was no better than Ian Mandel.

"*PMS Detective.* Bette Midler as a bitchy New York private detective who's always having a bad day."

"Whose idea is this?"

"Jonathan's. He thinks he could get Bette interested. Oh. No. Wait. I think Wendy Rubin's doing that one. Sorry. Okay. Whoopi Goldberg is hired as a teacher at a really exclusive Eastern prep school like Choate. And she turns the whole school upside down. You know, maybe she gets these white boys to sing gospel or whatever. Jonathan thinks we can have a lot of fun with this one." Dewey gave me a So-what-do-you-think look.

"What other ideas?"

"November eighth, 1965. Or November ninth. We don't know which yet. Someone's going to look it up. Anyway, it's the day the lights went out in New York."

"I thought Cantrowitz didn't want to do any period pieces."

"You're kidding? Well, this isn't really period. I mean, it's only 1965. It's not as if, you know, everyone has to wear long dresses or anything. Jonathan thinks it could work."

"It's not an idea. It's just a notion. It's just a date. What's the idea?"

"Well, you know how all those babies were born nine months after?"

"Yes?"

"It's everything that happens when the lights go out."

"What happens?"

"It's a love story."

"Between who?"

"I don't know. I'm not the writer."

That's refreshingly honest, I thought. "What else do you have?"

"Okay." She studied her list. "A man gets run over by a car and comes back as a dog and he's adopted by his own girlfriend." She looked at me hopefully.

"No thanks."

Dewey was starting to dislike me. She referred to her crib sheet, wanting to get the meeting over with. "Roomies. Picture Meryl Streep, Hume Cronyn, and a Sam Shepard type. Meryl Streep is a young novelist who has been widowed a few years before. She goes up to Maine to take care of her cantankerous grandfather while she tries to finish her latest novel. The grandfather realizes how lonely she is, and when he goes into town one day to do errands, he meets Sam Shepard at the Laundromat."

"It's a romantic comedy."

"Right."

"Sounds like it has possibilities."

Dewey immediately perked up. "So the grandfather tries to fix

Sam up with Meryl but Meryl says she isn't interested in dating again and tells the grandfather to mind his own business. When Hume Cronyn has a slight heart attack and has to go to the hospital for a week, Sam stops by the house with one of the grandfather's socks, which he found clinging to the side of the dryer."

"Let me guess what happens. Meryl is attracted to Sam, although she can't admit it to herself, but he stays for dinner, and ultimately, they sleep together. When she finds out the grandfather's been released from the hospital, the two of them start running around the house hiding his razor and aftershave, just like they're two teenagers sneaking sex."

"Jonathan already told you."

It wasn't until the detail of the socks clinging to the side of the dryer that the bell went off. Leisure World had been changed to Maine. Abe had been turned into Hume Cronyn. Instead of an old Jewish widower who doesn't want to get remarried, we now had a young attractive widow who feels the same way. Instead of writing a Ph.D. thesis, Meryl's writing a novel. Minna's telltale Mevacor was now Sam Shepard's aftershave. It was Hershel's *Vilna Redux* transmogrified into *Roomies*.

As many times as I've wanted to, this was the first time I've actually walked out of a meeting. I drove right to Miriam's house, wanting to tell her everything that had happened in the last twenty-four hours: Jerry Slotnick, sex, Wendy Wasserstein, Jonathan Prince, *Roomies*. But she wasn't interested. As soon as I was done Miriam began.

"It serves him right. After thirty-nine years he takes up with this Cockney Cunt. 'Happy Hunting. H.' On a Post-it. Son of a bitch. Here he's praying with the Lubavitchers like a good Jew and then he goes off with her. The hypocrisy. The little rabbi still can't believe it. He thinks of himself as a young playwright. He hasn't even written his best plays yet. Who's he kidding? I can't wait until his allergies kick in. Just wait until he has to carry food home from the market and his sciatic nerve starts acting up. Good. Let HER take care of him. And she doesn't cook. Did I tell you she doesn't cook? She cooks *shiksa* food. Hershel says food isn't important to him anymore. You know what he told me? He told me they drink together in pubs, he and the Tottenham Tart. He told me that he sat next to a man wearing a hat and that they had an interesting conversation. 'That's nice,' I said. What do you say to such a thing? He told me that Enid makes him do his own laundry and that he likes it. He knows how to match socks now. He realizes that if you turn the socks inside out, they look like another pattern and that's why he couldn't get them to match. Can you imagine that this is a revelation? He said I made a cripple out of him. He now knows how to make an omelette. Just wait until he has to do his own income taxes . . . he knows how to make an omelette," she spat. "And what's he going to do on the holidays? Go to the pub for Passover? Sure. He can have shepherd's pie for Passover with the *nafka*. She can feed him fish and chips. I thought he was Ibsen and Chekhov and Shaw all rolled into one. Jonathan can have his ideas. Did I show you what I do now?" She got up from the kitchen table. Since she'd discovered Hershel's betrayal, Miriam had stopped eating. Her round rouged cheeks were now sunken, her generous figure almost angular. "It's a prayer. But not a prayer to God. A prayer to the bad forces in the cosmos." She paused for a moment, as if summoning up the strength. Then she opened her dark, sparkling eyes and began her chant, acting out the words with arm gestures, looking like a stooped, knobby-kneed-cheerleader witch. "Stay his hand" (arm straight out, hand flexed, fingers point up). "Cloud his mind" (hand circles over the head). "Flatten his prick" (hand comes down hitting crotch). "Stay his hand. Cloud his mind. Flatten his prick." She sat back in her chair with a satisfied smile. "I do it when I'm walking at night. The neighbors may think I'm crazy but I don't care. If Hershel was smart, HE would have written something for Meryl Streep. Who wants to watch a play about Hershel's father? Who wants to watch a play about two old farts? Feh. Pooey. It serves him right, the son of a bitch."

"I don't think there's anything you can do about it anyway," I said, when I could finally get a word in. "Jonathan's changed everything around. It's not going to read anything like Hershel's play. And by the time it's gone through all the rewrites, probably even the socks will be gone."

"It's playing in Australia, did I tell you?" she said with sudden habitual pride. "The Australians love it. According to Hershel's agent, they've never seen anything like it."

It took me a while to piece together what happened next. Miriam, who was still desperate for the sound of Hershel's voice, who wanted to punish him and who wanted him back, got up at four-thirty the next morning and called him in London, eager to share the bad news. From what I gather, she told him Jonathan had stolen his play for Meryl Streep. Hershel then called his lawyer friend in L.A., the Writers Guild, and the Dramatists Guild. Finally he called his London agent and they agreed to meet for lunch.

They were on their way to some Indian restaurant and Hershel was understandably upset and distracted, maybe more than usual. They were crossing Oxford Circle and Hershel, momentarily forgetting where he was, didn't notice the arrow on the road and looked the wrong way. According to his agent, Hershel's last words as he stepped off the curb were, "Fuck that kid."

Miriam, always practical, picked out the cheapest wooden coffin. Hershel was wearing his old, familiar *yarmulke*, his head lying on a blue satin pillow. His wild hair and beard had been neatly trimmed by the mortuary and his only suit pressed crisply. The last time I'd seen him looking so presentable was the night Jonathan and I attended his play.

Miriam stood next to him and stroked his waxen cheek with the back of her finger. Her children came and comforted their mother, singly and in pairs, except for Noah, who, after viewing his father, sat down in a chair by himself in the corner of the room. I think Noah probably didn't know how to feel about his father. It was as confusing for him as for all of us. I'd always counted on Hershel and Miriam as a unit. A given. A reassuring constant. But, unlike Noah, I knew why Hershel had tried to escape from Miriam and never blamed him. She'd loomed over him, as she'd done with her children, waiting for the good report card to be brought home. But when he hadn't delivered, in spite of all her coddling, he'd felt diminished and angry by her voluble disappointment. It was easier to reinvent himself with a new woman, in a new place, than to remain with someone who was such a painful reminder of his failures.

Poor Hershel wasn't Ibsen. Jonathan Prince, by poaching Hershel's idea, had turned him into an Ibsen character. He'd stolen the child Hershel had created, he'd taken a piece of Hershel's soul, and Hershel, in utter anguish, had killed himself because of it. And just like Ibsen's Eilert Lövborg, he had failed to do it beautifully.

Hershel's coffin was lowered into the ground, and Miriam, following Jewish tradition, threw a handful of dirt into the hole. As she walked away from the burial site, just before she got into the car with her children, she turned and took one last look.

"Now I'll never get my Hirschfeld, the son of a bitch."

27
AND THAT'S HOW IT IS
1992

WISHFUL THINKING ASIDE, Wendy Wasserstein didn't do the
rewrite of my script. Once again, Jonathan had proved himself a
master of anticipation. He knew the script would never get made
and hired the most politic person in order to ingratiate himself with
Lance. And earn a coveted invitation to the old brown-shingled
house in Martha's Vineyard, where the white ironstone pitcher of
yellow daisies and tiger lilies always sat on the outside luncheon table.
I found out through Sparky that Freyda negotiated the deal.

After Whitney Topping failed to get her children's book published,
she'd decided to throw herself into screenwriting. Sparky slipped me
a copy of her script, but I threw it on the floor of my car and it stayed
there, along with an old plastic water bottle and a two-for-one pizza
flyer. In a few weeks I finally felt brave enough to read the first few
scenes.

THOSE SUMMERS
by
Whitney Lilly Topping

FADE IN:

EXT. FERRY TERMINAL—WOODS HOLE, MASSACHU-
SETTS—DAY

It's summer 1966 in New England. A Buick sedan, loaded with
luggage, pulls into the crowded lot and gets on line with the other
cars to board the ferry. We SEE a sign that says FERRY TO
MARTHA'S VINEYARD.

                                                    CUT TO:

INT. BUICK—DAY

Sitting in the backseat with her springer-spaniel puppy, TY-
LER, is eighteen-year-old MORGAN LAYNE, a beautiful
girl who is lost in her own thoughts.

Morgan's mother, KATHERINE, and father, WILLIAM,
sit in front. They are both wearing casual clothing for the
trip, although William, a successful banker, is more used to
suits than polo shirts.

                    KATHERINE
          When we get to the island we'll open up the
          house and then have lunch.

                    WILLIAM
          I just hope there's no damage from the winter.

                    MORGAN
          I think I'll take Tyler for a walk.

> KATHERINE
> (*always worried*)
> Just make sure you don't miss the ferry.

> MORGAN
> I won't. Don't worry.

                                    CUT TO:

EXT. FERRY TERMINAL—DAY

Morgan gets out of the car with the puppy. As she is about
to walk away we hear:

> ARTHUR'S VOICE
> Morgan!

MORGAN'S POV

ARTHUR GILES(18) is standing on the bow of the ferry waving
to her. We can see in his handsome face how much he has missed
her.

BACK TO MORGAN

> MORGAN
> Arthur!

She and the dog begin to run for the ferry.

                                    CUT TO:

EXT. FERRY BOAT—DAY

Arthur, who can't wait, runs to meet her halfway. They
meet on the deck just as the ferry whistle begins to BLOW.

It's funny what can happen almost overnight in Hollywood. Whitney became a screenwriter represented by Freyda and I was represented by no one, having quit the agency. It was no great surprise
when my contract wasn't renewed. Writers come. Writers go. I was
glad to be going. The only person who was sad about it was Mai Lei,
who dutifully helped me pack up all the scripts and books and notes.
I took a walk on the backlot for the last time and said farewell to the
little town, my front-porch swing, the skittish cat, and the lace curtains lifted so gently by the breeze. Maybe I was waiting for an epiph-
any, a sign, a clue as to what I should do with the rest of my life. It
came in the form of a studio guard in his golf cart, asking me if I
belonged on the lot.

Hart once described Florida as a place where old people think that
side-view mirrors are ornamental. I was remembering this when
Louie and Perle pulled up to the curb at the West Palm Beach airport.
Although Louie's arthritis prevented him from turning his head, he
became angry at Perle when she suggested I drive. By the time he'd
negotiated his way back to their condominium, and she'd screamed
"Watch it!" enough to deplete any normal person's adrenaline re-
serves, I was beginning to seriously believe in destiny.

On the plane, I'd already written the entire script for my trip because I knew my characters so well. My parents were old. Their
stories were sad. They were victims of bad doctors, unscrupulous
insurance companies, greedy car mechanics, incompetent handymen,
Aunt Lucille, and a cleaning woman named Carmen who wasn't "as
thorough as she could be." I'd come to the conclusion that one of
the reasons I avoided these get-togethers was that I felt powerless to
help. I sent them money periodically, but there was little I could do
to make their lives happier. What they wanted from me was reflected
glory and my star had dimmed.

Coward that I am, I'd tried enticing people to come to Florida
with me, said I'd pay for the hotel, went as far as offering to pay
airfare and incidentals. But there were no takers. My brother Jay was
in the middle of a trial and Jerry was romancing Marty to direct one
of those interchangeable peewee sport movies. Miriam was busy with
a whole new life.

She and Sparky had signed up for an adult-ed course at Santa Monica City College called Beads Beads Beads. *Have you ever admired beautiful necklaces, bracelets, or earrings and wished you could make them yourself? Learn to design and select beads and pearls as well as string, knot, and attach clasps and tips. You can do repairs or make new pieces right in class.* Miriam put Sparky on a healthy diet and got him walking. Sparky persuaded Miriam to stop dying her hair and created a whole new look for her. With her snow-white Lady Di coif, and her bright-colored clothes, she caught your attention in a crowd. The two of them drove to a breeder in Lancaster one weekend and picked out a Pomeranian puppy she named Boucher. In only two weeks he was trained to "go make a puddle," and Miriam declared him a genius. Little Macho and Hershel had both been replaced.

When we got back to my parents' apartment, Louie got right into bed, Perle reheated dinner, and I unpacked my suitcase in what was once Dora's bedroom. Upon her departure to the nursing home, it had been quickly converted to the junk room. I sidestepped the cardboard boxes and opened the sliding doors to her closet. Her neat little double-knit pants suits were hanging there as if one day she'd actually come home again to wear them.

I helped Perle wash the dishes because their dishwasher was on the blink even though I'd just sent them money to have it fixed. She'd called the repairman but was never able to get him to come back. She started to tell me again about Aunt Lucille's CRAZY diets, how she can't stick to them, makes a batch of cookies, and eats the WHOLE thing herself. But I interrupted, asked for the keys to the car, and escaped to the nursing home.

The smells alone make you never want to end up there. A mélange of overcooked food, Pine-Sol, floor wax, medicines, with just that faint hint of urine. The sad stench of institutionalized dying. An old woman with wispy, white hair was in the corridor, parked in her wheelchair with no one around to talk to. On her food tray was a harvest-gold plastic cup and flexible straw. Her hospital gown had slipped off of one bony shoulder. She reminded me of an overgrown, baby albatross I'd seen once in Hawaii. It'd been left alone all day in a field to fend for itself. For hours it waited helplessly for its provider to return. Why had this woman been abandoned? I wondered. Where was her husband? Still alive? Did she have any family looking out for her? I caught her eye and smiled and she reached out and grabbed my hand with an iron grip. That's when I saw the gray numbers tattooed on her arm.

"Take me with you, darling," she said, pulling me toward her. "Take me home. I want to go home."

"I can't just now," I said. "I wish I could but I can't. I'm so sorry." She held on tight. "Can I get you anything?" I said, knowing how empty and foolish it sounded. She turned away from me, then let go of my hand.

I headed for the administration office, trying to shake off a bad feeling, trying not to look back. I distracted myself by attempting to figure out who was the minimum-wage employee who'd stolen the watch I'd sent Dora. A woman behind the main desk informed me that visiting hours were over. I explained that I'd just flown in from Los Angeles and I had to see my grandmother NOW.

Dora was lying in her bed under a fluorescent lamp that hung on the wall above her. She was wearing a Lanz nightgown that someone had put on her backward. Her name was written across the tiny pink flannel flowers with a black laundry marker pen.

"Gramma?"

"Who's that?"

"It's Frankie. Your granddaughter, Frankie." I had one of those heart-thudding moments until I realized the only problem with Dora was that she wasn't wearing her glasses. She reached over and found them on her laminated nightstand and put them on.

"Mama said you were coming. I think they didn't want I should be surprised and have a heart attack."

In the next bed, behind a curtain, a woman was groaning. I walked over to see if she needed anything and I saw that she was wearing restraints.

"What's wrong with her?" I asked my grandmother.

"She's old."

Dora's hand was cold to the touch. On her feet were the little pink booties she'd crocheted.

"You must hate being here."

"What?"

"ARE YOU HAPPY HERE?"

"What choice do I have?"

I'd remembered to bring the photographs that my mother had retrieved from Dora's closet. I wanted to find out who these people were and Dora was the last person who still knew.

I took the photos out and held the first one in front of her eyes. I moved a chair over, sat down, and looked over her shoulder. I recognized my grandfather as a young man. Standing next to him, her arm through his, was a pretty full-faced woman wearing a dark hat and a light-colored traveling suit that reached the floor. She had a fur piece around her neck with four little animal tails hanging almost to her knees.

"I haven't seen these people for a long, long time," Dora said, taking the photograph. She was wearing chipped red nail polish, courtesy of Aunt Lucille on a duty visit. Polishing her mother's nails in a great hurry so she could run off to play bridge.

"Who's Grampa with?"

"That was his sister. She was drowned in 1907. The boat was going from Providence. They had a collision. It caught on fire. So she died and six more people from the family."

"How old was she?"

"She must have been about twenty."

"Was she married?"

"No. She was going home to get married."

"What was her name?

"Wait a minute." She thought for a second and looked at the picture closely. "It was my daddy's name. Shayna Devera. Shayna Devera in Jewish. And here they called her Rose. She came to visit the family and then to go home and get married."

The picture had been taken when Shayna thought her whole life lay before her. She was so young, yet she looked so sober and grown up. I wondered if she was wearing that very suit the day the boat caught fire. Had she lived, she would have been my great aunt.

"Who was she on her way to marry?"

"I never saw him. He was home in the old country. She was going back to the old country but she never made it."

"That's a sad story," I said. I don't know if she didn't hear me or it was so obvious it didn't require an answer. She picked up the next photograph.

"And this is an uncle from Israel. That's my father's brother. And this is my cousin Sophie when she first came here. She was maybe seven. First thing, she was in Canada about six months. They didn't let her into the country because her eyes were bad. I forget the name of it. The eye wasn't sick but it was a very small eye."

I looked at Sophie. She did have small eyes. "Who did she stay with in Canada?"

"In a hospital. They tried to send her back home but my father said, 'You can't send a child back when there is no family there.' So eventually they let her in and she lived with us."

"Is Sophie still alive?"

"Sophie's gone. He's gone, too. All of them are gone." Her eyes were moist, her nose a little red, and she reached over and took a tissue from the box on her nightstand but she didn't use it. She put it up the sleeve of her nightgown, just in case.

"Who are these dapper men?" It was a photo of two men; the one wearing a watch fob and cravat was standing, the other sat in a chair, leaning his elbow on a small round table, his legs crossed at the knee, showing high-button boots. He looked like Oscar Wilde.

"Those are the Berkowitz brothers. These are my father's cousins what we worked for when we first came to this country. With the Berkowitz brothers you couldn't strike. Because they were so independent. You couldn't say anything to them. So if any girl or man used to say something they used to say, 'Now listen. You can't boss us here. We could get more employees than we could get work for them. All we have to do is go down to the Castle Garden.' Where the foreigners come in, the boats. Did you see *Hester Street*?"

I nodded my head in affirmation.

"In America it's Ellis Island, in Jewish it's Castle Garden. So he used to say, 'I can't get enough chairs to put them all to work.' The factories at that time, they used to make money on the slaves. One time I got fired."

"Why?"

"What was the reason to fire me? We never worked on Saturday, and Friday in winter the sun sets early. So my father used to go home about four o'clock in the afternoon Friday and we used to go a half an hour later. One Friday getting on to four o'clock my sister Bessie had a toothache and I said to her, 'Go home with Papa. Go to the dentist. Why should you suffer?' Anyway, the foreman passed by and I said, 'Jake, my sister is going home, she doesn't feel good.' He said, 'What's the big holiday?' I said, 'It's *Shabbes* and the holiday is my sister has a toothache.' And he said, 'If you go home, don't come Sunday to work.' So we had to find another job. This factory was a bunch of foreigners and you felt like home. Till you get to know people, till you find out how to live in a country . . . But, I got a new job on Walker Street in New York."

"What kind of job?"

"Also with shirts. So the first day I go to work at seven o'clock. The elevator is not working until eight o'clock, so I go up the steps. It's pitch-dark. There is no light in the building, just walking, feeling it. When you come up on the floor there's a window shines in a little bit. So the next day I took a candle and matches. That time we didn't know from a flashlight, so I took a candle and matches and walked up. I worked there maybe two weeks when the Berkowitz brothers found out I was laid off, so they made for me to come back to work."

"Whatever happened to the Berkowitz brothers?"

"It's really funny. There were three brothers, partners, and everything was okay. Then their sons come in and when the children came in so the business wasn't good anymore. The sons were trying to take over. And they eventually went bankrupt. They were already American-born. They knew how to run the country."

"Visiting hours are over." It was a new face, a neckless woman with eyebrows tweezed off and penciled back on. She wagged a finger at me. "Fifteen lashes with a wet noodle." Behind the white curtain the woman had started moaning again.

"Why is that woman moaning like that? Is she in pain?"

"Oh, she just has bedsores. What's the matter, hon?" she said to the woman, although she'd just answered her own question. I put the photographs back into their envelope.

"I'll see you tomorrow, Gramma." And then it occurred to me to ask her something that had been on my mind. "Gramma, remember when I took you back to New York with me and Zippy met us in Grand Central Station?"

"Yes."

"And we were on the escalator and Zippy tried to tell me something and you asked her to be quiet."

"I remember. I remember."

"What didn't you want her to tell me? It was about my father, wasn't it?"

She could have said she didn't remember and I would have let it go. But Dora was incapable of telling a lie. She paused for a moment as if deciding whether to share a secret with me, as if she were weighing the consequences. Then she took my hand. "When your father lost his business and they had nowhere to go, I gave them my savings. So they could buy their place in Florida. He didn't want to take from me. But he had no choice. So I never mentioned it again. I'm only telling you because you asked. Otherwise, I wouldn't say anything."

"Don't worry. I won't tell him I know."

"It's better that way, believe me."

When he'd lost his business he'd had what Perle came to call in later years "a poor man's nervous breakdown." For the first few months he'd leave the house in the morning and disappear for the day, pretending to be at work. Then he stopped answering the phone because the collection agencies hounded him, refused to open the bills and threatening letters. He'd sit at the kitchen table with his head in his hands in a stupor of self-hatred and fear. Sometimes he'd cry. Louie knew how hard Dora had worked for that money, knew what her life had been, and he couldn't recover from the shame. And couldn't forgive her for having to save him. So after all those years I finally found out why Louie treated Dora so badly.

On the way down the hall, I saw a pay phone and stopped to call Jerry. Suzie patched me into his car but Jerry and I got cut off. Then I called Miriam and got her answering machine. I tried my brother but the sitter said he and my sister-in-law weren't home.

I sat in the phone booth thinking what my next move should be. A maintenance man was leading a buffing machine around the beige-speckled floor. He looked Cuban, and as I watched him work, I wondered how many children he had and how he'd managed to get to America. I thought about Dora's life. For all the hardship, her life had been much richer and more interesting than mine would ever be. I'd done nothing compared to her. I tried to forgive Louie, who'd been so tormented by the failure of his business that he'd never stopped grieving. And I tried to forgive Perle her willful sadness and having to pretend, for his sake, that they were better off than they were.

I understood something for the first time. My parents, who reside most of the year in Sunlake Village and who go to early-bird movies for a dollar, had shed new light on Hollywood. Up to that very moment I believed they had their own particular misery, which they lavishly and unstintingly spread among their three children. But they aren't unique. Hollywood is filled with people whose upbringings were just variations on my own. Jonathan, while having parents with more money and subtlety than mine, grew up under the same tyranny of expectation. What drove him to succeed in Hollywood is what drove me. And what finally drove Hershel away from Miriam and into the arms of the Tottenham Tart. It's what drove Freyda and Marty, Jerry Slotnick, Ian Mandel, Wendy Rubin and her lickspittle husband, Isaac, Judi and Joel, and the miserable array who were eating in the restaurant where I'd gone with Freyda the day I first laid eyes on Jonathan. No Jew can ever be successful enough to make up for all the sufferings of our forebears. We have an obligation and a responsibility to succeed. To justify our existence. For the sacrifices it took to get us here, after we were not only spared death but given all the advantages that money can buy, how could we not do everything in our power to make sure it never happened again?

As I was sitting in that phone booth, I realized Louie Fingerman, in his own way, was almost admirable. When he'd lost his business he fell from grace as a Jew. He'd rolled over and never got up again, unwilling to lie, steal, cheat, charm, or hustle. He was only willing to hurt the people closest to him, who understood and would never abandon him. Louie couldn't have made it in Hollywood. He lacked the killer instinct. Hollywood attracts a certain breed of Jew because success isn't that hard to attain here, provided you have the stomach for it. Jonathan reminded me of the Berkowitz brothers. But at least the brothers displayed some empathy toward those they exploited. You could forgive them because they'd started out with nothing and made something. Jonathan had started out with everything and made nothing.

It all seemed so clear to me how the tiny monsters like Jonathan were made. All his striving was only a means to power. Jonathan could only get the women and the respect he craved with power. He had no talent and he knew it. Jonathan was, at his core, essentially unlovable and he knew that, too. He felt no real passion in life, but he was smart. He recognized that if you're devious and shrewd, you could exploit those who live by a moral code. He shared with all the power types an immense freedom. Because when you divest yourself of your soul, anything's possible. Hollywood was the perfect environment for him. Invented by immigrant Jews, who in their yearning to belong built an imagined landscape, a cockeyed version of the wealthy, genteel, gentile world that had rejected them. But those shtetl Jews, those perennial outsiders, had succeeded beyond their wildest dreams. The powers that run Hollywood now no longer had to imitate a world they couldn't belong to, because the world now imitated them. They'd become the new aristocracy, the new insiders; every mediocre fool's, every ambitious nobody's fantasy of success. It was the ultimate assimilation. Hollywood was the royalty of America and Jonathan Prince wanted to be king. Only he couldn't create, so he did the only thing he knew he was really good at. He destroyed.

I dialed Miriam again. And this time she answered. I made arrangements for her to pick us up at the airport. Then I called the airline and bought another ticket, remembering at the last minute to order a kosher meal.

28

WE SHOULD GET TOGETHER ANYWAY

1999

I THOUGHT I was done, that I had said everything there was to say about Jonathan Prince, but a postscript plopped itself in my lap. Jerry had invited me to dinner at a small private club in the industrial section of Santa Monica. Not being a member himself, he'd pulled a number of strings to get a table, but the only reservation they would give him was for six forty-five.

I was glad it was going to be an early evening. It wasn't that I was worried about Dora, because I'd dropped her and the dog off at Miriam's. Miriam was cooking kosher chickens, which smelled of rosemary and garlic, and Sparky had rented *Waiting for Guffman* for after dinner. My new dog and Boucher had made a certain kind of peace, provided no food or rawhide bones were involved. All I wanted was to get back to watch the movie.

I was heading out the door to meet Jerry, but paused a moment. Dora, all dressed up, looking happy and puckish, was at the round dining room table carefully shuffling the cards. Miriam was next to her doling out pennies from a huge mayonnaise jar and Sparky was doling out the sugared walnuts Miriam served because they didn't get the cards greasy.

"Y'all have a good time," Sparky said to me, "and if Dora gets too tired, I'll bring her home and help her upstairs into the nursery." He turned to Dora. "How does that sound?"

"Who's tired? You'd think I was an old lady, the way you treat me."

"Deal, already," Miriam said.

They were Mr. Pincus and the widow Ida Mink playing kaluki around Dora's dining room table in her little house in upstate New York. I belonged with them. And would have done almost anything to get out of my evening. But I didn't want to hurt Jerry's feelings and there was no way to get in touch with him anyway. The club is so exclusive the phone number is unlisted.

Though its anonymous facade purposely resembles a warehouse, it wasn't hard to find the restaurant on the deserted, cheerless section of Olympic Boulevard. The valets were out in front in their red jackets, waiting for the famous people who'd be arriving later. The place was empty except for Jack Nicholson, who was in a corner booth with some industry people. I arrived before Jerry and was shown to the booth closest to the bar, a separate, vacant room with Frank Sinatra music playing too loudly. I studied my menu and snuck an occasional glance at Jack.

The occasion of this evening was Jerry and Gail Sylver Slotnick's third wedding anniversary. They'd invited me because I'd introduced them. Besides being the only other person I knew with white carpeting in the bathroom, Gail was suited to Jerry in ways I would never be. Jerry was looking for someone who would advance his career and I was becoming more and more like Yoshi. I couldn't stand to go to Hollywood functions anymore, didn't respect the movies Jerry made, didn't like the people he had to be nice to. We would have ended up not liking each other. And I didn't want to not like Jerry.

The other couple coming were Gail's business partner Nancy Bliss and her husband, Hal, who'd given the wedding at their house.

"What the fuck is this?" Jerry said, when he and Gail sat down. "Do you believe they make us come at six forty-five and the place is empty?"

"At least the lighting is nice. You don't see the wrinkles," Gail said.

"I'm going to call Don tomorrow and give him shit. He was supposed to tell them to treat us right. The place is fucking empty. I wonder how they make a living here."

"Doesn't Frankie look great, Jerry? I think I'm going dark with my hair. Enough with the blond already. I'm starting to look like an old Jew from Miami."

"The food is supposed to be good though. They got the chef from somewhere or other. Someplace good."

Jerry and Gail bantered back and forth, neither listening to what the other was saying. They were like an old married couple, but I couldn't figure out if this was comforting or depressing. At nine o'clock the place was starting to fill up and we were getting the not-so-subtle hint that they wanted us to leave. I didn't recognize any of the newcomers but Nancy Bliss knew one girl in the booth next to us who was the daughter of a television actor, and Gail had read one of the boys for an *After School Special*.

"It's a good thing Jack Nicholson is here," Gail said. "At least he brings the median age up. I love all the black leather and tattoos. I feel too clean."

"Too clean. Is that funny."

"I can't believe these kids are sitting there with their parents' credit cards and they're kicking us out. We have to come at six forty-five and THIS is the reason? I'm calling Don tomorrow and giving him shit."

We all got up to leave. It had started to rain, so Jerry took our parking tickets and ran outside to give them to the valet, while we stood just inside the door. That's when I saw Jonathan.

He was seated at the bar, in the corner. "Hey!" I was tempted to yell. "I threw out your Rolodex card a year ago and I've spent every day since then writing about you. What do you think of that?" But I wanted to observe Jonathan without him seeing me. He was sitting with a bucket of champagne in front of him. I knew what kind it was without even looking at the label. Shelley had informed me of Jonathan's latest decree in his march to Windsor Castle.

"Jonathan has become quite the Anglophile," she said when we happened to run into each other in Beverly Hills a few months before. "He only orders Bollinger champagne now."

"Am I missing something? Why Bollinger?"

"Prince Charles chose Bollinger for his bachelor party. Please. Where have you been? Our Prince Jonathan KNOWS these things."

We stood on the street for a good half hour while Shelley filled me in on Jonathan's personal trainer and his silver Porsche and his breakup with Katie, who had married the doctor after all. She told me that Jonathan had fired Henri Faroli after he caught him scamming on the bills. Not so coincidentally, Jonathan's name and phone number began appearing on most of the men's-room walls in West Hollywood restaurants. Jonathan was forced to change his phone number, but he'd gotten the last laugh: Jonathan had an underling call Henri, posing as a personal assistant to a supposedly wealthy New Yorker who was in need of a decorator to do his entire five-story brownstone. He talked Henri into buying a first-class ticket, which, he said, would be reimbursed. A suite at The Mark was supposedly waiting for him when he arrived in New York to meet his nonexistent client. I can just picture Henri, with all his luggage, in the elegant lobby of the small, discreet hotel, when he discovers there's no reservation. Turquoise eyes blinking in bewilderment, then fury, he shakes his head in disgust at the front-desk clerk, delicately wipes away the glistening spittle caught in the puppet lines of his mouth and demands to see the manager. When he finally figured out he'd been made to look the fool, what could he have said? But Jonathan didn't stop until Henri's reputation and livelihood were in ruins. Henri Faroli finally moved to Santa Fe and started over.

Shelley mentioned the valet service that shuttles people to Jonathan's Neutra house for the annual black-tie Christmas party and back down again. "If you were still on the Christmas party list I wouldn't have to be telling you all these things."

"So you're back in his good graces?"

"Of course. He may need one of my clients. Otherwise I'm sure he wouldn't have anything to do with me. Do you still get those stupid, pretentious Christmas cards?" I recalled the last Christmas card

Jonathan had sent me. Shelley had rewritten hers and sent me a copy:

Herein lies the tragedy of Hollywood: not that writers are poor,—
all writers know something of poverty; not that producers are
wicked,—who is good? not that executives are ignorant,—what is
truth? Nay, but that Jonathan Prince fucked the right people. —
W.E.B. Du Berg, *The Souls of Jewish Folk* (1991)

"I'm off the Christmas-card list," I said.

"Be thankful for small favors. Oh. Jonathan has become a Repub-
lican, did you know that? He's voting his conscience. But, of course,
now that Lance Topping has been fired—oops, I mean now that
Topping is making an indie prod deal, Jonathan is working directly
with Cantrowitz. So he'll probably become a Democratic fund-raiser.
Why is it that in Hollywood executives are never fired? I mean,
executives 'leave' to do 'independent production' and writers are
fired with vehement expletives. I just can't wait to open up the trades
one morning on the toilet and read that Jonathan is doing indie prod.
That's when I order the Bollinger. But, of course, it'll probably never
happen. Cantrowitz and Jonathan and some of the other industry
types just went on a wilderness adventure. They hired ten guides to
take them salmon fishing in the San Juan Islands. Like a Jewish Out-
ward Bound. Except, of course, they have their own private plane.
You know what gets me about this town? Most men either have to
kill it, climb it, or fuck it. In Hollywood you have to own it. They
can't enjoy an experience unless they've paid for it. I mean, can you
imagine these guys trying to enjoy the wilderness on their own?
Please. I mean. I was hiking just the other day in Temescal Canyon
and I passed Paul Fisher, remember Paul and the lovely Nicole? I
passed him walking with his daughter on some YMCA Indian Princess hike and he's wearing his CAA T-shirt and talking grosses with
some other asshole. What other business rewards ego and mediocrity
like Hollywood? What a town. I love it."

When we said good-bye, Shelley and I promised we'd call each other but, of course, we knew we wouldn't. Jonathan was our common link and it wasn't a strong enough bond to hold us together.

At first I thought Jonathan was by himself, which surprised me because I knew he hated to eat alone. Then I saw Paul Fisher move down a seat toward him, which surprised me even more.

"If she offered to blow me, I'd take her up on it, too," Paul said as if he was picking up the thread of a conversation started before. "We wanted a rock 'n roll president, we got a rock 'n roll president, so what do you expect? But do you get impeached for blow jobs?" Paul no longer resembled a sleek, pedigreed dog. He'd lost his arrogance. He was now more like a slobbering St. Bernard, bringing his master a drink. I'm sure Paul would have gotten Jonathan a cappuccino with his milk heated to one hundred and seventy degrees, if that's what Jonathan wanted. In Hollywood there's a statute of limitations on pride and shame.

Jonathan didn't say a word. His eyes roamed the room and he spotted me.

"Frankie!" He actually looked happy to see me.

"Hi, Jonathan."

He got off of his stool, made his way toward me, and gave me a kiss on the cheek. He was in a cocoon of blue cable-knit cashmere which I couldn't help wanting to touch. He held out his arm. "What do you think? Eight ply." Despite the personal trainer and the contact lenses, Jonathan was getting soft. He was already starting to look middle-aged. "You remember Paul Fisher."

My ex-agent looked at me and we shook hands but I could tell he hadn't a clue. And I wasn't going to help him out.

"You know it's funny, Paul and I were talking about you after Tom Hanks won for *Philadelphia*. I said, 'Remember that Frankie Jordan script?' It was too bad about that script. Joel and Judi were just totally the wrong people to have gotten attached."

"What's Joel up to?" I asked, almost curious.

"He's directing a western for Scotty."

"I thought Cantrowitz didn't like westerns."

"Scotty thinks the western is the great American art form," Paul said. "Say what you will about him, I think Scotty's a visionary."

"So what are YOU doing with yourself these days, Frankella? Still writing scripts?"

"On occasion. Actually, I'm just finishing a book."

"A book. Great. Novel? What's it about?"

"Maybe one day you'll read it." He took my avoidance to discuss it as a plea.

"I'd love to. Has anyone seen it yet? You have a publisher?"

"Not yet."

"I'll tell you what to do. Call the studio tomorrow and have Nicole Kahn send a messenger for it. It might be something we're looking for. You know, we should get together anyway."

I didn't say anything but I thought of an expression Dora had recently taught me: *Ain mol iz geven a chochmeh.* A trick is only clever once.

A beautiful, dark-haired girl walked over to Jonathan and leaned on the bar, taking the glass of champagne out of his hand. Her full lips were scarlet red and riveting. More stunning was her diamond ring, which you couldn't not notice. It was an "important" piece of jewelry an actress would wear but never own, returned to Harry Winston the day after the awards. But when Jonathan lifted her hand and kissed the ring, I knew this rock was a keeper. "Are we going to eat yet or what?" She sounded as contemptuous of Jonathan as she was that night he'd gotten her fired from her waitressing job.

"I'll go see about the table," Paul volunteered, getting up without having to be asked.

Jerry tapped my shoulder and said my car was ready. We said goodbye to Paul Fisher, Jonathan Prince, and his fiancée, whose name I never did get.

On the way out the door, I stopped to put on my coat and caught a glimpse of Jonathan's life as it would probably always be. His beloved had turned on her bar stool and was sitting with her back to him looking into the restaurant. Jonathan's fingers went slowly up the zipper of her black dress and gently stroked the back of her neck in a sensual way I remembered quite well. But instead of being mesmerized when she felt his touch, the dark-haired girl rolled her eyes and her face went rigid in pure annoyance. She sat there, very still, letting him think that he was pleasing her.

I drove through the steady rain, the windshield wipers *thwap thwapping* a slow, rhythmic beat, like my heart. I was glad it was raining. It felt moody and cleansing, much more fitting than a clear night with a big, gaudy moon. If this had been the last scene in a script, I would have put in rain, too. How many years, how much energy had I wasted hoping for justice or karma or even corporate nervousness to undo Jonathan? I'd wanted him toppled from his throne as all of Hollywood watched and applauded. But his punishment would be much more private, his tormentor disguised as a glittering prize. For the first time since I'd met him, Jonathan had finally managed to create something entirely on his own.

As for me, I was going home to the little room with the round table. With any luck, I'd get there just about the time everyone was sitting down to watch the movie. "So long, Jonathan Prince," I found myself saying out loud. "Thank you. For everything."

ACKNOWLEDGMENTS

Sondra Simon, who provides inspiration without ever trying. Frank Pierson, for showing me what to leave out, in big, bold strokes. Brad Darrach, who was the gentlest critic and the wisest friend. You are missed plenty. Loring Mandel, whose suggestions were too good not to take. Rick Carter, for helping me understand what I was trying to do. Lane Zachary, my trusted agent, for seeing me through from beginning to end. Betty Nichols Kelly, for her unwavering support and enthusiasm. And Chris Carter, who gave so generously of his time and whose opinion, insight, and honesty I trust, dread, and couldn't do without—thank you again and again and again.